Maya Blake's hopes of becoming a writer were born when she picked up her first romance at thirteen. Little did she know her dream would come true! Does she still pinch herself every now and then to make sure it's not a dream? Yes, she does! Feel free to pinch her, too, via Twitter, Facebook or Goodreads! Happy reading!

Maisey Yates is a *New York Times* bestselling author of over one hundred romance novels. Whether she's writing stories about strong, hard-working cowboys, dissolute princes or multigenerational families, she loves getting lost in fictional worlds. An avid knitter, with a dangerous yarn addiction and an aversion to housework, Maisey lives with her husband and three kids in rural Oregon. Check out her website: maiseyyates.com.

Also by Maya Blake

The Sicilian's Banished Bride
The Commanding Italian's Challenge
The Greek's Hidden Vows

Passion in Paradise collection

Kidnapped for His Royal Heir

Also by Maisey Yates

Crowned for My Royal Baby

Once Upon a Seduction... miniseries

The Queen's Baby Scandal
Crowning His Convenient Princess

The Heirs of Liri miniseries

His Majesty's Forbidden Temptation
A Bride for the Lost King

Discover more at millsandboon.co.uk.

RECLAIMED FOR HIS ROYAL BED

MAYA BLAKE

CROWNED FOR HIS CHRISTMAS BABY

MAISEY YATES

MILLS & BOON

First Published in Great Britain 2021
by Mills & Boon, an imprint of HarperCollins*Publishers* Ltd,
1 London Bridge Street, London, SE1 9GF

www.harpercollins.co.uk

HarperCollins*Publishers*
1st Floor, Watermarque Building,
Ringsend Road, Dublin 4, Ireland

Reclaimed for His Royal Bed © 2021 Maya Blake

Crowned for His Christmas Baby © 2021 Maisey Yates

ISBN: 978-0-263-28271-9

11/21

MIX
Paper from
responsible sources
FSC C007454

This book is produced from independently certified FSC™ paper
to ensure responsible forest management.
For more information visit www.harpercollins.co.uk/green.

Printed and Bound in Spain using 100% Renewable Electricity
at CPI Black Print, Barcelona

RECLAIMED FOR HIS ROYAL BED

MAYA BLAKE

MILLS & BOON

CHAPTER ONE

GHOSTED.

His Majesty King Lucca of San Calliano couldn't abide that word. He couldn't hear it without his jaw turning to granite. Without his fist clenching in volcanic fury. Without his temperature ramping up until he could see nothing but red.

Eighteen months ago, the media had delighted in labelling him *The Ghosted Prince*. After his breathlessly anticipated, spectacular, globally televised ascension to the throne of the kingdom of San Calliano, the daring few who believed themselves immune to his wrath had gleefully changed the moniker to *The Ghosted King*.

Apparently, it was immaterial that he was deemed one of the most forward-thinking heads of state of his time. That within a few short years he'd catapulted San Calliano back into economic success with a series of trade deals financial journalists still rhapsodised about. Hell, it didn't even matter that, as the world's most eligible bachelor, he'd dated stunningly beautiful women both before *and* after his one flawed encounter with the woman he'd thought trustworthy and above reproach.

She'd turned out to be merely beautiful on the outside.

His lips curled.

She would always remain *The One That Got Away*. The one who had turned her back on unimaginable wealth, immeasurable power and unfettered influence. The one romantics liked to believe had ripped his heart out, severely denting his playboy image in the process.

Except he didn't have a heart—certainly not the kind of heart that weakened men like his father, leading them into making shocking errors of judgement that reaped huge repercussions for the things they purportedly loved. That stained their family with disgrace that took painstaking effort to crawl out from under.

No, the strain of observing such a repeated barrage of flawed behaviour in his father had inured him against emotional entanglements long before he'd met *her*.

And yet...didn't you pave the way for that eventual near downfall yourself?

Sì. He grimly accepted that. He'd let untrammelled lust cloud his judgement. Allowed beauty and brains to blind him to the fact that those brains were being used against him, that behind her mesmerising smile lay a calculating soul. That smile had made him forget every last thing he'd learnt about discretion. Decorum. Circumspection.

He'd trampled over the hard lessons taught by palace tutors. Harsher lessons taught by his father's bitter and unforgiving hand.

For those spellbinding four months, Lucca almost believed he would've strained to remember his own name if asked.

He'd been bewitched. Entirely enthralled.

And then...

Ghosted.

No. He hadn't been discreet about his interest. He'd been even less so when she'd disappeared without a trace. When his every call had gone unanswered and her line had been disconnected soon after. He'd put himself through hell, imagining the worst, instructed his trusted investigators to spare no expense in finding her. Their failure had only incensed him more, driving him to take measures unbecoming of the Prince of a kingdom like San Calliano.

He'd dispensed favours like confetti to friends and enemies alike in a frantic bid to find her—leaving himself open to ridicule and exploitation.

Mio Dio, he'd even come within a whisker of *begging*.

She'd nearly stripped him of his dignity.

Ironic that her final act had restored it. Returning the most precious gift he'd given her, along with a handwritten note, shortly before his coronation, had finally driven him to reclaim his backbone.

He'd remembered the steel that had forged his kingdom's path through wars and strife, turning it into an empire that now commanded the world's attention and respect. He'd remembered that the royal blood coursing through his veins came with duty and responsibility, both of which he'd shirked with barely a thought from the moment he'd laid eyes on her—just as his father had with sickening frequency during his reign.

That reminder, and the fact that he was now King, had stopped him jumping on his plane the moment she'd been located three months ago. He had chosen instead to bide his time. To plot and strategise.

But those two handwritten words were seared in his memory for all eternity.

It's over.

Fury, quiet, stealthy and ruthlessly suppressed—because he'd never let himself forget again who he was—moved through him. With effort, he unfurled his fist, forced his vision to clear and took a deep breath.

Far below him the turquoise waters of the Mediterranean sparkled beneath a cloudless cerulean blue sky.

If Monaco was deemed the playground of the rich, San Calliano easily surpassed it as an arena of power and influence. A priceless crown jewel in a sea of ordinary gems that countless pretenders had sought to usurp in its six-hundred-year history.

However, for almost three decades his father had whittled away at its legacy—first with his precarious economic practices, and then by his wife's reckless actions.

Lucca himself had also, for a brief spell, nearly lost sight of what the San Calliano legacy meant.

Never again.

Another deep breath centred him.

Behind him, his tourism minister and her committee waited.

He hadn't spoken since that brief but unfortunate loss of control when he had surged away from the conference table after seeing *her* picture. Since they'd offered her up as a participant in the most exclusive event of his first year as King.

Lucca was ashamed of that flash of aberrant behaviour. But not as much as he was ashamed of knowing that even after all this time she affected him this much.

'Sire?'

He stiffened, even though he far preferred that title to *Your Majesty.*

Your Majesty seduced him back to a time when a connoisseur of lust, who had never obsessed over a lover, had lost his mind over a woman.

Against his will, he recalled their first meeting...the faintly mocking look in her liquid brown eyes as she'd dipped into a curtsy and huskily murmured, *'Your Majesty...'* knowing full well that he was a prince, not a king.

She'd teased him about it with increasingly sexual subtext—until she'd gasped it the first time he had penetrated her, embedding the sound of that title into his memory for ever.

Lucca despised her for that too.

It was one of the many sins he was very content to heap on her head.

Allowing that memory to increase his fury, he turned around to look at the enlarged pictures laid out on the polished antique conference table in his palace office.

Some people, like his tourism minister, mistakenly believed that despite the unsavoury headlines he'd got over her, hence her being offered up as a candidate now. And he had in the conventional sense. He'd dated several women since her, each more stunning than the last. But that sharp sting of betrayal, the memory of what she'd put him through in those frantic weeks, had never left him.

As a royal, he'd learned diplomacy long before his formative years; he knew when to hold a grudge and when to take the high road. When to bide his time, and when to show the full force of his power.

In this instance, he definitively was *not* going to be the better man and let it go. Not until he'd exacted retribution. To do anything else would be to risk being deemed weak, like his father. To remain the subject of lingering ridicule and whispers.

While San Calliano's reputation was fittingly restored in the halls of economic power, questions remained over his personal life because of her. And *that* he couldn't let stand.

So he stepped forward and stared down at the image of Delphine Alexander.

His ex-lover.

His *traitorous* ex-lover.

The woman who'd made a mockery of him, bringing ridicule to his kingdom years after his own mother had courted scandal and drowned them in disgrace, turning his father into a bitter, mean husk.

His mother's actions had been out of his control.

Delphine was another matter entirely. She'd pulled the wool over his eyes in a way that had seared his dignity and continued to stain his reputation.

He reached for the dossier accompanying her photo. Almost everything written in there he knew from his time with her. What he didn't know made his senses spark to life, his path to restoring the wrongs done to him seeming almost too easy once the plan had formed in his mind.

Still, he raised his gaze to the group seated before him.

While the ultimate decision lay with him, he'd learned the efficacy of listening to diverse views.

'She's your first choice?' he asked his minister, dropping the photo when he noted that his fingers were caressing the glossy outline of her cheekbones, her sensual full lips.

His minister nodded. 'Yes, sire. If we can convince her to come out of retirement, that is.'

Lucca was confident she would by the time he was done with her.

'Why her?' he pressed.

'Well, the other two are beautiful, of course, but Miss Alexander possesses a certain…*mystique* that we believe will truly capture the essence of the royal collection.'

Against his will, Lucca concurred. Her flawless dark caramel-coloured skin alone would illuminate the allure of the fabled San Calliano diamonds a thousandfold. He stopped himself from tabulating just how many extra ways she might elevate the occasion to mark the once celebrated but until recently defunct San Calliano Arts, Culture and Film Festival.

'You haven't approached her yet, have you?' he asked sharply, knowing how eagerly his whole kingdom was anticipating the week-long event.

Arabian thoroughbreds, a world-exclusive diamond show and a supercar exhibit, along with renowned works of Renaissance painters, were but a few of the gems his committee had come up with. Tickets had sold out in minutes and VIP invitations were like gold dust.

'No, sire. Since the show includes the San Calliano diamonds and you have a history with Miss Alexander we wanted to seek your input first.'

He dragged his gaze from Delphine's photo, but could only manage cursory glances at the other candidates before his attention was compelled back to her.

Lucca quietly despised his inability to look away. Despised the pull that had started across a clichéd crowded room in New York and still seemed to have power over him.

That link would be severed once and for all soon enough, he silently vowed.

'You're right. She's the right choice. But no one is to make contact with her. I will be the one to offer her the position.'

One month later

Delphie Alexander stared in shock at the sandy-haired man stretched out on the lounger beside her. He looked mildly hungover, but then that was a state of being he'd perfected over the years.

'Are you serious? You sold your share of the team?'

Hunter Buckman shrugged indolently, completely relaxed in the Qatari sun. That ingrained nonchalance had endeared him to her when they'd met several years ago, at the after-party of a runway show. But now that same nonchalance often left her gritting her teeth in frustration.

He never took anything seriously.

As sole heir to a multimillion-dollar Texas oil empire, he'd never needed to lift a finger to do an honest day's work. The problem was, *nothing* was what he did 90 per cent of the time. His attention span was flighty at best, and his hedonistic lifestyle exclusively dictated his interests.

But she'd hoped…*prayed*…his interest would be long-lasting when he'd let her buy into his latest venture.

'I'm sorry, Delly. The offer was too good to refuse.'

She bunched her fists in her lap, resisting the urge to scream. 'But you didn't even give *me* a chance to make you an offer.'

He grimaced, scratching his unkempt stubble. 'I knew you'd try to talk me out of selling. Or…' He paused, glancing away guiltily.

Her hackles rose. 'Or…?'

'Or bend over backwards to buy the shares from me.'

'And what would have been wrong with that?' She wasn't a stranger to hard work. She'd striven to succeed from the age of sixteen, when it had become clear that she only had herself to rely on, and hadn't looked back since.

Hunter avoided her gaze, glancing around before snapping his fingers at a passing maid. The staff were well-versed in their boss's predilections and thirty seconds later a chilled bottle of his favourite beer arrived. Delphie stopped herself from pointing out that it was barely 9:00 a.m.

He took a healthy slug before meeting her gaze. 'I knew you'd kill yourself trying to come up with the cash to buy me out. I couldn't let you do that. You've already been through so much.'

'So you were trying to spare my feelings?'

She couldn't stop the mild horror in her voice, or the shaming reminder that Hunter had seen her at her lowest point. He'd stood outside her bedroom door on endless nights and listened to her sob her heart out, first over her broken heart, and then over the deep despair of losing her precious baby.

When she'd finally stumbled out, wrecked and raw, he hadn't probed her with questions. He'd simply put her back together in his own unique Hunter Buckman way.

'How many times do I need to tell you that I'm fine?' she said now. 'All that…*business* is in the past.'

'Damn it, I knew you'd react this way. Delly…' He stopped and sighed. 'I was offered one hundred and twenty million dollars for it. That's a serious chunk of change.'

She winced, her insides churning as she swallowed the hard knot of reality. It would've taken her several months, perhaps even years, to come up with a financial package to counter that offer. And with multiple investors would've come multiple, and inevitably frustrating, demands.

She'd been thrilled with having Hunter as her sole partner, regardless of the fact that he owned 90 per cent of Hunter Racing and her a meagre 10 per cent. She'd poured her heart and soul, not to mention her entire savings, into the racing team for the last year—mostly from behind the scenes, since she hadn't been quite ready to face the world until recently, once she'd dragged herself out of her months-long desolation.

Fixing a distraught child's broken bike on the side of the road here in Qatar on one of her evening walks had been the defining moment that had sparked a flame and lit through her cold desolation, and it had set her on a new direction. A direction that not only gave her purpose and a means to dwell on something other than the child she'd lost, but also revived her father's memory through doing the thing he'd loved the most.

Her modelling days were behind her. Managing a racing team had become her new passion. A passion now at risk, thanks to Hunter's actions.

She swallowed the ball of frustration knotted in her throat. 'I only joined the team in the second quarter of last year. This was meant to be my first full year. You couldn't wait for me to find my feet before landing me with a different partner?'

'Come on...don't give me that,' he drawled in his lazy Texan twang. 'You found your feet in your first week as team boss. You pulled Hunter Racing up to fifth in the championship by the end of last season, after languishing in the bottom half four years in a row. Six races in this year, we're already third.'

Delphie massaged her temples as tension built. 'Yet you're walking away from the team?'

He shrugged again, his tanned torso gleaming under the sun. 'It doesn't spark joy in me any more, Delly. Not like it does for you.'

Joy.

A distant concept.

She'd arrived in Qatar firmly believing she'd never again experience that emotion. Nineteen months on, she knew it to be the truth. But she'd discovered she could still draw breath, despite her soul-shrivelling loss. Just as she could nurture the pebble-sized corner of her heart that still cherished the time she'd been given with her father before his death. In that place she'd found contentment. Enough to make facing the day bearable.

She swallowed, looking past the sparkling infinity pool to the gleaming waters of the Persian Gulf. Hunter had bought this house because it was infamously rumoured to have once belonged to a sultan's favourite mistress. But it had been Delphie's sanctuary when her life had fallen apart over a year and a half ago—

No. She wasn't going to think about that.

These days she could go for several blessed hours before King Lucca of San Calliano, his precious 'The List' or the child she'd lost crossed her mind. Not that the blade of memory didn't slash her just as brutally. But she'd learned to walk, talk and function without desolation dogging her every step—to breathe without the anguish of her loss threatening to drown her.

For the sanctuary Hunter had granted her unquestioningly under his roof, she couldn't be mad at her flighty friend. Nevertheless, she took several breaths before asking the vital question.

'Who's the buyer?'

Again his gaze avoided hers. 'The buyer was anonymous. You know how these offshore companies work.'

She exhaled slowly, praying for calm. 'I'm part-owner of the team. Surely I have a right to know who I'll be partnering in the future?'

'They want to wait until after the August midseason break to make a formal announcement. I signed a non-disclosure agreement as part of my deal, so I can't even tell you the name of the company.'

Delphie wanted to blame the light breeze for the shiver that coursed through her, but it didn't account for the sudden faltering of her heartbeat. The dryness in her mouth.

She dismissed her fanciful thoughts.

During the four months she'd spent in His Royal Highness Prince Lucca of San Calliano's bed, she'd never disclosed her love of racing cars. Nor anything pertinent about her family. Sure, he had known she had one, but she'd glossed over her estrangement from her mother, and cited the international demands of her modelling work as the reason she rarely went to London, where her mother lived with her new family.

With him she had explored a shared love of world cultures, their deep appreciation of gourmet food. And he'd given her jaw-dropping insight into how the diamonds in the South American mines his family owned went from rock to masterpiece—an exercise he'd had to learn first-hand by command from his father, the same way he'd been tutored in the oil fields his family owned around the world.

And in between all that, they'd delved deeply and unapologetically into sensual oceans that had left them spent and sated, with little energy for much else.

She hadn't known, for example, that she'd merely been a stopgap until he stepped up to marry a *suitable* woman on 'The List'—a document she'd been cruelly informed *she* would never appear on.

He'd been merely amusing himself with her, she had been told with brutal, cold-eyed efficiency, and all those deep-voiced promises he'd murmured in her ear in Italian had only been a part of his seduction technique. Delphie had learned, that unforgettable day in Paris, that even before she'd graced his bed, a long queue of women had been waiting in the wings to take her place...one of them destined to wear his crown as Queen.

That news, coming hard on the heels of her discovering she was pregnant with Lucca's child, had sounded the death knell of her foolish dreams. Or so she'd thought until true devastation had arrived...

She dismissed the fleeting thought that Lucca might have something to do with Hunter Racing. She'd returned the bracelet she'd fooled herself into believing was a form of commitment, and as she'd feared, but secretly hoped against, he'd excised her from his life.

She forced her gaze back to Hunter. He'd finished his

beer and was slowly peeling the wet label off the bottle, still avoiding her gaze.

'There's something else, isn't there?' she muttered, her nape tingling.

He was as close to dejected as she'd ever seen him. It was an odd look for him. Hunter Buckman epitomised carefree hedonism and was the life and soul of every gathering.

'I'm sorry, Delly, but the top two sponsors are also leaving after the August hiatus.'

She squeezed her eyes shut, the dream she'd nurtured, the one thing that had halted her rapid descent into despair, turning to ash before her eyes. 'Why? We're having our best season yet and suddenly you're selling up and the sponsors are deserting us?'

He exhaled loudly. 'They came on board because of me. They think you're an unknown quantity.'

Opening her eyes, she glared at him. 'Because I'm a woman?'

He grimaced and shrugged. 'You have a little grace period before they leave.'

'Yeah—two whole months to find sponsorship worth over three million.'

His face was sheepish but unrepentant. As happy-go-lucky as he was, she couldn't forget that he operated a highly successful empire that spoke to his hidden core of steel. She knew she couldn't talk him into reversing his decision. Nor could she lower herself into asking for the sponsorship money she needed.

Hunter had given her a sanctuary when she'd needed one. Despite his penchant for gossip he'd kept her whereabouts private, and never once asked why she'd arrived on his doorstep a heartbroken wreck nineteen months ago.

'Something will turn up, Delly. I have faith in you.'

His smile was pleading but cocky as he rose and sauntered off—as if he hadn't just dragged her dreams to the edge of a cliff and left her dangling there.

Delphie was grappling with the percussive ramifications

of Hunter's news when her phone rang. She started, then reminded herself that she was the boss of a successful racing team—not the emotionally wrecked ex-lover of the King of San Calliano.

Nevertheless, fresh from the unwanted memories of Lucca, she felt her heart hammer when she answered. 'Delphine Alexander...'

'Delphie! You're a hard woman to track down,' came the cigarette-hoarse voice she hadn't heard in almost two years.

She frowned. 'Rachel?'

'The very same. I'm honoured you still remember me. Listen, I'm not going to beat about the bush. I have a super mega assignment for you.'

'No!' The word ejected out of her, self-preservation kicking in as instinct warned her that she wouldn't like what was coming.

The cosmos was working overtime against her and she needed to stand her ground before she was flattened. *Again.*

'But you haven't heard what—'

'I'm retired, Rachel. Maybe that's why you had a hard time getting hold of me? So whatever you're offering— thanks, but no thanks.'

Silence throbbed at the other end of the phone, further agitating her nerves, while the same instinct screamed that she might not have a choice in whatever this was.

When Rachel sighed, she felt herself dragged another foot closer to the cliff's edge.

'Darling, I'm not sure what's going on, exactly, but...'

She paused and Delphie was stunned to sense that the formidable agent who struck fear into the hearts of many was gathering herself. 'This gig is paying three million. In the current economy that's a hell of a payday. The client says it's not a deal you want to refuse.'

Delphie was glad she was sitting down, because the ominous tremor that went through her would've taken her off her feet had she been standing.

'Who's the client?' she asked, despite her brain shriek-ing the obvious answer.

'Technically, the request came from the Ministry of Tour-ism in San Calliano,' Rachel confirmed.

Delphie's grip tightened on the phone while the tremors intensified. 'But…?'

'But I was personally called by His Majesty himself.'

The July heat beat on her shoulders and her hand felt clammy as she asked, 'What's the assignment?'

'It's a week-long gig. I'll send you a detailed email when we're done speaking. But to summarise—you're to present yourself at the royal palace in ten days. The Arts, Culture and Film Festival starts in two weeks. During that time you'll be required to showcase the royal diamond collec-tion. The last day of the festival is the royal ball, and you'll wear *the* San Calliano diamond necklace. Darling, it's an easy-peasy week's worth of fine dining and fabulous luxury. Surely it's worth coming out of retirement for that…espe-cially since the King is asking you himself?'

Delphie curbed hysterical laughter. While anyone with a reliable internet connection knew of her liaison with King Lucca of San Calliano, very few knew how it had truly ended.

The rumour mill had surged into working overtime, of course. And even in the depths of her despair Delphie had cringed at the headlines. The one about *The Ghosted Prince* in particular had triggered a twinge of sympathy—which had disappeared quickly enough once she'd found out that Lucca was hunting her.

She hadn't deluded herself into thinking it was because he was pining for her. It was a pride-salving exercise…the nick-name he'd acquired one his ego wouldn't take lying down.

That same apprehension snaked through her now, along with the renewed belief that Lucca was behind the events at Hunter Racing. *He* was responsible for Delphie finding herself on this cliff edge.

'Delphie? Shall I say yes?'

The unsettling tremors intensified. But they also brought anger. And a vicious refusal to return to that dark place she'd inhabited for far too long after leaving Lucca. She could never regain what she'd lost, but she wasn't prepared to let him steamroller over her dream either.

'No. Don't say anything. I'll give him my answer myself.'

Delphie stepped out of the shower in her suite at the San Calliano Grand Hotel just before six o'clock ten days later, determined not to be cowed by the series of mini earthquakes that had occurred since Rachel's phone call.

Her last race, the British Grand Prix, which should've been especially pleasurable since it had been on home soil, had turned out to be a nerve-shredding event. With rumours abounding, her two drivers had been testy because they were concerned about their future in the team, and the sponsors threatening desertion had still been playing phone tag—deliberately.

Since she hadn't been able to admit she was operating in the dark herself, she'd promised her team answers as soon as possible. Which, of course, had triggered more anxiety.

She'd grown increasingly certain that the new buyer was deliberately making her life a living hell. Suddenly the media were dogging her presence with suspiciously accurate details on what was happening in her team. Details only an insider could know.

With each new occurrence she had suspected Lucca's hand in it…

Unfortunately for him it had only firmed her resolve to refuse to bend to his will. With two weeks free before the next race, in Doha, Delphie had taken the bold decision to turn his offer down in person.

She swallowed her nerves, dried herself with extra vigour and stepped into the bedroom.

Even in her accommodation it seemed Lucca was playing puppet master. The double room she'd booked had miraculously been unavailable on her arrival. Instead she'd been upgraded to the royal suite, which cost tens of thousands of dollars for a single night's stay.

Her firm refusal of the upgrade had evoked shock from the reception staff, followed by genuine concern as to whether she would be able to secure accommodation elsewhere. Apparently, with the pre-festival season in full swing, every hotel, hostel and B&B in San Calliano was booked solid for the next fortnight. Just how the royal suite had come to be so conveniently available she'd stopped herself from asking, because she didn't really want to know. Didn't want confirmation that the ruler of San Calliano was pulling her strings.

All she needed to concentrate on was the meeting Rachel had scheduled an hour from now, with the man she'd done her best to block out of her life and her mind.

Delphie glanced at the clock, ignoring the mild quaking inside her as she mentally adjusted the time before her meeting to under an hour. Dropping the towel, she entered the opulent dressing room, selected the white sleeveless jumpsuit that always boosted her confidence. The stiff-necked collar and plunging neckline projected sophistication while maintaining professionalism.

After securing the gold belt, and slipping on matching platform heels, she passed a brush through her thick curls. The repetitive action soothed her, and by the time she set the brush down a minute later her breathing was calmer.

She was spritzing her favourite perfume on her wrist when the suite's doorbell chimed. Her leaping pulse mocked all her palliative efforts, and even though she reassured herself she still had half an hour before the meeting, Delphie instinctively knew who waited on the other side of the door.

She'd dismissed the butler who came with the suite earlier, and now every crumb of composure she normally adopted as team boss of Hunter Racing disappeared as she froze before the imposing, gilt-edged double doors.

For a nanosecond she wondered if her bravado had been

imprudent. If bearding this particular dragon should have been done from the safety of a thousand miles away.

Another door chime pierced her wandering thoughts, making her jump again. Without giving herself another second to dwell on it, she threw the doors open.

Her pulse spiked, pure adrenaline shooting through her veins as she looked into silver-grey eyes of King Lucca of San Calliano.

He looked the same yet...*different*. It took several moments to catalogue the devastating changes. Time had layered depth and gravity upon the man she'd once called her lover, steeping his already breathtaking aura in even more formidable power. Combining his imposing six-foot-four tower of masculinity and the pure royal blood flowing in his veins, he'd elevated himself from a prince to a god amongst men.

The fact that he'd been gifted more than his fair share in the looks department merely added to the unholy sensuality that had thickened with his elevation from Prince to King: a weapon he'd wielded mercilessly in his pursuit of her when they'd first met. A weapon that had eventually weakened her defences, plunging her headlong into a soul-searing experience she'd limped away from with her heart in shreds when she'd discovered there was no future for them.

Courtesy of 'The List'.

The style and elegance cultivated from his royal ancestral Italian roots arrogantly ensured he would command attention in a burlap sack. So the sharp suit she knew had been hand-stitched by royal tailors merely emphasised his superbly honed physique, his broad shoulders, tapered hips, slicked-back hair and the neatly clipped designer stubble he sported, all but ensuring the breath she'd tried to take what felt like an aeon ago remained locked in her chest.

'You're early,' she finally managed to blurt, after withstanding his sizzling head-to-toe scrutiny.

Unnervingly cool eyes observed her and he didn't answer, further ruffling her already strained nerves.

A full minute passed.

A minute in which she dragged her gaze past him to the granite-jawed bodyguards stationed at intervals along the corridor. Their gazes were trained rigidly forward, but Delphie knew they were acutely attuned to every movement she made, and that they could turn lethal in defence of their liege—as she'd witnessed first-hand when a hapless paparazzo had deigned to get within three feet of Lucca at an event two years ago.

When her gaze returned to him he was still watching her with that deadly wolverine intensity, and the ghost of a smile playing at his lips.

'*Ciao*, Delphine,' he drawled in his slightly accented baritone, immediately plunging her into singeing sensual memory.

'I wasn't expecting to meet with you *downstairs* for another half hour,' she said, emphasising the venue for their meeting to give herself some much-needed detachment. Because while the royal suite was vast, and multiroomed, it reeked far too much of other private, intimate places they'd inhabited in the heady past.

Spaces where every surface had been game for sexual play…every corner of every suite a playground for their unquenchable sexual appetites. She'd screamed his name in more hotel rooms than she could count—a thought that made her inner core clench hard while the vice around her chest constricted with an apprehension that solidified the thought that, no, she shouldn't have come.

She should have let Rachel deliver her refusal and stayed far, far away.

But she was here now. And, as she'd learned from both the distant and recent past, hiding away from the difficult things in life didn't make them magically disappear.

She was here…and she wouldn't succumb to any weakness.

She watched him slide his hands into his pockets, rock slowly on his heels. 'You've been reverting to type and playing hard to get for the past two weeks. Perhaps I arrived early because I felt like indulging your game and giving the impression that I simply couldn't wait one more second?' he replied, his droll tone making a mockery of his words. 'Or perhaps I was eager to disabuse you of the notion that you have any standing in what comes next?'

He shrugged indolently, his lips once again curving in a hard smile that sent cold shivers down her spine.

'Either way…are you going to invite me in, Delphine?'

CHAPTER TWO

Delphie wanted to back away from him, but to do so would be as good as arching her neck, displaying her jugular and inviting him to deliver the mortal blow.

So she summoned the poise she'd painstakingly learned under Rachel's tough tutelage when she was just seventeen, turned her back and strolled with feigned nonchalance into the spacious living room and its to-die-for vista, flaunting the best of San Calliano's capital, San Lorena, at sunset.

The stunning city was a masterpiece blend of old-world charm and modern architecture, which under normal circumstances Delphie would have spent hours exploring. Instead, she was struggling to remember to breathe, intensely aware of the man who'd sauntered in behind her after ominously shutting the door, his presence filling up the room to the exclusion of all else.

With nowhere to go once she reached the floor-to-ceiling windows, she turned and faced him. 'Since you seem to know which room I'm in, I'm assuming you're responsible for all this?'

From the priceless Venetian wallpaper to the Aubusson carpeting and the gold-edged paper set upon the polished antique writing desk, every inch of the suite was testament to the sort of wealthy echelons Lucca moved in.

'I thought you would appreciate it. We both know you appreciate the finer things in life,' he confirmed.

'No,' she denied. 'You're the one who commands the

highest premium out of every corner of your life. I merely came along for the ride.' It had turned out to be a more precarious roller coaster than she'd anticipated, and when she'd stepped off she had known she was changed for ever.

Hard cynicism twisted his lips. In the setting sun, his deeply tanned skin gleamed with vitality, making her fingers itch to explore its warmth the way she'd once loved doing.

'It's unbecoming in you to attempt to paint yourself the simpering sycophant when we both know you're nothing of the sort.'

A punch of pride raised her chin. She wasn't going to admit she would've followed him anywhere, turned herself into whatever shape he desired, simply to remain at his side. Hadn't discovering just how deeply that desire ran, on top of finding out she'd been nothing but a passing fancy, with her true, *temporary* place in his life unveiled with callous brutality, been the reason she'd fled?

'Think what you will, but I didn't ask for this.'

'You refused the plane I sent for you—and my invitation to stay at the royal palace. Now you disparage my generosity.'

The bite to his words and the tension in his shoulders fed her own. She fought the urge to swallow, and shrugged. 'I prefer to pay my own way.'

'Really? The rumour is that you're a little light in the pocket. Are you sure you can afford to throw my hospitality back in my face?'

'And how would you know that?'

His smile was pure arrogance, declaring that he was top of the food chain and didn't care who knew it. Hell, he was extremely happy to flaunt it.

'Do you really need to ask, Delphine?'

The sensual intonation of her name reminded her that he was the only one who called her by her full name. Everyone else adopted a different version of it. She herself had always preferred the softer Delphie...until he'd uttered her name the first time they'd met.

He'd captured her hand, raised it to his lips and rasped, 'I'm Lucca, and I intend to be your lover before this weekend is over.'

It had taken longer than a weekend for her to land in his bed, but his attention had never wavered once he'd set her in his sights.

His attention didn't waver now either, but Delphie knew it was for an entirely different reason than lust and possession.

'I've been following your recent activities. Congrats on placing third in this weekend's race, by the way.'

She sucked in an anxious breath, unnerved, but strove to keep her emotions out of her voice. 'First the offer of your plane? Then a room upgrade and now congrats? All so you can have the opportunity to hear me say *no*? Because, in case Rachel wasn't clear, I don't model any more.'

He strolled to stand before the window a few feet away. This close, his scent filled her nostrils, threatening to flatten her with another layer of memory…mainly of her snuggling close, naked.

Compelled by his silence, she turned her head, watching his gaze settle on a distant church spire for an endless minute before he abruptly faced her.

'We both know you came for many other reasons than to refuse my offer. We have a lot to talk about, Delphine. But first I want to talk about this.'

'This' was the piece of paper he'd plucked out of his pocket and now held up to the setting sun. *'This'* was a stark reminder of her wrecked soul and the dark despair she'd dwelt in for several long months.

'This' was the hardest two words she'd ever written.

'You…you kept the note?' Her question was a hoarse, shocked whisper, the ice unravelling in her belly making her quake.

He shrugged, an offhand gesture the direct opposite of the cold flame in his eyes. 'Call me sentimental.'

She barely kept herself from snorting. 'Sentimental implies—' *Caring.* She bit back the word at the last moment.

'Perhaps sentimental is the wrong word… Perhaps I kept it for verification reasons.'

Warning darted up her spine. 'Verification?'

'I wanted to look you in the eyes one day and ascertain for myself that you did, in fact, write this note. *Did* you, Delphine?' he queried, his tone like silk wrapped around barbed wire.

She stiffened, completely and painfully aware the truth might well destroy her.

The Lucca she'd known had been proud and arrogant.

The one who stood before her now was multiplied by a thousand, with an armour of forged, merciless steel stamped into his core. While his sensual lips promised mind-melting pleasure, his eyes promised dire retribution, and his body was wrapped in titanium control she might have fooled herself into thinking she controlled once upon a time, but now knew she would never break.

As she stood there, poised between regret and panic, he slowly held up the note, the stark words *It's over* filled her vision.

'Answer me,' he breathed.

In that breath she caught banked fury. The dent she'd caused to his pride.

She'd heard the stories, of course. Even in hiding, the activities of one of the most powerful men in the world had filtered through. Maybe because she'd allowed them to.

Hunter had taken delight in delivering morsels of gossip in those first few weeks, until she'd stopped him. But not before she'd discovered that she'd left behind a furious prince, soon to be King, who wouldn't forgive her actions in a hurry.

Yet she couldn't lie. She already held a secret much greater, much more devastating than this. She couldn't compound her sins with a falsehood he would prove in minutes.

'Yes, I wrote the note.'

For the longest time he didn't speak. But his face, his body—hell, even his altered breathing—did the talking for him. Then… 'And when you were busy attempting to erase

me from your life, did you stop to think that I might be...
concerned?'

She gasped. 'What?'

His nostrils flared, and even that small action sent goose-
bumps all over her skin.

'Our association was high profile. One that drew attention from both benign and unsavoury corners. Did you consider how I might feel about your disappearance when you
were busy taking the coward's way out?'

'Don't you dare call me a coward! If you knew—' She
sucked in a breath, shocked at what she'd almost revealed.

His gaze sharpened, turning steely.

'If I knew what, Delphine? Enlighten me.'

She shook her head. 'It doesn't matter.'

His face tightened. '*It doesn't matter?* How did you arrive
at that conclusion?' he asked, his voice edged in icy fury.

'Because you've moved on. Weren't you dating a count-
ess six months ago? And a president's daughter and a tech
heiress before that?'

Two of those three women had been on 'The List', lending credence to its authenticity. Until then she'd shamefully
harboured the secret hope that 'The List' was a lie—that the
stranger who'd visited her that day in Paris had been pursu-
ing his own nefarious ends.

She knew differently now.

In recent months Hunter, believing he was administer-
ing the bite-sized shock therapy she needed to return to the
land of the living, had blithely dropped Lucca-centred gossip into their conversation, oblivious to the fact that each
morsel was a dagger between her ribs.

His fist closed over the note with a ruthless, wince-in-
ducing crunch. Then he reverted to the suave, cultured ruler
his people adored. The man whose words leaders of the free
world hung on to with alarming sycophancy.

'You know who I've been dating?' he drawled. 'Have
you been keeping tabs on me? Why, Delphine, it's almost
as if you care.'

She forced her chin up. 'I care only in relation to this meeting and a need to know your whereabouts. Nothing more.'

If she'd hoped to come within a whisker of putting him in his place, she was doomed to failure. Because his conceit only fattened, a veritable feast of a smile curving his lips.

'How passionately you protest. You're aware that you could've listed anything on my very public business schedule but instead chose to point out your knowledge of whom I was seeing *in private*?'

The images his words conjured up flayed layers off the tight vault she now kept her heart in. Images of what he'd done with her *in private*. The singular attention he'd showered upon her. The magnificence of his lovemaking.

Especially that.

'Or are your questionable sources allergic to the perusal of the financial pages?' he continued when she remained silent.

'You're the one who's made all this personal by exerting your power to impress and influence me. I'm simply accommodating your game. For now.'

A single clench of his jaw. Then, 'You'll accommodate it for however long I please. Do you forget that you're the one who sought this meeting?'

'I haven't forgotten. So why don't we get back to that?'

Please.

The plea remained locked in her throat. She'd already lost so much. She had no more to give. 'You keep harassing Rachel, who in turn harasses me. I came here to tell you to stop.'

'That's not the only reason you came, is it?' he tossed at her as he turned away, to all intents and purposes entirely bored with the conversation.

Strolling from the living room to the adjoining office, he approached the immense desk carved in elaborate scenes from his kingdom's history and polished to a flawless shine. He tossed the crumpled note on the buffed surface and dropped into the throne-like chair.

Then, across the space between them, he proceeded to treat her to another slow head-to-toe scrutiny. His gaze lingered in the places he'd claimed once upon a time were his favourite parts of her body—the hollow of her neck, the inside of her elbow, her breasts…

'Stop it,' she snapped, intensely aware of the electric tingles under her skin, the husky weakness of her protest, the low throb in her abdomen…the tightening of her nipples.

She raised her arm on instinct, to hide her body's reaction, an irrational part of her a little terrified that he'd see beyond her arousal to the evidence of her soul's devastation. Somehow glean that she'd carried—and lost—his child.

Only when her hand brushed the lintel did she realise she'd followed him from the living room, was now frozen in the doorway between the two rooms.

'Why? Because *"it's over"*?' he returned tightly, one long finger rising to stroke his full lower lip.

'Yes,' she managed, mentally balling her fists against the assault on her senses.

'Have you tried telling that to your body?' he taunted. 'Because from where I'm sitting, it looks as if it hasn't quite received the memo.'

'Lucca—'

He jerked upright in his chair, his elbows landing on the desk and those mesmerising eyes pinning her to the spot with cold lethality. 'That will be *Your Majesty* to you. You no longer have the right to use my first name.'

Her jaw sagged before she could stop it, her breath stalling in her lungs. 'But…but I thought you didn't go for all that *"pompous protocol"*?' His words, not hers.

One corner of his lips quirked, then his face hardened into an impenetrable mask. 'I am no longer the man you knew.'

Her insides quaked, but she succeeded—barely—in not showing outwardly how that affected her. Because, dear God, she believed him. The merciless intensity in his eyes, the cruel slash of his sensual lips and even the warrior-like way he carried himself now struck deep apprehension in her. Along with a heavy dose of alarming arousal...

'So you desire to be worshipped now?' she asked, attempting contempt and achieving far less.

'In the right circumstances and with the right person... absolutely,' he replied, his voice stuffed with conceit.

She licked her lips, the sting deep inside her already mourning the loss of being allowed to use his name. As if she didn't have enough problems... 'Fine. Your Majesty—'

He stopped her with a curt *tsk-tsk*. 'That won't quite do, *cara*. Try it again—minus the attitude. Make me believe you. Or, trust me, it will indeed be *over*.'

Every ounce of the power bristling from him assured her that he meant it. This was a test she absolutely needed to ace if she had any hope of getting further.

She reminded herself that she'd been extremely successful in her previous career because of her ability to conjure up the right act for any situation. Fashion houses and photographers had loved her for her ability to pull off the right emotion, the right pose, even the right personality on command.

Modelling was far more intricate than simply pouting and strutting down a runway under spotlights. And she'd been a natural long before she'd stepped on her first catwalk. She'd learned to hide her feelings, to pretend she was happy in order to keep the peace. To keep her mother from having to take sides lest Delphie find herself on the wrong one.

In the end it had been all for nothing. She'd been an outcast in what she'd thought was her home, forced to accept the hard truth. She hadn't been wanted, hadn't fitted into her mother's new life, and no amount of conformity or smiling through her anguish would ensure a safe haven or her mother's love.

She strode towards Lucca now, watching him shift ever so slightly in his chair, his gaze flicking to her hips and the swell of her breasts for a nanosecond before he resumed that alarming iron-willed control.

She'd changed. They both had. She'd known that long

before she'd stepped off the plane this afternoon. So why, now she was confronted with the man he'd become, did a piece of her mourn the old Lucca? Especially when discovering that he wasn't the man she'd thought she knew in the first place had fuelled her flight?

'Your Majesty, I arranged to have an hour of your time. I would be most grateful if our meeting could commence.'

His searing mockery flayed another layer off her skin, then he waved an imperious hand.

Delphie sank into a chair with relief. She needed this meeting to be over as quickly as possible. Wanted to be done so she could start the arduous process of once again blocking him out of her life.

Except if he was truly behind the acquisition of Hunter's shares she might not be completely free of him. But that was a risk she was prepared to take.

She'd already lost so much—far more than she'd imagined possible. She couldn't lose sight of what mattered now.

'I know I'm not the only model in the running for your diamond campaign,' she began.

'Ah, those questionable sources again?' he drawled, an almost bored look in his eyes.

Almost… But she saw beneath the ice to the steady but intense smouldering beneath. The one that evoked a rumbling volcano beneath a snow-capped mountain. The fire was there all right. All it needed was a trigger to erupt.

She recalled that same smouldering magnificence, amplified and focused exclusively on her. She'd gloried in it, immersed herself in it body and soul.

'Rachel told me. Is she wrong?'

'No, she's not.'

'Then my refusal shouldn't be a problem.'

'It's a problem if you require my assistance in your little venture but choose to start negotiations by displeasing me. I admit that's quite a mystery to me. Have you truly forgotten how rewarding pleasing me is, Delphine?'

For a traitorous few seconds her pulse leapt and her core

tightened in sickening anticipation. Until she read his face. Her mind might have delved into the deeply carnal, but Lucca was extremely focused on business.

'Your Majesty...' she started, then trailed off when he reached into his jacket, extracting a thin, folded piece of paper, which he slid across the immense desk, his laser-sharp eyes on her face as she hesitantly reached for it. 'What is this?' she asked, cringing at the noticeable tremble in her voice.

'Look for yourself,' he invited.

She was almost scared to. She knew it would affect her on a deep level. That invisible strings were tightening around her even though she'd fooled herself into thinking they were on an even keel.

With a slow indrawn breath, she looked down at the paper. Even though the words blurred before her eyes, they registered fiercely in her brain.

'No...' she whispered. Despite her instincts warning her for the better part of two weeks, she'd still, on some cellular level, refused to believe it.

'What exactly are you objecting to?' he drawled lazily, a predator toying with his prey. 'The evidence of your own eyes? Or the fact that I've swept the ground from under your feet?'

She raised accusing eyes to him, her insides congealing with all the ramifications. 'You planned all of this.'

The fingers steepled in front of his lips stopped her from seeing his smug smile, but she knew it was there. Knew he wouldn't let this triumphant moment pass.

'Planned what, exactly? Offering you a lucrative job that will temporarily bail you out of the hole you find yourself in? Or ensuring what comes after that is entirely in my control? If so, yes—on both accounts,' he supplied readily.

Delphie glanced down, furiously focusing on his words. 'He wouldn't...'

But he had. Hunter had known exactly who he'd sold his stake to. She might have suspected, even hoped, one of San

Calliano's numerous wealthy subjects had bought the shares, and not the King, but deep inside…she'd *known*.

'By *"he"* I presume you mean Buckman?' Lucca bit out, with more venom than she'd anticipated.

She swallowed. 'You bought the team from him…'

'His entire stake—*sì*. Which grants me the controlling share,' he said, thick relish in his voice.

Her insides trembled harder. He was in control of the one thing that meant anything to her. The only thing that had stopped her from sliding into the dark pit of despair. 'Why?'

Cold eyes regarded her without remorse. 'Because I could.'

'Because you want me under your thumb!' she returned heatedly.

He nodded with raw, naked triumph, his thumb slowly caressing his lower lip. '*Sì, cara,* that too.'

She gasped. 'You're not even going to bother denying it?'

One muscled shoulder lifted in a regal shrug. 'Why should I when it's the truth?'

'Why?' she demanded again.

'Because I want you for exactly the purpose Rachel told you about.'

She frowned. 'You paid one hundred and twenty million dollars to get me to do three million dollars' worth of work? That doesn't make sense.'

His smirk was mirthless and the eyes that combed her body were alive with volatile emotion, as if now they'd got down to brass tacks he wasn't bothering to hide behind his icy hauteur any longer.

'No, as delectable as you are, not even *you* are worth that, *cara*. The festival assignment will just be the start. I have other assignments for you to undertake.'

'And if I refuse?' she taunted, partly incensed by the trap she could feel closing over her and partly quaking at what was to come.

'If you refuse, the sponsors you've been trying so hard to retain will be the least of your problems,' he stated, and that cool voice sounded as if it was wrapped around a deadly blade.

'What exactly do you want?' she demanded.

He rose to his imperious height, then leaned over the desk until his body was front and centre of her vision, leaving her in no doubt to his seriousness. 'For starters, *The Ghosted King* will be ghosted no more!' he snarled.

She gasped. 'That's all this is to you? An ego-salvaging exercise?'

'You lost the right to question my reason for anything when you disappeared from my life without the courtesy of informing me you were leaving.'

Her mouth dropped open as the true picture of his intentions reared into focus.

And in that moment Delphie knew she had to appeal to his better self—if such a thing existed in the man who now stared at her with zero mercy.

She'd ghosted a prince turned King, and he intended to exact payment for the slight.

'Luc— Your Majesty,' she hastily corrected when his gaze froze over. 'I thought the…the note would be enough—'

'The note you didn't bother to send until two months after you disappeared, you mean? Along with the gift I gave you?' he interjected, his breath exiting in a harsh exhalation.

She pressed her lips together and held the words deep in her chest. Because anything she said right now would unravel everything she'd kept under lock and key. The last thing she wanted was for him to learn that theirs hadn't been an ordinary affair for her. That in those final days in Paris she'd hoped for something more.

She desperately didn't want him to know that discovering she carried his child had given her one last, desperate hope. Until even that had been dashed by a cruel stranger's visit. Most of all, she didn't want Lucca to learn just why it had taken her so long to raise her head above the parapet after fleeing to Qatar.

'I didn't expect you to look for me that intently. I thought you'd move on soon enough.'

'You had me at a rare disadvantage there. Had you given me the chance, I would've given you my blessing to move on and never spared you a second thought again.'

The sheer conceit behind the statement left her breathless for several seconds. 'I didn't want anything from you. Not then, not now.'

He straightened and casually strolled around the desk to stand behind her. Delphie felt his gaze drill into her crown but refused to look up. After an age, she sensed him closer, shivered when his minty breath brushed her ear.

'Really? Then I guess there's nothing worth negotiating. This meeting is over.'

She heard his footsteps retreating while actively managing the meltdown in her pelvis. While cursing her body's full-blown reaction to his proximity.

By the time she'd vaulted off the chair and chased him down he was at the door, one hand poised to open it.

'Wait!'

He pivoted with the grace and elegance of a man who knew his worth. A true monarch used to commanding his loyal acolytes.

'Let's get one thing straight, *cara*. I am no longer the man you knew. I suggest you revise any inclination you feel to sway me to your way of thinking by using whatever wiles you possess.'

That bubble of hysteria forced its way up again. She'd never once dreamed she could wrap him around her finger when they were together. Sure, their affair had been one of those comet-like blazes across the sky, with lust the fuel that had kept them going long after his usual notoriously brief attention span, when their liaison should've burnt out. But she had harboured hopes...

In the end much to her detriment.

'Trust me, I wouldn't dream of it.'

'Trust you?' His lips curled. 'Shall I remind you how the

"fool me once" saying goes? Perhaps *you* should trust *me* that I'm no fool, *cara*.'

She inhaled sharply as pain lanced her. Licking suddenly dry lips, she fought to maintain her composure. 'Can we talk about this properly? I'm willing to hear you out.'

He kept her waiting for an age, settling his eyes with uncanny focus on her face before strolling back into the living room and dropping on to the sofa. One arm extended along the back of it, he patted the smooth, plump seat next to him with his other hand.

'Sit down.'

Every rebellious cell in her body rose in opposition. Thoughts of taking back her agreement to talk, of walking into the bedroom, throwing her things into her suitcase and storming out with a carefree *To hell with it* flew through her mind. She could grab the next flight and be back at her apartment in Qatar by midnight. Better still, she could rent the fastest sports car available and drive until every last alarming concern about her future dissipated under an infusion of pure adrenalin and several hundred horsepower.

His mocking smile as his fingers continued to tap elegantly on the seat said she hadn't done a great job of concealing her thoughts. That he was confident of his victory.

Their battle of wills lasted a minute and felt like a year. But, spurred on by the thought of getting through this as quickly as possible and the more harrowing aversion of returning to that place of bleakness if, heaven forbid, he made good on his threats, Delphie approached.

Ignoring the seat he'd indicated, she chose the one farthest from him, uncaring what he read into it.

'You'll take the modelling assignment,' he said before she'd drawn breath. 'According to my organising board, you're the best candidate. And I'm inclined to agree.'

She didn't fool herself into thinking he was being complimentary. His intentions were far too cold-blooded for that. Delphie pursed her lips. 'Rachel told me about the job. Can you assure me there won't be any unforeseen extras?'

A terrifying glint lit the eyes narrowed on her face. 'Such as…?'

'Can you assure me that one week won't suddenly become two? That I won't be asked to work ungodly hours?'

'Some flexibility may be required… It's not as if you don't know what your line of work entails. What's the big deal?'

'I have a life to be getting on with. One you're disrupting with these demands.'

'Tell me about that life,' he invited smoothly, much like a snake coaxing a rabbit for a visit to its dark cave. But that intensity remained, as if he was holding his breath for… *something*.

Delphie curbed the shiver that threatened to reveal her angst about the whole situation. 'This isn't a social meeting, Your Majesty. My life isn't your concern.'

His eyes turned Arctic. 'You should be careful, Delphine. There's nothing to be won by this animosity towards me.'

'Really? You say you're not the man I knew. So far everything you've shown me has proved that to be true. So shouldn't I be arming myself against whatever it is you're planning?'

Her accusation merely garnered a lazy shrug. But that look didn't dissipate from his eyes. And the room continued to hold its breath. 'You catch more flies with honey than vinegar…isn't that the saying?'

She tilted her head, infusing maximum cynicism into her expression. 'Is His Majesty comparing himself to a fly? How terrifying for the poor flies.'

For a nanosecond she caught a glint of humour in his eyes. Then it vanished, leaving her with a sharp reminder of how they'd used to laugh together. How the rich, decadent sound of his laughter had filled every cell of her body with contentment and achievement, because she'd never seen the intense Prince Lucca of San Calliano being carefree with anyone else when they were together.

Now she blinked the thought away, knowing that to dwell on the past was especially foolish.

'Do the job required of you and I see no reason for there to be any extraneous demands on your time.'

Relief piped through her bloodstream, but she didn't relax. Because, if anything, her tension was mounting, signalling that the crux of the matter was yet to be addressed.

'In that case, I'll do it.'

He leaned forward, resting his elbows on his knees. Nothing in his expression indicated that he was pleased by her agreement. As she'd suspected, the assignment was a mere conduit to his true intentions.

'*Bene*. That should lay the foundations for what comes after that.'

Every atom of her body froze. 'And what comes after that?'

'You make reparation for the damage you caused by your sudden disappearing act nineteen months ago.'

CHAPTER THREE

Lucca watched myriad expressions dart across her face. Shock. Alarm. Wariness. Then full-blown outrage.

He cringed at the clichéd knowledge that the last emotion looked most beautiful on her. Everything about Delphine Alexander was stunning, but her fiery spirit—that ingrained refusal to kowtow to his position or back away from his sometimes imposing passions—had kept him fixated on her far longer than he'd intended, with the somewhat dismaying realisation that time had flown by without his registering.

He secretly admitted he would've preferred it if she'd lost some of that allure during their time apart. But, no. Her absence might not have made him grow fonder, but her beauty and spirit had gained nuanced, completely engrossing new layers. Initially he'd been unable to pinpoint it, but gradually he'd unearthed the secret.

It wasn't simply the passage of time, but life experience that had claimed the girlishness in her and steeped her in true womanhood. She had an iron-forged strength and stamina that invited him to look deeper into her eyes, ponder her experiences, wonder what crucible fires she'd endured.

Against his will, he wanted—*needed*—to know everything. Just as he'd needed to know why he'd never been enough for his parents. Why his mother especially had been so deeply indifferent to everything happening under her roof, instead chasing the hedonistic pleasures she'd treasured above all else.

He ruthlessly pushed the thought out of his head.

'Are you joking?' came Delphine's shocked reply.

He wanted to laugh. Then he wanted to block his ears from hearing that rich, sultry voice that so enthralled him… like every inch of her body.

Now he knew where she'd hidden herself in the months after her departure he was a little jealous of the Qatari sun, because it had turned her creamed coffee skin a shade deeper, lent it a glow he wanted to explore with his fingers, his mouth and his manhood, for hours. He wanted to discover which curves the sun had missed, trace every tan line with his tongue…

Cursing his body's eager reaction to his thoughts, he summoned a hard smile. 'Be assured that nothing I say tonight stems from humour.'

'But…but we broke up, Luc—*Your Majesty*! Since when is an ex-girlfriend required to pay for ending a relationship?'

Something lanced his gut at hearing the descriptor. Was it because *girlfriend* seemed so…so tame for the position she'd held in his life? She'd strayed dangerously close to becoming his consort—an unparalleled position in his life— to becoming a person he could tackle almost every subject under the sun with.

Almost.

Because he'd been reticent about discussing his childhood or his parents with her—from a deep desire not to appear flawed in her eyes, perhaps? Or simply because their time together had been a sacred space and he'd refused to let the stain of his childhood blemish it?

He shook himself free of the alarming thoughts. Concentrated instead on her outrage. 'There was a certain protocol to be observed,' he told her. 'Your abrupt departure threw that process into chaos.'

Her shrewd eyes narrowed. Something tightened in his gut, because even now he couldn't quite step away from how the whole thing had made him feel…the heavy weight in his stomach as the worst possible scenarios had unspooled in his head.

'Why didn't you simply send out a press release?' she asked, and he caught a trace of bitterness in her voice. 'Isn't that how the usual *process* goes?'

Lucca felt a sting of shame because, as frantic as he'd been to find her, it hadn't even occurred to him to do that. He'd all but banned his advisers from discussing Delphine.

'And what if you'd resurfaced soon after that, with a story of your own to sell? All it would've garnered would have been further unwanted attention.'

Her outrage grew. 'At what point during our time together did I give you the impression that I'm the sort of woman who sells stories to the tabloids?' she demanded, deep affront in her beautiful eyes.

He shrugged its effect on him away. 'You proved conclusively that I didn't know you at all when you pulled your disappearing act. How was I to know what you'd do next?'

'Not that! A man in your position doesn't function on facts and figures alone. You said as much once, if I recall. Couldn't you trust your own instincts?'

Lucca was bracingly aware of how much he'd revealed of himself to her. A fact he deeply regretted.

'I was a prince then. I'm a king now. I don't have the liberty of trusting everyone who pleads their innocence.'

She launched herself upright, granting him the full-scale, breath-stealing view of the five-foot-ten curves and valleys of her body. The material of her jumpsuit perfectly delineated her flat stomach, supple thighs and the proud protrusion of her breasts, the buttocks honed by a daily exercise routine, and the long, graceful arms that had clung to him in ecstasy once upon a time. All of it colluded to launch flames into his groin, stirring his manhood to life.

'That's a cop-out. What's really going on here? And what exactly does "reparation" mean, anyway?' she demanded.

Lucca dragged his thoughts from the power her body had wielded over him back to the present. To the sharp reminder that he needed to be circumspect in the information he divulged now.

His advisers and security team had gone to a lot of trouble to ring-fence any detrimental information lingering after his mother's activities, but to achieve his goals now he needed to make it unequivocally clear that refusal wasn't an option.

'You came dangerously close to causing irreparable damage to my kingdom's reputation with the act you pulled—do you do know that?'

Shock lit her chocolate-brown eyes and she slowly sank back down into the chair. 'What...?' Before he could reply, she shook her head free of the emotion. 'No. All I did was leave. I get that it might be a novelty for you, but—'

'Don't be naive, Delphine. You may have chosen to believe our liaison was a regular one, to stop yourself from being overwhelmed by the experience, but the reality was far different. I wasn't a nobody and you had certain obligations—one of them being how things would end between us.'

Her full lips pursed, reminding him of how he'd loved to bite her lower lip when she did that. How much he wanted to do that now, damn her.

'First, I wasn't overwhelmed—' she said.

'Weren't you?' he countered.

'No,' she stated, but her gaze evaded his.

He hid a smile. It soothed his pride that she'd been just as mindless as he.

'Second, I don't recall signing my life away in blood simply for the chance to date you. If I recall, you came after *me*.'

Because she'd been an instant fever in his blood he hadn't been able to overcome—not without a full and immersive experience. Even now, remnants of the fever lingered, stealing through his blood like seductive poison.

'It may not have been explicitly spelled out for you, but you're an intelligent woman. Were you not aware of certain protocols in the normal course of our days together?'

'You mean how we couldn't go to a restaurant without phoning ahead and having it vacated just for us? Or how your bodyguards cleared the shops in a mall before we could visit? I'm assuming that now you're King whole towns need to be evacuated before you deign to set foot in them?'

He wanted to smile because, *mio Dio*, no other person dared to speak to him the way Delphine did. Without fear. Without sycophancy. With that sexy, husky, *taunting* tone that set his blood on fire.

He'd never bothered to read the dossier his security team had gathered on her within weeks of the start of their relationship—he had even gone as far as to delete it, because he'd welcomed the novelty of her—but, wherever she'd gained her thick vein of pride and fearlessness, he couldn't let it stand in his way now.

'For reasons I won't go into, it has always been imperative that there be no hint of impropriety about my liaisons. Your actions triggered rumours that continue to undermine certain aspects of my rule.'

She frowned. 'What rumours?'

His jaw clenched. He was unsure whether he was more annoyed at her obliviousness to them or the fact that he had to lower himself to repeat them. 'Unfounded ones that need to be conclusively laid to rest,' he replied.

'And they relate to this modelling assignment...how?' Wariness remained in her voice.

'You'll be accompanying me to functions while wearing the San Calliano royal diamond collection during the festival. Naturally there will be rumours of a reunion between us. Rumours we will do nothing to dispel.'

Her eyes widened again. 'I... You're not serious!'

He merely stared back, let his expression speak for him. Again she surged from her seat—this time to pace the area in front of the coffee table. And, *Dio* help him, he couldn't look away from the captivating roll of her hips, the elegant swing of her arms, the delicate line of her neck and jaw and those dense corkscrew curls he'd loved to sink his fingers into...couldn't stop his gut clenching tight as wild lust attacked him at the sight of her body.

It had been this way from the instant he'd laid eyes on her—a need that thrusting inside her hot, tight body again and again hadn't assuaged one iota.

'Why? What purpose will it serve?' she asked.

'I thought it was clear, *cara*. If it isn't, let me spell it out for you. This time *I* will control the narrative. *I* will decide where and when it ends.'

'You want me to…?' She stopped and shook her head, disappointment and another emotion he couldn't quite pinpoint briefly dulling her eyes before she exhaled. 'So really this isn't a modelling assignment. I'm supposed to act as if I'm besotted with you?'

'Just like you did last time, yes.'

Her long, lush lashes swept down, shielding her gaze from him, sparking embers of anger inside him. He wanted her to deny she'd been acting then. Wanted her to acknowledge the euphoric madness that had engulfed them both before she'd inexplicably fled his life and his bed.

But all she did was take another breath before raising that proud chin. 'It sounds like you have a PR problem on your hands. Why should I do anything to help you?' she challenged.

'Besides the fact that you owe me an explanation that you still haven't given me?' he countered, noting the shell of bitterness hardening his words.

She was demonstrating the same indifference his mother had always shown when he'd demanded to know why she behaved the way she did. Shrugging it off as if it didn't matter.

As if he didn't matter.

And now Delphine's answer was to turn her back on him. The same way his mother had done far too often. She went to the window, gazed out at the bright lights of his capital.

During their time together his diplomatic duties had mainly stationed him in the States and South America. They'd only visited San Calliano once, briefly, when his father had summoned him home.

Lucca had kept her in his private royal residence, away

from the royal palace, and flown out with her as soon as he'd been done with his father. He hadn't been in a hurry to introduce her to his royal life—perhaps for fear that his family's sordid past would lead to second thoughts, perhaps even rejection?

No matter.

He was above that now. His priority was his people, and ensuring his kingdom remained above reproach and rumours.

When she turned to him, determination flared from her eyes. 'Relationships end all the time. I believe my note stated my views on ours.'

Her note.

The two-word dent to his pride still stung more than he cared to admit.

'So you routinely and arbitrarily decide when the men you indulge in liaisons with don't deserve the courtesy of an explanation?' he bit out, aware that his emotions were overruling his will. A far too frequent occurrence when he was with her.

'Why do we need to perform an autopsy on us?' she demanded. 'Just accept that things weren't working for me and let's move on, shall we?'

He'd surged to his feet and was bracing his hands on the window, caging her in, before he'd taken a full breath.

'Things *"weren't working"* for you?' he growled in disbelief. 'When only the night before you disappeared you'd clung to me in bed, scoring my back with those vixen nails as you screamed, *"Again, Lucca. More, Lucca. Please, Please, Please, Lucca."* Lie to yourself all you want, *dolcezza*, but don't attempt to insult my intelligence by telling me blatant lies.'

Her nostrils fluttered on a shaky breath and he was satisfied to see her pulse racing at her throat, her fingers fluttering uselessly at her sides. 'Sex wasn't…*isn't*…everything,' she said finally, and he had to grit his teeth as her sweet breath washed over his jaw.

'Perhaps not. But it was a very big, very visceral thing for us. So unless that miraculously changed overnight…'

A shadow passed through her eyes, sending alarm bells clanging in his head.

'Was that the reason, Delphine?' he pressed, an almost rabid need to know tearing at him. 'What changed?'

She attempted to brush past him, but he halted her dismissal by catching her wrist.

'You do know the more you withhold your explanation the more determined I'll be to get to the truth?'

'Why does it matter so much?' she flung at him.

'Because I detest secrets and subterfuge. I prefer to see the field on which I'm playing. That stunt you pulled is why we're here right now. Hiding things from me will only push me to dig further. Is that what you want?'

'I didn't enjoy your company any more. Is that truth enough for you?'

A roar built in his chest, climbed into his throat. He could feel her racing pulse beneath his fingers. And, *sì*, he didn't want to accept another rejection—especially one he knew was false at worst, and a smokescreen at best.

So he did the one thing he'd promised himself he wouldn't do.

Heaven help him, how could he *not* when she pushed his every button? When her unique crushed roses scent wove unadulterated delirium around him? When her succulent lips were this close and her body, whether she knew it or not, had angled itself ever so subtly closer to his during their little heated exchange?

He took her mouth with his in what he'd intended to be a brief counterattack to sabotage her false claims.

Of course it wasn't that easy. Nothing was ever easy with this woman. Of course she tasted much more intoxicating than he remembered. And, *santa cielo*, when her lips clung to him, he might be a king, but he was only a man.

A very tried, very tested man.

He deepened the kiss, heard her soft moan of acceptance

and wanted to roar in triumph. Instead, he cupped her full breast, groaning deep when he brushed the stiff, welcoming peak with his thumb.

A thick shudder went through her before she pushed her chest into his fingers, as gratifyingly eager for his touch as he was to grant it. Supple flesh that had haunted far too many of his dreams eagerly filled his hand, and when he trailed it down, cupped her bottom, he was even more gratified when she strained against his erection.

Only when their prolonged kiss threatened to turn into the frenzied madness that had so encapsulated their time together did Lucca disentangle his tongue from hers. Only then did he drop his hands from her firm buttocks, drag his body a necessary but painful foot from hers.

He gazed into her heated eyes and watched the frantic rise and fall of her chest with unabashed satisfaction, even while he licked his lips, eager for one last taste of her.

'I think I've just proved that the sex isn't why you left.'

'You bastard,' she hissed, dragging the back of her hand across her kiss-swollen lips, attempting to remove the evidence of his possession.

Lucca didn't care. Other erogenous zones gave him the corroboration he needed. The intoxicated look in her eyes, for example. The subtle twitch in her thighs as her unfulfilled desire came crashing down.

He pivoted and placed another several feet between them, because in that moment he didn't trust himself not to delve in for a second, third, fourth taste.

Per l'amor de Dio—he was a king! Such base desires should be beneath him. Especially since they had been the root cause of his father's downfall, with his mother's blind pursuit of hedonistic outlets. And the foundation of his dysfunctional childhood—the reason he'd vowed never to fall prey to such emotions.

He dragged a hand through his hair. 'Regardless of how you feel about the matter, this is what's going to happen. After the festival, and your last race before the August hiatus, you'll stay here in San Calliano—specifically, in the palace. To all intents and purposes we'll be a couple reunited. When I'm satisfied the rumours have been laid to rest, we'll devise a suitable uncoupling.'

The haze of lust receded from her eyes, replaced by shock, then fury. 'That's… I can't just uproot my life at your behest!'

'Unfortunately, that is what I require,' he stated ruthlessly.

'And what do I get in return for this…this absurd performance?'

'I'll ensure that your team stops haemorrhaging sponsors, for starters. I'll even throw in a few extra million to speed up whatever development the team needs. I don't need to tell you what public backing from me will accomplish.'

The stubborn light remained in her eyes. 'This is blackmail.'

'No, it's a negotiation,' he replied firmly. 'You have something I want. You require something I have. Tell me how this is different from any business negotiation?'

She took a long, audible breath and, aggravatingly, Lucca found himself holding his own.

After an age, she exhaled. '*If* I agree to this *business* transaction, there will be no sex. Nothing remotely similar to…to what just happened. Is that understood?'

His gut tightened, ferocious rebellion seizing his muscles. 'Are you sure you want to hobble your own needs like that?' he asked.

Naked need flickered through her eyes, then immediately, alarmingly, dulled. 'My needs will be taken care of.'

Rage turned his vision red. '*Come l'inferno lo farai!* Like hell they will,' he translated bitingly when she stared blankly at him. 'Accommodate even a look of interest from another man and this deal is over! And not just that. I will ensure that you—'

'Calm down, Your Majesty,' she said, with a toss of her head. 'I get that it defeats the object if I blatantly start dating someone while pretending you're my sun and moon. I meant that I have a perfectly adequate vibrator that can see to my needs.'

Shock bolted through him. 'Sex toys?'

He wasn't a caveman. He was well-versed in pleasure-enhancing gadgets—had even indulged his partners with the odd one or two before the novelty wore off. Still, the thought of Delphine using one…

One of her perfectly shaped eyebrows quirked. 'You look surprised… This *is* the twenty-first century, you know,' she stated drolly.

Lucca fought to dismiss the image—the progressively more enthralling image—and sauntered back to her. 'Does that mean you will yield to my demands?'

The humour evaporated, and her expression was once more apprehensive. 'I want everything in writing—just so there's no misunderstanding.'

Something kicked in his chest. A cross between triumph and relief. 'You'll have it.'

Again she hesitated. When her gaze dropped to his lips, then to the opening in his shirt, Lucca curbed a smile. She wasn't immune to him, despite her stipulations.

Suddenly he was looking forward to the many ways she intended to fight this thing between them. Because in making her eat her words he might also get the answers he needed to the questions that continued to eat away like acid inside him, long after she said, 'Yes, I agree.'

Delphie asked herself why she'd said yes as she perused the contract papers the next morning.

The three stoic-looking lawyers in attendance were mostly easy to ignore. The man she couldn't ignore was the orchestrator of all this. His cosmic re-entry into her life had left her shaken, staring at the ceiling into the early hours, wondering how deeply she'd doomed herself by coming here.

Lucca was attired as sophisticatedly as he'd been last night, having swapped the dark suit for a lighter one, but again sans tie. The hair she'd frenziedly dishevelled last night was neatly combed this morning and, although she'd been too overwhelmed to notice last night, she saw that it was longer, the strands brushing his collar. In the light of day his designer stubble was even more inviting, framing his full, masculine lips and making her aware of every word that dropped from them...

'Delphine?'

She started, heat pulsing through her when she realised he was addressing her. 'Yes?'

The sharp gazes of the lawyers indicated that she hadn't added his correct title, but she shrugged it off. She was already committing a few errors of judgement in agreeing to this absurd deal. What was one more?

'Is everything satisfactory?' Lucca asked.

She detected a hard edge to his tone and realised she'd been staring at the document for five minutes. After taking half an hour to read it. Twice.

She couldn't stall any longer. 'Yes,' she said, and then, holding her breath, scrawled her signature on the designated line.

The lawyers sprang into action, witnessing the document and handing her a copy before, bowing to their King, they made themselves scarce.

Rising from the desk, she went to the window, the view this morning calling to her. There, she allowed the warm sun to linger on her skin, desperately trying to ignore Lucca's leonine focus on her.

The dark gold palazzo trousers and matching halterneck top she'd worn for this meeting were perfect for the temperate San Calliano weather. But as she withstood his lingering scrutiny a deep awareness invaded the room, her tingling body confirming just how much of her bare flesh was on show.

Everywhere his gaze touched resonated deep in her pelvis. Much as that kiss yesterday had affected her. She'd thought herself immune to such base sensations after the harrowing months she'd endured since leaving him. Last night had shown that she had capacity for unlimited physical desire. That he only needed to lay a finger on her for her body to go up in flames.

Dear God, she'd all but clawed at him in her frenzy for that kiss...had spent many hours unable to help herself reliving it frame by frame.

Her only reprieve had been promising herself that it wouldn't happen again.

Unable to withstand the silent scrutiny, she pivoted to face him. 'What now?'

'Now you have breakfast with me, while my staff relocate you to my palace.'

Her belly dipped and somersaulted in alarm. 'I thought I wouldn't need to do that until the festival was over?' She'd been banking on distance to shore up the defences that had suffered a huge blow at the first temptation last night.

He shrugged. 'It's been brought to my attention that there's a shortage of hotel rooms. A few days won't make a difference. Besides, the collection you'll be showcasing is at my palace. It makes sense for you to be there for security purposes.'

It will make a difference to me! she wanted to scream.

But dissolving into hysterics would solve nothing. She was in this thing. She just needed to see it through and then she could carry on with the new path of her life. The path that reconnected her with the father she'd loved and lost far too soon.

As if summoned by the will of his King, the butler assigned to the royal suite appeared and bowed deeply. 'Would Your Majesty and madam like anything to eat for breakfast?'

Lucca simply stared at her, one eyebrow sardonically cocked, daring her to countermand his edict.

Maintaining her composure, she turned to the butler. 'I'll have an egg white omelette, decaffeinated coffee with cream and a bowl of fruit. His Majesty will have fruit muesli, Indonesian black coffee and two grapefruits. We'll take it outside on the terrace, please.'

'Right away, madam.' To his credit, the butler didn't show one ounce of surprise at her knowledge of his King's breakfast preferences as he executed another perfect bow and retreated.

Unable to resist, she glanced at Lucca to find his lips twitching with faint amusement. 'Feeling the need to flex a little power, *cara*?'

'I'm just not in the mood to play games,' she replied, even while her stomach hollowed with dismay at her rashness. Because by accurately reciting his breakfast choices hadn't she just revealed that she hasn't forgotten a single thing about him? That her exit from his life hadn't been born of a lack of interest?

She veered towards the French doors leading to the wide wrap-around terrace, eager to flee her own roiling emotions.

'You're aware you've already set tongues wagging, aren't you?' Lucca said, rising to follow.

She paused, glancing over her shoulder. 'Isn't that what you want? As far as I'm concerned, the earlier this starts, the earlier I can be done with it.'

All traces of humour left his face, leaving it a hard, mesmerising sculpture she wanted to explore with her fingers. She stepped outside, simply to stop herself even thinking about that temptation.

He arrived behind her at the table, pulling out a chair before she could. In the process he leaned close, his face aligning with hers.

'We may have an agreement, but I'd still caution you to stay on my good side, *cara*,' he breathed.

His breath washed over her neck and the curve of her shoulder, dragging up a shiver she couldn't hide. Nor could she ignore the chilly warning in his words. While their time together had seemed like an attempt to hit every high note of an affair with a short shelf life, she'd caught occasional glimpses of the core of steel he needed to be the future ruler of a prosperous Mediterranean kingdom that held clout on the world stage.

Like when a heated call with his father had led to her previous trip to San Calliano. He'd never told her the reason behind it, and she'd never asked, but his stern, rigid demeanour throughout their visit had quietly terrified her.

Now she looked up into his face and saw raw, unapologetic ruthlessness in his eyes. She swallowed, aware that she was risking rousing a predator that could ravage her every vulnerability. 'You can't want this thing prolonged more than necessary, surely?' she probed.

An inscrutable look filmed his eyes. 'My primary duty is to ensure my kingdom's reputation. I'll do whatever is necessary to achieve that. Sit down, Delphine.'

The rigid instruction sent another bolt of warning down her spine. While it lit a fire of rebellion inside her, she accepted that she needed to pick her battles carefully. So she sat down, reaching for the crystal pitcher of orange juice already placed on the pristine laid table. Out of courtesy she glanced at him and, when he shook his head, poured herself a glass.

'Why motor racing?'

Her hand shook and she hastily placed the jug back down. 'What?'

'Motor racing is a world removed from modelling. Most models start their own brand or agency, and generally stay within their sphere of knowledge. Why such a curious deviation?'

She pressed her lips together, fiercely unwilling to state the reasons why. By silent mutual agreement they'd shied away from sharing personal details about themselves when they were together, and Delphie was even more reticent to open herself to him now, when there was clear animosity between them. But she'd already aroused his displeasure. Moreover, when it came down to it, he held sway over whether her precious team thrived or floundered.

So she gritted her teeth and answered. 'My father was a mechanic. He could fix anything with an engine, but he especially loved fixing classic cars. I picked up a few things when I was younger.'

His eyes narrowed. 'You speak of him in the past tense.'

She braced herself for the lash of pain and it came full force, the passage of time having done nothing to dampen it. 'He…he died when I was twelve.'

The laser harshness in his eyes lessened, and she swore she caught a wave of compassion before his lashes swept down. *'Condoglianze,'* he murmured.

The unexpected sentiment eased her pain. 'Thank you.'

'And your mother?' he asked, that intense look returning.

A different sort of pain arrived, sharpened by the blade of estranged rejection and bitterness. 'She's alive. Lives in London,' she added.

The butler's arrival with their breakfast halted conversation, bringing the welcome break she needed. And when he'd departed, she scrambled to change the subject.

'What's my first assignment?'

For a pulse of time he didn't speak. Then, 'The official opening of the festival will take place at the San Calliano art museum at ten a.m. tomorrow. The press will be there, so I suggest you put on your game face.'

Pride made her stare bold. 'I have no problem projecting the image required of me.'

His eyes darkened with a touch of scorn. *'Vero,* I'm beginning to see that you possess a veritable range of talents. Not all of them particularly savoury,' he said, a thick vein of bitterness in his voice.

And, as much as she loathed to admit it, in that moment she experienced a brand-new strain of distress…this one caused directly by the man who'd taken her to the highest highs, then sent her plummeting to the depths of despair.

CHAPTER FOUR

FIVE HOURS AFTER their progressively more stilted breakfast, she was ensconced in a royal apartment that put her hotel suite to deep shame.

Every inch of the San Calliano royal palace dripped with grace, elegance and opulence, the likes of which she'd only ever seen in extreme digitally-enhanced magazines, from its pale baroque magnificence, pristine manicured gardens and stained-glass windows to the vaulted Renaissance-themed frescoes depicting scenes of the love and war that had forged the kingdom.

She was slack-jawed as Lucca guided her through a few of the main staterooms, where immense crystal chandeliers illuminated rich tapestries and history blended with magnificent modern decor. Then he excused himself, tasking two high-ranking palace aides to show her the remainder of the breathtaking palace perched high on a hill overlooking San Lorena.

Entering the palace at his side, she'd seen a visible change in Lucca. The unyielding, imperious countenance had reappeared, his nods had been curt and his words polite but clipped. Not that she'd understood any of it, since Italian was the official language. His streamlined body had been held equally military-rigid, and he'd given no quarter as he strode down the vast hallways.

His departing words had been brief and to the point. 'I

have duties to attend to for the rest of the day. You'll be collected to dine with me this evening.'

Before she'd been able to reply he'd walked away, the man he'd introduced as his chief of staff already rattling off reports in rapid Italian.

Now, thankfully alone, she explored her suite, trailing her fingers over the silk walls, a solid bronze bust of some royal ancestor, whose proud patrician features resembled the current King's, and the thick embossed paper stamped with the royal crest. She paused in awe before an authentic Botticelli painting while her bare feet luxuriated in deep gold carpeting.

Delphie had declined lunch after the palace tour, her stomach rebelling at the thought of food. Nevertheless, shortly after the aides had taken their leave, a butler arrived with a tray of delicate sandwiches and a pot of fragrant tea.

Hoping tea would calm her nerves, she sipped a cup as she continued to acquaint herself with her suite. Discovering a coffee table book on San Calliano, Delphie perched on the deep emerald velvet divan and opened to the first page.

An image of Lucca, dressed in full green and gold royal military regalia, had her breath catching. According to the annotation, the photo had been taken on the morning of his coronation. He looked *magnificent*, the deep purpose and pride in his eyes leaving absolutely no doubt that he was born to be a king.

Delphie found herself wondering for a reckless moment what would've happened if she hadn't opted for self-preservation and had allowed things to reach their inevitable conclusion. Would she have been present at his coronation? An ex-lover who'd agreed to be thoroughly contemporary and remain friends?

She snorted painfully beneath her breath. That would've been impossible. Not with the life-altering events that had occurred before *and* after her flight out of his life.

She continued to leaf through the book, her heart skipping each time she saw Lucca's image. But, going through it, she noted that while there were many pictures of his father, his mother rarely featured. Information about Queen Alessia of San Calliano was minimal, and the only pictures of her were as a stunning newly crowned queen in her late twenties.

Curbing her curiosity as to why her story was so abbreviated, Delphie turned to San Calliano's history. She was totally absorbed in how the kingdom—young in comparison to its larger neighbours—had gained power through its oil and diamond holdings in strategic countries across the world, when a firm knock came at the door.

Her heart leapt—until she remembered she wasn't seeing Lucca till that evening. On less hesitant feet, she approached the door, only to feel the tension ease out of her at seeing who her visitor was.

'Nicola! What are you doing here?'

Nicola Barbieri threw out her arms and hugged Delphie, before kissing her on both cheeks. Easing back, she smiled, her dark topaz eyes sparkling with joy as she sailed into the room. 'I'm here to do your fitting.'

Delphie had hit it off with Nicola, then an intern, at their first meeting in a major fashion house in Milan six years ago. The dark-skinned woman's bold sense of style and friendliness in the cut-throat world of fashion design had been refreshing, and they'd stayed loosely in touch over the years.

Of course, Delphie had lost her connection with most of her acquaintances when she'd fled to Qatar, but it was heartwarming to see a friendly face.

'But…how did you even know I was here?'

Nicola's smile widened. 'I didn't. I submitted my name to the tourism committee when I heard they were scouting fashion houses for the festival. Imagine my shock when they rang yesterday morning to say that not only had my designs been picked but *you* were the one I'd be dressing! I really should've gone ahead and spent a small fortune on lottery tickets.'

Delphie laughed, but part of her grew a little unsettled.

Lucca had known she would agree even before he'd arrived at her hotel last night.

She suppressed the disturbing thought as Nicola tossed her long, luscious dreadlocks over her shoulder and snapped her fingers. Two women entered, each pushing two rails of clothing. Another followed, wheeling a trolley stacked with accessories.

'This is my team,' Nicola announced proudly. 'We'll be here every morning to get you ready for the festival. And to dish on all the gossip, naturally,' she added under her breath.

'You have your own fashion label?' Delphie's pride for her friend pushed through her chaotic emotions.

Nicola nodded. 'House of Barbieri is small, but we're making inroads in the fashion arena. Dressing you will definitely put me on the map.'

Delphie linked her fingers in front of her. 'I haven't modelled in a while, so maybe don't hold out too much hope?'

Nicola waved her away. 'You have more style and grace in your little finger than most models dream of having their whole career. I'm not worried. Are you ready to get started?'

At her nod, the designer went into enthusiastic work mode.

Three hours later, her hitherto near-empty dressing room was filled with enough jaw-dropping designs to equip London Fashion Week.

On a whim—and because deep down she didn't want to be alone—Delphie had invited Nicola to stay for a drink, smiling when the woman happily accepted and dismissed her team.

'So… I have to ask. Are you and His Majesty back together?' Nicola whispered, casting a quick glance at the departing butler who'd served their refreshments.

Delphie tensed, struggling not to let that minute sting of what-might-have-been show. 'No, we're not. I'm just here on assignment.'

It was better to let events unfurl on their own. Besides, she'd agreed to let Lucca handle the narrative and couldn't risk jeopardising that. Ensuring the future of Hunter Racing was the most important thing.

Nicola grimaced good-naturedly. 'Well, some of us are incurable romantics and we're dreaming of a fairy-tale reunion. Who knows? It might yet happen.'

Sharp pain she thought she'd left behind months ago lanced between Delphie's ribs and she pursed her lips to keep the gasp from escaping. 'Please don't hold your breath, Nicola. This really is just a job,' she insisted.

Because these flashes of traitorous wishing for things that couldn't be needed to stop. She'd entertained deep feelings for Lucca, discovered she was pregnant with his child and then, courtesy of her unwanted visitor in Paris, been enlightened about the existence of 'The List'—and her guaranteed absence on it—in a matter of twenty-four hours.

Those twenty-four hours had shattered her dreams, and the devastating loss of her baby had shredded her soul completely.

Now she was back in Lucca's life under false pretences, and she couldn't lose sight of the fact that this was nothing but a ruse.

Nicola watched her, a far too speculative gleam in her eyes, before she shrugged. 'I never say never. If I did, I wouldn't be where I am today.'

Delphie sipped her tea to avoid responding, and after another small pause turned the conversation to safer territory.

Glancing at the coffee table book, she toyed with asking Nicola if she knew about Lucca's family history—specifically his mother—but dismissed the idea just as quickly. Probing any subjects she was supposed to know about already would only attract attention.

Far too soon Nicola took her leave, and Delphie headed for a quick shower before dressing for dinner.

The green waterfall-hem dress she chose from her own wardrobe was stylishly casual and comfortable—deliberately chosen not to give any impression that she was trying too hard. Because she wasn't. Still, her critical gaze lingered in the mirror for seconds too long, ensuring her hair wasn't too busy or the amount of leg on display didn't border on risqué.

Impatient with herself, she turned away from eyes that were a little too bright and...*excited*.

A chunky silver-linked chain from her favourite London jeweller added to her sense of security and confidence as she slipped her feet into silver heels, added a few more accessories and convinced herself she could withstand a couple of hours dining with Lucca.

At ten to seven, a knock came at her door. Fully expecting to see Lucca, she experienced a dart of disappointment when one of the aides, Domenica, smiled politely at her. 'I'm to escort you to dinner with His Majesty,' she said in heavily accented English.

Delphie understood the ten-minute lead time as they traversed countless stunning hallways and dozens of courtyards. She lost count of the frescoes, paintings, statues that graced the palace before, finally, they entered a wing with a bolder, more masculine decor and a corridor filled with family portraits. She knew they were family because each one bore a strong resemblance to Lucca.

She was so busy admiring the grandest one of all that she didn't sense his approach until he spoke.

'My great-grandfather Gioseffo,' his deep voice murmured close to her ear. 'He was famous for his over-the-top extravagance. His had to be the largest portrait, painted by the most renowned Italian artist at the time.'

Delphie spun on her heel and encountered brooding, merciless silver-grey eyes. He was without a jacket and his midnight blue shirt clung to his broad shoulders, muscled arms and streamlined torso.

She stopped herself from conducting the zealous top-to-toe scrutiny her senses demanded, and stopped herself from being swallowed whole by his overwhelming presence.

She turned back to the portrait. But all the grand painting did was reinforce the formidable magnetism of the San

Calliano royal males. The hauteur brimming in their eyes and the power that rippled from the paintings.

She glanced to the side when she heard light footsteps and saw his butler approaching with a silver tray holding two flutes of champagne. Lucca took both and held one out to her.

'Shall we have a toast?' Faint amusement ringed his voice.

She hesitated. 'To what would we be toasting?'

This version of Lucca was lethal—a cunning predator who might well devour her to achieve his specific goal. She intended to look before she leapt anywhere with him. Because letting down her guard wasn't an option.

'To getting what we both want, of course.'

Since she had no counterargument to that, she clinked glasses with him, acutely aware that his sharp gaze remained on her as they sipped the vintage champagne.

'Come, let me introduce you to the rest of the clan,' he invited, his voice even-toned.

Rather than set her at ease, it ramped up the nerves dancing in her belly. 'Where are we, exactly?'

She stepped beside him as he started down the long corridor. On either side of them arched doors led into large, breathtaking rooms.

'You're in the King's private wing of the palace. Where did you expect to be?'

Another layer of tension piled on her already ragged emotions, and her fingers clutched the glass tighter. 'Somewhere neutral,' she said, before she bit her runaway tongue.

He paused mid-stride, one eyebrow raised. 'Neutral?' he echoed. 'Are you expecting a war, Delphine?'

She inhaled slowly, praying for equilibrium. 'Last night you set out a timeline, which I agreed to. Today you seem to be in a hurry to alter it.'

'And how have I done that?'

'Come on… Moving me into the palace today instead of after the festival… Bringing me here to your private wing when you know it'll spur the rumour mill into overdrive…'

A gleam shimmered through his eyes. 'Perhaps I don't see the harm in striking while the iron's hot?'

'Is this how it's going to be? You arbitrarily bending the rules?'

One corner of his mouth lifted. 'I have personal experience of how flexible you can be, Delphine.'

The overtly sexual connotation made her gasp. 'You can't say that!'

'Can't I? Is there another rule that says I can't reminisce on our past liaison? Or are we to pretend it didn't happen at all?' he enquired.

There was a definite bite to his voice. One that warned her to tread carefully.

'I prefer to stay in the present,' she said. 'If that's not too much to ask.' A large chunk of her heart was still shattered from her loss.

For a long stretch he simply stared at her, his gaze probing far too deeply. 'Perhaps it might be. I haven't decided yet.'

He proceeded down the hall, introducing her to his ancestors with a brief but captivating history of each one. But just when she told herself it might be okay to relax, she saw his tension mounting. She glanced from Lucca's stiff face to a portrait that couldn't be more than twenty years old. She recognised the man from the coffee table book.

'My father—King Silvestro of San Calliano,' Lucca confirmed tersely, every emotion wiped from his expression.

His tension hollowed out her stomach, its effect eerily familiar. It was the same sensation she'd felt with her stepfather every day, from the moment he'd placed a ring on her mother's finger. The same tension she'd felt eventually with her mother, in the days before their final estrangement.

'You look like him,' she said, simply because it was a truth apparent to anyone who looked at the portrait.

An austere smile twisted his lips. 'I would like to think that's where our similarities end.'

She searched her mind and couldn't recall an answer to the question that now rose, so she asked, 'Is he still alive?'

Lucca nodded. 'On advice of his doctors, he stepped down from his reign. He spends the better part of the year in the winter palace.'

Even though her senses warned her there was more to his father stepping down and Lucca becoming King, she couldn't stop herself from asking the next question. 'And your mother?'

A flash of emotion dangerously close to anguish crossed his face before his expression froze into neutrality. His profile grew colder, his cheekbones standing out in sculptured relief as his gaze remained fixed ahead. 'She died ten years ago.'

Sympathy welled inside her. 'I'm sorry.'

He shrugged, the movement as stiff as his profile. 'She was appropriately mourned.'

His words might have sounded callous, but again she caught something in his eyes that indicated he was more affected than he portrayed. Delphie knew all about presenting an outward countenance that didn't match the inside.

'Didn't she get a portrait?' She looked around her. 'It seems women don't feature anywhere in this space.'

His nostrils flared slightly, as if the question angered him. 'My mother's portrait is among the formal paintings displayed in the public staterooms.'

'But you don't have one here?'

His gaze slashed to her, his eyes narrowed laser beams. 'Believe it or not, there's a protocol that dictates where things go in the palace, even when you're the King. All reminders of my mother—including what she looks like—are stored where they should be. Including but not limited to my very excellent memory.'

She opened her mouth. Perhaps to do something foolish, like challenge him. Tell him his answer had only revealed what he was trying to hide.

A discreet clearing of throat from the hovering butler stopped her.

'Dinner is served, sire.'

When Lucca placed his hand in the small of her back and guided her through the door into an opulent dining room, she told herself she didn't withdraw because to have done so would've sent the wrong message to anyone watching—including the six staff standing at discreet attention, ready to serve them.

He pulled out a chair at the corner adjacent to the head of the solid, twenty-seater table, laid with snow-white damask and priceless candelabras. The silverware looked too pristine and exquisite to touch. She was a little relieved when the butler stepped forward with an empty tray and glanced discreetly at her half-finished champagne.

The antipasto had her eyes widening. She looked up from the bruschetta with Parma ham, layered with roasted peppers and drizzled with truffle oil, to find Lucca examining her keenly.

'Your favourite—unless your culinary tastes have changed?' he drawled.

She wanted to say they had, but what would be the point of lying on such a small issue? 'No, they haven't.'

Satisfaction thawed a layer of the frost on his face as he picked up a bottle of red wine—also a favourite that he'd introduced her to—and poured her a glass.

She debated the wisdom of drinking around him, then shrugged it off. Last night had proved she was susceptible to Lucca's strain of sexual wizardry whether she was stone-cold sober or not. Besides, she wasn't planning on it happening again.

'Your fitting went well, I hope?' he asked halfway through the starter.

Delphie nodded, then asked the question that had teased at her senses all afternoon. 'Did you request Nicola specifically for me?'

He shrugged. 'I remembered that you'd worked together in the past. I thought you'd feel more at ease with someone you knew.'

She told herself his thoughtfulness meant nothing deeper.

He was merely orchestrating the easiest way to achieve his goals. Still, she couldn't stop herself from murmuring, 'Thank you.'

'Prego,' he murmured back, his eyes lingering on her mouth for a charged spell. Then he nodded at the hovering butler to clear away their first course.

'Nicola told me this is the second year of the festival's revival. Why did it stop in the first place?' she asked.

He stared into his wine glass without answering for a few seconds, his face hardening. 'Because my mother lost interest in organising it and my father refused to have anyone else take over.'

'Can I ask why she lost interest?'

His lips flattened and he took a large sip of wine before setting the glass down. 'My mother did *as* she pleased *when* she pleased. It was endearing to some, troubling for others, and ultimately detrimental to the kingdom. She decided that organising an arts and culture festival to elevate San Calliano's image on the world stage wasn't something she wanted to dabble with any more, so didn't.'

'You sound as if you disliked her.'

A harsh bark of laughter left his throat. 'How very diplomatically put.'

'Luc— Your Majesty, I don't mean pry, but as you said yesterday, I need to have some level of knowledge if this thing is going to work.'

'Then tell me something I didn't get around to discovering about *you* when we were together,' he lobbed smoothly back at her.

Her breath caught, and she felt the ground shifting precariously beneath her feet. 'There's nothing important—'

'Since we have agreed that I will control the narrative, perhaps let me decide what's important?' he said, lounging back in his chair with an air of false ease.

'You forget that I've attended social events with you in the past,' she said. 'You're a master at deflection. Besides, aren't you the King, as you keep reminding me? Can't you simply order people not to pry into your business?'

'Deflection only lasts until people begin to wonder what you're hiding. It's that stage I wish to avoid reaching. As for ordering people about—I don't wish to be tarred with the same brush as a dictator,' he murmured, his eyes on her face.

Delphie bit her lip, knowing she'd just be aggravating the situation by suggesting he'd already done so with her. The amused gleam lurking in his eyes said he knew she was holding back.

Their second course arrived, granting her a reprieve from confrontation, although she remained keenly aware of Lucca's probing gaze on her. And despite the faintly alarming direction of their conversation, the first bite of gnocchi with grilled courgettes and olives melted in her mouth.

He pounced as soon as they were alone again. 'Did you go to Qatar straight after leaving Paris?'

Her fingers tightened around her fork as she struggled to control her alarm. 'Yes.'

A tic throbbed in his temple. 'Using Buckman's jet?'

She started, then wondered why she was surprised that he knew Hunter had a private plane. He must have done his homework before buying his motor racing team. 'Yes,' she answered again.

Displeasure gleamed in his eyes before his lashes swept down. 'Why Qatar? Why not home to London? Or New York?'

She carefully set her cutlery down and wove her fingers through the linen napkin in her lap. 'London hasn't felt like home in a long time.'

And New York bore far too many anguished memories of their affair.

Qatar had been far enough. A place to nurse her wounds, to regroup before she decided when best to tell the man destined to choose his bride via a royal list that she carried his child.

Only fate had spared him that news, while robbing her of her precious child.

Delphie toyed with telling him now. Then swallowed as bitterness soured her mouth. What purpose would it serve except to dredge up more pain? Besides, he'd moved on quickly enough. He'd returned to the women on his precious 'List' as she'd drowned in despair.

'Because…?'

She exhaled in a rush of quiet pain. 'Surely no one will expect you to divulge such personal details about me?'

'Perhaps not. But I want to know. Why hasn't London felt like home?'

The steely pressure of his query said he wasn't about to back down. She reassured herself that nothing she was revealing was as monumental as the secret buried in her heart. That she needed only to show the surface for him to see the bleak plot line of her childhood.

'My mother remarried two years after my father died. My stepfather made it clear I wasn't part of the new family he intended to start with my mother. Two months after I turned seventeen, and a couple of weeks before my mother had my little brother, I was spotted by a talent scout from Rachel's agency. I'm sure you can guess the rest.'

His lips tightened. 'I would prefer not to. Did your mother not support your decision? Oversee your career? Seventeen is still young.'

The blade of memory sliced deep, drawing fresh pain. 'She was tired of being caught in the middle, between her second husband and her daughter. I… I tried to force her to take my side by threatening to leave school and take the modelling contract. She didn't object. In fact, I think she was…relieved.'

'So she washed her hands of you when you were seventeen instead of fighting for you?' he bit out.

'Not immediately. I took a few modelling jobs during the school holidays—enough to pay my way through university. But it soon became clear that the new baby took priority over everything and that I wouldn't be welcome back once I went to uni. So I…stopped going home.'

His thunderous frown grew darker. 'And your mother never reached out to you?'

Delphie exhaled shakily, fought hard to shake off the dejection. 'It doesn't matter. You wanted to know why London isn't home. Now you know.'

'So why Qatar?' he charged again, sending her breathing into fresh disarray.

'Because I wanted to hide from the world.'

'No. Because you wanted to hide from *me*,' he parried acidly, his eyes boring into her, daring her to deny it.

'Does it stroke your ego to push that line of reasoning? Did it not even occur to you that you were the last person I was thinking of when I left?' she tossed back.

Initially she'd wanted to hide from the reality that she'd been nothing more than a plaything to him, that his royal path was set in stone and would in no way or shape be altered on the strength of a meaningless fling. And then she'd *needed* to hide because her heart had been shredded into a million useless pieces.

'Forgive me if I find it hard to reconcile the woman I was with the night before with the stranger who left without a word. I don't think I'm in any way overstating it when I say you were into me as deeply as I was into you,' he stated, with the assurance of a drop-dead gorgeous king who knew every single ounce of his worth. And revelled in it.

She'd never known the name of the cold, vicious man who'd delivered the news about 'The List'. She'd been too busy absorbing the new reality that she carried the baby of a future king who was destined to marry someone else. That just as she'd been rejected by her mother in her new life, she and her baby were about to become pariahs in Lucca's.

Because there'd been signs. Their affair had taken place in impersonal, if opulent, hotel rooms. Her sole, lightning-fast visit to San Calliano had been shrouded in secrecy and far removed from the scrutiny of the royal palace. As if he was keen to ensure that lines weren't blurred… That she didn't get the wrong ideas and hope for something she'd never have…

'I'm afraid it's a reality you'll just have to get used to,' she answered, relief piercing her when her voice emerged smoothly.

To put an end to the conversation she resolutely picked up her fork, calmly finishing a respectable amount of food before, accepting that her appetite was gone, she reached for her sparkling water.

'You should count yourself lucky,' he stated after several minutes had passed.

'Why?'

He didn't raise his gaze from the deep burgundy swirls of his wine.

'Because I wasn't quite myself in those weeks after your disappearance. Had I discovered you'd simply lost interest, after I'd spent considerable time and effort in attempting to locate you, things wouldn't have been quite this…civil.'

Her breath locked in her lungs, her skin tingling hot, then cold from the calm, merciless delivery of his words. 'I accept that you're the almighty ruler of your own kingdom, but I'm fairly certain you can't go around making such outlandish statements. This isn't the Dark Ages.'

A sardonic smile whispered over his lips but didn't touch any other part of his face. 'The blood of my ancestors runs through my veins, *cara*. And sometimes I simply have to embrace who I am.'

The primitive throb in his words wove a certain dark magic through her, much to her chagrin. But when Delphie's heart began to race and her pelvis heated in response to the steady, brooding gaze he levelled on her, she swallowed and dragged her own gaze from the chiselled perfection of his face.

'Would madam like dessert?' the butler murmured from a few feet behind her.

She knew the question was directed only at her because

Lucca didn't indulge in sweet things. His vice was rich black coffee, several times a day.

Fairly certain she couldn't swallow another morsel, she shook her head. 'No, thank you.'

The moment the words left her lips, Lucca surged to his feet. 'Come, we'll finish our conversation in the living room.'

As they were exiting the dining room, she felt his lingering gaze on her. 'What?' she demanded.

'You're wearing my favourite colour. Exquisitely, I should add.'

Something inside her leapt at the compliment, and she wondered whether this was why her subconscious had gravitated towards her choice tonight. She shook herself free of the fanciful thought before it could take root. 'It's just a co-incidence.'

'*Se lo dici tu...*'

'I don't know what you just said.'

His smile widened. 'I said, if you say so.'

'I do,' she insisted.

His reply was to place his hand in the small of her back and guide her into the next room, where she stopped and gaped in awe. 'You have your own ballroom?'

The room was several sizes smaller than the ballrooms she'd briefly toured that morning, but it wasn't one single degree diminished in splendour.

'It's for more intimate gatherings.'

Her mind immediately flew to no-go areas, her senses agitated by thoughts of all the women he'd been rumoured to date recently. Jealous bile rose in her throat and, despite sternly lecturing herself that she was over it, she couldn't seem to swallow it down.

'Is that a look of jealousy I detect, *cara*? Should I be grateful that your expressions are still as easy to read or is it now a double bluff?' he enquired, that bite of acid still in his tone.

Her heart lurched, then banged against her ribs. 'It doesn't matter to me what you do in your private life or who you invite into your private space.'

'That's not strictly true, is it? Last night proved that some private things are still very much of interest to you. That level of chemistry comes with a certain…possessiveness.'

'Thank goodness, then, that I have some semblance of willpower to stop me from throwing myself at you every second of every day.'

His brooding gaze swept down, sinfully lush eyelashes veiling his expression. 'Yes, that would be tedious. But I wouldn't be averse to watching you try for an hour or two when my schedule allows,' he stated drolly.

Dark, unwanted delight shivered through her. 'I wouldn't hold your breath if I were you,' she snapped. And then, since it seemed she couldn't help herself, she tossed in, 'Are you seeing anyone?'

His lips tightened. 'Wouldn't it be the height of ludicrousness for me to attempt to salvage my kingdom's reputation while sullying it with a side tryst?'

Put so dryly, she felt heat creeping into her face. Still she fixed her gaze on him. 'Is that a no?' she pressed. 'Because I wouldn't want some poor woman discovering second-hand that she's moved down on your *list*.'

Far too much bitterness stained her words and her breath froze in her lungs, the possibility that she might have given herself away snaking horrifically through her. Because that was exactly how she'd felt when that vile man had visited her in Paris. Learning she wasn't special in His Royal Highness Prince Lucca's life had dredged up the anguish her mother and stepfather had made her feel. Ultimately unimportant enough to be discarded.

In her quiet moments, Delphie knew she'd partly fled because she hadn't wanted that possibility confirmed. Had rejected Lucca before she could be rejected.

'Despite what the media likes to print about me, I don't date a new woman every week, Delphine. The last woman to grace my bed was—'

'I don't need the details, I'm sure,' she interjected, because the vice around her chest was in danger of crushing the air out of her lungs.

It was only when he smiled stiffly and waved her out of the ballroom that she breathed again. 'Of course you don't. You're not interested any more, are you?'

The words sounded exactly the way she was sure he'd intended—as a taunt.

'And I'm sure if I were to kiss you again you'd absolutely hate it.'

'Yes, I would. So don't try it.'

But, as much as she wished it, Delphie couldn't find another emotion to replace the disappointment that seeped into her veins as he returned to being a polite, if imperious, host, escorting her through the jaw-dropping rooms of his private wing.

Nor could she find the strength to move away when he kept his hand on her waist throughout the tour.

CHAPTER FIVE

LUCCA STOOD ON his balcony the next morning, his gaze resting on the view that normally pleased him. The palace and the whole kingdom was abuzz with excitement about the upcoming festival. But while he should've felt satisfaction at this swing from the apathy and distrust that had spilt over from his father's last two decades of rule to hope and optimism for the future, all he could think about was *her*.

Seeing her again last night had only confirmed his suspicions.

She was even more entrancing than he remembered.

And she was hiding something.

Perhaps nothing vital—because his life had continued smoothly after those unfortunate few weeks following her departure, after all—but something with the potential to trigger another media frenzy?

She wasn't in another relationship, casual or otherwise. He'd made it his business to check this time. Nevertheless, the suspicion wouldn't relent. And, contrary to what he'd said to Delphine, he still trusted his gut just as much as he did facts and figures.

Why rely on them when he could rely on his gut too? With the exception of Delphine, it had aided him thus far. It had kept him from becoming like his father and turning a blind eye to personal matters that could have had crucial consequences on his kingdom. So he needed to—

'It's time, sire,' his personal aide said from behind him.

Lucca took a breath, tried to infuse purpose and duty into his veins even while his mind strayed into recollecting how Delphine's skin had felt beneath his fingers. How her eyes had sparked fire at the thought that he might be dating another woman. After she'd cut him off, Lucca hadn't felt the need to confess that, while he might have dated, he hadn't taken another woman to bed since Delphine.

She'd forced him to take a long, hard look at himself, to realise how close he'd come to losing all sense of who he was.

Perhaps that was what disturbed him the most.

He swung away from the view, an almost tangible layer of irritation and disquiet prickling his senses. Now was not the time to doubt himself. He was the King. He'd established himself on the global stage in most of the ways that counted. Attaining his goal of elevating himself and his kingdom above reproach would achieve the rest.

As for uncovering Delphine's secrets…he'd get to that in time.

He followed his aide through staterooms and the portrait room and into the vast receiving room. He'd presided over enough state affairs to perform his duties in his sleep. Which left his mind free to replay their dinner last night. To think of the revelations about Delphine's family life he was a little ashamed to discover he hadn't bothered to find out the first time around.

Because he'd been so captivated by her.

Discovering Delphine had been for the most part on her own since the age of seventeen shouldn't have bothered him the way it had. His admiration for her courage in the face of rejection and adversity shouldn't have found a surprisingly malleable sympathy inside him. Above all, her palpable pain at being estranged from her mother shouldn't have made him wish, for a very brief moment, to commiserate. To share his fraught experiences with his own mother with her.

They weren't the same.

If they were, she wouldn't have betrayed him. Left him without a thought as to what chaos her absence might cause.

'Your father's chief of staff is also here. He wishes five minutes of your time.'

Lucca stiffened at his aide's words, curbed the strong urge to refuse.

The man who'd been his father's closest confidant had rubbed Lucca the wrong way even as a child. And as a grown man, he knew Marco Coppi had wielded a heavy hand in some of his father's more questionable decisions about San Calliano's destiny. Especially the heinous decision that had almost plunged San Calliano into vicious scandal and international disgrace.

It stuck in his craw that at every turn his father still defended Coppi's actions—had even kept him in his role after, finally facing up to his faults and realising his ineffectual rule had led to San Calliano's steep decline, he'd stepped down from the throne. Lucca had wished he would find comfort from knowing that with both men residing far away in the winter palace they would keep out of trouble, but increasingly Coppi had found excuses to inveigle himself into palace affairs.

He returned to the portrait room to find the older man planted in front of a portrait Lucca had found himself examining far too many times in the past.

The subject's beauty was the delicate, flawless and classical kind that stopped grown men in their tracks. Lucca had seen it happen in real life too, when his mother had only needed to enter a room to capture the attention of every red-blooded male and hold it for as long as she pleased.

Queen Alessia of San Calliano had thrived on that slavish devotion—wielded it like a weapon that had ultimately decimated her husband and her son, and nearly brought the kingdom to its knees. The fact that she hadn't cared one iota about the damage she'd caused, right up to her very dramatic death, sent a river of bitterness rushing through Lucca's veins.

At his approaching footsteps, Coppi turned. His bow stopped short of the required level of respect. Another act meant to needle Lucca.

'*Buongiorno*, sire. Your father wishes me to deliver his personal contribution to the festival's equestrian award directly to you.' Coppi reached into his pocket and handed over a thick envelope.

'You could've had this messengered to me or delivered directly to the festival committee. You didn't need to travel all this way yourself.' Lucca didn't bother to curb his scepticism.

'It was no trouble to do my duty. It never has been. Besides, it gives me a chance to share in the excitement. You'll remember that your mother stopped organising the festivals—'

'I don't need the reminder, Coppi,' he interjected.

Handing the envelope to his aide, he turned away.

Coppi cleared his throat. 'Your Majesty, if I may?'

Lucca gritted his teeth. '*Sì?*'

'Your father has some thoughts on certain aspects of the festival. Your choice of model for the diamond collection—'

'Is none of your business. Or my father's,' he butted in tightly.

A hard, malicious gleam illuminated the older man's eyes but he quickly veiled it. 'I'm merely relaying your father's sentiments, sire. He feels that she is not the right choice for such a pivotal task. Perhaps it should be worn by the woman who will become your Queen. Perhaps someone from "The List"?'

The unwanted reminder of the archaic agreement he'd signed on his twenty-fifth birthday turned Lucca's river of bitterness into anger.

It had been his mother's actions that had necessitated such an agreement, and at the time he'd fully concurred with his advisers' urging. It had been a way to remove emotion from a union that rightly demanded political precision, dedication to duty and faultless character from both future King and Queen.

For the most part he'd forgotten its existence. Until Delphine's disappearing stunt had forced self-examination, reminding him of 'The List' and its merits. There would be no obsessive lust or star-crossed nonsense dictating his actions when the time came to choose his Queen.

So why did Coppi's reminder feel like barbs under his skin?

'It seems both you and my father have forgotten that he is no longer King. Matters of state are now *my* responsibility,' he said icily, drawing satisfaction in watching the older man stiffen. 'Now I have a festival to open. You know your way out of my palace.'

He left the room feeling even more incensed. But that emotion changed to something visceral, the punch in his gut merciless, the moment he stepped into the receiving room and saw the figure standing a short distance away, flanked by two aides.

Delphine looked breathtaking—a unique wildflower in a field of house plants. The gold lace overlaying the burnt orange calf-length silk dress lent an extra glow to her beautiful dark skin. Her glorious hair had been tamed, much to his irritation, into straight sheets that caressed her shoulders, and her light make-up lovingly emphasised her perfect cheekbones, her full lips and alluring eyes.

What drew his eye above all else was the La Mattina diamonds resting at her throat, highlighting the graceful lines of her neck and her delicate jawline.

How *right* they looked on her.

He approached, struggling to keep his roiling senses under control. '*Buongiorno*, Delphine.'

Mio Dio, how her scent tortured him. Her throat moved in a delicate swallow, drawing his attention to her neck once more.

'*Buongiorno*, Your Majesty,' she responded perfectly in her husky voice, reminding him of both the benign and the risqué Italian words he'd taught her. Words she'd saucily repeated to him when he'd least expected it, often with the result of sending his libido haywire.

Aware he was in danger of raising more than a few eyebrows with his feverish interest, he held out his arm. 'You've been briefed on the schedule?'

She nodded. 'You're officially opening the festival at the Museo d'Arte before we visit the equestrian show, and tonight you're hosting a VIP dinner for a few hundred dignitaries.'

'Molto bene,' he said, a swell of satisfaction wiping away the aggravation caused by Coppi's visit.

He started for the doors leading outside, where his motorcade waited. But just then her gaze swung past him and Lucca felt her stiffen.

Glancing at her, he spotted the quickly veiled alarm. 'Something wrong?' he asked.

'Wh-who's that man?'

Lucca swung his head, followed her gaze to Coppi and stiffened himself. 'Marco Coppi. My father's chief of staff. Why?' he asked, a spike of protectiveness rising up and stunning the hell out of him.

She cleared her throat and shook her head, her lashes dropping to veil her expression. 'Oh…nothing. He just looks… I thought he was someone I knew.'

Her gaze rose and a bright smile replaced her alarm.

For several seconds Lucca wanted to probe further, but this wasn't the right time nor the place. Not with palace staff and invited dignitaries milling around.

Putting it out of his mind, he escorted her from the palace to the waiting limousine.

In the car, she kept her gaze on the window, her expression serene and contemplative.

'My diamonds look exceptional on you,' he said, aware of a curious gruffness in his voice. The compliment was warranted, but above that he wanted the coolness between them to be dispensed with.

For the sake of appearances, he assured himself.

Her eyes widened a touch as she glanced at him, and her almost reverent hand caressed the row of cushion-cut diamonds, the facets of the matching pendant earrings catching the morning sun.

'Thank you,' she replied, her voice alluringly smoky. 'I've read about them. They belonged to your grandmother. Did she really wear them to breakfast every morning?'

Lucca settled back in his seat, allowing a small smile to be triggered by a fond memory—rare in his childhood. 'My grandfather was a romantic. He gifted the diamonds to my grandmother the morning after their wedding night and she named them La Mattina. And, yes, she wore them each morning, regardless of the occasion.'

'You sound…nostalgic.'

He shrugged. 'He was a great man. I didn't have nearly as much time with him as I would've wished for.'

A shade of reserve left her eyes, the liquid depths warming. 'You miss him,' she stated with a hint of surprise.

His lips twisted. 'You think me such an ogre that I don't feel fondness for any relative?'

She stiffened again, her lips pursing. 'I didn't say that.'

He sighed, regret lancing him. 'You're right. I miss him. He was bold and fearless and not afraid to go after what he wanted.'

The eyes that met his held less irritation but more wariness. They also held the kind of temptation he'd first been drawn to. The kind of temptation he knew he should be wary of. And yet wasn't her bold daring what had dragged him into her seductive web in the first place?

'You want to be like him,' she said, her voice echoing with conviction.

It sent a peculiar sensation through his gut. Why on earth would he want her to know him this intimately? She was here to do a job, after which he'd send her packing.

Are you sure?

He tensed against the mocking taunt. 'If at the end of my life I'm half the man he was, I'll be proud.'

That circumspect smile curved her lips again, her eyes once more warming. Before he lost himself in them, they were thankfully pulling up at their destination.

'We're here already?' she exclaimed with faint disappointment.

'That's one advantage of travelling in a motorcade, *cara*,' he replied, although the journey had been far too brief for him too.

'Or a disadvantage if you're not ready,' she muttered, sliding her hand down her dress.

'Another reason I chose you for this role is your ability to master it even in your sleep,' he stated, then drew satisfaction from watching her jaw drop.

He stepped out on to the red carpet and turned to help her.

The sounds of adulation from the crowd grew by several thousand decibels as they caught sight of her. Her professional smile was firmly in place, her shoulders back and her chin angled up in a pose his deportment tutors would've been proud of. And when he pulled her arm through his, the crowd went wild.

'I think you're well on your way to achieving your aim, Your Majesty.'

Lucca curbed a sudden urge to tell her to drop his title. He wanted his name on her lips, spoken with that groin-stirring husky pitch. A fact that mildly irritated him.

'Then it's all been worth it,' he said tersely.

The arm caught by his jerked, but her expression didn't alter. 'I'm glad.'

'Are you really?' he muttered, pinning his smile in place as he tried to read her inscrutable eyes.

'Why shouldn't I be?' she returned.

'You forget, I'm intimately familiar with your body, *cara*,' he murmured.

She opened her mouth, but was stopped from speaking

as the small group comprising the museum's curator and other specially selected dignitaries approached.

Still, he caught the fire in her eyes as she locked gazes with him for a split second, before duty and diplomacy forced a switch into imperial mode.

In that gaze Lucca was reminded far too vividly of how it had felt to tangle with her—in bed and out. How he'd tumbled far out of his normal straitjacketed role as Prince into being a man he didn't recognise. A man who'd found himself, in the weeks prior to her disappearance, yearning for a different life.

The reminder sent a timely rod of purpose up his spine. So what if she looked magnificent in his diamonds? As if she was born to be right here, on his arm, in this moment? Her actions were a timely lesson that he was at serious risk of losing himself. Of forgetting how his mother's behaviour had decimated him and those around him.

He swallowed the knot of bitterness in his throat, walked Delphine to her allocated spot and then moved to the podium.

Jagged satisfaction moved through him as he was forced to put thoughts of his past aside in favour of matters of state.

And when he stepped down from the podium to applause and flashing cameras from the media, he was once again in control.

Delphie's head spun at the mercurial unfolding of events as the hours passed.

For the first few minutes that morning she could've sworn she'd caught glimpses of the man she'd met almost two years ago. His compliments had lulled her into lowering her guard, the melting feeling inside her reminiscent of their early time together. Before the visit from his father's chief of staff—the man she now knew as Marco Coppi—had enlightened her as to her ephemeral role in Lucca's life.

Seeing Coppi so unexpectedly had wrenched that feeling away, harshly reminding her that the stunning diamonds, the clothes, her very presence beside Lucca, were all for a role she'd soon need to leave behind. That no matter how much a tiny part of her wished this was reality, and not some orchestrated drama, she couldn't let the feeling take root.

More importantly, the reminder had reaffirmed why she was doing this—to heal herself after losing the baby she'd yearned for from the moment she'd known of its existence and to strengthen her vital connection with the father who'd been her world—the connection she'd abandoned under the guise of survival, when deep down she hadn't wanted to confront the pain of missing him.

Nevertheless, she couldn't compel her gaze away from the man now conversing with the head of his royal polo team a few feet away.

Lucca couldn't have looked more dashing if he'd tried. It was a sin, really, how good he looked, even with that stubborn lock of hair repeatedly dropping on to his forehead.

As if sensing her regard, he swung his head her way.

Her heart thudded wildly as she saw the answering flare of heat in his eyes. He knew exactly what she was thinking…how she was feeling. And as he made his excuses and advanced towards her she lost the ability to breathe.

'Are we leaving?' she asked, then cringed at her breathlessness.

'Why, Delphine, you almost sound hopeful,' he drawled in that deep voice that found its bullseye in her pelvis. 'Do you wish to be alone with me?'

She glanced at the crowd straining against the perimeter fence of the San Lorena polo grounds. 'No, I don't. But I think your subjects are getting restless.'

They cheered every time he waved at them, and it couldn't have been more apparent how much his subjects adored him.

'They will behave themselves. If they don't, do you doubt that I'll protect you?' he enquired, his voice deep, confident and far too thrilling to her senses.

She couldn't help a decadent shiver. 'Don't you have bodyguards to do that?'

A smile lifted the corner of his lips. 'I thought you'd appreciate the personal touch. You always did before.'

The liquid in her glass threatened to slosh over her hands. 'What are you doing?' she whispered fiercely.

He stepped closer, one eyebrow quirked. *'Che cosa?'*

'Why keep making references to our past? I thought we agreed we wouldn't?' she demanded, far too shakily.

'You insisted. I don't recall making such an agreement.' Amusement drained from his eyes as he continued to watch her. 'And perhaps there's a method to my madness. Maybe referencing our time together will frustrate you into telling me what I want to know.'

Her heart lurched, then dropped to her stomach. 'It won't.'

He lowered his head until they were breathing the same air. Until she had to lock her knees to keep from surging up to brush his lips with hers.

'So confident... Let's see how long you hold out over the next six weeks, *cara*.'

With that soft but deadly spoken gauntlet thrown, he took her arm and led her to another group eager to soak in their King's attention.

While that sensation of being caught in a cyclone continued to gather strength inside her.

Another speech and a formal dinner later, they were back in the limo, heading to the palace.

Delphine averted her gaze, determined to fight the maelstrom of sensations inside her, while beside her Lucca scrolled through his phone. She knew the exact moment he glanced her way, his incisive gaze heating her skin.

'My festival committee tells me the first day was a success.'

Compelled against her will, she glanced over to see him loosening his tie. At the glimpse of his strong, tanned neck, she felt heat invade her being.

'I thought that was obvious from all the screaming adoration and applause,' she said, a little more tartly than she'd intended.

Perhaps it came from watching pedigree women fawn over him at every opportunity, triggering a cursed urge to know which ones had been added to his precious 'List'. Or perhaps it stemmed from her alarming inability to control her body's reaction to him.

'The people of San Calliano are a passionate lot. They're zealous in their appreciation. They're especially pleased to see a real-life exhibition of their most prized possessions,' he said, his gaze lingering at her throat.

She bit her lip to stop herself commenting on the myriad enthusiastic women at the VIP gathering who *didn't* hail from San Calliano. 'I'm glad playing my part helped things along for you.'

His lips firmed and displeasure flashed in his eyes before he snuffed it out. 'Don't you want to know what they're making of your reappearance at my side?'

A fine tremor went through her. 'If it's the result you wanted to achieve then I don't need to know the finer details.'

'They're speculating on how long you've been back in my bed,' he delivered anyway. 'On whether our time apart only made us realise how much we missed each other.'

Her fingers tightened around her clutch, his words rousing dangerous memories of how those first days after Paris had seemed like hell.

God, how she'd missed him.

She'd never imagined one human being could hold such emotional power over another until leaving Lucca had enlightened her.

She could never return to that...

'Are they? That's a shame, since we'll be disavowing them of all that romantic nonsense in a few weeks.'

Again his lips firmed, but he said nothing as they pulled up to the palace. Delphie didn't have enough bearings yet

to know where they were, but a few minutes later she recognised the corridor leading to her suite.

He opened the doors after dismissing the bodyguards
who'd trailed after them. 'Have a nightcap with me,' he said,
as if the quarters were his, not hers. But then, since the palace belonged to him, her suite technically *was* his.

She remained in the short entrance hall leading into the
living room, unwilling to expend more emotional resources
fighting this…this *intense need.* 'Do you mind if I don't?
It's been a long day and I'm tired.'

She hadn't expected him to meekly accept her refusal—
he was the King, after all, and even if he'd accepted her
dismissal she'd expected he would do so with haughty
pride—but what she hadn't expected him to do was stride
back to where she stood, capturing her wrist and leading
her to the sofa.

Shock rattled through her when, after seeing her seated,
he dropped into a squat before her and gently tugged off her
heels. 'Wh-what are you doing?'

Silver-grey eyes speared into her in that breath-stealing
way that told her he could see into the heart of her every
need. 'Relieving a little of your stress. What else?'

'Lu— Your Maj— Oh…' She was aware that she sounded
far too much like the women from today, but she couldn't
help her groan of appreciation as his thumbs dug into her
stiff arches.

For a full minute neither of them spoke as he worked
her muscles. Then, 'Good?' he drawled, his gaze rapt on
her face.

Delphie resisted the urge to melt into the sofa by pushing
her balled fists into the plump cushions. But she couldn't
help her eager nod as his fingers wrought magic on her
tense muscles.

Another arrogant smile played at his lips. 'You can express yourself vocally, you know. I wouldn't even condemn
you if you moaned again,' he stated thickly.

She pressed her lips tighter together to stop another moan

from escaping as he cupped her ankles with warm, firm hands. When he drew the hem of her dress up to her knees and closed his hands over her calves, Delphie knew she was straying into dangerous territory.

'I... I think I'm fine.'

'You *think*?' he mocked.

She cleared her throat. 'I'm fine,' she stated more firmly, tugging her legs away. 'Thank you.'

Brooding eyes combed her face, then rested on her mouth. 'So polite... Even when you're being untruthful. Even when you want more.'

She rushed to her feet, half terrified that she would jump him if they remained in such close, intensely hot proximity. 'I'm not doing this with you, Your Majesty,' she said, as frostily as she could manage around the constriction in her throat and the deep pull of arousal between her legs.

He rose lithely to his feet, his regard even more ferocious as it trailed down her body and up again. His towering presence filled the room, while decadent need flooded her body.

Helplessly, Delphie's gaze dropped to his groin, and she gasped at the powerful imprint of his erection.

When her eyes flew back to his, she encountered pure silver fire. 'Oh, but we *are* doing this,' he countered. 'We've been doing this since the moment we set eyes on one another. Deny it all you want, but it's going to change nothing. You will admit your every truth to me. I guarantee it. *Dormi bene, dolcezza.*'

Once again he left her standing, staring after him, but this time with a bigger ball of fear in her stomach and greater yearning in her heart.

Long after she'd relinquished the diamonds into the safekeeping of her aides and taken a long shower she was still tossing and turning, reliving every moment of the day.

She was terrified that Lucca wouldn't stop until he'd got the truth of why she'd left.

Until he uncovered the devastation that daring to wish for more had brought to her door.

CHAPTER SIX

THE NEXT TWO days were much like the first day of the festival. Delphie dressed in stunning gowns that matched a progression of magnificent jewellery each morning, following which she left her suite and walked through the palace to meet Lucca—to increasing speculative attention from the palace staff.

But on Thursday the compliments she'd so foolishly come to anticipate from Lucca were starkly absent.

She felt self-conscious as his charged gaze remained fixed on the large snowflake-shaped pendant between her breasts. It darted to the smaller snowflake cascade earrings that made up the Desiderio di Natale diamond set—reportedly a gift from his father to his mother—before dropping to take in the pale pink chiffon gown with overlapping panels that showed hints of her skin when she moved.

The design was slightly more risqué than Nicola's previous three offerings, but she'd worn far less on the runway, and this occasion of the film festival called for even more glamour, so Delphie had embraced it.

Hell, she felt far sexier than she had in a very long time, triggering a memory of how she'd used to feel dressing for Lucca, anticipating his appreciative looks and the sometimes lustful consequences of wearing her outfits.

Those feelings swirled through her now as she withstood Lucca's regard. 'Is something wrong?' she asked, after several more seconds had passed.

His nostrils flared before his enigmatic gaze met hers once more. 'The only other person I've seen wearing this set was my mother. I didn't expect it to be part of the collection.'

She tensed at his hard tone, barely stopping herself from reaching up to touch the pendant. 'I'm sorry, I had no idea. If I'd known—'

'It's all right, Delphine,' he interjected. 'I should've remembered that we know very little about each other besides the physical.'

She was still reeling from that curiously stomach-hollowing observation when he added, 'And I much prefer the diamonds on you than I did her.'

Shocked at his words, she glanced around to see if they'd been overheard.

He laughed under his breath. 'Are you worried about me being undiplomatic, Delphine?'

'Aren't you afraid you'll reverse everything you're trying to do by saying things like that?'

He shrugged. 'My choppy relationship with my mother isn't exactly a secret.'

What exactly had happened? She curbed the urge to ask and replied, 'Like you said, I wouldn't know.'

'No, you wouldn't,' he murmured thoughtfully before holding out his arm. 'Shall we?'

Despite it being clear that the subject of his mother was closed, questions were still pinging through Delphie's brain as they were driven from the palace to the opera house—the venue for the formal opening of the film festival.

Unable to withstand the lingering tension any longer, she took the bull by the horns. 'Why was your relationship with your mother choppy?'

Her gut clenched as his head swung sharply towards her. Eyes like winter lightning slashed her, his jaw clenched tight. For a taut stretch of time she thought he wouldn't answer. Then he exhaled audibly.

'It's only a matter of time before you hear some outlandish version of it, so perhaps it's best you hear the truth from

me. My father was much older than my mother when they
first married. According to palace sources, it was hailed
as a true love match, despite their age difference.' A thick
vein of bitterness trailed through his words. 'But even as a
child I knew there was an imbalance in their relationship.'

'What sort of imbalance?' she asked, careful to keep the
alarm out of her voice.

During her fateful conversation with Marco Coppi he'd
stated that exact word—*'imbalance'*. Only he'd been far
more cruel in his delivery…had tossed in far more bruising
words. Words like *'lacking pedigree...' 'Not queen material...' 'A frivolous fancy...'* Words she'd never imagined
could wound until she heard them.

Coppi had meant to put her in her place, and in so doing
had repeated words far too reminiscent of her stepfather's
scathing rejection and her mother's reluctance to upset the
balance of her new family. It had shown Delphie the reck-
lessness of falling further under Lucca's spell, especially
with the earth-shattering discovery that she carried his child.

How could she not have fled after that?

She dragged her focus to the present, watched shadows
dance over his face before he answered.

'The simple truth was he was obsessed with my mother,
while she was completely indifferent to his feelings. She was
unfaithful to my father. Repeatedly. After the first handful of indiscretions—once she knew her position as Queen
would remain secure, regardless of what she did, and that
my father couldn't bring himself to tackle the situation—
she threw the last scrap of discretion out of the window.'

Delphie gasped, sympathy swelling inside her. 'I'm sorry.
It couldn't have been pleasant for you to be caught in that
kind of atmosphere.'

'It wasn't,' he confirmed tightly, storms of emotion criss-
crossing his face. 'As a child, I didn't understand it. When I
was old enough to grasp what was going on, I clashed with
my father over it.'

Having witnessed her own mother rowing with her stepfather over her, Delphie understood more than she wanted to admit. 'I'm thinking it didn't resolve anything?'

He gave an abrupt shake of his head. 'None whatsoever. It was a miracle if either of them remembered there was an offspring to be considered in the grand tragic opera of their lives.'

Lucca heard her soft gasp, watched concern and sympathy build in her eyes and asked himself why she would pull the kind of act she had when this side of her existed. Unless this was false too.

He'd looked deeper and called himself ten kinds of fools for craving what wasn't there. Hadn't he done the same with his mother? Searched for consideration and care, which had rarely materialised?

He shifted in his seat as knots of emotion built in his chest again.

As a grown man he had realised his parents' actions had changed him fundamentally. But he wasn't ready to expose that side of himself to Delphine. Didn't want to disclose that he'd gone against the grain of his own warning to trust her. Only to have her betray him.

'You said you clashed with your father... What about your mother?' she queried softly, her eyes still soft with emotion. 'Did you ever talk to her about it?'

His unease grew, those barbed knots scraping over wounds he'd thought hardened with the passage of time. 'Yes. But she was an expert at trivialising it. It was always everyone else making a big deal of something she considered natural.'

Delphine's jaw dropped. 'She thought being unfaithful was *natural*?'

The question brought up another rancid memory. His mother laughing as she went into another what's-the-big-deal? diatribe and his father losing his mind.

'She thought limiting herself to one purported soulmate was *unnatural*.'

He watched her eyes widen, and then her gaze boldly probed his. She wet her lower lip before asking, 'You don't share that sentiment, do you?'

'Being indiscriminate to the point of miring one's kingdom in scandal isn't my idea of exemplary rule.'

Her sensual lips pursed. 'That wasn't what I asked.'

He wanted to demand what right she had to ask him such a question—why it mattered to her at all since she'd ended their relationship. And yet he found himself answering, allowing the rusted door of his emotions over his mother to creak open.

Was it because the memory of talking with this woman long into the night about every other subject under the sun made this a little easier too?

He shifted under the weighted question but answered anyway. 'No, *dolcezza*, I find infidelity an abhorrent trait.'

Something resembling relief lit her beautiful eyes and he wanted to latch on to that expression, probe its true depths. But doing so would reveal his own peculiar need. He wasn't ready for that. Not after just exposing his childhood pain and his adult bewilderment.

'Did they manage to resolve their differences?' she asked.

Lucca glanced out of the window, for once wishing the journey would end. But the opera house was at least ten more minutes away, and it seemed having thrown the door wide open, by mentioning the diamonds she was wearing, he couldn't pull back from exposing more of his sordid past—even the event that had plunged San Calliano into international disrepute.

'My mother was independently wealthy before her marriage to my father. She knew she could buy herself out of almost any unsavoury situation. So my father tried increasingly desperate measures.' His fist balled on his thigh at the dark memory. 'The final one was to lock her in the cellars of the winter palace for a month.'

Delphine gaped at him. '*What?* No!'

'*Sì,*' he confirmed grimly. 'The scandal was never officially confirmed by the palace, but enough people leaked it to the press for it to become an open secret.'

'What did your mother do?' she whispered.

'The one thing I commend her for. She never confirmed it—perhaps because she knew she'd gone too far with her latest dalliance since she'd almost started an international incident—but she did pack her bags and move to Paris the very next day. She was killed in a car accident six months later.'

'Did you ever get a chance to say a proper goodbye to her?' Delphine asked, her voice barely above a whisper.

Lucca knew words like *closure* and *acceptance* and *reconciliation* mattered to certain people, but they'd never mattered to him because his mother had been a stranger long before she'd left San Calliano. *Left him.*

So why did his gut wrench with bitter anguish whenever he thought of her? Why did he wish he'd made an effort one last time to confront her, show her what her rejection had done to him and demand accountability for her failings? Acknowledgement of her own flesh and blood? Why did he lie awake at times, racked with guilt that he hadn't done enough, maybe closed himself off from her far too soon?

He pushed Delphine's question and his own feelings aside and cupped her cheek, revelled in the silky-smooth skin caressing his palm. He'd wanted to make her see. Now he had.

'You now understand why your disappearance caused more interest than might usually be warranted?'

It was certainly why those who knew of Silvestro's treatment of his wife had vowed to stop it happening ever again. It was also why Lucca's own advisers had warned him to ensure the hard-earned clean image of San Calliano wasn't jeopardised under any circumstances. Why they'd urged him that perhaps it was time to activate 'The List'.

Shocked understanding dawned in her eyes. 'Lucca… I… My God, they didn't really think you'd done something equally nefarious to *me*, did they?'

Did she know she'd used his name instead of the progressively snippy but sexy *Your Majesty* she usually threw at him? Did she know what the smoky texture of his name on her lips did to his insides?

'We may not have spent much time in San Calliano during our affair but, trust me, our every move was well-documented. Your abrupt disappearance from my life and my efforts to locate you raised questions—ones even tact and diplomacy couldn't resolve without issuing outright lies.'

A flare of alarm, hastily veiled, flashed through her eyes, sending his hackles rising.

'But they didn't really think you'd locked me up in a basement somewhere, did they?' she probed again.

He shrugged, his fingers finding their way down her throat to her throbbing pulse. 'My father before me had done it—why not the son?'

Her long lashes swept down, veiling her expression from him. He fought the urge to cup her chin, force her gaze up to his so he could read better this woman who'd succeeded in tilting the ground beneath his feet even long after her departure.

When she raised her gaze again, her expression was shadowed, reaffirming his notion that she was hiding something. 'How are things between you and your father now?' she asked.

He tensed, then breathed out as the car drew to a halt. 'That's a conversation for another day,' he said, with a welcome punch of relief.

'Wait,' she said, before he could get out. To his surprise, she laid a hand over his. 'I know what it's like to be a child in difficult family circumstances. I'm sorry you had to go through that.'

Something thick and vital turned over inside his chest. *Mio Dio.* Few people had turned him inside out as Delphine had. And for the life of him he hadn't yet discovered a way to circumvent that phenomenon. The more he tried, the less effective his struggle became.

And, yes, that unsettled him greatly.

So he busied himself with the role he knew best.

Being King.

'It's time for you to charm your audience once more,' he said.

Delphie took her seat in the opera house beside Lucca after another dazzling red-carpet ceremony and a photo op with a string of A-list celebrities that would've left her dizzy once upon a time. A time before she'd met Prince Lucca of San Calliano...

After her years in the fashion industry, and the excesses she'd witnessed first-hand, she'd thought she'd be jaded by another sun-drenched, heaven-kissed locale that catered to the rich and powerful, but with each discovery of San Calliano's many wonders she couldn't help but be drawn into its charm. It stood head and shoulders above Monaco and the French Riviera, and deserved its title as the new international film festival destination.

The movie that was to formally open the festival was a melodramatic love story, fraught with impossible odds and heart-wrenching obstacles from the start.

Delphie realised she was ill-prepared for it when she felt the furtive scrutiny of the audience, and as the drama on-screen ramped up, so did her emotions. Because she'd discovered another misstep on her part: she hadn't paused to read a synopsis of the movie or about the defining moment of the story—the loss of a child.

Her heart began to hammer as the soul-wrenching events unfolded.

Delphie didn't realise she was shaking until Lucca's hand grazed hers. She tensed, but couldn't bring herself to move, fearing she'd draw more attention.

'*Cara?* Are you all right?' he murmured, his breath washing over her ear.

She suppressed a shiver and hastily nodded, but when she tried to speak her throat was clogged. With emotions. With memories. With their conversation in the car that had drawn her anguish for what he'd had to endure as a child.

With her own loss and longings scrambling to rip free from the titanium vault she'd placed them in.

Her eyes begin to mist. She blinked the tears away, but emotion continued to suffocate her.

'Is it too much? Do you want to leave, *dolcezza*?' Lucca pressed.

Dolcezza. She'd refused to read anything into how easily he'd slipped back into the endearment he'd used for her in the past. Refused to entertain the idea of being his sweetheart, especially now.

But now the term caught her on the raw, striking at the soft, unguarded centre of her emotions. Dragging her to a time she didn't want to remember—especially as the female character on-screen howled her pain at her loss.

'No. I'm fine,' she managed to croak, thankful for the dark interior of the spectacular opera house.

Lucca didn't reply, but when his lips brushed over the back of her hand the roar in her ears almost drowned out the hushed whispers in the room, and the spark of guilt in her belly added to the maelstrom of emotions.

'You will admit your every truth to me. I guarantee it.'

Her insides quaked as she recalled Lucca's words. Somewhere along the line she'd convinced herself that her loss was hers alone, but now, as she cast her own furtive glance at Lucca's imperious profile, she wondered whether that was true. Whether he didn't deserve to know the truth she'd told herself was better kept locked in her heart.

He turned his head then, met her gaze full-on, and her heart dropped to her feet. She told herself she was imagining the craving in his eyes, and when he glanced away a moment later she was sure that was true. But he continued to grip her hand through the rest of the movie, unknowingly containing her emotions, stopping them from spilling out.

She escaped as soon as she could after the movie ended, excusing herself to the ladies' room. If Lucca suspected it was an excuse, he chose not to comment, merely nodding at one of his bodyguards to accompany her. She curbed her

objection, recalling that she was wearing priceless royal
gems that needed to be guarded.

In the VIP ladies' room, she caught her reflection and
gasped at the raw, naked emotion swirling through her eyes.
No wonder Lucca had wondered if she was all right...

Swallowing, she breathed in deep, ran her hands under
cool water in a frantic bid for composure. Minutes later, she
accepted it was futile. But she couldn't stay there for ever,
so she touched up her make-up, practised a few more deep
breaths and headed out.

The flash of a camera temporarily blinded her as she
stepped back into the small foyer leading out of the ladies'
room. Then a woman planted herself in front her, a discreet
microphone extended to Delphie.

'Miss Alexander, I'm with the San Calliano *Gazzetta*.
Care to answer a few questions?'

'Are you supposed to be here?' Delphie asked, suppress-
ing her unease.

The woman shrugged away the question, her keen eyes
locked on Delphie. 'Did you enjoy the movie, Miss Alexander?'

She strained for every crumb of composure. 'Yes, it was
very moving.'

The woman's gaze lingered on Delphie's pale cheeks. 'Is
that why you were distressed?' she pressed.

'With respect, that's none of your business.'

Delphie started to walk away, but she followed.

'How do you feel about the diamond collection you've
been hired to exhibit this week?'

The question was benign enough for Delphie's steps to
slow, even though her senses remained on high alert. 'I've
read the history of how the San Calliano diamonds helped
build this kingdom. I know what they mean to its people
and I'm proud to have been given the opportunity to showcase them.'

'The last woman to wear the Desiderio di Natale diamond

set was the Queen. As King Lucca's ex-lover, do you have any such aspirations?'

Her stomach dipped wildly, even as a chill racked her body. But alongside the iciness a flame flickered inside her.

Like hope.

Like yearning.

Rightfully, it was snuffed out. Because even though Delphie hadn't fully grasped the flame's meaning, she'd accepted it was a futile, foolish kindling. A shadow of a shadow that could never exist.

It took every ounce of her past modelling experience to maintain her composure as the microphone was thrust further into her face. 'Of course not. I'm simply here to do a job. Once it's done, I'm done too.'

She hurried away, exhaling with relief when she saw the bodyguard poised a few feet from the auditorium entrance. Casting a quick glance over her shoulder, she saw the journalist fall back.

'Signorina Alexander, His Majesty has been called away. I am to escort you back to the palace,' the bodyguard said in halting English.

Her relief evaporated, replaced by a bereft sensation that alarmed her as she followed the bodyguard back out on to the red carpet. Several more flashbulbs went off, but without Lucca she didn't have to stop and acknowledge them— a situation for which she was grateful.

She'd just handed the diamonds to the aides, slipped out of her dress and into a silk dressing gown, when a firm knock had her retracing her steps back from the bedroom.

From the imperious urgency of it, she knew who waited on the other side before she opened it.

Lucca stalked past her, tension riding his body as he stormed into the living room. Before she could ask what he was doing there, he whirled to face her, his nostrils flared. '"Once it's done, I'm done too"?' he quoted accurately. Leashed fury bracketed the words.

'You're angry.'

He muttered something pithy in Italian. 'Perhaps you should try giving another interview—attempt the impossible and be a little bit more dismissive.'

'She ambushed me in the ladies' room. What did you want me to say? You didn't want me to gush sentiment about you, did you?'

'Yes!' he sliced at her. 'Why the hell not?'

She sucked in a stunned breath. 'Lucca—' She froze as his name dropped unguarded from her lips. About to correct herself, she was shocked into further silence when he arrived in front of her, a control-wrecking pillar of masculinity, and placed his forefinger on her lips.

'I only stepped away for twenty minutes and you threaten to wreck everything we've achieved this week.'

She curbed the urge to ask where he'd gone. She had no right. 'I only told the truth,' she whispered.

He exhaled audibly, his eyes darkening while his finger slid languorously over her lower lip. For a short, taut stretch neither of them spoke, and the only movement was his electrifying touch.

'Why do you find pleasure in aggravating me so much?' he demanded, his deep tone faintly bewildered.

She would've been amused had her every effort not been focused on *not* chasing the path of his caress with her tongue. 'Do you want me to spell it out for you? You're used to *yes men* jumping to fulfil your every desire. You hate me for standing up to you.'

His head lowered, his finger dropping from her mouth to be replaced by the faintest brush of his lips. 'No, I do not. Trust me, *cara*. That's the very last thing I hate about you.'

Before she could ask what he meant they were colliding, straining against each other in a fireball of desire that promised to consume them. Their kiss was hot and torrid, fused with breath-robbing urgency. His tongue stroked hers with lusty possessiveness, his hands trailing down her sides to grip her waist, holding her in place as he ravished her.

With a helpless moan, Delphie threw her arms around his neck, rose on tiptoe to meet the power of his kiss. Deep down she questioned her own sanity, but even that evaporated under the blaze of desire.

The shudder that unravelled through his tensile frame sent an answering shiver through her. She clenched her fingers in his hair, half terrified that this would end way too soon. Before she'd had the chance to lock a substantial memory in place for the future. Before every inch of her body was saturated with the unique brand of his sexual mastery.

Because even before they'd parted she'd feared she would never experience anything like it again. In the time since she hadn't felt the smallest inclination to test that theory. And now, falling headlong into his drugging kisses, her frantic hands moving over his body in a mad exploration that had them both groaning and shuddering, she was absolutely convinced she never would.

So she needed to gorge and hoard.

When he boldly cupped her bottom and moved her along the powerful outline of his erection, she gave a hoarse cry and revelled in their carnal dance.

When he growled, bit her lip then soothed it with a decadent lick, she dug her fingers into his nape and encouraged him.

And when he uttered a thick curse and dragged himself away, stalking to the far end of the room, she sucked in a life-sustaining breath and told herself it was for the best.

'I did not come here for this,' he growled, his fingers stabbing through his hair.

'Then why did you come?' she asked shakily, once she could speak again.

Even from across the room she saw a tic ripple through his jaw. But the disgruntlement he'd entered with was now tempered by something approaching…*concern*. An emotion that shook through her. She didn't want him concerned for her. Concern implied…*care*. And she couldn't afford to let that flame flicker back to life.

'I wanted to check on you,' he said. 'You seemed distressed by the movie.'

The reminder sent another wave of alarm through her. She glanced away before he could read her reaction. 'I told you I was fine.'

He gave an abrupt nod, the corners of his lips turning down. '*Sì*, I can see that for myself now. And the interview?'

Mentally replaying the conversation, she cringed inwardly. 'Maybe I could've expressed myself…differently…'

One eyebrow quirked mockingly as he paced back to her. 'Maybe?'

'The question about being Queen was unexpected—not to mention way off base.'

Something glinted in his eyes, far too quick for her to catch. 'I can see how that would throw you.'

She caught the belt of her robe between her fingers, pulled it tight just for something to do then felt her lungs squeeze when his gaze dropped to her waist, her legs.

Again something flickered in his eyes—this time charged with a heat that made every cell in her body strain for… *something*.

'Were you about to head to bed? At only nine o'clock?'

She shook her head. 'Not to sleep. I have some work that needs my attention.'

His gaze drifted with heated intent over her body. 'Work that can't wait till morning?'

She shook her head, faintly panicking that he would linger for a nightcap. That she would join him. Because even now, when clarity should've reasserted itself, she couldn't stop her gaze from roving over him. From lingering on the full, sensual lips she'd so thoroughly explored minutes ago. From drifting lower to the still prominent erection he wasn't bothering to hide.

'Not if I don't want to lose another sponsor by morning. They all seem to be deserting the team.'

'Which ones?' he clipped out with a frown.

She named them.

Regal authority brimmed from him. 'It will be taken care of.'

Pride straightened her spine. 'I don't want any special favours.'

His eyes narrowed. 'I gave you my word that I'd stop you haemorrhaging sponsors. I believed my message had reached the relevant parties. It's clear it hasn't, so I'll take care of it.'

'Oh… I…'

He drew closer, his eyes fixed on her mouth. 'Here's where you say, *Grazie*, Lucca.'

'Lucca? You're not going to demand I use Your Majesty?'

'A few minutes ago you were moaning my name. It felt rude to insist on it then. And now I feel we've crossed that bridge. So…?' he drawled.

'*Grazie*, Lucca.'

'*Prego, dolcezza.*' He trailed his knuckles gently down her cheek, smiled conceitedly when she sucked in a shaky breath. 'And, just for my sanity, no more interviews to devious paparazzi. *Sì?*'

He lingered for several contemplative seconds after she'd nodded her agreement, and through it all Delphie forgot to breathe. Which was just as well since the air was thick with unfulfilled lust, and her body was screaming for her to throw caution to the wind.

Instead, she locked her knees and watched him stride to the door with languid ease.

There, he paused, casting her another heavy, contemplative look that lasted moments but felt like a year.

And then he was gone and she could breathe again.

Propped against the wall, every moment of the day seemed to crash down on her, until she felt as if she might drown just from the relentless power of the shifting of her axis.

CHAPTER SEVEN

SHE WOKE ON Sunday, the final day of the festival, with mingled relief and apprehension. Her pure white jumpsuit with trumpet sleeves and a plunging neckline showcased the final spectacular diamond set—a three-tiered necklace, headband and earrings.

There was something wild and decadent about these diamonds that excited her. Or perhaps it was learning there was no profound or melodramatic history attached to these gems. According to the descriptor card within each of the exquisite velvet boxes, this particular set had been completed by the royal jeweller only a month ago, to commemorate this year's festival. As foolish as the notion was, Delphine felt quiet pride in being the first to showcase the Primavera.

She was stroking the large teardrop emerald that centred the necklace when Nicola re-entered the room. The designer had lingered in the suite after the fitting, her gaze a little sad now as it met Delphie's.

'Those diamonds are my absolute favourite. And they look spectacular on you,' she said with a smile as she tweaked another curl Delphie was sure didn't need tweaking.

Delphie smiled. 'Thank you.'

Nicola sighed. 'It's been a wild and awesome week. Normally I whine about diva models and their endless demands, but it's been a joy to dress you. I only wish we'd had a chance to have more than that one drink,' Nicola said.

Delphie bit the inside of her cheek to stop herself from

telling her she would be back in two weeks. She'd already incurred Lucca's wrath with that interview. And while she adored Nicola, and could count on her discretion, her soft-hearted friend would most likely read all the wrong things into it. Things Delphie had to stop herself from entertaining.

'Hey, maybe I'll come to one of your races. It'd be a trip to see you in action. And all those hot drivers… *Sì, sì, sì…*' She sighed gustily as she fanned herself.

Delphie smiled. 'I'd like that. Let me know when you want to come.'

'Great, it's a date,' Nicola said, then kissed Delphie on the cheek and left.

Alone once again, she took one last look in the mirror, assuring herself that the dullness in her eyes had nothing to do with leaving San Calliano in a few short hours.

Leaving Lucca.

She berated herself for the bruising sensation in her chest when she should be concentrating on more important things—like the upcoming race. But even then her thoughts veered inexorably towards Lucca, and the welcome news she'd received this morning.

As if conjured by her thoughts, she saw him striding to-wards her. Like her, he was dressed less formally, with a suave neckerchief tucked into the open neck of his light pur-ple shirt, his bespoke jacket and matching trousers a lighter shade than he usually favoured.

Her breath stalled in her lungs as she took in the perfectly groomed stubble and the way it emphasised his wickedly sensual lips. The way the wool blend of his trousers moulded his muscled thighs.

It took several alarming seconds for her to realise they'd stopped dead half a dozen feet from each other, their gazes locked in heated investigation. Of what, exactly, she was too scared to think.

Despite silently extending his arm, as he had all week, she knew something was changing. Probably had *already* changed. And when they stepped outside to find a sleek supercar in place of the usual fleet of vehicles, she wasn't altogether surprised.

'No motorcade?'

'No, I wanted to try something…different.'

Foreboding echoed again, warning her of something fundamental but out of reach…changing.

She forced down the need to overreact and breathed in and out as he settled behind the wheel of the Ferrari and accelerated out of the palace with speed she was sure would leave his bodyguards tearing out their hair.

She even managed to force her vocal cords to work once she'd dragged her senses away from the decadent thrill of watching Lucca work the engine. 'I heard from the sponsors this morning. Whatever you did worked. Thank you.'

A look flickered in his eyes. 'You're welcome. You see how easy things are when we work together?'

She tensed. 'There's a difference between working together and me letting you take control.'

A wicked smile curved his lips. 'But isn't it pleasurable to relinquish control for a while? Isn't there joy in knowing you can cede it for a while, then take it back?'

She swallowed, her body aroused far too quickly by the potency of his words. 'When have you ever ceded control?' she tossed back.

The sliver of amusement evaporated, leaving shadows in his eyes. 'You don't think you seized control from me when you disappeared without a trace?' he queried with a tight growl.

Delphie grimaced inwardly for redirecting him to the raw subject of their separation. A part of her wondered if it wasn't subconscious. Whether that mounting guilt inside her was feeding the need to rake over what was clearly an aggravating issue for Lucca. Or was she pushing for more, looking for a deeper meaning that wasn't there?

'Well, you've taken back your control by summoning me here this week, so I'm thinking we're square on that front,' she said, infusing as much brisk finality into her tone as she could manage.

That enigmatic look weaved through his eyes again, before he returned his gaze to the road. 'You would like it to be that straightforward, wouldn't you, *dolcezza*?'

Something sneaky snagged in her midriff. 'What's that supposed to mean?'

'It means I'm far too familiar with living in the unknown to ever take things as "square", *dolcezza*.'

She gasped softly. 'You don't mean…your mother?'

A hard expression clenched his features. 'No, that is behind me.'

'Is it? Because it sounds to me like you're allowing the past to colour your outlook on the present.'

'And how would you like me to look at the present, or indeed the future, Delphine? With guileless optimism? Shouldn't the template that states that people, given the chance, will take and take and then disappoint you be my mantra?'

She swallowed, aware that she'd waded into dangerous territory again. She couldn't deny she hadn't taken from him, because she had—even if she'd felt justified in fleeing without divulging that knowledge.

'Caution is good—prudent, in fact. But what good is closing yourself off completely from everyone and everything? Even a king can't exist in isolation.'

He pulled up to the exhibition centre, where the last big event of the festival—the San Calliano Supercar Show—was taking place. But he didn't step out immediately. Instead, ignoring the hundreds of flashing cameras and the throng screaming for their King, he turned to her. 'Is that what you learned while sequestered away at Buckman's property?'

She clenched her fingers in her lap to stop their shaking and forced herself to meet his censorious gaze. 'No. I knew it before then. I knew it when I returned home at seventeen, despite knowing I wasn't wanted. I know it now because it hurts that I don't have a family any more and it's partly my fault.'

A frown clenched his brow, even as a look approaching sympathy flickered through his eyes. 'Hold your mother responsible for being a bad parent,' he said. 'But never yourself for wishing for what was due to you—the care and support every child deserves from their parent.'

'Didn't you hope for that too, even as you blamed your mother for her indifference?' she asked, foolishly anxious to dissipate the shadows in his eyes.

His gaze swept down and his nostrils flared as he audibly inhaled. 'But I'm a quick study, *dolcezza*, and I didn't have the luxury of superfluous emotions. Men in my position rarely do. I swiftly accept the futility of an action and move on.'

She wanted to ask if he'd moved on from her. And if so, how quickly. She didn't, of course. Because—again—she had no right. And, more, she was terrified of his answer.

When he alighted and rounded the car to help her out, she told herself that the emotion moving through her was relief.

But the mocking voice taunted her for the lie.

Because she didn't want to be relieved.

Despite being the one to flee, she knew the reason she hadn't completely got over Lucca was because, far too frequently in the past nineteen months, she'd wondered what would've happened if she'd stayed. If she'd disregarded Marco Coppi's cruel words, told Lucca about the child they'd created and let fate take its course.

A mere half hour later, while circling the latest supercar from a renowned German manufacturer, she let her gaze stray to the right and met the eyes of the very man who'd set her life on a different course.

As if conjured up by her churning thoughts, Marco Coppi stood beneath a grey VIP awning, his cold gaze fixed on her. Ice cascaded down her spine, sending a shiver through every cell as she veered away as calmly as she could manage.

Unsuccessfully, it turned out.

'What is it?' Lucca asked sharply, obviously noting her reaction.

'I… It's nothing important.'

'Yet you're clearly distressed—just as you were before. How do you know Coppi? Tell me, or I'll summon him and discover the truth for myself.'

'You will admit your every truth to me. I guarantee it.'

She swallowed hard. 'We met briefly a long time ago.'

His eyes narrowed. 'Where?'

She tried to distance herself from the searing memory, but it was etched far too deeply into her psyche. 'Paris. You remember my last photo shoot?'

'Of course,' he replied, his voice ringed with bitterness. 'How could I not? It was the day before you left me.'

Her insides quaked at the soul-shredding reminder of that day and everything that had followed. 'He wasn't very pleasant, if you must know.'

Lucca's head swung towards Coppi, his displeasure barely sheathed before he turned back to her. 'What did he say to you?'

She shrugged, aware of their audience and, more importantly, of the need not to divulge her true emotions surrounding that day. 'I don't recall the exact words. He was concerned about my place in your life…concerned that you were behaving uncharacteristically. He wanted to warn me not to read anything into the fact that I'd lasted longer than any of your previous…dalliances.'

A muscle rippled through his jaw and she was thankful he was facing away from the crowd when she saw the incandescent flames leaping in his eyes. 'It was not his place to say such things to you.'

A deep weariness settled on her shoulders and, much as she'd have liked to hate Coppi for his part in what had happened, she knew it'd been…inevitable. 'Maybe not, but he was looking out for you, nonetheless. You were the Prince, on the brink of becoming King. He was doing his duty. You can't fault him for that.'

Sharp grey eyes narrowed on her face. 'You almost sound as if you defend him.'

She shrugged. 'Like you pointed out, certain protocols are necessary for the smooth running of the royal line.'

His head twisted again towards the older man, and he took a step.

Panic flaring, Delphie placed a hand on his arm. 'No.'

Lucca glanced down at it, then after a moment looked into her face. His gaze was filled with bristling purpose. 'Our month together will be without interference from any source. You have my word on that.'

Which was exactly what she feared. Because if the past week had been a harbinger of things to come, those four weeks in August would be a study in hiding every scrap of extraneous emotion she'd felt for him in those days before she'd fled Paris.

Containing the guilty secret that she'd not only fallen pregnant with their child but lost it. Trying to stop herself falling desperately, foolishly in love with a man who had only ever been on short-term loan to her.

A man who still commanded dizzying emotions from her she feared she hadn't completely purged.

Those thoughts plagued her for the remainder of the festival—long after she was packed and ready to leave San Calliano.

Now, while she waited for the chauffeur, she paced the living room, unable to stop memories surging up from the shallow grave of her mind.

The first time she'd suspected that she might be carrying the heir to the San Calliano throne had been the morning of the photo shoot. A quick trip to buy a pregnancy test had brought shock and awed acceptance. Then worry over when to tell Lucca. Immediately? Or wait to see if her often erratic period made an appearance, even though deep inside she'd *known* it wouldn't.

She'd eventually talked herself into doing it immediately, once she was done with work and Lucca had returned from his meeting.

Except someone else had been waiting for her when she'd returned to their suite.

Someone who'd shown her that the rosy scenarios she'd concocted in her head were simply dreams, and that the reality of 'The List', of Lucca's true path, would be leaving her out in the cold.

And because even then she'd been terrified of the depth of her feelings, of her yearning for the Prince, whose attention had been like basking in pure sunlight after years of darkness following her father's death and her mother's abandonment, she'd taken the only remaining option left for her.

She'd intended her retreat to Qatar to be nothing more than a breathing space until she told Lucca about the baby. A little distance away from the overwhelming cascade of events.

Only fate had stepped in again.

Theirs had been an affair she'd been deeply wary of starting and then ferociously fearful of losing. Once the dust had cleared, she'd known her only option was to keep away. Raking over a doomed relationship and the loss of her precious child would've been doubly shattering.

Would he care now if she told him? Could she risk shattering her heart all over again by having the memory of their child rejected by its father?

Pushing the harrowing thought she wasn't ready to face aside, she hurried across the room, intending to call and ask where the car was. But she froze as the door opened and Lucca entered.

The circumspect look he'd been levelling at her since she'd confessed Marco Coppi's behaviour was still in place, perhaps even sharper than before. Each glance probed be-

neath the surface. Searching. As if she was a conundrum…
one he was determined to solve.

Her heart lurched wildly as they stared at one another,
the tight, charged silence that was theirs alone filling the
space between them. Had she been of that frame of mind,
she'd have sentimentally pondered if this was where, in the
movie, the hero burst through the doors to declare his un-
dying love. But she knew it would be something far less
melodramatic than that.

Apparently concluding a festival wasn't a simple matter
of giving a final speech and being done with it. The aides
had informed her earlier that His Majesty would be tied up
with his festival committee for a couple of hours. And perhaps a little cowardly part of her had hoped to be spared
this…this ceremony of a departure.

'Am I free to leave now?' she demanded, cringing when
her voice emerged with a touch of breathlessness instead of
the cool professionalism she'd wished to project.

He didn't answer immediately, nor show any sign of being
riled by her demand.

At some point he'd discarded his jacket, so she was
treated to the ripple of his biceps beneath his pristine shirt
and the strong column of his throat as his powerful body
filled her vision.

'Why do you play these games with me, Delphine?' he
breathed calmly, his eyes fixed on her face.

She notched her chin up, determined not to show further weakness. 'What games? What are you talking about?'

'We cannot be in the same room without the visceral urge
to tear the clothes off one another. And yet you pretend to
be anything but affected.'

She glanced blindly at her watch. 'Lucca, I have a plane
to catch. I'm not sure why any of this—'

His nostrils flared and a layer of anger filmed his eyes.
'Don't you know by now that indifference is one very effective way to push my buttons? Or is that why you do it?'

Mild panic laced with heavy excitement churned through

her stomach. 'I just want to get out of here, get back to my team—'

But he wasn't listening. He was running his hands through her hair, a frenzied intent in his eyes. An intent that ignited her own need, made her move closer when reason demanded she resist. Made her melt when she should head for the door.

'You're still here because I wanted to say goodbye. I was willing to leave it up to you as to whether we did that civilly or not. But, since you never make anything between us easy…'

'Lucca…' His name was a helpless craving on her lips.

His lips slanted over hers in a carnal kiss that swept the ground from beneath her feet, leaving her swimming in a sea of desire so deep all she could do was dig her hands into the trim flesh of his waist and hold on as he masterfully, thoroughly, kissed her.

She was gasping for breath when he finally lifted his head. 'Tell me you feel indifferent about that.'

Delphie scrambled for something solid, only to find the hard muscle of his six-pack. The irony that the very danger she should've backed away from was the thing she now clung to wasn't lost on her. Still, she tried to bluff her way through it. 'So you have the power to turn me on…?'

'Like no other man does,' he completed, a primitive possessiveness throbbing in his voice.

She couldn't deny it—not when her blood ran hot and her sex pulsed with an emptiness only Lucca had been able to fill. Not when in all their time apart it hadn't even occurred to her to seek another man's arms.

Lucca, among his other sins, had ruined her for other men. That thought sparked rebellion to life.

'Yes, fine! You make me wild and needy and so horny I can't see straight. Is that what you want to hear?'

The fingers in her hair clenched and his other hand dug into her waist, his gaze devouring her. 'That's a start,' he allowed, his voice thick and deep.

With monumental effort, she disengaged her fingers from his firm body. 'Well, that's all you're going to get. Because, Lucca, all those things are secondary to what matters. We both know that.'

Tension doused a layer of the aroused flames in his eyes. 'What the hell are you talking about?'

'I'm talking about the transience of passion. What happens when it fades? What will you chase then?'

His nostrils flared again, but before he could launch another heavenly assault she pivoted on her heels and headed for the door.

'I've done everything you've asked for. I believe I'm free for the next two weeks?'

'Delphine—'

She ignored his warning tone. 'No. I won't allow you to make any more demands,' she threw over her shoulder.

Thick, powerful arms were folded across his chest, his feet planted wide apart, lending him an even more commanding appearance. 'I wasn't going to,' he declared sardonically. 'I was merely going to say that your flight has already left but my jet will take you wherever you want.' Before she could breathe out in relief, he added, 'And I'll send it back for you two weeks from today. I suggest you don't attempt to alter our agreement in any way while we're apart.'

'If that's a dig at my pulling a disappearing act, save your breath.'

The blazing fire in his eyes sizzled her skin. Thankfully, he didn't say anything, merely strolled with easy-limbed grace to where she stood, took her face between his hands and lowered his lips to hers.

After another thorough exploration that almost triggered a tsunami beneath her feet, he raised his head. 'I don't need to say it. There's nowhere on earth you can hide from me. Not this time. *Ciao, dolcezza.*'

She stumbled away from him with shaky legs, hating herself for wishing with every step that she was going in the opposite direction. Because she already missed him with a ferocious need that made her wonder where her self-preservation had gone.

Digging deep and reminding herself that she'd been more or less alone for over a decade and didn't need anyone, especially the force of nature that was Lucca, was what kept her head up, her spine straight, as she boarded his jet twenty minutes later.

As she'd been escorted through Customs by important-looking officials and personally handed into the jaw-dropping opulence of the royal jet by sharply dressed attendants, Delphie had wondered cynically if this was Lucca ensuring that she didn't forget that, for now, he owned her.

She tried to tell herself it didn't matter. That there would come a time, somewhere in the nebulous future, when Lucca would be nothing but a memory. A breath-robbing, stomach-clenching memory, but a memory nonetheless.

Those self-affirming words returned to mock her later when, upon opening her suitcase to change into more comfortable clothes, after arriving in her apartment in Doha, she saw the wide, flat velvet box laying on top.

Fingers shaking, she opened it, her gasp filling her bedroom. She was still staring, jaw agape, at its contents when her phone rang. She considered ignoring it. But her feet moved of their own accord, her fingers pressing the answer button.

'*Ciao, dolcezza.* Did you have a smooth flight?'

Delphie shut her eyes against the raw sensuality in his voice. Opening them again, she let her gaze fall on the diamonds sparkling in the late-afternoon sunlight.

'Why did you have your aides pack the Primavera diamonds?' she demanded. Then, realising her hands were shaking, she flung the box on to the bed.

'They are my gift to you. Are you pleased?' he drawled.

'Am I…? They're priceless diamonds!'

'Hardly,' he drawled. 'Very few things in life are price-less. Diamonds aren't one of them.'

She tensed, something about him waxing philosophical raising her hackles. 'Such as…?'

Silence. Then, 'Ask me again in a month,' he said cryptically. 'Now, answer me.'

She struggled to remember his question. 'Yes, the flight was smooth, thank you,' she added. 'Did you want something specifically, Lucca?'

Another drum of silence pounded before he answered, 'I've lined up two more sponsors for you. They'll be in touch tomorrow. Vet them as you see fit and report back to me.'

Again she found her jaw dropping. 'I… Thank you.'

'Should I be insulted that once again my generosity surprises you?' he demanded tersely.

Fingers tightening on the phone, she sank on to the bed. She didn't want to confess that it had been a while since anyone had considered her needs. Not since her father died.

Her mother's preoccupation with her new marriage had left her out in the cold long before further cracks had ripped them apart. Long before her stepfather's disapproving glances had turned into stinging criticism and strained distance.

Her half-sibling's arrival had worsened the strain. The hard choice to leave the family sphere had broken something inside her. Something she'd been terrified would never heal.

Until she'd made the mistake of looking for healing in Lucca.

Until the sorcery he'd wreaked on her body and soul had skyrocketed towards her heart.

She'd suspected she was in trouble long before that final day in Paris, and the intensity of the resulting devastation was the reason she couldn't allow her emotions to soften.

'I can't accept the diamonds,' she said, even as she let her gaze stray to the flawless gems, recalling how they'd felt against her skin, recalling Lucca's intense reaction. She shivered again.

'Return them. I dare you,' he sliced icily at her.

It took her a vital second to grasp why he was so livid. 'Lucca, I returned that bracelet because it was a family heirloom. It was your grandmother's. I couldn't keep it.'

'There are no sentimental attachments to these diamonds so that settles the matter.'

She opened her mouth to argue, then decided against it. This conversation wasn't going the way either of them had intended. She needed to quit while she was ahead.

'Thank you for checking up on me,' she said, hoping to defuse the charged atmosphere.

'Thank me by ensuring the podium finish you've been promising in the next race,' he said tonelessly. Then hung up.

If she'd hoped for distance after that, she was to be woefully disappointed. Each night Lucca called for an update, demonstrating an in-depth, breathtaking knowledge of motor racing and team management.

Against her will, Delphie found herself talking through driver dynamics and race tactics with him. And when she relayed her own solutions to engineering issues, she preened inwardly at his approval. Then immediately berated herself for it.

Yet it didn't stop her heightened sense of anticipation when race day arrived. As much as she was looking forward to seeing her hard work translated on to the track, she knew the tight ball of excitement in her stomach was because by day's end she would be back on Lucca's royal jet, on her way to being delivered to the King of San Calliano, despite knowing every moment of the next four weeks would be pretend—

Her thoughts screeched to a halt when she walked into her trailer and saw the man lounging in the armchair.

'What are you doing here?'

Lucca slowly rose to his feet, filling up the small space. 'I'm here to watch my team—what else?'

She'd mistakenly thought the burly bodyguards she'd

seen outside were for one of the many Qatari royal family members who gravitated to events like this.

He looked unbearably suave in light-coloured trousers and a navy jacket. Under the light slanting through the windows his dark hair gleamed with vitality, making her fingers itch to bury themselves in the tresses. His gaze dropped to her lips and they tingled wildly.

She spun away from him, taking far longer than necessary to formulate an answer.

'I thought we agreed we'd announce your involvement with the team after the August break?'

'The official announcement—*sì*. We never agreed that I wouldn't attend the last race.'

'Why didn't you tell me?'

He gave a far too self-assured smile. 'Perhaps I didn't want to throw you off your game.'

She sucked in a quiet, hopefully sustaining breath, and almost groaned when it did nothing to quell her roiling senses.

'Are you going to turn around and look at me, *dolcezza*?'

Girding her loins, she turned. 'Tell me you're not here because you think I'm running away...'

His eyes darkened with a flash of displeasure, which he quickly neutralised. 'I told you—you won't get away from me this time.'

She should be offended. And yet that primitive throb in his voice echoed low in her belly...evidence of how far she'd fallen. Because suddenly she didn't mind being caught by Lucca so much.

She shook her head, a little terrified by her own thoughts. 'I need to get to the garage.'

'Not for another half hour. We have time.'

Wild, unfettered tingles danced up her spine, then slowly reached around to engulf her body in a tremulous embrace. 'Time for what?'

'To tackle a couple of issues.'

That tingling embrace grew tighter, squeezing the air from her lungs. 'Issues?' she echoed.

'*Sì*. First of all, you haven't said hello properly. It seems to be a recurring theme with you.'

Her core clenched hard at the reminder, her fingers tingling with the need to turn his words into action in the way it had pleased them both. But she couldn't uncage that needy woman she'd been. She had led her down a dangerous path that had ended in heartache and loss. She couldn't afford to regress that way again.

'It wouldn't happen if you didn't insist on appearing when you're not wanted,' she accused, denying the fact that she yearned for his breath against her cheek, the heat of his skin…

Her traitorous gaze dropped to his sensual lips and she almost groaned at the cruel temptation—at the desire that made her want to rip that jacket off his broad shoulders, yank the expensive cotton off and reacquaint herself with every inch of that sculpted torso.

Her gaze flew up to find eyes of quicksilver and lightning locked on hers, one eyebrow quirked as if he knew the silent battle she fought. Then his body shifted, his lips going slack, as if anticipating a savouring of his own.

But, maddeningly, he kept his distance. Until the small space crackled with strained sensations.

'Let's start again, shall we?' he said. '*Ciao, dolcezza,*' he breathed from across the room.

'Hello, Lucca,' she croaked finally.

Then they said nothing, simply staring at each other as sensual heat built and built and built.

Terrified she would drown in temptation again, she forced herself to speak. 'You said a couple of issues… What's the other?'

Slowly, desire drained from his eyes, and for a second she wished she hadn't reminded him of whatever was on his mind.

'I saw Buckman on my way in.'

'Yes. And…?'

His jaw rippled. 'And I saw that he has VIP access to my team.'

'It's *our* team, remember?'

'You will revoke it immediately,' he stated.

'He's just a friend, Lucca.'

A different fire lit his eyes. The kind that promised lethal consequences. 'I don't care. To the eyes of the world he's the man you fled to after you left me. I won't be made a fool of again. Is that understood?'

'Why is this such a big deal?'

'You can glare at me and raise that beautiful chin in defiance. But this particular rebellion I *will* quash. My mother brought endless shame on my family…made my kingdom the butt of gossip and pity. I lived through endless cycles of scandal and vicious rumours. Never again. I mean it, Delphine.'

The echoes of long-suppressed pain in his voice and in his eyes convinced her that this was more than just a display of territorial possessiveness or jealousy.

She swallowed, the fire of rebellion dying down a touch. 'If it means that much to you, then fine. Consider all his future invitations revoked.'

He examined her features for another long minute. Then, satisfied with what he saw, he turned on his heel and exited the trailer.

Another minute passed before she realised she'd sagged against the wall, her fingers clutching her middle, and she accepted that whatever beast she and Lucca wrestled, it was far from slain.

CHAPTER EIGHT

THAT BRACING THOUGHT lingered as she changed into her team uniform and headed to the garage before the countdown to the race officially begun. Lucca's overwhelming presence there heightened speculation in the garage as preparations started to send the cars to the grid.

She wanted to hate him for it, but she couldn't deny his presence had the desired bolstering effect. Her temperamental drivers unearthed their best behaviour and the team, already on their A-game, stepped it up another admirable notch.

Even her five-minute conversation with Hunter went smoothly, with her friend handing over his VIP pass with a harmless smirk. 'I got the feeling this would happen.'

'You're not annoyed?' she asked, faintly surprised.

'Hell, no. At least he sent you to do it. I feared for my hide when he spotted me this morning. Talk about if looks could kill… This way I escape intact and I can also make sure you don't hate me for selling my shares to him.'

Her previous dismay at his actions melted away. An inevitability shrouded the whole thing and made it a wasted effort to hold a grudge against Hunter. 'I could never hate you.'

He started to raise a hand to her cheek, then checked himself and patted her shoulder instead, after a quick glance over her shoulder. Her tingling senses told her they were being watched by none other than the man under discussion.

'Thanks, Delly. And put in a good word for me with the

King when you can, would you? I'd like it very much if I don't get demolished the next time we meet in a boardroom.'

She pressed her lips together to stop herself from making promises she couldn't keep. And from correcting his assumption that she held any sway over Lucca.

Don't you?

She ignored the tempting voice, said goodbye to Hunter and made her way to the pit. Her senses tingled more wildly a minute later, and she didn't need to turn around to know Lucca was behind her. But what she tried to deny with her eyesight he multiplied with his intoxicating scent...

'Are you staying here for the duration of the race?'

His voice was a rumble that went straight to her toes.

'Yes.' It would be far better than subjecting herself to his overwhelming presence.

His lips tightened for a nanosecond. 'Then I'll see you afterwards. Good luck.'

She saw the lingering female looks that followed him as he left and tried not to let them bother her. He wasn't hers. Would never be. The quicker that reminder settled into her bones, the better off she would be.

Resolute, she turned her back on him, drawing the headphones over her ears.

Two hot and sweaty hours later, she raced across the pit lane and into the garage, her smile a mile wide as she exchanged high fives with her crew.

And then she turned to Lucca.

His gaze raked her flushed face, a hint of a smile flirting with his lips. 'Second and third positions. *Congratulazioni.*'

She shrugged but for the life of her she couldn't stop smiling. 'It was a fluke. Mostly. But I'll take it.'

'No, it wasn't,' he disagreed, and there was a sharp glint in his eyes as he reached out to tuck a tendril of hair behind her ears. 'You made crucial calls on a knife-edge and they paid off. Accept your rightful accolades.'

A deeper flush heated her cheeks. *'Grazie.'*

The growl of engines as the cars returned sent her crew out into the pit lane. She followed, hyper aware of Lucca next to her in the boisterous crowd that pinned them closer together.

'Your bodyguards must be going mental,' she said, more to ease the awareness inside her than anything else.

'They'll survive,' he rasped drily.

They stayed through the podium celebration, where Delphie unsuccessfully tried to dodge the spray of champagne from her ecstatic drivers.

Laughing, she swiped at the stream of champagne dripping through her hair and down her throat. Then her laughter faded, a punch of heat attacking her belly as she caught Lucca staring at her. He nudged her into a quiet corner and dug out a handkerchief to wipe at the moisture collecting between her breasts, his gaze lingering heatedly on her flesh before rising to sear hers.

Then he stepped away from her as if that charged little moment hadn't happened.

'I think it's time to put the rumours to rest, don't you?' Lucca asked when they were back in the garage.

Glancing at the expectant faces of their team, she nodded. 'Okay.'

Lucca stepped forward, raised his hand and achieved immediate silence. 'As you've probably guessed, I'm the new owner of this team, along with Delphine.' His lips twitched as a loud roar of approval immediately went up in the room. 'She's led the team admirably and I have every confidence she'll continue to do so.'

Another round of loud cheers went up, and Delphie blushed as Lucca sent her a sidelong glance.

She stepped forward. 'I'm proud of you all for what we achieved today. It wasn't quite the top step, but I know we'll get there.' More cheers. 'Unfortunately, I can't stay to celebrate with you, but enjoy yourselves and rest well during your break. Now that we've claimed the podium, I don't want us to let it go. I intend for us to stay there for a very, very long time. See you all in a month.'

About to head for the door, Delphie paused when Lucca cleared his throat.

'One last thing. There will be a team name change at the next race. We'll let you know what it is in due course.'

'What on earth was that about a name change?' she demanded as soon as she'd slid in beside him in the limo and the driver was heading for Hamad International Airport.

She hadn't wanted to exchange words with him in front of the crew. And then she'd been stunned and a little annoyed to discover that her belongings had been packed and taken away, both from her personal trailer and her apartment.

Again, Lucca was moving at dizzying speeds.

Ferocious eyes turned her way. 'You really expect me to leave Buckman's name on *my* team?'

She wanted to assert her 10 per cent stake, but saved her breath. As much as it annoyed her, they weren't equal partners.

'No. You're far too primitive for that, aren't you?' she said instead.

His eyes drilled into hers. 'And don't you forget it.'

She struggled not to let the fierce possessiveness in his eyes excite her. It didn't mean anything.

'And what do you plan on naming it?'

His gaze scoured her face thoroughly, as if searching for the answer there. When it settled on her mouth she strained not to lick across her lips to relieve the hungry tingling.

'I was thinking Delphine Racing… But if that's not agreeable, you can come up with your own suggestion.'

Her lips parted in shock. But alongside the shock something essential and fundamental shifted within her, rendering her speechless. And so very afraid.

Because the emotion attached to it was absolutely terrifying. It felt vital. Life-sustaining.

And because she couldn't…*wouldn't* name it, she withstood his gaze as he placed his own interpretation on her reaction. His eyes grew icy and distant. 'Why do you expect everyone to disappoint you?' he asked, with a cold sort of curiosity.

'Wh-what?' she stammered, grappling with what was happening to her.

'Is your mother responsible for sowing such a soul-deep mistrust? Or was it a concerted effort by others?'

'Lucca, I… I don't know what you're—'

'Fermare.'

She let him cut across her weak interjection because she couldn't deny he was right.

'Perhaps I was too blinded by other things to see it clearly before, but I see it now,' he went on. 'You operate from an arm's length position. And I want to know why.'

'What makes you think I owe you any insights into my psyche?' she asked.

'Perhaps because I've just gifted you something you won't throw back in my face this time?'

She swallowed, utterly overawed by his generosity. To have the name her beloved father had given her in vivid green livery on her racing cars… Her father…

Pain rippled across her senses, throwing her back to a more harrowing time she'd buried deep down.

'Tell me,' Lucca insisted, his breath washing over her face, heat from his body stopping the chilling loneliness of memory.

Avoiding his gaze, she concentrated on the hollow of his throat, on the steady pulse beating there. 'I was ten when my father was diagnosed with cancer. He had this…this *confidence* in everything he did, and he made me think *I* could achieve anything I set my mind to. So when he told me he would beat the cancer I believed him. I was old enough to know it was the kind of thing parents tell their children to spare them pain, but… Lucca, I *believed* him. I believed him right until I heard him tell my mother to swear she would look after me. Right until I sat next to his hospital bed and watched him take his last breath. I believed him.'

Somehow her hand had settled on Lucca's chest, and his steady heartbeat was helping her form difficult words.

'And then, what seemed like five minutes later, my mother was getting married to another man. A man who despised me. I don't know if she used my stepfather as an excuse to go back on her promise to my father, or she did it because she had no choice, but... She didn't live up to her promise to love me the way my father did. And for that I hated my father a little bit. For leaving me. For a long time after his death I refused to think about him. Not... not until...'

'Until you left me?' Lucca pressed tightly. 'Until you went to Qatar?'

She exhaled shakily. 'It was the most innocuous thing... I was going for a walk one evening and I came across a young girl. She was crying because a couple of spokes on her bicycle wheel had come off. It was an old bike. Several parts were missing. I didn't have the heart to tell her it was better off on the rubbish heap. It took me a couple of hours to fix it, but in that time I remembered every moment I'd spent with my dad, fixing broken things. I mended the bike, then I went home, ashamed of myself for attempting to forget him. When Hunter offered me a ten per cent share of his racing team, I jumped at it.'

'But that wasn't it all, was it?' asked Lucca. 'You'd convinced yourself that remembering him wasn't enough somehow?'

Her heart banged against her ribs as his softly spoken words cut through her. She pulled away from him. 'Yes. It reminded me that nothing in life is guaranteed.'

'And that's the only way you'll accept the good things in life?' he said. 'On the basis that they arrive with a gold-plated guarantee?'

Anger she hoped would seal the vulnerable wounds she'd exposed flared high. 'Don't patronise me!'

'Everything you've described to me is natural. We're born with a set of ingrained expectations that are either nurtured or smothered. Either way, we have a right to feel a certain way about it. I more than anyone know how it is to despise a parent.'

'You want me to get over it? To move on? Is that what you're trying to say?'

He shrugged, then reached out to trail a hand over the hot skin of her cheek. 'I'm saying that if it's a guarantee you require, let me tell you this. This thing between us that starts here and now will be finished four weeks from tonight. Free yourself from thinking about what comes next for the next month and just...*be.*'

His words held far too much temptation and she shook her head. 'I... I can't.'

'Because you're afraid,' he declared. Condemned.

And that ignited a little bit more of that fire inside her. 'Because I won't be dared into forgetting myself the way—' She stopped, sharply inhaling.

'The way you did before?' he elaborated, his eyes laser-sharp. 'Is that what you're stopping yourself saying?'

She pressed her lips together. 'You wanted to know why. I've told you why. Now you tell *me* why you own ninety per cent of the team but are giving me naming rights.'

'You really think I'll keep a team name that belongs to the man you fled to when you left me? Put yourself in my shoes, Delphine.'

She did, only for a split second, and absolutely detested herself for the rancid rush of jealousy.

'But you're the majority shareholder.'

He gave an expressive shrug. 'I care about ensuring a business is successful. I care about the bottom line. I especially care about the things I own and the pleasure they bring me. Slapping names on things, however, not so much.'

'Except when that name is Hunter Buckman?'

His eyes blazed unholy fire. *'Esattamente.'*

He should've been pleased that he'd peeled back yet another layer of the conundrum that was Delphine Alexander. It should've satisfied him to learn she'd been as wild for him as he'd been for her during their time together. That beneath her blinding beauty there resided a semblance of humanity, a capacity to feel hurt.

But as he settled back into his seat and watched her walk towards the back of his plane to freshen up, the stone of dissatisfaction inside him grew larger. Because the deeper he delved, the more layers he uncovered. If she had all this emotional capacity then why hadn't it applied to *him*? Because he didn't deserve it?

It was driving him mad.

He was sure he was officially breaking some obscure record for dwelling this long on one woman, when in his regimented past he'd sworn never to ponder the whys and wherefores of any woman the way he'd done with his mother.

Bitterness laced through the dissatisfaction as he found himself once again circling the mystery of why the woman who was supposed to have loved him the most...hadn't.

He'd always chosen women who clearly adored him, who weren't coquettish with their expectations, and had dispensed with them when his own interest waned. It had been a simple and effective process.

Until Delphine.

It didn't help that his advisers had started dropping subtle hints about 'The List' since the end of the festival. He'd ignored every one of them. And rightly so, he assured himself. Because how could he give his wholehearted commitment to a new venture when another remained open-ended?

Delphine reappeared—a speed bump threatening to stall what should be a smooth process in his life—and he found himself rapt as his gaze raked over her stunning body.

She'd changed into her favourite colour—the gold three-quarter-length satin trousers lovingly moulding her thighs and hips. He shifted in his seat and swallowed as flames lit up his groin. Her top was the sort of wide-shouldered style that slipped to one side with her movement, showing off delicate collarbones and a delectable throat. The material moulded her shapely breasts and trim waist. Thin gold bangles tinkled, drawing attention to her delicate wrists, the elegance of her slim fingers.

Mio Dio, but he wanted those fingers on his flesh so damn badly—

'Would you like something to eat?' He interrupted his own thoughts before his body gave him away.

Expecting a battle, he felt his senses calm when she nodded. 'Yes, please. I'm starving.'

And how pathetic was that? That he should find contentment in the simple act of feeding her?

He suppressed his intensely irritated feelings and summoned the hovering stewardess. He rose as the woman approached. 'Order for me too, Delphine. I'll be right back.'

He paced the conference area of the plane, making necessary but non-urgent calls simply to dissolve this feeling of obsession over the insufferable woman who occupied his thoughts.

On a decisive strike, he made a call to his most senior adviser, scheduling a meeting a month and a day from today to discuss 'The List'.

Because, like it or not, life needed to move on.

Satisfied, he returned to the table, convincing himself his kingdom was in better shape because he'd paid it due attention. He even managed to pull off the concept of charming host and indulgent King for the rest of the flight, discussing Delphine's goals for the racing team and dispensing advice where necessary.

And when she pleaded tiredness he showed her to the plane's master suite and retreated, despite his rabid urge to join her.

He had a whole month ahead of him, after all, to unravel this conundrum and dispense with the mystery of Delphine Alexander once and for all.

Thereafter he would dedicate the totality of his focus to his kingdom without a single backward glance.

* * *

'Is something wrong?' she murmured from beside him, her smoky, seductive voice sending several shards of desire through him. 'You've barely said two words to me since we landed.'

His lips twisted bitterly. *Sì*, something was wrong. He might have sensed the inevitability of it, but he hadn't expected to be trounced so spectacularly, so soon.

The flight had been a litmus test of withstanding their sexual chemistry while conducting civil conversation. Failure had started as a dull, painful throb in his groin and had soon overtaken every atom of his being, mocking him with his inability to stem the tide of his needs.

'Are you feeling neglected?' he asked.

Her answering shrug compelled his gaze to her smooth bare shoulder, tripling the need rampaging through him.

'We don't need to talk if you don't want to. I just… It seems unlike you, that's all.'

His mouth twisted harder. 'And you know me so well?'

She let out a heavy sigh, her fingers massaging her temple. 'Maybe I don't. But seeing as you've got your way, can't we at least call some sort of truce?'

'So very reasonable, aren't you?' he taunted, unable to keep the cynicism out of his voice.

The flash of disappointment in her eyes made his gut clench. 'You're clearly itching for a fight,' she murmured calmly.

That riled up his anger. Who was she to be disappointed in *him*?

His gaze dropped to her mouth, twenty-twenty recollection providing him with an X-rated picture of how most of their past arguments had concluded. He stifled a groan when the pink tip of her tongue slid across it.

'Are you going to give me one?' he demanded.

'Not tonight. I'd prefer to bask a little longer in my achievements today, if you don't mind.'

Feeling like a heel on top of his already roiling emotions, he wanted to growl.

Thankfully, they arrived at the palace then, and he exhaled in relief. The usual contingency of staff would stop him from doing anything foolish—like pulling Delphine close and taking out his frustration on her willing mouth.

Ignoring her searching look, he turned to the waiting staff. 'You remember Domenica from before? She'll be your personal aide for the next month. Any needs you have should be addressed to her.'

He turned away as Delphine and Domenica exchanged pleasantries, the need to get away from her, to be alone, to wrestle his emotions under control, triggering him into movement.

He knew he was being discourteous, but he was past caring.

The antique clock was striking midnight in his private wing, and the fact that there was still no clear-cut path to solving the riddle of Delphine drew a frustrated growl from him.

He barely registered where his agitated strides had taken him until he arrived in front of her door, knocking before he thought better of his actions.

Her approaching footsteps rushed the blood faster through his veins and something kicked him wide awake the moment she opened the door, wearing a thigh-skimming silk nightgown and matching robe.

'Did I wake you?' he asked.

'No.'

'May I come in?'

She stepped aside, and the light pouring in from the living room silhouetted her perfect legs.

Walking through, he saw a tea set laid out on the coffee table, imagined her curled up on the sofa with the hot beverage and grimaced at the enticing, sexy image.

'Is jet lag keeping you up as well?' she asked, the polite

tone she'd adopted in the car emerging once more to grate on him.

'Perhaps. Perhaps not.'

She nodded warily, as if unsure how to handle his response.

His lips twisted. 'But I think I'll need something stronger than tea to solve my issues.'

She stiffened, but her gaze flicked to the extensive liquor collection on the antique cabinet a few steps away. 'Can I get you a drink?'

'*Grazie*. You know what I like.'

He had the perverse pleasure of seeing electric awareness light through her eyes, and her movements were not quite so calm as she crossed the room and poured his favourite cognac.

Their fingers touched as she handed him the glass, and he heard her breath catch before he turned towards her living room window to stare at the bright lights blanketing his capital. Now he was here, the restlessness that had riled him for hours was lessening—a state he begrudgingly attributed to her.

'The view is amazing,' she said. 'But I'm sure it's even better from your own suite?'

'Is that your way of asking me to get to the point?' he responded, without turning around. A sip of expensive cognac further dulled the edge of his angst.

'You didn't come here to drink and admire the view.'

He turned around, saw her perched on the sofa, her eyes boldly on his. She was a gazelle aware of her power. A sleek, breathtaking, dangerously seductive gazelle. The only woman whose allure could drive fever through his bloodstream with one flicker of her eyelashes.

All of a sudden the only thing that mattered was getting the answers he deserved.

'I don't like mysteries, *dolcezza*. And you've quite successfully wreathed yourself into one.'

'You can't be losing sleep over *me*, surely, Lucca?'

He despised the edge of bitterness in her voice. As if she had a right to feel affronted. When he was the one who'd nearly lost his head over her. Lost his—

He stiffened, a dark desire to rile her surging through him. Since one subject always elicited a charged response, he harked back to it in the vain hope that it might lead to other answers.

'Tell me why you left me in Paris, Delphine. Did something happen or was it just Coppi's visit?'

Shock and wariness tensed her body. Her gaze dropped and her fingers clenched in her lap. 'I told you it wasn't important.'

'Perhaps not to you. But it is to me. You see, it's not the first time Coppi's meddling has affected me. He was whispering poison in my father's ear long before I was born, and I believe he was the instigator of that unfortunate cellar affair with my mother.'

'Then why do you still keep him around?'

'I don't. But my father does. And, while he may no longer be King, he's entitled to certain accommodations.' He watched her, quietly dismayed at his desperation for answers. 'You say it's not important... So what's holding you back?' he taunted.

Her eyes sparked with a different light, a mixture of panic and defiance, before they lowered and swept away from his. And even before she spoke Lucca felt he'd lost a vital connection. As if a weighty subject had been tackled and decided without his input.

And the agitation came roaring back.

Delphie's heart hammered as she stared into Lucca's implacable face. She knew evading this now would simply feed his formidable thirst for answers. But this was only one facet of the mystery he was determined to unravel. Dared she hope he would leave it alone once she satisfied this curiosity?

She licked her lips, dug deep for composure.

'Coppi was waiting when I returned from my photo shoot.

In a nutshell, he said I wasn't the sort of woman a king takes as his queen, or even the right pedigree for a royal mistress. He said I was just an exotic tipple whose flavour you would grow bored with eventually. He wasn't indelicate enough to state it was because of the colour of my skin, but I knew that was right up there in his top three reasons,' she replied, her voice heavy with bitterness.

She didn't know why she didn't mention 'The List'. Perhaps because, even now, she feared Lucca would confirm Coppi's assertion that she hadn't ever been part of his future plans?

Lucca's jaw tightened. 'Those were his reasons. They were never mine. The colour of your skin has no bearing on my attraction to you except insofar as it adds to your beauty. To me you have always been far more than a breathtakingly beautiful Black woman.'

Delphie couldn't afford for his words to touch her. Because when everything was said and done 'The List' remained an insurmountable obstacle to even the smallest of hopes. That and the loss she was yet to confess…

She dropped her gaze before he read that truth. 'It doesn't matter.'

'Like hell it doesn't. Look at me,' he commanded.

She dragged her gaze up from her lap and met ferocious intent in his eyes.

'When I have time, I'll dig up my family tree and prove how many of my progenitors married whomever they chose. Right now you will look at me and know I mean it when I say *his reasons were never mine*.'

Maybe on some fundamental level she believed him. Lucca was still undeniably attracted to her. But… 'It still doesn't mean we wouldn't have ended.'

At her answer, he prowled to a stop a few feet from her. This close, she saw his fingers clenched around his glass.

'The mystery still remains, *dolcezza*. Why were you in such a hurry to quicken our end? Did you want to reject me before I rejected you? Like your mother did?'

She gasped. 'What? I… Of course not. That's absurd.'

'You lie.'

Eyes that saw far too much drilled into her.

'At some point did you feel it was no longer just a fling? Did you flee in case it didn't unfold the way you wanted it to?'

Her stomach knotted. His words were far too close to the truth for her liking. 'What if I did? It's called self-preservation. Isn't that another form of what *you* do? End a relationship before a woman gets too attached?'

He had the grace to look guilty for a second, before ingrained hauteur slotted into place. 'Perhaps. But I never pretend to be something I'm not. You, on the other hand, denied yourself and me the honesty of confronting what we felt about each other. You made assumptions and literally ran from them.'

'No…'

'Yes. At least have the courage to face up to what you did.'

'I do! I am.'

'No…'

The word seethed out of him. He was livid. And bitter.

In his shadowed eyes, disappointment, resignation and traces of pain lurked. She recognised the emotions because she'd experienced them during that final row with her mother. When she'd seen that no matter what she said, her mother had already given up on her. Her mother had washed her hands of her, chosen her second marriage, and there had been nothing Delphie could do about it.

Registering that she, Delphie, had done that to Lucca, staggered her. The pebble of guilt that had started to chafe inside her even before she'd snatched up her suitcase and sprinted for Charles de Gaulle Airport grew into a rock, then a boulder, as he condemned her.

'You ran and hid yourself so effectively I couldn't find you. Perhaps you wanted to punish me for what you felt. For disappointing you by not being mediocre and indifferent and judgemental, the way everyone else had been in your life up until then?'

The vice around her heart started to shatter under the on-slaught of his words. And she was frightened. Terrifyingly alarmed at how vulnerable he'd leave her when he was done. But even as the titanium shattered, the guilt grew. As did her need to defend herself, to make him see that ultimately her actions had protected him.

She jumped up, paced away from the incisive gaze boring into her skin, demanding the terrible truth buried in her soul.

'It wasn't all about you, Lucca.'

'Like hell it wasn't. I consumed you just as much as you consumed me—'

'And while we were busy consuming each other we made a baby!'

He froze mid-sentence, the imperious hand he'd lifted to make his point poised just above his temple, his eyes wide orbs of staggered shock.

Somewhere beyond the shock waves engulfing them both she heard his glass clatter on to the carpet, spilling its amber contents. The ominous sound shattered his stasis. Breath exploded from his lungs and he went ashen.

'Lucca, say something—'

He came roaring to life, his chest expanding on another sharp breath. 'Repeat what you just said, Delphine,' he rasped, his voice a cracking glacier.

She didn't play for time by asking what he meant. Not when she'd unpinned a grenade and thrown it at his feet. Not when they were both shell-shocked, waiting for the worst devastation to register.

She licked her lips. 'I said...we made a baby. I... I was pregnant when I left Paris.'

Eyes filled with thunderstorms dropped to her stomach, then immediately flew back to her face as his throat worked. 'You were pregnant with my child when you left?' Disbelief rang through every syllable. 'No. *Impossibile.*'

'Yes...' she confirmed with an anguished whisper.

He charged across the room, a warrior set on annihilation, and grasped her arms. 'You kept the existence of my child from me?' He breathed choppily, as if he'd ran a marathon. 'My child? My *heir*?'

'Lucca, listen to me—'

'Why? Our time together was...' He stopped, shaking his head in bewilderment. 'I treated you with respect, gave you as much of my time as I could, considering my duties. But obviously I made a mistake somewhere. Because...' His fingers tightened on her arms—not enough to hurt, but a testament to his bewilderment. '*Non capisco*. Make me understand. What did I ever do to you to warrant such treatment?'

'You didn't do anything.'

His eyes dropped to her stomach again, and something heartbreaking moved through his gaze. The look was so profound, she linked her fingers over her stomach. Because now, with the protective shield gone, that look speared straight into her heart, forcing her to relive her devastation all over again.

He saw her action and his eyes frosted over, his nostrils thinning as he locked gazes with her.

'Where is my child, Delphine?' he rasped, his voice throbbing with a thousand blazing emotions.

CHAPTER NINE

In her heart of hearts, Delphie had hoped she'd never have to confess her loss. *Their* loss. That she alone would have to bear the burden.

'Lucca…'

'Tell me!'

'I… I lost it,' she confessed through numb lips.

'What?' The question was a hoarse, shaken rasp.

Sorrow tore through her heart. 'I'm sorry, Lucca, but our…our baby didn't make it.'

A different sort of transformation overcame him. The proud, noble warrior staggered, tremors visibly shaking through him as he backed away from her. The backs of his legs met the sofa and he dropped on to it, his fingers clenching in his hair.

For an interminable age he simply stared at the carpet. His eyes were pools of torture, his throat moving in useless swallows. When he raised his head, a terrible bleakness was etched into every corner of his face.

'Tell me…' he demanded again, this time in a ghostly whisper.

She knew exactly what he was asking for. Details. Details she'd sealed in a precious box and stashed at the centre of her heart. A box she didn't want to prise open. 'Please, Lucca…'

'I have a right to know, do I not?' he demanded, the regal command that was stamped into his very soul emerging. 'When did you know you were pregnant?'

'Th-the day I left. I got a test on the way to the shoot…
because I suspected…'

His eyes narrowed into ferocious slits, condemnation
stamped into his every cell. But thankfully he didn't speak,
just silently commanded her to continue.

'I… I wasn't sure how you would feel about it, but I
planned on telling you…later.'

'You would've known how I felt by simply telling me,'
he supplied icily.

Her lips firmed. 'We'd taken every precaution, even when
we got carried away. I wondered if there might be some
doubt on your part.'

His lips flattened. 'Watch yourself, *dolcezza*. You continue to cast aspersions on my character with no basis whatsoever.'

'Fine. *I* had doubts—okay?'

His jaw clenched tight. 'You had doubts about having
my baby?'

'Believe it or not, most women do—even if only for a
fraction of a second. It's not inhuman to wonder what kind
of parent you'll be. Whether you have what it takes to care
for another human being. And—not to stroke your enormous
ego—you were a prince, bound for the throne. I was just the
woman who'd been reminded I was good for nothing but a
brief tumble in your bed. I needed a minute to process it all.'

'You took a hell of a lot more than a minute.'

She shut her eyes for a sustaining second. 'Coppi didn't
just inform me of the many ways I wasn't your equal, Lucca.
He also told me about "The List".'

'What?'

'Your precious list of potential future queens. Remember?'

He tensed, then a veil descended over his face. 'I fail to
see how a protocol enacted years before we met plays into—'

'Are you serious? Just for a second, think about how that
made me feel.'

His eyes narrowed, and she knew he was ready to flatten her with more condemnation.

'But you know what?' she went on. 'I decided it was better that I knew. We'd gone to great lengths not to probe each other's personal lives. Maybe because we knew our bubble couldn't withstand it.'

'Don't presume to speak for me, *cara*,' he bit out.

'Then why didn't you tell me about it?' she challenged, quietly anxious for something...*anything*...to lessen the tight knot suddenly suffocating her.

His inscrutability increased, rejection of her demand bristling from him. 'Perhaps you're right. It was none of your business.'

She suppressed a gasp, even as he continued.

'It still doesn't give you the right to flee without telling me you carried my child.'

There was no escaping this truth. 'Once I knew I wanted to keep the baby...' She paused at the slight easing of tension in his shoulders. 'I wondered how you'd feel about becoming a father. How it would factor into your life. And I... I took another minute.'

'Funny how none of those minutes included picking up the phone to call me, isn't it? And what did you conclude once you were done *processing*?' he demanded tightly.

Delphie took a breath as memories of childhood rejection collided with raw, more recent loss. 'As your adviser had reminded me, I was a nobody and you were a prince. I was terrified that you'd care enough to take the baby from me. Then I was even more terrified that you wouldn't—that my child would be subjected to what I went through. But then it all became...moot.'

Silence fell as they both absorbed that final, simple word.

'When?' he asked eventually, in a voice scoured with bleak acceptance.

'Three weeks later. I woke up in the middle of the night with cramps. The doctors tried, but they...they couldn't save it.'

He surged forward, his hands clasped tight between

his knees as his gaze bored deeper into her. 'You were in hospital?'

She jerked out a nod.

'How long?'

'A few days. They threw out first trimester miscarriage statistics that I suppose were meant to comfort me, but instead they made me feel insignificant.'

He swore underneath his breath, his nostrils flaring as he stared at her. 'Were you in much pain?' he asked, his voice racked with desolation.

How to answer that without exposing her shattered heart? In the end it felt safest not to distinguish between the unique and varied strands of anguish she'd suffered, there in the hospital bed and in the harrowing months afterwards.

'Yes.'

His jaw clenched tight, as if he was holding every scrap of emotion inside. He clawed his fingers through his hair then wrapped his large hand over his nape.

Just for something to do, besides sit there mired in the jagged jaws of memory, she surged to her feet, returned to the liquor cabinet and poured him another drink.

He took it, but didn't drink it, his eyes fixed in the middle distance, completely shutting her out. And because her heart quailed at that look, Delphie found herself sinking to her knees in front of him, tilting her head to attempt to connect their gazes.

'Lucca—'

His eyes snapped to hers. 'Did you plan to keep it? If the unthinkable hadn't happened, would you have had my child?'

Scalding tears stung her eyes. This answer was much simpler. 'Yes.'

Something heavy, soul-stirring shifted in his eyes—a moment of shared pain. Perhaps even sorrow. Then he visibly collected himself. '*Grazie*. But now it's my turn to take a minute.'

She shifted closer, seeking a connection. Perhaps it wasn't

there, but she attempted to anyway. Because if he felt even a fraction of her ever-present anguish… What? She wanted to ease it for him?

'I know it's a shock and I—I'm here if you want to talk.'

Another flight of shadows moved over his face. 'Perhaps it's better we tackle it another time.'

'Okay. If that's what you want.'

Slowly, his eyes grew inscrutable, but they didn't move from hers. Still pinning her in place. Then he lifted the glass and sipped the cognac. Swallowed.

Her gaze moved to his strong throat, to the sheen of liquor clinging to his bottom lip. The sound that left her throat was involuntary. And damning.

The atmosphere pivoted.

Away from pain.

Away from regret and recrimination.

Not too far, but enough to permit other sensations.

Sensations that shouldn't have a place in this time and space but seemed almost…*inevitable*. Par for the course when they were this close to one another.

'You ran and you hid and you fought against coming back. And yet here you are, *dolcezza*, conquered by your needs,' he said, his tone reeking of satisfaction.

Some part of Delphie didn't want to admit that perhaps he knew her more than she knew herself. Because that would be catastrophic.

'I don't need you,' she said.

She knew it was the wrong thing to say when his features hardened to flint.

'I'm almost inclined to make you take back those words, make you burn for me the way you do so beautifully. But, on a night like this, wouldn't that just make me a monster, like my father?' he questioned jaggedly.

Her heart squeezed tight. 'No, Lucca. You're nothing like your father…'

A tremor moved through him and he shook his head. 'Hush, now. I'm hanging on by a thread here, *dolcezza*.'

She swallowed, the yearning to take him in her arms clawing at her. But she knew enough to respect his space. To stay put when he rose abruptly.

She witnessed the shock waves flashing through his eyes before he neutralised the telling emotion.

'This news you've delivered needs getting used to. I think it's best if we say goodnight now.'

She rose, reluctance thick and heavy in her limbs as she retreated.

At the door to her bedroom, she turned. She remembered how utterly her loss had consumed her in that hospital bed. Remembered her desperate need for a shoulder to cry on.

Her need for Lucca.

The thought of him retreating to suffer alone made her heart twist.

His eyes locked with hers and she spotted what he didn't want her to see. The naked anguish burning in his gaze. She stumbled towards him, and for a moment his eyes blazed with his need for the lifeline she yearned to throw him.

But then his austere, regal presence reasserted itself. Pivoting on his heel, Lucca left her suite.

A sob caught her throat as she stumbled into her bedroom. Her head told her to accept his wishes, but her foolish heart, which still bled for her pain, railed at her for retreating.

For an hour she paced her bedroom, until an unstoppable compulsion drove her to the dressing room. She dressed without paying much attention to her attire. It helped that everything in her new wardrobe was geared for style and elegance, so she didn't have to think about disgracing herself once she left the suite.

Heart in her throat, she made the long, circuitous journey, fear of rejection looming larger with her every footstep.

What was palace protocol for visiting the King in the middle of the night? Had Lucca even returned to his private wing?

Did she need to call ahead to announce herself?

When she spotted Lucca's personal aide, Delphie exhaled in relief—and then with apprehension when he frowned at her. 'Miss Alexander, may I help you?'

She prayed for the poise of her modelling days to come to her aid and pulled her shoulders back. 'I would like to see His Majesty, please.'

To his credit, the man didn't check the time or indicate in any way that this was highly unusual. But his infinitesimal pause before he nodded felt like an aeon in Hades.

But then, once again, Delphie found herself in the hallway of portraits—only this time with every pair of eyes flaying her with deep censure.

She didn't hear the aide retreat, but she definitely felt the real-life scrutiny boring into her skin as she turned to face Lucca.

Lucca's shirt was undone and untucked, his feet bare and his hair sexily dishevelled.

'What do you want, Delphine?'

His tone was flat. Lifeless. That frightened her. She didn't want to be responsible for Lucca being...*less*.

Despite the icy lake in her stomach, she forced herself to speak. 'I know I'm probably the last person you want to see, but I... I remember how much I didn't want to be alone when...' She stopped and took a breath. 'I just... Let me be here for you, Lucca.'

He regarded her curiously. 'Do you know what I've done this last hour?' he asked.

She shook her head.

'I've replayed everything that happened that last day.' He sucked in an uneven breath. 'I remember you not answering your phone when I called to say my meeting had overrun. I recall deciding not to call the hotel room because I didn't want to disturb you if you were resting before dinner. I recall my aide telling me that my father and Coppi were passing through Paris on their way to Germany.' Balled fists shoved into his pockets and he rocked lightly on his feet. 'And I have realised that had I taken slightly different views in light of these facts, things would—'

Her hand shot out, pre-empting that harrowing view. 'No. Lucca…you can't think like—'

'When *you* were "taking a minute", did you wish things had gone differently?' he asked, in that same toneless voice.

A harsh bark of laughter seared her throat. 'Only every second of every day. But that just causes more pain. We can't change the past, no matter how much we'd like to.'

Eyes dim with dark, stormy emotions, he turned, his long strides taking him away from her. She followed in slower steps, her heart bouncing in her chest when he approached his bedroom. Stopping in the doorway, she felt her breath snag in her throat when he emerged from his dressing room moments later, clad in silky pyjama trousers and nothing else.

With another hard look her way, he crossed to his bed. But somehow her crossing the threshold felt…momentous, despite her altruistic intentions.

Pausing in the act of discarding half a mountain of pillows, Lucca said tightly, 'I'm not sure exactly what this support role entails, but I hope it doesn't involve you haunting my doorway for the rest of the night?'

In her wild bid to *'be there'* for him she hadn't considered that Lucca might want to sleep away the news. Which was hypocritical, because hadn't she done the very same thing? Sought oblivion in sleep because reality had been too devastating?

Caught in the emotional tug of war between heart and mind, she hesitated some more.

Lucca's face shuttered. 'Either come in or leave, Delphine. I'm in no mood to accommodate half measures.'

And since that only left her with one choice—because what sort of person would she be if she retreated now?—she entered.

He watched with cold, dispassionate eyes as she chose

the wide armchair beside his regal fireplace. Because, of course, the bed was out of the question.

His fingers tightened on the pillow he held, then after a moment he went into his dressing room and emerged with a thick cashmere throw. Shaking it out, he draped it gently over her.

Throat clogged by that unexpected gesture, she looked up at him. 'Thank you.'

For an age, he stared down at her.

Then abruptly he crossed the room, slid into his vast kingly bed and stared at the ceiling.

'Lucca…'

Sighing heavily, he turned out his bedside lamp. 'No more talking, Delphine. Go to sleep.'

Astonishingly, she did.

Delphie wasn't sure what woke her. Her own distressing dream, in which she fought to cling to some precious thing to no avail, or something else. But when she blinked her eyes open she was no longer in the armchair.

She was in Lucca's bed. Her head pillowed on Lucca's shoulder.

He was wide awake, his gaze on her belly. When he locked eyes with her, she knew his turbulent emotions had roused her. Remembered too that she'd woken up a short while ago and slid into his bed of her own accord, her craving to be close to him overcoming all sense.

He made a jagged sound, the tips of his fingers hovering over her womb.

She swallowed, her own churning emotions eating her alive. 'Do you want me to leave?' she whispered.

His nostrils flared and fire blazed in his eyes. 'No. But you stay on one condition. No more running.'

She exhaled shakily.

Dear God.

She'd fought and fought and fought this. But Lucca was right. She'd fled before things had reached their natural in-

evitable conclusion. And a part of her had always regretted that decision.

Because it smacked of the same cowardice and fear that
had stopped her leaving home all those months before she'd
finally made a move. It smacked of letting herself down
when she'd vowed never to allow the possibility of rejection to stand in her way.

And wasn't facing this and besting it a testament to the
fact that she was stronger?

'I'll stay,' she responded, her voice fracturing at the edges.

He relaxed, and some of his tension receded, but she
didn't fool herself into thinking his shock and devastation
and bitterness were gone. No, they were still there, barely
contained. But they'd been overtaken for now by other
base emotions. Lust. Oblivion. Any other outlet for pain.
All finely channelled into a live electric wire that writhed
between them, galvanising her every breath and blink and
heartbeat.

He pulled away, situated himself in the middle of the em-
peror-sized bed then beckoned her. 'Come here, *dolcezza*,'
he commanded gruffly.

Apprehension and excitement danced a dangerous tango
inside her as she rose on her hands and knees and crawled
to him.

In her supplicant stance, the V-neck of her wrap-around
dress put her breasts on show and caused unholy flames to
lick in his eyes. She was about to be consumed whole. Her
instinct for self-preservation might have deserted her, filling those vital spaces with sharp anticipation, but Delphie
was confident she would rise, if not like a phoenix, then in
some other version of herself.

Hadn't she always?

When she reached him, she boldly met his gaze, watched
the corded muscles in his throat move as he swallowed.

'You see what you do to me? Even after all this? Still?'
he rasped, his deep, regal voice tinged with bewilderment.

She could barely manage a nod, her emotions churning harder as another sensation stirred into life. Feminine power. Drugging and empowering. It pushed her to touch him, stroke him, caress him, stretch out and gain momentum as he hissed in reaction.

He might be King, but in that moment she reigned supreme.

Even when he flipped her over, speared his fingers into her hair and commanded her gaze, she still held equal power.

Still made him shudder.

'Do you like this, Your Majesty?' She drawled his title throatily, trailing her hand down his front to grasp his manhood.

Delphie recognised that they were no longer playing games, but something in her pushed him to remember that they'd shared happier moments in the past. And perhaps in remembering that amongst all the devastation, they could both heal.

And he could move on...choose someone from 'The List'...

She shrank back from the sharp, lethal edges of that thought, forced her mind to the present. To the very male, very virile power of the King of San Calliano, thickening beneath her touch. To the flooding of arousal and hunger that plumped her sex and beaded her needy nipples.

His hand traced down one cheek to her jaw, then her neck, then boldly cupped one breast. She gave a low moan as he kneaded her eager flesh, then toyed with her nipple.

'Take me out,' he ordered roughly.

'Yes, Your Majesty,' she responded, gleefully revelling in his reaction at her sultry, teasing obedience.

His eyes darkened to midnight tempests, his torso clenching as her shaking fingers tugged down his pyjamas. His sensual lips parted, his breath hissing out as she stroked him. Their eyes still locked, melded in a confluence of desire, she caressed him, heard his breathing grow choppier.

'Give me your mouth, *dolcezza*,' he rasped, in a voice gravelled with lust.

She didn't need more bidding after that. Because this was soul-searing familiar territory.

She'd thought they'd explored every inch of each other once upon a time. They hadn't. Because he hadn't been a king back then. And there hadn't existed this terrible, devastating loss between them.

Delphie knew they were both altered on a cellular level now, likely for ever. And even as she closed her lips over him, felt him shudder wildly beneath her touch, she suspected there would be no going back.

She suppressed that thought, earthed herself in the present and pleasured him with her tongue, her hands, her mouth. Lost herself to the intoxicating taste and texture of him until her every breath existed just to gratify him.

'*Santo Dio,*' he groaned after long minutes, before he cupped the back of her head, urged her on and growled his pleasure when she enthusiastically complied.

Just when she thought she'd dragged him to the point of no return, he proved he had reserves of iron control left. He released her breast and captured her chin, drew her gaze up to his. 'Strip,' he commanded thickly, with a naked, almost pleading need.

A tug on her wrap dress and it came off with gratifying ease, discarded without a thought. She started to rise, to ease off her panties, but his hand moved to her shoulder, holding her in place.

Tendrils of decadent lust moved through her as she manoeuvred the panties off and watched his feverish gaze devour her breasts, her belly, the shadowed place between her thighs.

Still watching her, he kicked away his own clothing.

Delphie gawked in appreciation as miles of vibrant, tanned, hard-packed flesh were exposed to her avid gaze. Her fingers yearned to stroke, to reacquaint herself with his golden perfection. And she did—to her heart's content.

Just as he took free rein over *her* body.

Her breath stuttered in her lungs when he rose and

plucked a condom from his bedside table. Eyes on her, he took his shaft in his hand and stroked, taunting her with her need.

At her traitorous moan, he smiled, then waited another long, agonising moment before handing her the prophylactic. Memories flashed through her mind of the times she'd done this, the pleasure they'd both found in it.

Delphie shuddered in delight when the solid heated column of his body bracketed hers. One hand trailed from throat to breast to belly, lingering there while he looked deep into her eyes. Her throat clogged, words deserting her. They stayed locked like that for an age. Then, with a jagged exhalation, Lucca parted her thighs and with one sure, powerful stroke penetrated her.

Delphie threw her head back and moaned with shameless abandon.

Sweet heaven, she'd missed *everything*.

His low, animalistic grunt of triumph and pleasure when he entered her for the first time. The way he held himself still and unyielding inside her afterwards, as if ensuring she felt every magnificent inch of him. And then that slow unravelling of pleasure where each stroke reclaimed a piece of her soul.

Delphie felt tears prickle her eyes as sensation overwhelmed her. 'Oh, God,' she whispered, awed by the wonder of it.

'*Sì, dolcezza. Anch'io.*'

Me too.

The confession was raw, with a tight edge. As if he couldn't help himself. As if he was bewildered by it.

But she was beyond thinking. Beyond feeling anything but the wicked sorcery he evoked so effortlessly within her. 'Please. Don't stop.'

A rough laugh erupted from him, also edged in bewilderment. 'Your pleas will only receive consideration if you use the right form of address,' he teased wickedly.

She dragged her gaze to his, encountering fevered eyes. 'Please, Your Majesty.'

With a low growl, Lucca dug his fingers into her hair, directed her lips to his and captured her mouth in a searing kiss that drove every thought from her head.

Pleasure liquefied her insides. Delphie made no attempt to contain it, because to do so would be pure folly. And like a true connoisseur he honed it to his bidding, each thrust, kiss and caress directing her towards one specific destination—nirvana.

She arrived with a muted scream he claimed for his own, devouring it even as he continued to pump inside her. The hand gripping her hip rose to band her waist, holding her in place as she convulsed and came apart.

His groan of satisfaction only heightened her release, and she was still climaxing minutes later when he flipped her on to her stomach.

Delphie opened lust-glazed eyes to watch him over her shoulder, his towering body dominating her. His incisive gaze devoured her every expression, every tremble and gasp taken as his due.

'Again,' he commanded roughly.

Gathering her close, he wrapped both arms around her, containing her in his hot, steely embrace, pinning her with his body so there was no escape—not that she wanted to escape—as he thrust repeatedly inside her, groaning with each stroke, sending her higher and higher, until she was nothing but a morass of bliss…until the untamed animalism of the act pushed her to the brink of another kind of shattering she was certain would mark her on a fundamental level.

And the heart she'd been so terrified of bruising opened up, stretching and yearning for that marking.

When it came, she screamed. Long and unfettered and raw. The kind of response she'd only ever achieved with Lucca.

Above her, all around her, he continued to stake his claim, his groans growing hoarser in her ears, words in his native tongue growled against her ear as he hunted down his own climax. It arrived with a force that swept her along with it, triggering another release she was powerless to stop.

They shook and gasped, struggled and barely found enough air to sustain their lungs. And when the silence thickened, and reality arrived, they clung harder, fighting the inevitable, even though they both knew that while they might have held it at bay for now, the dam would be breached sooner rather than later.

Lucca knew he was using sex to cauterise the gaping, bleeding wound made by her news. He should've sent her away, dealt differently with the anguish gouging at the soul he'd believed had shrivelled into uselessness after his mother's treatment of him. But for the first time in his memory the thought of dealing with a situation on his own terrified him.

He knew that once he faced it the enormity of what he'd lost as he'd stumbled around, completely oblivious, would tear deeply at him. Would probably reveal things he wasn't ready to accept.

Like how deeply he mourned the loss of a child he hadn't even known he'd helped create... An extension of himself he'd always thought of in an abstract sense, but had now discovered had existed—if only for a short time and already passed into memory.

His child.

His heir.

Gone.

He wanted to rail at the unjustness of it all.

He wanted to rail at *her*.

But Delphine's own pain was real. Perhaps that was her sole saving grace. What he was enduring now, she'd endured for longer. She'd grown his child within her and literally felt the loss.

Was that why he'd accepted her comfort? Or was that primal pull at work again?

Her hands framed his face, drew him away from the chasm of bewildering loss. He wanted to ask her how she'd dealt with it. How she wasn't ranting at Fate every hour of every day. But he knew better than most that parenthood was a different and individual thing. Both his parents had doled out different versions of it, neither of which he wanted to emulate. Ever.

So, no. He and Delphine…they weren't in this together. She'd made sure of that. *Dio*, he'd had to *drag* the truth from her.

For her own selfish reasons or to save him this pain?

The dividing thought gave him pause. And then he stopped thinking altogether when she lifted her head and brushed his lips with hers. 'Lucca—'

'No.'

Whatever she was about to say, he didn't have room for it. The swell of emotion moving through him—an emotion he now stunningly read as grief—felt too large to toss anything else into the mix. So, yes, his remaining recourse was sex. Because when he was inside this woman everything else ceased to exist. That was what he craved right now. Complete and utter oblivion.

'No talking. The only use I have for that mouth right now is kissing. *Baciami, dolcezza*. Make me forget.'

The soft understanding in her eyes made him close his own, waiting for her to heed his command. Just as he wasn't ready to confront his pain, he wasn't sure he was ready for softer feelings from Delphine. Not when this strange chasm inside him yearned for her against his will. Not when he felt much too emotionally needy for comfort.

She'd said she wouldn't run.

But what if he reached out and she did?

Life had taught him the folly of such actions.

So, instead, he chased oblivion with every ounce of his being.

Of course, reality was waiting in the wings, biding its time until he woke a mere hour later, Delphine still entangled in his arms.

He held his breath, futilely willing everything he'd learned not to be true. But it crashed back even harder, battering his senses with double the force.

Mio Dio, he would've been a father by now. What kind of parent would he have been? Firm, but caring? Emotionally removed so as not to contaminate his child with his own flaws? Or hopeful of doing better than his own examples?

The burning questions propelled him from the bed, his restless feet taking him to the living room and the liquor cabinet.

Alcohol was a poor tool for divination, but he poured himself a drink anyway—which remained untouched ten minutes later as he stood on the balcony, staring at nothing and wondering if the black hole in his chest would ever heal.

He heard her before she spoke…braced himself for whatever was coming.

'I wasn't planning on keeping the baby from you.'

Her voice was smoky…low, but firm. He disguised his involuntary groan as a snort, his shoulders cording hard with tension. He wanted to insist on the *no talking*. But a king must face his tribulations.

'You don't believe me.'

Still staring unseeing at the view, he wished the anguish away. 'Do you care what I believe? Does my opinion matter at all in anything that you do?'

She inhaled audibly. 'Don't say that—'

He whirled to face her and almost wished he hadn't. She'd thrown on one of his discarded shirts, and from her lust-tousled hair and bruised lips to her shadowed thighs, every inch of her body reminded him of what they'd done to each other in the last few hours. Hours spent chasing oblivion just so he wouldn't have to deal with *this*.

'Why not?' he challenged, aware his voice was cold and harsh, but not caring very much in that moment. 'You discovered you were pregnant with my child and your first instinct was to keep it from me and vacate my life.'

'It wasn't.'

His eyes narrowed. 'The only other explanation is that you had planned to leave me anyway.'

She couldn't hide the raw truth and he saw it, his face tightening.

'And here we are again.'

She stepped forward, closing the gap between them, and for the first time in his life Lucca wanted to retreat. Because he was torn between pulling her close and safeguarding himself from this...this *craving* he had for her.

'Why are you so hung up on that? It wasn't like...' she started, then frowned and paused as some sort of realisation struck. 'Oh, God...'

Delphie watched his eyes narrow, his expression chilling but wary. As if he was alarmed at what she might see.

'Whatever you're thinking, you're wrong,' he said.

'Am I?' she asked. 'You don't want to talk about the baby, so why not dissect this and be done with it? You tell me I can't live my life holding people at arm's length, that I should move on, and yet you're stuck, aren't you? You hate me for leaving because I pulled the rug from beneath you before you could do it to me. And now you're wondering when, where, how it would've happened. You don't have the closure of dumping me and you hate me for it—because it feels far too close to what your mother did to you.'

His face turned pale, then livid with anger. 'Do I need to remind you who you're talking to?'

She flung out her arm, swatted away the warning. 'Don't pull the king card with me, Lucca. Part of the reason we sizzle together is because I'm not afraid of you. I can call you on your bull any time I like. You'll rant and rave, of course, because it's in your alpha blood to do so. But deep down you don't hate it.'

His expression didn't show an ounce of give. 'And do you also forget that I know how to shut you up?'

She shivered. 'No, I haven't forgotten your superior sexual prowess. But I don't let that scare me away. Tell me the truth. Is that why?'

'What if it is? Is it wrong to not wish to leave things open-ended?'

'Fine. Let's play this out. What would you have said to me if I'd told you I was leaving?'

His nostrils flared. Then he shrugged. 'I have no idea, because I wasn't done with you then. I'm not done with you now.'

Before she could stand her ground and insist, he was sweeping her off her feet. She ended up flat on her back in bed, much as she'd been a few hours before.

She stopped him with her fingers on his lips before he could claim hers. 'You can't always interrupt a conversation like this.'

His eyes narrowed. 'As you seem determined to forget, I'm a king. I can do whatever the hell I want.'

But even as she succumbed to the mastery of his love-making Delphie was aware of the chasm that existed just beyond the bubble Lucca seemed determined on creating around them.

He went out of his way to deny it, finding inventive ways to avoid talking about the subject that ticked between them like an emotional time bomb. And in the days that followed she allowed herself to be swept away by the magnificent tide that was King Lucca of San Calliano.

CHAPTER TEN

THE WEEK PASSED in a whirlwind of public and private engagements during the day and in the evenings.

Lucca's attention on her when they were in public was singularly focused and endless.

Meals were lavish, sumptuous affairs, prepared with painstaking attention to every favourite dish she'd ever consumed.

Delphie only needed to express an interest with a look or a word to have it manifested.

In private, Lucca seemed determined to best every previous bout of lovemaking. He'd been insatiable before. Now he was borderline obsessed with driving her out of her mind.

She'd agreed to stay. And the wronged King was hellbent on torturing her with reminders of not just how things had been like between them before she'd walked away, but with thoughts of a different, heart-rending version of what their future might be like if they were meant to be.

Which they weren't.

She knew that in her heart.

She'd confronted him with 'The List' and his only response had been that it was none of her business. And, as much as she wanted to rail at him, wasn't she the one who'd insisted they were over? Wouldn't digging deeper only cause her more heartache?

Yet daily her battle to reinforce the foundations of her resistance crumbled a bit more, dragging her deeper into the relentless tide that was the magic of Lucca's existence even as her heart twisted in growing anguish with each sunrise that spelled one day less with him.

One day less that he'd refuse to acknowledge their loss, despite the occasions when she'd caught him staring at her belly with a flash of bleakness in his eyes when he thought she wasn't looking. When his hand lingered on her belly when he thought she was asleep. Or when a distant look entered his eyes and he glanced away, jaw clenched, when the subject of children arose in company.

She reminded herself that it had only been a week. She'd needed *months* to drag herself from the depths of despair.

Aside from those brief, stomach-churning moments, the well-orchestrated publicity of their reunion took San Calliano by storm. The media devoted countless column inches to the news, at first with cool cynicism, and then with increasing indulgence as the kingdom got swept along with the ruse.

Within the week everyone was intrigued with the model-turned-motor-racing-boss who'd seemingly recaptured their King's attention.

The palace staff were a little more reserved, treating her with courteous coolness whenever she encountered them. Considering what had happened with the previous King and his wife, and in her own encounter with Coppi, Delphie understood their reservations. In fact, she told herself it was a good thing, because it was a crucial barrier that kept her from being completely swept away.

Nonetheless, it didn't come without a pang of dejection. And it was that lingering dejection that propelled her out of Lucca's private residence a few days later.

Finding herself with a rare few hours to herself, she wandered to the garages that held Lucca's jaw-dropping private collection of cars for yet another visit.

Classic. Contemporary. Vintage. The priceless collection was serviced by a team of fifteen mechanics who kept it in pristine shape.

The head mechanic approached when she entered.

'I don't mean to disturb your work,' she said.

He smiled. 'It is no disturbance, *signorina*. Not when you appreciate cars like we do, eh?'

Delphie smiled, a little relieved. '*Grazie*. Do you mind if I wander around?'

He waved her on. '*Per niente.*'

Like a child set loose in a sweet shop, she lost herself in horsepower heaven. She was halfway through the seventy-five-car collection when a tingling in her body announced Lucca's arrival.

She straightened to find him two cars away, his gaze fastened on her. 'What are you doing here?' she asked. 'You're not supposed to be back for another three hours.'

He gave a very Latin shrug. 'My last appointment cancelled on me, if you can believe such a thing.'

She rolled her eyes. 'Pull the other one, Lucca.'

A rare grin slashed his devilishly handsome face, making her breath tangle in her lungs. '*Bene*. I grew tired of circling the same tedious subject with an intransigent team who bicker about non-issues. I threatened to dissolve the whole committee unless they came back tomorrow with convincing reasons not to. Does that sound more like me?'

Delphie found herself smiling back, her spirit joyous just at the sight of him. 'That's definitely more like you.'

That moment of levity lingered, spinning a cocoon around them. He stepped closer, wrapped an arm around her waist and brushed his lips against hers. She fought not to melt. And even when he stepped away that curious joy remained.

He turned to examine the car she'd been admiring. 'I'm told this is your third visit here. Should I be jealous, *dolcezza*?'

She trailed her fingers over the superb burgundy paintwork of a vintage Mercedes with a chrome steering wheel and hubcaps. 'Probably,' she teased. 'I mean, very few things top the magic of a well-put-together engine and chassis.'

His lips twitched with the remnants of his smile. 'Paint a scene for me. Tell me how you would spend an afternoon with a car of your choice.'

That tug-of-the-tide sensation returned. Stronger. Irresistible. And it felt a little bit special that she was sharing knowledge she'd acquired from her father with the man she...she—

Her thoughts stalled, a panicked little pang threatening her joy. She pushed away the startling definition threatening to form and concentrated on their conversation.

'This little beauty is made for long drives on the winding roads of the French Riviera. If you want to be a little more showy...' she moved two rows down and caressed the grille of a matte black Bugatti Veyron with broad silver stripes '...this is the one for a fast drive down to Monaco. You'd leave the engine running long enough to dash inside, place a single bet and leave.'

Eyes twinkling, Lucca snorted. 'For starters, San Calliano's casinos are far superior to Monte Carlo's. And why a single bet?'

Panic bloomed large and she turned away, afraid he'd see it. 'Because the house always wins. And the temptation to... to gamble it all needs to be resisted at all costs.'

A throb of silence greeted her, and she swallowed the knot of apprehension clogging her throat. Had she said too much? Laid bare the secret yearning she'd had no choice but to let go two years ago?

'Next?' he said, a mysterious roughness in his voice.

Delphie breathed a quiet sigh of relief that he hadn't probed her reckless answer. She stopped in front of a nineteen-twenties Rolls-Royce, a study in classic elegance. 'This I'd take to a secluded beach at sunset, to watch the golden light move over the darkening water while dancing barefoot in the sand.'

He didn't prompt her for more, but the dream she'd spun once upon a time, featuring him as the main character, wouldn't let her go. Her feet slowed when she reached the

Alfa Romeo 33 Stradale, easily in her top five most spectacular cars in the world. The blood red paintwork gleamed under the recessed lights, its sleek lines making her yearn for the feel of the engine beneath her. But she was supremely conscious of the man prowling behind her, watching her every move with eyes she feared saw everything.

'This one presents endless possibilities,' she said, her fingers trailing over the uniquely sloping hood. 'You can take it easy with her or go fast—head for the hills with the wind in your hair, or park under the stars and lie on the hood after a skinny-dip in a lake with the moonlight on your skin.'

Inexorably, her gaze sought his. Across the low, wide bonnet his gaze snagged hers, then raked over her face, his nostrils flaring slightly as he braced his hands on the polished surface.

Without taking his eyes off her, he uttered a torrent of Italian that had the head mechanic hurrying over. Another exchange and the older man bobbed his head reverently.

'Sì, Sua Maestà. Un momento.'

A minute later, he returned with a set of keys.

Lucca took them and turned to her. 'So, what are you waiting for?'

She gaped. 'Really?'

He cast an exaggerated glance at his watch. 'The day is wasting, dolcezza,' he drawled.

She glanced down at her clothes.

'Sei bellissima, Delphine.' Lucca pre-empted her before she could speak.

She rushed to the passenger door, then froze when Lucca rattled the keys again. Catching his meaning, she widened her eyes. 'I get to drive?'

'Only if you hurry.'

With a delighted yelp, she lunged for the keys before he changed his mind, earning wicked laughter from him. Rushing around to the driver's side, she barely curtailed a moan of appreciation as she slid behind the wheel. Then she hesitated. 'But…what about your bodyguards?'

Reclining in the passenger seat, he draped one muscled arm commandingly over her seat and shrugged. 'It will drive them insane, I suspect.'

She bit her lip. 'Lucca—'

'It's now or never,' he interjected firmly, a curious tone in his voice.

Her hand shook as she inserted the key, instinct warning her that his last statement had been about more than just her driving his precious car. It was the reason she didn't glance at him as she eased the car out of the garage.

Perhaps he'd somehow suspected all along that this would happen, because by the time she hit the road outside the palace a trio of SUVs were following close behind. But her joy in the classic car overcame the obtrusive presence of Lucca's security detail. Not that he seemed to mind, from the way he stretched out his legs, his fingers teasing through her hair as he gave her firm instructions on which roads to take.

After several minutes she noticed the roads were quieter, the scenery growing more spectacular by the mile. When she tentatively released the throttle, Lucca's fingers stroked her neck encouragingly.

'*Ebbene, dolcezza*…show me what you can do.'

With the road mostly clear before her, it was too tempting to refuse. She stepped on the gas, delighted laughter spilling from her as the sports car roared into life beneath them. Even the momentary pang of guilt for leaving his security team behind drifted away beneath the joy of driving.

A quick glance at Lucca showed an indulgent smile playing at his lips, rather than apprehension at the speeds she was travelling. 'Enjoying yourself?'

She laughed. 'Am I ever!'

He chuckled and relaxed deeper into his seat.

A thrilling hour later, they ended up on a quiet country road on the outskirts of San Calliano, near the border with France and Italy. At some point Lucca's hand had relocated from her neck to her thigh, almost as if he wanted to experience the drive with her. Through the thin cotton sundress his hand stroked back and forth, heating her insides and rousing her body into life.

Seeing a sign she vaguely recognised, Delphie turned down a road bordered by tall poplar trees. After another mile, the trees gave way to long grass, and she gasped in delight when they went from tarred road to gravel and then on to a large swathe of secluded beach.

With the tall trees behind them and the beach before them, they'd found the best of both worlds. 'My God, that was exhilarating! And this is breathtaking,' she said of the view.

Lucca extracted his phone, dialled and murmured a few words before hanging up. Then he turned sexily brooding eyes on her.

For the longest time he simply stared at her, until self-consciousness assailed her. 'I wasn't going too fast, was I?'

He shrugged. 'Somewhere around a hundred miles an hour I discovered I found this extreme petrol head side of you…stimulating.'

The hand on her thigh moved decisively. Commanding. Claiming. A breathless scrutiny of his body showed her full effect on him. Her breath hitched as his fingers delved beneath her dress, their destination unmistakable.

'Your bodyguards…' she started feebly.

'I sent them away,' he responded huskily, undoing her seat belt with a decisive click. 'We won't be disturbed.'

With a moan torn from her soul, Delphie lunged for him. He met her halfway, urgent hands encouraging her from her seat and into his lap. Their lips met in a clash of searing passion, her body already moving over his in a dance that broadcasted her desire.

With a thick groan, Lucca moulded his hand over her buttocks, encouraging her. When breathlessness drove them apart he drew down her neckline, baring one plump breast to his gaze while his other hand delved beneath her panty line.

'Tell me you want me,' he commanded, ruthlessly torturing her nipple.

Barely able to draw breath, she gasped, 'I want you, Your Majesty…' unable to deny the towering emotions roiling through her.

'No. No more of that. *Lucca*,' he amended thickly.

Flaming eyes absorbing her every hitched breath, his fingers expertly explored her body, grunting in satisfaction when she cried out in delight.

'Lucca!'

She writhed on top of him, chasing the bliss he delivered to her scant minutes later. And she'd barely caught her breath when he lowered his zip and freed his shaft. Her breath caught all over again when he positioned himself at her hot entrance. Long fingers spiked into her hair, keeping her attention trained on him.

'You're mine,' he declared in a pebble-rough voice.

That declaration burrowed deep, settling far too close to her heart for comfort. But then he surged inside her and Delphie was lost, feeling a sliver of relief lacing through the sensations buffeting her, because she didn't have to examine why those two words both terrified and pleased her. Why she wished the hands that held her in place would hold her for much longer than the month they'd agreed.

And as her cries mingled with his thick grunts she mourned the day when all this would be in the past. When her life would be diverged from his for ever and this unique, fragile euphoria she'd only ever found with him had conclusively ended.

They swapped seats on the drive back, with Lucca taking control of the wheel. Their silence was heavy, but companionable, and when he drew her hand on to his thigh she didn't resist. Because her greedy heart craved moments like this, to hoard for when this was all over. For when her memories would be the stitches that held her together.

* * *

Three Saturdays later, she woke to a note on Lucca's pillow. She plucked up the luxurious cream vellum card and read the bold, beautifully scrawled words.

Join me at the stables. A steward will escort you.

Her heart performed a balletic somersault—an alarmingly frequent action lately—and thirty minutes later, dressed in a sleeveless purple calf-length jumpsuit with white polka dots and ruffled edges complemented by silver accessories, she alighted from the steward-driven buggy in front of an immense whitewashed barn that constituted the royal stables.

A flight of stairs led her to a sun-drenched terrace above the stables where Lucca, dressed in pristine riding gear that elevated his good looks to dangerous levels, stood.

'You've been out riding?'

The devastating smile she'd got used to recently was notably absent. 'You were sleeping so soundly I didn't wish to wake you,' he said, pulling out a chair for her.

Breakfast was laid on a pristine white cloth, royal silverware glinting flawlessly in the morning sun. 'What's this?' she asked.

He shrugged. 'It's your birthday week. I thought we'd start the celebrations early.'

Her mouth gaped. 'You know when my birthday is?'

Censure glinted in his eyes and she regretted her blurted question. She remembered his accusation that she was always thinking the worst of him. As much as she wanted to reassess that particular indictment, his refusal to discuss their loss had stopped her. As did the cooler atmosphere between them now.

Were they finally going to discuss their baby?

Did he forgive her?

Blame her?

Or was he secretly relieved he'd learned about it after the fact?

In her alone moments those questions had plagued her. Held her in peculiar limbo she wasn't sure how to extricate herself from.

'I'm sorry, I didn't mean to imply...' She stopped and shook her head. 'Is something wrong?'

His nostrils flared. 'I have something to show you. Let's eat, then we'll get to it.'

Delphie's belly clenched. 'You don't sound very happy about it,' she observed as he poured her coffee. 'I don't need...whatever this is, Lucca.'

He redirected his gaze to the stunning view of the palace grounds for a minute, before spearing her with stormy eyes again. 'Unfortunately, need or not, this has been neglected far too long.'

His cryptic words were punctuated by the butler's arrival, silencing the questions that rose to her lips. She ate simply to be civil, her insides roiling with apprehension. Something ominous hovered in her immediate future.

When he rose twenty minutes later, she almost took the coward's way out and demanded he tell her. His pursed lips and mildly dismal look silenced her.

Downstairs, they passed dozens of stable hands, who bowed respectfully to their King, and then headed for the southern end of the stables. Above a half-open stall a stunning horse, its silky white coat speckled with faint grey dots, peeked out, eyes bright with curiosity.

Murmuring softly to the horse, Lucca caressed its forehead, then stepped aside and gestured Delphie forward.

'Wow, Lucca. She's beautiful. Wait, it is a she, right?'

He gave a brisk nod. '*Sì*, it's a mare—descended from a sultan's pure thoroughbred stables in Saudi Arabia.'

'Does she have a name?'

Lucca caressed the mare's crest, his gaze avoiding hers. Her stomach tightened further. 'Lucca?'

'I named her Lady Delphine, after her owner,' he said, his voice tight.

Delphie froze, mouth gaping. 'What? Her owner... *Me?* You bought me a horse?'

Narrowed censorious eyes met hers. 'I bought you a horse.'

Heart banging against her ribs, she swallowed and asked, 'How long have you had her?'

Again he shrugged, as if the answer wasn't important. 'Nearly two years.'

This time shock arrived with a prickling of tears behind her eyes. 'Lucca...no...' She wasn't sure exactly what she was denying.

His twisted, faintly pitying smile seared her insides. 'Oh, yes, Delphine.'

The horse whickered softly at hearing her name, earning herself another gentle caress and a miniature carrot treat from the King.

Delphie swallowed the lump thickening in her throat. 'I... I don't know what to say.'

That sparked fire in his eyes.

Stepping around the gorgeous horse, Lucca planted himself in front of her, one eyebrow regally elevated in cynical mockery. 'Don't you? Then let me tell you how I imagined this going, shall I? Two years ago I would've brought you to San Calliano on your birthday. I would've introduced you to your mare. You would've been delighted.'

He drew closer with each word, until there was nothing but a whisper between them.

'Perhaps delighted enough to gift me one of those magnificent smiles that spark a fever inside me and remind me that I'm a red-blooded man in the company of the most beautiful woman on earth.'

He caught her wrist and twirled her around so she faced the solid wall of the stable. Then he leaned in close, his body a living, breathing column of heat at her back, his breath washing over her ear.

'And then I would've seduced you in an empty stall, so we didn't scandalise your new horse. Now, you have an impressive imagination, *dolcezza*. Tell me what would've happened next,' he urged thickly.

She wanted to reply that this was his story, and therefore only he could provide the details. But she was caught up in a fever of might-have-beens, floored by the beauty of the gift she'd denied him the chance to present her. And when he stepped closer, the fever swallowed her alive. Words tumbled from her lips.

'I would've worried about how to care for a horse. You would've reassured me. And then my delight in my gift would've been complete.' She twisted her head and looked into his taut, clench-jawed face. 'We would've made love then, and perhaps you would've shown me how to ride a horse afterwards.'

His chest rose and fell in a heavy sigh. '*Bene.* So you can guess at my disappointment when this didn't transpire the way it should've, *si*?' he pressed.

And then she knew in her soul that these past three weeks had been building up to this. 'Lucca—'

'Did you doubt I'd be an adequate father?' he rasped, his face a bleak mask of torture. 'Is that your reason for taking extra time to yourself?'

She turned fully to face him. 'No! Lucca, if that's why you've been avoiding the subject, please know that I didn't. For the most part I was terrified about my own abilities. Yes, I did wonder how it would play out between us—but not because I didn't think you'd be a good father.' She stopped to absorb the slice of pain into her heart. 'Sometimes I wonder if going from doubt to wanting my…our baby too much was what…' She shook her head, words failing her.

He paled, then his face tightened. 'You think your miscarriage was some sort of payback?'

Her throat worked. 'I don't know. Maybe…'

He gripped his nape, stormy tension vibrating off him. 'If it is, then I'm guilty too.'

She inhaled sharply. 'What?'

'Look at the examples I had. Perhaps history was destined to repeat itself and the Fates deemed I was better off without that test.'

Pain intensified in her chest. 'So you're…fine with it?'

His eyes darkened with shock. 'No! I would never be *fine* with such a loss. But I cannot overlook the flawed blueprint of my childhood.'

She reached for his arm, the urge to turn him from that line of thought ramming urgently through her. 'But don't you see? The fact that you know it's flawed means you'll avoid those same mistakes. Just as I vowed to never turn my back on my child the way my mother did with me.'

'That's no guarantee that other, possibly worse mistakes wouldn't have been made.'

Her hand dropped, her insides icing over. 'You don't truly believe that. You're convincing yourself of that just to avoid the pain.'

His lips firmed. 'I wouldn't know, would I, Delphine? You made sure to deprive me of the real-time experience of it, remember?'

She gasped in horror as he turned and strode out of the stall. But his steps slowed as he reached the wide entrance to the stables. Pivoting smoothly, he faced her once more, his face a contortion of shadows.

Delphie felt her heart drop to her feet, knowing that whatever he was about say would flay her.

'For what it's worth to you, I do know one thing. I would never have turned my back on you or our child, Delphine.'

She watched his broad back as he stepped outside into the sunlight, the sun itself worshipping him almost as much as she did.

When he'd disappeared from view, she dropped, feeling useless and devastated, to her knees, every truth she'd tried to avoid for two years, every touch she'd welcomed and every look she'd tried to second-guess to save her heart, mocking her in the face of the overwhelming emotions shrieking inside her.

She loved Lucca.

Had loved him probably from that first moment he'd pinned her with those devastating eyes and claimed her with that smile that said it was useless to deny him.

The horse...*her* horse...whickered softly again, her doleful eyes resting on Delphie with a hint of reproach that suggested that perhaps she was two years too late in acknowledging that emotion.

CHAPTER ELEVEN

LUCCA CHARGED INTO his private office, aware he sought sanctuary there to avoid Delphine.

The incident at the stables had been…unplanned. Hell, nothing in the past three weeks had gone as he'd intended.

Yes, the aim to put some distance between what his father had done and the whiff of scandal surrounding him had been achieved, and he'd restored his reputation with his people. But that, in turn, had prompted clamours for a new queen.

All because of Delphine.

The woman he'd tried to stay emotionally detached from.

He'd failed repeatedly and consistently enough to draw concern. Concern that she still held such effortless power over him. Concern at the hollow ache residing in his chest at the thought of her departure next week. Concern that those words she'd spoken at the stables were in danger of burrowing through his reservations and finding fertile soil. Concern that perhaps his outlook on fatherhood needn't be so dire. That, given another chance, he would grasp it with both hands.

Was that what presenting her with the horse had been about? To gauge her feelings on what might have been? Perhaps even make her yearn for the things he'd been too unnerved to admit he wanted when he bought the horse?

Except he'd made a hash of it.

He'd found himself discussing the one subject that had continued to flay him since she'd dropped her bombshell.

He paced his office, his mind in turmoil. Perhaps he should end it now. The end goal had been achieved.

The acute desolation that struck him at that idea made his gut clench hard.

Swallowing, he forced himself to think it through. When every thought pattern arrived at the conclusion that he wasn't ready for her leave, he froze. Everything was beginning to make some sort of inevitable sense.

He would *never* be ready. Not when it came to Delphine.

Which left him with two choices.

Ignore it and move on anyway.

Or lay himself bare?

'It would please me if you wear the diamonds I gave you,' he said.

She was about to step into her gown for the ball he was throwing for a handful of new ambassadors before they took up their posts.

Any other woman would have preened and then read endless connotations into his request. Delphine merely regarded him with calm composure before nodding. 'Of course. If that's what you want.'

No! he wanted to rail. He didn't want her calm or collected. He wanted to see her anguished because they only had one week left. He wanted to know that she felt this same weight on her chest as he felt on his at the thought of never seeing her again. He wanted to know if she went to sleep dreading the passage of time and awakened yearning for permanence, as he'd done far too frequently lately.

But she remained cool… Hell, *regal*, even. As if she had found the serenity jeeringly eluding him.

Or the indifference.

Acid boiled in his belly at those words. With an inner shake of his head, he dismissed them. The past three weeks had convinced him she didn't harbour *that* particular feeling towards him. No one could fake the passion she exhibited in his bed. Or the genuine interest she'd taken in San Calliano and everyone she'd met while at his side. He'd even been surprised and thrilled to hear her practising Italian with her designer friend Nicola.

He had cause to celebrate in that regard, at least. Not all women were like this mother. But Lucca didn't feel like celebrating. He might have arrogantly snarled *'You're mine!'* as he'd taken her that evening in his car, but every instinct shrieked at him that she wouldn't be for much longer.

'Do you mind fastening it for me?'

While he'd been lost in the vicious circle of what to do about this woman who held far too much importance in his life, Delphine had finished dressing. The shoulder-baring saffron-coloured silk gown, with its cape-like sleeves draping to the floor, was impressive enough, but it was the woman who wore it that elevated the outfit and her into a riveting sight.

He watched her glide towards him, a vision he couldn't look away from. *Mio Dio*, she looked like a…like a… He sucked in a sharp, shocked breath.

Her eyes widened. 'Lucca? Are you all right?'

It took every self-control technique he'd learned to keep him upright. To make him nod and reach for the necklace she needed help with.

When she faced away from him at his prompt, he closed his eyes for vital seconds, sucking in a slow breath to calm his racing heart before fastening the necklace. Then, because his willpower was deplorably weakened, he brushed his lips over her nape.

Her tiny gasp restored a little of his equilibrium.

Enough to clear his head.

Enough to allow a little bit more of that shocking revelation to take root inside him.

'Shall we?' he said.

After the handful of events she'd attended at Lucca's side, Delphie knew how the evening would unfold. Endless introductions and small talk followed by a meaningful prearranged conversation with a chosen few. But tonight, it felt as if Lucca was assessing her interactions with an enigmatic expression she couldn't quite read.

'What do you think of the ambassador from Malta?' he asked between conversations.

'He seems a little too blasé about important issues.'

'I agree. And the ambassador from South Africa?'

On and on it went, with each answer keenly considered or probed with further questions, his possessive hand on her back as he steered her through the room.

As if she mattered.

'You're mine.'

No. He'd only said that in the heat of passion.

Despite her reminding herself of that, a tiny bubble of hope bloomed in her chest, expanding as she danced in his arms and applauded his speech.

The emotion gathered strength, urging her to take a risk. It grew even stronger as she stepped on to the terrace for a breath of fresh air towards the end of the ball, after Lucca's aide had pulled him aside to take a call.

Was it that sensation building inside that made San Lorena appear even more beautiful from the wide terrace?

For the first time in a long time, Delphie toyed with the possibility of calling this place home.

She was in love with Lucca. And he...he didn't seem to mind her presence.

Dared she hope it could be more?

Approaching footsteps made her turn, but her smile froze when she saw who had joined her.

'Good evening, Miss Alexander.' Marco Coppi's greeting was cool, his gaze on the diamond necklace when he reached her even cooler.

'Can I help you, Mr Coppi?'

His lips twisted. 'It seems not, seeing as my advice to you has fallen on deaf ears.'

Her fingers tightened around her chilled champagne glass as she held on to her composure. 'Don't be so sure. I did listen to you once—to my regret. But I won't be making the same mistake again.'

Malice flared in his eyes, but slowly he regained control. 'You're a formidable woman. I will grant you that. But everything I said to you before still holds. Perhaps you should remember that before you make future plans?'

Where she'd cowered and crumbled before, she pulled her shoulders back now. She knew what rock-bottom felt like. Whatever happened with Lucca, she'd survive.

Wouldn't she?

But you didn't know you loved him then. Now you do...

She ignored the seismic quaking of her heart and answered the man before her. 'I will. Thank you. Now, if there's nothing else?'

She felt his hard gaze boring into her as she returned to the ballroom, fresh air be damned.

Her gaze met Lucca's eyes across the ballroom. She watched his eyes narrow and knew she hadn't quite shored her emotions up as much as she'd hoped.

Still, she went towards him, with every step knowing that she wouldn't walk away this time. Not until she knew once and for all if she had a chance with King Lucca of San Calliano.

Her steps faltered as his aide murmured in his ear. She watched Lucca frown and nod sharply, and then, with a clipped, regretful smile her way, he walked out.

'I'm sorry, Miss Alexander,' the aide said when she reached him. 'The King's been called away on urgent business.'

Concern lurched in her heart. 'Is everything all right?'

'The situation is still unfolding. He may be a while. I'm to escort you back to your suite.'

'Thank you,' she murmured.

She didn't bother going to bed, because she knew sleep would elude her. And when she gave in, scouring social media and seeing the news reports of an explosive device going off near San Calliano's southern border, her churn-

ing thoughts vacillated between worry for Lucca and fear
of what the future held in store for the love she'd finally
admitted to herself.

Her restlessness drove her to the balcony, her fingers
stroking the diamond necklace she'd been unable to take
off due to its complicated clasp. The diamond Lucca had
gifted her...

Because he was this generous to all his lovers or because
she meant more to him?

Her emotions were deeply entrenched in a quagmire when
she heard his footsteps three hours later. She turned away
from the view she fervently hoped wouldn't be her last of
San Calliano, her heart catching at the dark shadows in
his eyes.

'Is everything all right at the border?'

He nodded. 'Environmentalists making a point. I've invited their leader for a meeting next week,' he said, while
spearing her with a long, searching look. 'Why did you seem
so distressed earlier? Should I be worried that you were seen
talking to Coppi at the ball?'

This wasn't the way she'd hoped to start their conversation, but it was still an opportunity. 'I don't know—
should you?'

His face hardened...a regal sculpture that captivated her
more. 'This has gone on long enough. Believe me, as of
today, he's banned from the palace.'

'Is that going to solve our problems, though?'

He stiffened. 'What do you mean?'

The vice around her heart squeezed so tight she could
barely breathe. This was the most important conversation
of her life. She knew it down to her marrow.

'Three weeks ago you asked me to stay. You accused me
of running before—' She stopped, cleared her throat. 'But I
can't do this any more, Lucca. Not until I know.'

Fury mixed with what looked suspiciously like panic

flashed across his face. 'Need I remind you that we have an agreement?'

'I haven't forgotten. And instead of packing my bags and saying to hell with the consequences I'm staying. To talk.'

A tic appeared in his clenched jaw. 'I suppose I should be thankful that this time I get to ask you why you're thinking of packing your bags.'

He growled the last word. And she watched as tension mounted in his body until she could barely see beyond his overwhelming aura.

'If this talk includes a request that I set you free—'

'"The List",' she blurted, through fear-dried lips. 'Tell me it's an overblown, archaic thing that old men set in their old ways bandy about to make themselves feel important.'

Shock rippled across his face and his jaw clenched tight. For a soul-shredding age, he didn't speak. When he did, she couldn't miss the stark resignation in his voice. 'Delphine…'

Oh, God.

'So you endorse it too? When do you intend to activate it?' she blurted, because that was the one question that haunted her above all else.

Again a look crossed his face that pulverised her already shredding heart.

'Oh, my God. You already have.'

He spread his hands out, a curiously supplicant gesture that looked almost wrong on him. 'Wait, Delphine. Let me—'

'When is it all happening? Next month?'

His hands dropped.

'This month?' A choked sound left her throat. *'Now?'*

His lips flattened. 'Yes. I gave the order on our way back from Doha.'

Delphie felt the blood drain from her head. Felt her knees knock and her stomach hollow. But she was absolutely *not* going to crumble in front of him.

Too shattered to form words, she pivoted and entered the

bedroom. She refused to look at the bed—refused to let her gaze linger on anything that would remind her of Lucca.

'Are you not going to ask me why?' he bit out, prowling behind her.

She stopped dead in the dressing room, for a moment wondering why she couldn't see. Then she realised she'd failed. Her emotions were leaking out of her in the form of hot, gulping tears.

Still, she struck out blindly for where her suitcase had been stored.

'What the hell are you doing?'

Fury rose to mingle with pain and she rounded on him. 'Are you serious?'

He opened his mouth, no doubt to slice her open with another imperious put-down, but she beat him to it.

'You're about to parade your potential wives under my nose and you have the nerve to ask me why I'm packing my bags?'

He froze, then swore viciously under his breath. A layer of ice thawed in his eyes as he stepped forward. 'Delphine—'

'Don't. There's nothing you can say to make this humiliation acceptable.'

'No, you will not leave. Not in this state.'

Anguish twisted harder inside her. 'I'm sorry if my tears don't feed into your narrative. I guess I'm not as accomplished an actress as you hoped. But I'm sure you can spin this too.'

'I don't wish to spin anything!' he growled.

But she was done listening. 'A few times now you've invited me to put myself in your shoes. How about you do the same? Imagine if I had a list of men, waiting for me to pick and choose, who would replace you when I tossed you from my bed. Imagine I could have one of them right there in that bed behind you before sunrise.'

He growled. He actually had the audacity to growl his displeasure, his hands bunching into terrifying fists, his face a bleak mask.

She would've laughed had she not been choking on fresh tears.

'Does it hurt, Lucca? Does it make you want to burn the world to the ground?'

'Dammit—*sì*, it hurts! Ask me why I did it, Delphine.'

About to refuse, she paused. Because his voice was ragged, desolate. A man at the end of his tether. Not at all the proud and powerful King who awed her with his very existence.

'Why did you do it?'

His jaw rippled and he drew in a long slow breath. 'I signed "The List" at twenty-five because I was absolutely determined I wouldn't make the same mistake my father did and choose a wife based on emotion. Three weeks ago—' He stopped. Swallowed. 'I activated it because I was terrified with the way you consumed me. I already dreaded a future without you, and I mistakenly believed giving in to my advisers' demands would make me feel in control. But, *mio Dio*, I've never been in control where you're concerned, *dolcezza*. Not the first time I saw you, not when you made me laugh, spun circles around me with your intelligence, and not when you gifted me with the honour of your body that first time and every time after.'

He lurched towards her and her eyes widened to see him stagger under the weight of his emotions. But still she shook her head, too overwrought to take his words in. 'What are you saying, Lucca?'

'That I need you! That I'm nothing without you.'

Every cell in her body froze. Even her heart was afraid to beat. When it did, it slammed hard against her ribs. 'What?'

'*Per l'amore di Dio*, don't leave me again, Delphine,' he rasped, his face a rictus of desolation. 'Every day you were absent from my life I felt incomplete. Every day since you arrived back in my life—even the day you shared your loss with me—I've felt less alone.' He stopped, then shook his head decisively. 'I can't go back to how it was before. I refuse.'

She squeezed her eyes shut, fighting the dizzying pull of his words, and gasped when he caught her arms.

'*Please.* I can't live without you. Tell me what I need to do to make you stay. I will do anything, *Mia Regina.*'

Her eyes flared open. 'Did you just call me…?'

His shaking hands slid up to cup her jaw. 'My Queen. You're the only queen for me. I knew that two years ago but I didn't have the balls to say it. You slipped through my fingers and everything felt broken. When I got the chance to get you back, even temporarily, I seized it. *Because I can't live without you.*'

His voice shook with those last words and her whole world tilted.

'Stay. *Per favore.* Please stay.'

Raising her hand, she placed it over one of his own. 'What about "The List"?'

'Damn "The List"! My future will not be held hostage by an archaic council who think they know what's best for me. You've urged me not to let the past dictate the future. I will choose the woman of my heart or none at all!'

'The woman of your heart…' she whispered, awed by the power of his words.

Fresh tears clouded in her eyes. He brushed them away.

'Don't cry, *il mio amore.* You've shed enough tears for today—for a lifetime. I'm sorry I didn't take care of this before it caused you pain. *I love you.* My heart has known for two years that it belongs to you. My head needed a bit of time to catch up,' he mused, a strange light in his eyes.

Delphine cupped his cheek. 'Tell me again. Please.'

'I love you. I can't imagine a future without you.'

'Oh, Lucca. I love you too.'

Flames lit his eyes, warming her in the power of his love. 'So you'll stay? Become my Queen? Bless our home and our kingdom with gorgeous babies when you're ready?'

Her heart tumbled over, right into his keeping. 'When you lay such a dream come true at my feet, how can I refuse? I love you,' she reaffirmed, feeling hope and love finally sprouting free and unfettered in her heart.

He pressed his forehead to hers. *'Oggi, domani, per sempre.'*

Today. Tomorrow. For ever.

EPILOGUE

Five years later

'I SAW NICOLA leaving earlier.'

Delphie hid a smile at the naked interest so woefully disguised behind her husband's statement. 'Oh, really? I thought you were stuck in meetings all day?'

She felt more than saw his shrug as his arms wrapped around her from behind. 'My office is blessed with wonderful views. And that racing green colour you convinced your friend to paint her little sports car is very distinctive.'

'Hmm, so it is,' she replied, deliberately infusing her voice with a lack of interest.

'Delphine…' There was a faint thread of warning in his voice, but it was shrouded by thick anticipation. 'I've been a good husband and put our little hellions to bed. I think I deserve a reward, *si*?'

She laughed and finally turned in his arms, winding hers around his neck. Despite his good-natured grumbling, he adored bedtime with their children. Four-year-old Prince Rafael and three-year-old Princess Sofia had learned very quickly the ploy of prolonging bedtime with a father who utterly doted on them.

It was what had given her time to prepare his surprise, momentarily forgetting that the love of her life had a knack for ferreting out secrets.

'So it's your birthday week…' she mused.

Interest sharpened in his eyes. '*Sì*, it is.'

'Our racing team has placed first and second for the fifth time in a row...'

'Thanks to your excellent leadership,' he added.

'And my mother is coming for another visit next week.'

'The children can barely contain themselves about Granny's visit.'

Her mother's acceptance of her invitation to their wedding had mildly stunned Delphie. She had Lucca to thank for that as well, with his prompt not to write off her relationship with her mother just yet. He'd applied the same reserved hope to his father, although that particular journey was a little bumpier than hers. Delphie knew it was what drove Lucca to be the best father he could be to their children; he was scrupulous about history not repeating itself.

'So, I'm in the mood to celebrate. Big time.'

A wicked smile broke out on his face, rendering him the kind of impossibly handsome that knocked the air out of her lungs.

She sauntered away from him, exaggerating her movements, knowing his eyes were riveted on her. Picking up the champagne flutes she'd filled a minute ago, she presented him with one. 'I thought about a horse. But you have so many of those.'

'*Sì*, I do.'

'Then I considered another car...'

He grimaced. 'I only have two legs and a very busy schedule, *dolcezza*. No more cars.'

'Hmm... Then I thought about a challenge...'

His eyes lit up. 'I love challenges.'

'Well, how about this? Since Sofia has been begging us for a sister, I thought...'

Strong arms tightened around her waist, pulling her close enough to feel the tremor that moved through his body.

'*Yes*. It would be my honour.'

Delphie laughed. 'I haven't even finished telling you what the challenge is!'

He swallowed, a faint flush scouring his cheeks as he waited.

Delphie knew the one thing he yearned for. Another baby. But he'd been patient. Waiting until she was ready.

With each pregnancy, they'd drawn even closer, their shared loss contained in loving memory, in a special place in their hearts, making each gift of a child more treasured.

She was ready for their next miracle now.

She drew the dressing gown from her body, displayed the specially commissioned lingerie Nicola had just dropped off for her. Watching him swallow, she leaned up, whispered in his ear. 'Your challenge is to put a baby in me before your next birthday.'

'*Santo cielo, sì,*' he responded gruffly.

An hour later, she moved her fingers through his damp hair, her body replete as he stared down at her.

The love that shone from his eyes awed and humbled her. 'I love you, Lucca.'

'*Grazie, Mia Regina.* For this life I never dared to dream of which you've so generously made come true. For the rest of my life I will honour you with every breath, every beat of my heart. *Oggi, domani, per sempre.*'

* * * * *

CROWNED
FOR HIS
CHRISTMAS BABY

MAISEY YATES

MILLS & BOON

To Megan, Jackie and Marcella.
What's better than alpha heroes?
Alpha heroes that you get to write with your friends.

PROLOGUE

THEY WERE THE most notorious, shocking, dissolute group of rakes to ever grace the hallowed halls of Oxford. And given the school's illustrious and rather lengthy history, that was truly saying something.

Of course neither Prince Vincenzo Moretti, heir to the throne of Arista, nor his friends, Sheikh Jahangir Hassan Umar Al Hayat, Prince Zeus and Rafael Navarro, bastard child of a king of Santa Castelia, would ever say it themselves.

There was no need.

Their reputations preceded them.

With great pomp and circumstance. From the mouths of men who envied them, wishing only to find themselves ensconced in the afterglow of their power, as if it might give them even the tiniest bit of access to the women that they enjoyed, or the excess that they acquired with the snap of a finger.

And of course, from the women.

The women who declared themselves ruined for all other men, who sighed wistfully about the pleasure they had experienced at their royal hands and would never experience again.

For surely, no man alive could match the prowess of these ruthless royals.

And they could not. Vincenzo himself had no qualms about basking in the benefits of such a reputation.

Of course, his father believed that he would put on the public face required of him for all the world to see. All the while, seeking his own pleasure and lining his own pockets, as their people lived in spartan circumstances.

Vincenzo had begun to combat that with the establishment of many charities, using covert networks he had created outside of his country to bring money in that his father could not touch. Money that appeared to be foreign aid that he would keep his hands off in the name of keeping relations strong between other nations.

But that was not Vincenzo's only plan. No. He was playing a long game. He could not move, not now. His mother's health—mentally and physically—was fragile. Especially after the scandal three years ago that had rocked Arista. After...

Eloise.

He refused to dwell on her.

He would not.

The destruction of the monarchy would end his mother. And he could not bear that. He would protect his mother. No matter what.

His mother had loved the palace once—and Arista. And the one thing she enjoyed still in life was her role as Queen. He could not let her see what he would do to the royal family. The royal line.

For he would not produce an heir. Never. He refused. He would not carry on the royal line of Arista. He would allow his country to change hands. To go into the hands of the people. And he would make sure that his father knew this before his death. This legacy... It was the only thing his father cared for.

And Vincenzo would see it destroyed.

Yes, his reputation as a notorious, shocking, dissolute rake was truly one that would make even the hardest of harlots clutch their pearls. But if they knew what he really was, if they knew what he truly intended to do... They would expire from the shock.

"A toast," he said, looking around the room that served as their clubhouse, where they conducted their meetings—all of them already earning their own money hand over fist, carving their own place in the world apart from the legacies of their dubious fathers. "To being unexpected."

"It could be argued," Rafael said, "that your rebellion might be seen as deeply expected."

"It will never be expected by our fathers. Who are far too prideful to think that anyone could surprise them in the least. But I have no trouble playing a long game."

"No indeed," Zeus said, looking down into his glass of scotch. "But I think, my friend, that you will find I am not a patient man. I prefer the game short. Hard and brutal."

"I'm all for brutality. But I find brutality is much more effective when meted out strategically."

"I didn't say I wasn't strategic," Zeus said, grinning broadly. "I said I wasn't patient." He lifted a shoulder. "Brutality now. Brutality later. Brutality all around."

He waved a laconic hand and settled more deeply into his resolute lounging position.

"I admire your thinking," Jag said, one leg thrown out in front of him, his arm slung over the back of the couch. He elevated casual disdain to high art.

"For my part, I intend to let my father's kingdom…" Vincenzo swirled the glass and watched the amber liquid spin, an aromatic tornado. He lifted the scotch to his lips. "I will not produce an heir. Ever."

"How nice for me that it is not expected," Rafael said. "As a bastard, it is my younger legitimate brother who will inherit control of the kingdom, and the concern of carrying on the line is his. Not mine."

"My father cares so greatly for the reputation of our country," Jag said. "My greatest delight would be to find a woman he would see as desperately unsuitable."

"Only *one* woman?" Zeus asked. "I myself intend to acquire an entire stable of them. But no heir. Never that."

"A toast to that," Vincenzo amended. "To unsuitable women, revenge served hot or cold and to never falling in line."

CHAPTER ONE

ELOISE ST. GEORGE did not feel merry or bright. The snow falling outside felt like an assault, as did the roaring fire, beautiful evergreen garland and cheery Christmas tunes. Yet she was responsible for it all—save the snow. A resolute rebellion against the depression that was threatening to swallow her whole.

Christmas Eve.

She was without a Christmas tree. Since it was still back in Arista. With him.

She had hung garlands, wreaths and other hallmarks of cheer. She had baked cookies and decorated them, had made herself a beautiful dinner. But she wasn't feeling… Any of it.

She had made Christmas a happy time for herself all these years, in defiance of her upbringing. She'd always been happy to celebrate it alone, in her historic stone house in Virginia, which could not be more picturesque.

But alone felt… Alone this year. Truly, deeply.

With all the snow piled outside, she'd managed to get Skerret, her foundling cat, to finally come inside from the cold.

The little gray creature was curled up by the red brick fireplace in a contented ball, purring.

It should be wonderful.

It wasn't.

She put her hand down on her rounded stomach.

It would have been wonderful. If not for Vincenzo Moretti.

And the fact she was currently carrying the heir he had vowed to never create.

Seven months earlier...

This was the address he had been given, but Prince Vincenzo Moretti could not reconcile the crumbling manor before him with the woman he knew Eloise St. George to be. He remembered her vividly.

She had lived at the palace from the time she was six years old, and he had found her disruptive. He was four years her senior and at ten he had been deeply serious. He had also suspected that her presence was emblematic of something that was wrong in the palace. He had been correct.

Her mother had come to the palace to be his father's mistress. He didn't advertise that, of course. Not the Upright and Honorable King Giovanni Moretti. He gave her an official job title to conceal her real purpose. But even at ten, Vincenzo knew.

He could see it in the decline in his mother's health.

He had resented Eloise at first. Had seen her as the mascot of his father's perfidy and her mother's sins.

But reluctantly, slowly, over the years she had become his... Friend.

A shock for an arrogant princeling who had never befriended anyone in his life.

Then he'd gone off to university and met Rafael, Zeus and Jag. And when he'd returned home...

Eloise had been a woman. And things had taken a turn.

He'd found her beautiful. Captivating. She'd seemed fragile and still so innocent. But when she'd... When she had told him she wanted him, he'd turned her away. Out of deference to her youth, her innocence.

Because she had not chosen life in the palace. Had not chosen a life where she was forced to know him and he'd felt that she should... Go and experience life and men she had chosen.

But her true colors had been revealed after. Not innocent. Not his friend.

Not...

It did not matter except in the way she might be useful to him now.

The way that she might enhance his plan.

His father had been involved in one scandal. Only ever one.

Eloise.

She had become the symbol of an old man's folly. A man who could never have resisted the wiles of an eighteen-year-old beauty hell-bent on seduction.

His father's only sin.

While publicly, Vincenzo committed many.

For all the world to see, Vincenzo was a disappointment. A man who glutted himself on every indulgence available, a man who engaged openly in the kinds of behavior his father engaged in privately.

But in secret, it was Vincenzo who was saving

Arista, and they would never know it until after his father died.

But he would not save it in the manner his old man wished. For he would not produce an heir. He would let the monarchy burn.

And he would be all the gladder for it.

His father was an old man now. And it was time to begin dismantling his legacy. His facade. For he wished to do it where his father could still see. Exposing his financial malfeasance and his mistreatment of his wife. The beloved Queen of Arista.

His poor mother had been... Disgraced in the end.

His father had told the country she'd fallen into a depression and had blamed a weak spirit.

Not his own actions of course.

His father had damaged his mother's legacy, and Vincenzo would *destroy* the King's.

And it began here. Though he had not expected this ramshackle collection of stones with ivy climbing up the side of it. Nor had he expected the crooked wrought iron gate with honeysuckle wound through the spires.

Eloise St. George he would've expected to live in an ultramodern flat paid for by her latest conquest. Somewhere near clubs and shopping and all the other vices her kind enjoyed. But not this. This place out in the middle of nowhere. Clearly, he had seen that it was near nothing when he had looked it up on the map, but he had expected something grander.

Or that perhaps she had built her own row of shops that had not yet appeared in the mapping program. For he could hardly imagine the girl that he'd known moldering away in the countryside. Least of all in a place like this.

He pushed open the gate, which creaked and caught on a vine that grew out of the cobbled walk.

It was a hazard, this place. He slammed the gate shut, though it did not close all the way, and he strode up the walk, careful not to catch his foot on any of the uneven stones. Nature, it seemed, had taken over this place. There were hedges, large trees wrapped in creeping vines. Most of the garden was shaded, with sun, golden as it was in mid-May, breaking through each time the breeze twisted the leaves.

It was hot. Far too hot for the bespoke suit that he was wearing, but it was not in his nature to yield to the elements. He preferred to force them to bend to him.

Why she had chosen to make her escape here in this rather rural corner of the United States he did not know. It made no earthly sense to him. Which in and of itself was a mystery, because Eloise should be simple. Her mother certainly had been. And as far as he'd been able to tell, Eloise was the same.

Her mother, protected by her title of Personal Assistant had spent lavishly and lorded her position over the household staff.

And Eloise, he had been certain, was driven by much the same things. He might have believed she was different once.

But he'd learned.

Yes. Eloise was no different than her mother. Which was why he was confident that he could enlist her services. Either through blackmail or bribery. It did not matter to him which.

He stood at the front door, blue with a cheerful wreath hung at the center. He could not imagine Eloise taking the time to hang a wreath at the center of her door.

She must have staff to see to such things.

Perhaps that was the piece he was missing.

Perhaps this was where her protector had installed her. Within a close enough proximity for his pleasure, but far enough away perhaps that she would not interact with his wife and children.

Yes. Eloise was exactly the sort of woman who would play mistress to a wealthy married man.

It would suit her. She had the cheekbones for it. Among other things.

He rang the doorbell. And there was no response.

Perhaps she was out.

He took a step off the path and around to the side of the house, checking for signs of life.

It was not a terribly secure property, and if nothing else, perhaps he would let himself in and see what information he could gather about Eloise and her current situation.

When he went around the side of the house, he heard a small sound.

It was… Humming.

Tuneless, rather terrible humming.

He paused and listened. He could not make out what the tune was, as it was just so sporadic and tone-deaf.

But there was something strangely charming about the cheer that seemed injected into the sound. And that was deeply strange as he could not remember being charmed by much of anything, least of all something cheerful. Not in his entire life.

When he rounded the corner, he was shocked by what he saw. The back of the most luscious figure he had seen in... He could not remember how long. The woman was bent over, working on something in the garden, and the trousers that she was wearing conformed to her ass in an extremely pleasing way. She stood, and he saw that the woman had wide hips, a narrow waist, and he was terribly hungry to see the front of her.

His second thought was that he had the wrong house. Because the Eloise he knew had that sort of gaunt, haunted look that her mother had, the hungry look of a woman who cared more to be attractive in photographs than in person. More angles than curves.

This must be the gardener, but if there was a gardener for the house then what had they been doing all this time? The place was wild as far as he could tell. He preferred things manicured and tightly kept. And this... Well, it was not.

The humming suddenly stopped. And the woman jumped, startled as if she sensed that she was being watched, and she turned. Her blue eyes went round, and her mouth dropped open. She was holding a potted plant, with a cheerful red blossom on the top. And then she dropped it, and the pottery shattered on the stones below.

"Vincenzo."

CHAPTER TWO

ELOISE COULD NOT stop the flutter of her foolish, traitorous heart. This was like a dream. Like every shameful dream she prayed wouldn't be there waiting for her at night when she fell asleep, but always was.

For she had never forgotten him.

The man with the dark, compelling eyes, who made her feel things that no other man ever had. Who had awakened a desire inside of her when she was only fifteen years old and had held her in thrall ever since. Even though her seduction attempt had ended in a refusal, all these years later she could understand it in a way an eighteen-year-old hadn't, the memory of the one and only time she had ever been close enough to touch him still lingered in her mind and made her tremble in her sleep.

But that wasn't her worst memory of Vincenzo. Her most painful. No. It had been the way he'd sent her away. The way he'd believed… Everything.

Everything except what she'd told him.

She'd been so certain they'd been friends. That he'd cared for her.

But that final moment between them…

He'd made it clear he'd never really cared for her at all.

Did that stop her body from responding to the steamy visions of him that floated through her sub-conscious at night?

No. No, it did not.

He occupied her dreams. He occupied her fantasies…

He was currently occupying her garden.

"Eloise," he said.

And she could see that he… He had not known it was her.

She was vaguely embarrassed by that, but only for a moment. Because she was accepting of the shape that her body had taken in the years since she had left the palace. She liked the changes in herself. The changes that had occurred when she could finally con-trol her own life. When she could decide what her pri-orities were. When she no longer had to live beneath the shadow of her mother and her impossible standards.

Still, it was always vaguely hurtful to realize that you were so different you were not even recognizable.

"Yes," she said. "Quite. But you… You cannot be here by accident. Because this house is not on the way to anything, least of all anything that you would be headed to."

"Indeed it is not," he said, sliding his dark jacket from his broad shoulders and casting it onto a white chair that boasted intricate iron scrollwork, with one careless finger. It seemed a metaphor for his existence here. The very masculine object covering the delicate, feminine one.

He turned his wrist and undid the button on his cuff, rolling his sleeve up and revealing a muscular forearm before doing the same to the right side. She blinked, watching with deep interest. Interest that she tried not to feel. And definitely tried not to convey.

"Why are you here?"

His dark eyes met with hers and her heart slammed against her breastbone. He was still the perfect image of masculine beauty. And she feared that for her he always would be. The way his tanned skin gleamed in the sunlight, that same light catching in his dark eyes and displaying a dangerous fire there. She had always thought his eyes so compelling. They were so dark they were nearly black, and she wanted to get lost in the depths of them.

She had embarrassed herself horribly as a teenager staring at him, or at least, she would've liked to embarrass herself horribly staring at him. But he had never noticed. He had practically acted as if she was invisible. Again, with hindsight, she was grateful for that, and had she not horrifically misstepped he would probably never have noticed her at all.

But she had.

And she felt covered in shame about it even all these years later. That she'd believed she loved him. That she'd believed he loved her.

No. Forgive yourself. Forgive her.

She did try.

She had tried to change her life entirely. Step away from the path her mother had wanted her to be on. To find out who Eloise St. George was all on her own. Not a girl living in the palace and the shadow of her mother's great and terrible beauty. Not a girl who had been taught that the only value she had was in her beauty. That girl who had believed, in spite of all that, she might really find a fairy tale. When she'd left Arista, it had been under a cloud of shame. Every newspaper in the world printing lies about her and touting them as verified truths.

It had hurt her. Profoundly. As had Vincenzo's belief in them. But when she'd gone, when she'd found life outside the palace... Away from her mother, his father and Vincenzo himself...

She'd gained perspective. She'd realized how many things had been built up in that palace that simply weren't real. Her mother's ideals had no bearing on the life she lived out here, in the sunshine, amongst the flowers. The King's gaze didn't follow her here, and while the press might have tried to ensure she had no real peace or opportunity to get work, enough time had passed—and she'd managed to make for herself a good reputation in her field and she'd never struggled to get work.

Reality was rich and deep and warm away from the cold stone of Arista.

It felt like an illusion now.

Parts of it.

One thing she was confident in was that her feelings for Vincenzo had been real. They had not been based in a desire to snare herself a rich protector. They had not been about anything other than the fact that he had captured her from the moment she had first laid eyes on him at six years old. As silly as that was. Of course, back when she had been a child, there had been nothing sexual about it; it was simply that she had found him... Wonderful. There was something about him that reminded her of a knight in shining armor.

He had been kind to her. One of her few experiences of kindness. And in her memory, in spite of how things had ended between them, he was still that mythological figure.

But the way he was looking at her now…

There was nothing heroic about it. And she was quite certain that he had not come to save her.

You don't need to be saved.

"I'm here to take you back with me, Eloise." He did not look away from her, his dark gaze unwavering. Her chest went tight, her throat. She could feel her insides trembling.

"To Arista?"

Thinking of Arista, of returning there made her feel cold inside. And why he would want her to come back when he'd paid her to go away in the first place…

"Yes," he said.

"Vincenzo… Has something happened to your father…? Or my mother…?"

"No," he said. "But I require you, for a very specific purpose. You will not be returning with me in whatever capacity you might imagine. You see, you are an important instrument in my revenge against my father."

She blinked. "I am?"

"Yes," he said. "And I think you will find that there is sufficient reason for you to return with me. Whether you wish to or not."

"Vincenzo," she said, trying to force a smile, because after all, they had been a part of each other's lives for a great number of years, and there was no reason to be grim. "If you need my help, you have only to ask."

And she couldn't say then what was driving her. She could tell herself it was that she cared for him, whatever had passed between them. She could tell herself it was because she wanted to do something to ease the darkness coming off him in waves.

But what she did not tell herself was that it had anything to do with the tendrils of pleasure that curled around her stomach when she thought of revenge.

He made a compelling picture. A dark avenging angel standing before her, asking her to indulge her basest self.

You don't own that pain. That rage, none of it is yours. You let it go.

She breathed in deep and smelled the lilacs.

And thought of vengeance still. If only a little.

"I have only to ask?"

She forced a smile. "Of course. I'm sure that we can discuss whatever it is you're planning. There's no reason for you to come here all dark and angry and threatening. No reason to threaten me at all. Can you go over there to the shed?"

"I'm sorry?"

"To the shed. My broom is in there. And you made me break my plant."

"*You* broke your plant," he said.

"Yes," she said, feeling slightly testy. "But it was because you startled me. So would you be so kind as to get my broom."

"Perhaps you have forgotten who I am?"

"I haven't. You're the one who didn't seem to know who I was. I said your name immediately. How could I fail to recognize you? I could not. Ever. And I think you know that. Please get my broom."

"And…"

"And then we will discuss your plot."

"It is not a plot."

"It sounds like a plot to me. Complete with intrigue. Vincenzo, I am no great fan of your father, neither am I particularly fond of my mother. There is a reason that I have not been back to Arista in all these years. Depending on what you have in mind... I will help you."

"Just like that?"

She hesitated "Of course."

"I will get your broom, and then you will explain to me what you've been doing this past decade and a half."

"Oh, a great many things," she said, trailing behind after him as he went to the shed.

He opened the door, and fished around inside until he grabbed a broom. "Why did you follow me if you sent me on the errand? You could've easily retrieved the thing yourself."

"Yes, I suppose," she said. "I didn't mean to follow you. It just sort of happened. But I am intrigued. What has happened? What are your plans?"

"Nothing more has happened than what has been happening in my country ever since my father ascended to the throne. He is corrupt. He has kept your mother in secret as his mistress while masquerading for all the world as an overbearing, pious leader who has inflicted a false morality upon the entire country that he himself is not held to. I, as you know, am his great public shame, and yet what he's done to my mother over the years is unconscionable. I will expose it. And I will do so by making a public display that will destroy him."

Hearing him say those words, while omitting any

mention of her made her breathless and a bit dizzy. "And what do I have to do with it?"

"I may not approve of you, Eloise, but the fact is my father's…dalliance with you is another example of why he must be dealt with. Only you were ever hurt by it, not him. Do you not find that unfair?"

Even more unfair, considering she'd never touched him. And never would.

But the truth hadn't mattered to the press.

Or to Vincenzo.

"Life is not fair, Vincenzo, or did no one ever tell you that?"

"I aim to balance the scales. By taking everything he has."

His dark eyes glittered with a black flame, and an answering heat smoldered in her stomach, but she did not allow that to show.

Instead, she scrunched up her nose, looking up at him, backlit as he was by the sun. "That does all sound a bit intense. I don't suppose you've ever tried therapy?"

"Therapy," he repeated, his voice flat, the broom still in his hand, which was an incongruous sight. She had to wonder if Vincenzo had ever held a broom before. She did not imagine he had.

"Yes. I have found it incredibly helpful. I no longer get angry. Now I garden."

"You garden."

"Yes," she said. "Of course, now I have one less flower." She took the broom from his hand and went back over to the scene of its destruction. "But that doesn't matter. I can always plant more. That is the wonderful thing about nature. It is incredibly resilient.

It grows, and it thrives, often in spite of us. I find it quite cheering. Bettering myself is one of my pursuits since leaving Arista. But only one of them. I went to school for horticulture. I made a lot of friends. I traveled around. I…"

"With my money?"

Heat lashed at her. "You gave it to me."

"I paid you off."

"Did you want revenge on me? Or on your father."

"It is only that you speak of those accomplishments as if they are yours when we both know how you paid for them."

"Do not look at me like that," she said. "How is it that you've managed to finance your life?"

"I have made my own way."

"From the starting position of 'billionaire prince,'" she said. "Your father, your lineage, gave you your start in life. I had to… I had to make the best of what I was given. I will not apologize for it."

His appraisal of her was decisive and cold, and she felt as if it had cut her down to her bones. "I don't require your apology."

"And I don't require your approval, so now we have that out of the way, what is it you want from me?"

"It's simple," he said, and she did not like the way he said that. Simplicity for a man with the sort of power and bearing Vincenzo Moretti possessed meant nothing to mere mortals such as herself.

Simple could mean flying a private jet to an equally private island, or rallying the whole of the media to listen to him speak. It could be climbing a ladder to collect stars from the sky.

Simple for Eloise was something else entirely. An

evening at home with a cup of tea, or an afternoon in the garden.

Definitely without her mother in her vicinity.

He was looking at her. As if "it's simple" was all she needed to know.

"If 'simple' involves reading your mind, you have the wrong idea of 'simple.'"

"It's not a negotiation," he said. "Nor am I asking for your help, I'm demanding you come with me. I see no reason to continue to speak in your garden."

"I said I would help you. You can stop looming so menacingly." She turned on her heel and stalked toward the house, throwing the back door open and going inside.

It was warm.

There was no air conditioner, and by late afternoon not even the stones could keep the heat at bay. But she didn't mind it. It was hers. And, all right, Vincenzo might dispute that, because she had taken that horrible money he'd flung at her to run away and had used some to purchase this house. But it felt like hers. It felt like home. And she'd been the happiest here than she'd been anywhere.

And yet he made her feel like she had one foot back in that life again.

You agreed to help him...

But she knew him.

The threats were not empty, and she wouldn't win if she argued. And if she didn't choose to go with him, she would be forced to go.

One thing Eloise could not bear, not ever again, was to have her choice taken away. And in this instance she knew she could change it, retain her power.

She had shocked him with her easy offer to help.

She wanted to keep shocking him.

She had spent her life in the palace at Arista on the defense. She had been out of place in every way. Her mother had always been a hard woman, who saw Eloise as an accessory to play dress-up with when it suited her, and a doll to discard when it did not.

The King had not paid any attention to her, until he had.

And Vincenzo? He'd been her only ally.

Until he wasn't.

"I will have to pack. And I need to see if my neighbor can feed Skerret."

His brow creased. "What is...that?" he asked.

"My cat. Well, she's not my cat entirely. She looms around the garden—a lot like you, actually—and I feed her."

He arched one dark brow, his expression beautifully insolent. "You have not fed me. Should I be offended?"

"Likely." But she was busy texting her neighbor Paula to see if she could leave food for the poor little tabby while she was away.

Paula responded with a quick yes. And when she looked back up at Vincenzo, it was because she could feel the impatience radiating off him in palpable waves.

"There is a breathing exercise I learned," she said. "It helps with tension."

"You are not my therapist."

"You don't have a therapist," she said. "I think we already covered that."

"No, I do not. But when we get back to Arista...you will be playing the part of my mistress."

Her mouth dropped open and she couldn't help it. She laughed.

"Your *what*?" She couldn't stop laughing. She laughed so hard tears streamed down her face, because he could not be serious.

To her great shame she had followed his… Trajectory, she would call it, for the last ten years. She had seen him in the news with an endless parade of women. All perfect. All gorgeous. All… Very not her.

"I do not believe I said anything that was difficult to comprehend."

"Oh, no, I comprehend, I just think you're way off. There is no way anyone would believe that I was your mistress."

"The world is unaware of *our* complicated history, *cara*."

Cara. He had never called her that. She had heard him call other women that, though. He used to bring them to the palace, after ostentatiously arriving in the country with them on his arm.

She could remember the fury of his father—always—when he had done so.

He is a disgrace.

Trying to humiliate me.

Trying to diminish the Crown.

She wondered now if he had been. All along. If Vincenzo had truly set out to tarnish the institution from day one.

But mostly the word *cara* echoed inside of her and made her feel light-headed.

She shook it off. "They are all too aware of…"

"Your affair with my father? That is why I want you. You were made to take all the scorn upon yourself. An eighteen-year-old temptation no man could resist." His dark eyes went blank, and she was glad. She'd defended herself already back then; she wouldn't keep doing it. But hearing him repeat the things the tabloids had said wasn't easy.

"Why bring me back?"

"A triumphant return, Eloise. On my arm. A reminder of when his mask slipped, and then we will tear it off together. We will force the reality of truth upon the masses. These are different times. Even I have changed in how I see things. A man of his age has a certain power. A man of his position more still. You were an eighteen-year-old girl and for all that I disapproved...you were given sole blame. I think if the world is forced to look at it in this new time they would see him for what he is. A predator with no morals."

He wasn't wrong. Things had changed. Too late for her, but they had.

"But why would anyone believe you're with me?"

"I'm a man of great debauchery—no one will find it hard to believe I've taken on my father's former... You."

"No, that's not what I mean."

She stared at him and waited for him to figure it out. He only stared back. Enigmatic and hard, like a sheer cliff face.

"Are you going to make me say it, Vincenzo? Because I knew you were a bastard, but I thought being deliberately cruel to me might be a bit beneath you."

"Explain to me how I am being cruel?"

"I am not beautiful. Not by the standards those people use to measure it. And sample sizes are hardly going to fit this figure."

He laughed. He dared laugh! That dark chuckle rolling through her like a lick of flame. "Sample sizes? *Cara*, I am not your mother. I do not need to debase myself bargain hunting. Whatever I provide for you will be fitted especially to your exquisite curves."

"Exquisite?" She had never been called anything even adjacent to *exquisite*. "I am not your type," she said.

"Beautiful? Lush? Beddable? That is not my type?"

He said it as if he were reciting a shopping list.

Milk.

Bread.

Beddable.

Beddable. She couldn't get over *that*.

"I am round," she said, her voice flat.

"Lush," he said, his voice far too seductive. "The narrow view on beauty your mother fed you…"

"To be clear," she bit out. "I am not insecure. I like my life. I like my body. As much as I like cookies. But I do not want to subject myself to what will undoubtedly be a heap of criticism from the press. I have been there and I've done it all before. And this time I know exactly what they'll do. With glee. Don't you think they'll put photos of me side by side and speculate on my weight gain?"

"But you are not eighteen," he said, his voice fierce. "And you will not run this time."

"You mean I will not be banished?"

"Let us go."

"I should pack a bag."

"You will want for nothing. By the time we arrive at the plane, a seamstress and a rack of clothing will be there waiting. You will be fitted and the items altered en route to Arista. By the time we arrive, you will look every inch mine."

Mine.

She shivered.

Then she shook it off.

This was not a fantasy. He might be a prince, but in this case she had a feeling he was less knight in shining armor, and more the dragon who might eat her alive.

CHAPTER THREE

ELOISE SEEMED TO have a personal mission of being unexpected. He had expected her to do one of two things when he had demanded she go with him: to cry hysterically and call him a brute before ultimately capitulating to his blackmail. Or to flirt while succumbing to his bribery.

She did neither.

Instead she had looked up at him with round eyes and a seeming lack of artifice and had said she would help him.

She reminded him more of the girl he'd known than the woman he'd made her into in his mind when he'd discovered her association with his father.

But now he wondered if she'd changed in that moment, or if he had. And it was a discomfiting thought.

Even now as they boarded his private plane, comfortably fitted with many rooms and all the amenities a person could ever want, she looked… She did not look *bored*, or as if she was stepping into her due. Rather she had an expression on her face of a woman who was surprised and delighted by her surroundings.

Perhaps *delighted* was an overstatement. But there was something fascinated in her gaze, and it was not the sort of bright avarice that he might've expected with a woman such as her. No. It seemed to be more interest.

Enjoyment.

There was a purity to her response that... Took him off guard. For he had never applied the concept of *purity* to Eloise St. George.

"Is there something you wish to say?" he asked as he settled onto the soft leather sofa in the main seating area of the aircraft.

"Only that it's quite grand," she responded. "The plane."

"It is to my advantage to have everything well in its place for when I travel. I must be able to function as if I were in my own home."

"Well naturally," she said. "It must be so horribly taxing for you to travel to and fro as you do. I myself have been quite stagnant for much of my life. Though, of course my mother enjoyed traveling with your father on occasion. And sometimes I went too. A testament to your father's great kindness," she said, the words biting. "That he would bring not only his assistant, but her child. But his plane is not quite so spectacular."

"Indeed not," Vincenzo said.

He could not quite figure out what game she was playing, and that caused him a hint of concern. Concern was a foreign feeling, as was the sense that he could not read another person.

He *knew* plenty enough about Eloise. A mere week after she'd come to *his* room—tried to seduce him. Told him she loved him, kissed him—the story had broken about her affair with his father.

And he'd... Well he'd considered himself a saint for

sending her away. Desire had been a living, breathing beast inside of him and even then he'd known. She was far too young. And most importantly, she would barely remember life away from the palace. They had grown up together, and in some ways they'd grown up alone.

She'd thought she loved him because she was too innocent to know better.

And so he'd told her no. Told her they couldn't…

What a fool he'd been. An even bigger fool for the pain he'd felt when he'd discovered that she had never loved him—she only wanted to align herself with a crown.

And any would do.

He had learned. He had learned since then to harden himself.

"Have a drink," he said.

As soon as he said those words, his stewardess appeared and walked over to the bar. "What would the lady like?" she asked.

"Oh," Eloise said. "A club soda would be nice."

"A club soda," he said. "Please do not hesitate to put a larger dent in my bar than that."

"I don't often drink."

It surprised him. For he had imagined…

He had imagined a whole woman in his head that it seemed did not exist. And that was what he was finding here.

He had imagined Eloise sharp and pointed, like her mother. Had imagined her with heavy makeup and a daring taste in clothing. He had thought she would feign boredom at his plane, consume his entire bar and demand to know how she would be compensated for all of this time spent inconvenienced.

But she looked different. Spoke different. Acted different.

He was certain he was rarely wrong, and yet with her, it seemed he was.

"If you are saving it for a special occasion, then let us make this one. For we are rather triumphantly returning back to Arista, are we not?"

"I don't know that I find it triumphant to return to Arista."

He waved a hand and his stewardess poured two glasses of champagne. She brought them over on a tray and he took them both, before handing one to Eloise, who stared at the fizzing liquid blinking rapidly.

"You do not feel triumphant, Eloise? You are… A horticulturist with a… I suppose it is what passes for a home in some circles. Do you not feel pleased with yourself?"

He found himself waiting. Waiting for the truth of her to be revealed. And it was a strange thing, he acknowledged to himself, that he had not done exhaustive research on her before he had gone to look for her. For in most circumstances he would've walked into the situation already knowing all the answers. He would have made sure that he had them. But he had been so certain that Eloise St. George could not surprise him. That she was the exact same tawdry, sparkling bit of cloth that her own mother was, and cut right from it. Why should he do research?

"Nothing that I am is designed to make my mother proud," Eloise said, lifting the champagne to her lips. She looked somewhat surprised when the liquid touched her tongue, and he had to confess that either she was a very good actress, or she truly did not often drink.

He was leaning toward her being a very good actress.

"You know how I feel about her," she said softly.

"I thought I did," he said. "But then, I thought I knew you once."

"I never lied, Vincenzo," she said softly, "whatever you might think."

Her eyes were sincere, and this woman sitting in front of him was…

She was not a surprise.

He had created a fictional Eloise in his head because he had wanted to banish all images of the girl he'd once cared for. Had fashioned her into a mold that would make it easy for him to do that. The same mold as her mother.

But if…

If that night, when she'd kissed him. When he'd held her in his arms for a brief moment before sending her away. If he'd imagined who she might become then, he might have seen the person sitting before him.

He hardened himself. For that was a nice thought, but it was all it was. And he knew well how adept some people could be at fooling the masses, and while he had never fancied himself a member of said masses, he knew that Eloise had tricked him once.

He would not allow her to do it again.

"Lies. Truth. None of it matters now."

"It does to me. I don't enjoy sitting with a man who despises me."

"And yet you have agreed to help me. Why would

you do that if you did not wish to return? Why would you do that if you hate me so?"

"I never said I hated you."

His gaze flickered over her, and her cheeks went pink. His blood warmed. "You should."

"Why? Because you hate me? It doesn't work that way."

"I don't hate you, Eloise. If I hated you, I would have done this without you. What I want to know is the manner of your investment in this."

"I have always thought…" She did not look at him; rather she looked over the top of her champagne glass, straight ahead at the back wall of the plane. "We were not so different, Vincenzo. Your father does not care for you any more than my mother cares for me. We are simply caught in the middle of their games. That was why we were able to become friends. Me, a girl from America who didn't even know princes existed outside of fairy tales…and you, the heir to a country. I care for you. It was only that friendship that carried me through. And so I would happily act as your friend now."

The word cut him.

"*Friends*," he repeated.

"Please don't embarrass me," she said, her voice going tight. "Please do not bring it up."

It was anger that drove him now and he felt a sick shame with it. He was better than this. Better than the sort of man who was led around by emotion. Better than his father. And yet he couldn't help himself. "Are you speaking of our last encounter, when I sent you away, or of the night when you were eighteen and you…"

He looked up at his stewardess and gestured for her to leave the room. The woman stared for a moment, then caught herself before retreating to the staff's quarters.

He turned his eyes back on Eloise. "The night when you threw yourself at me with quite the brazen…"

"Oh, yes, I was so very brazen," she said, her tone tart. "Kissing you with all that experience of mine and crying and saying I loved you."

In some ways he was surprised that she even remembered it. And he had to wonder what the purpose of bringing it up now was. But he would've brought it up, she was correct. So perhaps using it against him before he could use it against her was the game.

"It is a vague memory for me," he lied. "Any number of women fling themselves at me, Eloise, and you were simply one more."

She looked wounded, and for a moment he regretted landing the blow. For the pain in her blue eyes did not seem to be manufactured. And if it was, she had manufactured it quite quickly and had managed to cover any sort of shock she might be experiencing.

"All for the best, then," Eloise said, taking another sip of champagne. She sat down on the couch, her feet—clad in white sneakers—pressed tightly together, along with her knees. Her shoulders seemed to be contracted, as if she was trying to shrink in on herself.

He took the moment to look at her. Really look at her. She had a red handkerchief tied around her head, her blond hair tucked into an old-fashioned-looking roll. She was wearing a bright blue button-up shirt knotted at the waist, trimmed to accentuate her full bust and small midsection. The pants she wore were red like her handkerchief and cuffed at the ankles. She looked like a 1950s pinup waiting to happen. All he would have to do was unfasten the top few buttons of her blouse. No doubt her cleavage was abundant. It was a shame that it was done up all the way so that he could not see it.

And it bothered him. Bothered him that he was sitting there counting buttons and trying to gauge how many it would take to reveal her glory.

She was subtle. She had no makeup on today, but her skin was bright and clear, her eyes that pale cornflower blue. Her lips a pale pink, full, the top lip rounded and slightly fuller than the bottom.

He remembered that.

The color of her eyes, the shape of her mouth. But her face had been much narrower then, while now it had rounded. Her cheekbones were high and elegant, but not razor-sharp, and he found the new arrangement of her features pleasing.

He could not think of any man who would not.

The truth was, she was an entirely lovely creature. He had been prepared to resist the creature he had made her into in his mind. He had not been prepared to confront the woman she was.

But it might be a ruse. "Tell me, what are your current entanglements?"

"My...entanglements?"

"Lovers. Employers."

"I'm a horticulturist. Though I am between jobs at the moment."

"Between jobs?" He could not work out if she was speaking euphemistically or not.

"I was working at a large estate up until last month.

But the owner sold it, and…" She closed her eyes, as if the memory was painful. "The greenhouse that I was in charge of curating was done away with. It was quite a lot of work. Had some beautiful mature plants, all gone now so that someone can have a new pool area. I had enough money that it was not immediately necessary for me to get more work. So I've been considering starting my own nursery. I haven't gotten that far. But it is something that I'm in the early stages of planning."

He could not help himself. He wanted to know… Why? He kept trying to remember if she had particularly liked plants and flowers back when he'd known her and could not recall that she had. "And why horticulture? Why are you invested in that particular vocation?"

"I just like the idea of growing things. Of leaving the world a little bit more beautiful. I actually don't want to be notorious. And you know… It doesn't really matter if I am. For I will just fade back into obscurity. I will go back to the garden. It doesn't matter to me. I want to be able to live on my own terms. I know you might not believe that, but it's true. My mother controlled everything in my life. What I thought, what I did, what I ate, what I wore. And I like being myself. I like leaving the world fuller, rather than simply taking from it."

She was not going to answer his question, then. And he had to wonder if the person who owned the manor house she had previously worked at had also been her paramour. That would make sense. That she had not simply lost her job, but been removed as his mistress. Perhaps she was in between lovers then.

She seemed to have little concern for money, and

while he knew that she had been given some money by his father, and she had presumably been earning money at her job, he could not credit that it was enough to truly support her.

Especially not in the lifestyle she would…

But he was forced to look at her again and ask himself what lifestyle she was truly paying for.

Well, he did not need to itemize the cost of her clothing. She was in an outfit that she had been gardening in. That was not a true reflection of her life. And just because the woman liked to dig in the dirt did not make her truly unexpected.

"Are you finished with your champagne?"

"I suppose."

"Let us go for your fitting."

"My fitting?"

"I told you, that you would be fitted here on the plane."

"Oh, yes, but I…"

"All of the clothing is in my study. Along with the seamstress."

"I don't even know what to say to that. That feels a great amount of excess. Being fitted thirty thousand feet above ground."

"We have not reached cruising altitude yet."

She blinked. "Indeed."

He walked over to where she was and extended a hand. She looked up at him as though it were a shark.

"You must be comfortable with my touch."

Her eyes went round. "Must I?" He had the distinct feeling he was being mocked.

"You must *appear* to be," he amended.

She squinted, then took hold of his hand, and the

contact of her soft skin against his was like a punch to the gut.

How he would like her hands to be wrapped around other parts of him.

It would be helpful if he could think of her as dowdy. But he was a man with far too much experience of the female form to look at that outfit and not understand exactly what she would look like naked. How she would appear when the layers of her clothing were stripped away.

She was not dowdy at all.

She was the embodiment of sex. Sex he would like to have. Quite a lot. And that outraged him.

He'd thought he would be immune to her now.

He was... He held on to his memories of that moment finding out she'd been with his father so that he would keep her at a distance. It should not be so easy for her to make him want her.

It should not be so easy for him to forget.

When they walked into the study, her eyes went even rounder than they'd been previously. "This is incredible," she said. "I had no idea that a private plane could be quite so... It is a palace unto itself."

"Yes. As I told you. I spend quite a bit of time flying."

There was a rack of gowns and a smooth, immaculate man ready to do his bidding.

He went to his desk and sat on the chair. "Begin," he said.

"You cannot possibly... You cannot possibly expect me to undress in front of you," she said.

Why was she so modest now? She had climbed into bed with him once, her thighs on either side of his as she'd kissed him earnestly, and now she didn't want to undress in front of him?

Do you want her to?

"You may lower your dander," he said. "There is a screen for you to step behind. But I will be approving each and every gown. So I will be here the entire time."

It turned out that the entire experience was an exercise in torture.

He had not intended to dress her subtly. And so the gowns that had been provided by Luciano were not subtle in the least. Gold and glittering, bright and tight. Creative shapes designed to accentuate curves, and cutouts that flirted dangerously with revealing parts of her body that only a lover should see.

"I..." She looked at herself in the mirror, and her face contorted with shock. She was currently in a gold gown with a deep V at the front, exposing the rounded curves of her breasts. The back was low, and the vision of the two dimples that he knew were just above her rounded ass was making him hard.

"This is far too revealing," she said.

"Are you uncomfortable?"

"I am."

"Do you think you look bad?" He felt the need to comfort her, and he could not untangle his feelings for her.

He was not a man who trafficked in uncertainty, and he hated this. Not enough to be cruel to her. Not now.

"Women of my shape do not wear dresses like this," she said.

"And why is that?"

"I am a strong breeze away from a wardrobe malfunction, and that's just the first issue. The second is that it's… Clearly made for a runway-ready sort of woman, and not…"

"Runways are changing, or have you not noticed?"

Her cheeks went pink and he wondered if he had said the wrong thing. In his opinion, the change was welcome. He was the sort of man who liked variety. To him, these changes were only good.

"It does not matter if they are changing," she said. "I would still be a novelty, not the accepted. I will be in the same room as my mother and I will look like…"

"You will look like what?" She had been confident and happy when he'd taken her from the garden, freely offering herself to his revenge, and he could see her changing before his eyes.

As if the closer they were to her mother, the further she was from her confidence.

When he'd decided she was a liar, he'd decided everything about her was a lie.

Their friendship. Her relationship with her mother. Her feelings for him.

What if some of it were true?

"I think it's fierce," Luciano said. "For what it's worth."

Eloise grimaced. "I… I appreciate that. But I do not feel fierce. I feel… Round."

"You say that as if it is a bad shape," Vincenzo said.

"Do not play dense," she said. "When I think you know that hip bones are much more de rigueur than hips."

"I understand that it is your mother's preference, but that has little bearing on the truth of actual beauty. It is not so narrow, I feel. And who are you trying to impress? Your mother? As you said yourself, she recognizes only a very specific thing. But I wish to show you to the world, and I guarantee you that your sex appeal will not be missed."

"People will compare. And they will comment."

"Perhaps. But I am your lover," he said, the words making his gut tight, increasing the flow of blood down south of his belt. "And I find you glorious. If Luciano were not here I would strip the gown off you and lay you down on the floor."

He intended it to be a performance. Establishing the connection between the two of them, but it felt all too real. It felt all too much like the truth.

He drew closer to her, and he had not meant to. She smelled...

The same.

And it took him back.

To the girl she'd been.

Worse still, to the boy he'd been.

He leaned in, as he traced a line from her neck down across her bare shoulder. And he whispered in her ear.

"And I would have you screaming my name inside of thirty seconds. That is what I see when I look at that dress."

And he forgot. Why they were here. And that it was now.

And that he was supposed to keep her at arm's length.

There was no distance between them now.

She turned scarlet. From the roots of her pale hair, down all the glorious curves of her body.

"I just... I just wonder if there is perhaps a more subtle way to accomplish this."

"I have an idea," Luciano said.

He took an emerald green gown off the rack and handed it to her.

She went behind the screen, and when she appeared, she was somehow all the more maddeningly beautiful. The gown was crushed velvet, off the shoulder and conformed itself to her curves, while not revealing overly much skin. It was tight all the way down to her knees, then flared out around her feet.

"This I like," she said.

"It will do," he said, keeping himself away from her this time. "But fit the gold one to her as well. And use the rest of the measurements to fit some casual clothes too."

"I like a retro style," she said.

"I have a good handle on your style based on the outfit you had on today," said Luciano. "The gowns will be ready by the time we land, and the rest of the items should be there within a day. I will call ahead to my studio and have my staff get to work."

"Thank you," he said. "You may get dressed," he said to Eloise.

"Oh, may I?"

"Yes."

"May I also use the bathroom?" she asked, disappearing behind the screen.

"You do not need a hall pass."

"It's only that I thought I might."

She appeared a moment later, dressed again, but still tying her shirt up at her waist, and he wanted to round the desk, step toward her, hook his finger through the knot and undo it. Then undo all the rest of the buttons. Sadly, Luciano was still in the room, and also, he was never going to touch her in that way. Not for purposes other than performance.

It is perverse, he thought. And in some ways… Expected. He was a royalty, and very little was forbidden to him. So of course the luscious apple he should not take a bite of was the one he craved most of all.

She scampered out of the room then, and he thanked Luciano before leaving. She had used the closest bathroom, and he waited outside the door for her to appear. When she did, she nearly ran into him, her cheeks going red.

"Let me show you to your room. Where I think you will find the lavatory much more to your liking."

"I don't see anything wrong with that one."

"You might like a bath," he said.

"Oh, might I?"

"Yes. Are you intent upon being angry about all that I offer? May I remind you that you did come of your own accord."

"Yes," she said. "I did. Because I could not stand the idea of someone controlling my life yet again. It is something I cannot bear. And so I made the decision to come back with you. It was easier. It was better. Better than… Better than the alternative."

Guilt, which was an emotion he was entirely unaccustomed to, lanced his gut. She was tearing him in pieces. With memories. Memories that challenged his certainty.

And with herself. All that she was, and no matter what he knew about her, it didn't seem to matter. Didn't seem to keep him from wanting her.

He gritted his teeth and gestured down the hall, toward a glossy mahogany door. "This is you," he said.

He opened the door to reveal an expansive suite with a large, plush bed. He knew for a fact that the bathroom was ornate and very comfortable. He also knew that if he stepped in there, he would be tempted to invite her to draw a bath that included him.

And he did not like this feeling of being off-kilter. He could not afford it. Not now.

"I shall perhaps need you to explain to me what it is you expect," she said.

She looked vulnerable. She looked young. She looked like everything he knew she was not. And she absolutely did not look like her mother's daughter.

Was this how it happened? Was this how a woman sank her claws deeply into a man?

No, that isn't fair and you know it. Her mother's claws were not sunk into his father any more than his fangs were not sunk into her. They were together of their own accord, toxic of their own accord, and while Cressida St George had played havoc with his mother, his father happily engaged in hurting both of them.

"Rest," he said. "It is five hours yet before we land in Arista. We will go to my apartment first. Before we go to the palace."

She nodded. "All right."

"And we will engage the press."

She looked frightened, and he had to wonder if it was genuine. It seemed so.

"You needn't worry about instructions," he said. "You need only to follow me, and do as I say. And look at me as if I am the sun, the moon and the stars." And then he could not help himself. "You did so once."

"Yes," she said, her eyes suddenly filling with tears. "But that night you barely remember knocked me out of the sky. And I have not tried to reach for the stars or the moon since."

Then she closed the door in his face and left him to wonder why his chest hurt.

CHAPTER FOUR

SHE HAD A BATH, but she did not rest—it was impossible to rest, knowing that she was landing in Arista. Impossible to relax after what had happened...

She had made a fool of herself. She had exposed all of her insecurities. She was far too honest. She had reminded him of that night between them, one he said he didn't remember. *He didn't remember.*

She had loved Vincenzo Moretti more than anything. And she had never thought she would ever want a man. She hated the way her mother was with her lovers, and even though she'd only been six when they'd moved to Arista and her mother had taken up with the King, she could remember the men before.

She had told herself she would never let herself fall apart over men. That she would never depend on them. Vincenzo had always felt different.

She'd seen him as a friend first. A protector. By the time she was fifteen, her heart felt like it was going to pound out of her chest when he was near. When he went away to school, coming back so rarely, she'd thought she would die.

She'd had no one, those lonely years, and she had lived for the times he would come home to visit. Which was why, when he graduated and came to Arista for a visit, she had decided to give herself to him.

To make sure he knew how much she loved him.

She'd been eighteen and, in spite of everything, full of hope.

She'd borrowed one of her mother's dresses that she'd never even worn. Tight and sexy and hopefully something that would capture his attention.

She'd sneaked into his room at midnight and he'd been in bed, shirtless. He'd been so beautiful her heart had caught in her throat. She'd nearly wept.

"What are you doing here, Eloise?"

"I had to see you."

"You could have waited until breakfast."

"No. No, I couldn't."

She'd crossed the room and, with trembling limbs, climbed onto the bed, positioning her body over his. "I... I want you, Vincenzo. I love you."

She leaned down and kissed him. Her first kiss, and it was everything she'd ever wanted. Because it was him.

And for a moment, his hand went around to cradle the back of her head, and he kissed her back. She could feel him growing hard between her legs, and it sent a thrill through her body.

But then suddenly, he was pushing her away.

"Eloise, no. You are too young. You can't know what you want."

"I do know," she said, running her hands down his chest. "You. I want you. I love you."

"You don't know any other men. Go. Go away to school. Go away from here. Kiss other men. And if

*when you come back you think you love me still... You
will always be my Eloise."*

But she wasn't. She hadn't been.

He'd been so quick to believe the lies his mother
had told about her, that the press had told about her.

"Go away from here, Eloise."

*His face was like stone. "Vincenzo, I didn't... I
would never."*

*"Take this." He held a check out in front of her.
"Go and do not return."*

In the end, she thought perhaps she wasn't lovable.

Now of course she realized that was not the case.
And she could not define herself by what the people
around her could not or would not give. It was not her
responsibility. She could only be true to herself. She
could not take on the baggage of others; she could not
make it about her. She'd had therapy. She knew that.
But something about being around him made her feel
eighteen again. Desperate to perform and do the right
thing, and she hated it.

And the way he had looked at her...

Like he thought she was beautiful now. But she
couldn't understand that. She didn't understand any
of this.

When she went back into the bedroom, she was sure
she was going to have to dress in the outfit she had
come in, but to her surprise, a pair of soft white linen
trousers and a white linen top had been laid out for her,
along with a white lace bra and matching underwear.

It looked positively bridal, which was ridiculous,
because he wasn't even pretending that they were to
be married.

No, he was aiming to parade her before the world

as his mistress. And she knew what he really thought of that. What that meant to him. It was exactly what he saw her mother as. And she did understand. They had both been traumatized by aspects of their lives, and she knew that.

It was just that… It was just that she despised how small this made her feel. It wasn't even her fear of the press. She had no remaining fear of them in truth. They'd already skinned her alive when she'd been a younger, more tender person.

It was how much it reminded her of being that needy, lonely girl, who wanted so badly to be whatever he might have wanted her to be. To be whatever her mother might've wanted her to be. She had become who Eloise wanted to be, and she was happy with that. Except…

Well, she had shut down the part of herself that wanted to be seen as attractive by men. The way that her mother was, the way that her mother had always been in those relationships concerned her. And what had happened with Vincenzo had worried her even more. Had convinced her that she could not be trusted to enter into that sort of relationship. And this only confirmed it, really. Because she was back to being insecure, back to feeling uncomfortable, back to being all of the things that she had tried to let go of. She was thinking about her body through the lens of other people, and she had determined to stop that.

Are you thinking about it in terms of other people, or him?

No. He had been… Complimentary.

The memory made her face warm.

There was a stern knock at the door, and she went

to open it. And there he was, resplendent in a fresh dark suit, his black hair pushed off his forehead, his expression enigmatic.

He was far too much, this man. Perhaps he always had been. At any rate, he was far too much for her.

"We will begin our descent soon," he said. "Come and sit."

Her stomach tightened up, butterflies swirling around. Arista.

She had lived in America until she was six, until her mother had met King Giovanni Moretti at a party where she had been with another man, and he had been with his wife. Up until then, Eloise had enjoyed a fairly comfortable life with a nanny who had cared a great deal for her.

She had not seen her mother often, but when she had it had been nice enough.

Then the King had brought them to Arista to live. And everything had changed. She had been turned into a secret. Isolated. Kept separate from the rest of the world. From friends. From everything.

Her palms felt sweaty. She had never thought that she would return to Arista. Being confident and healthy and happy was easy in Virginia. It was easy in the new life she had carved out for herself, which consisted of quiet evenings at home, gardening and monthly meetings with her flower arranging club. She had made for herself a quiet life with people who didn't know who she was. With people who didn't know who her mother was. With people who didn't have any idea what she had been like when she was younger. Where she had been headed.

But now she was going back to the scene of all she

had been created to be, to her mother's barbs and his father's cold indifference.

Two yawning, empty corridors that recognized her loneliness and amplified it. Created an echo in her chest that expanded throughout her entire body.

She hated it. And she hated the idea of it even more.

But what if he's right? What if this is your chance at redemption? Revenge.

"You do not look well," Vincenzo commented as she sat down on the leather sofa.

"I am not," she said, shaking off her uncomfortable thoughts. "I don't enjoy the prospect of going back to Arista."

"You said you'd had therapy."

"I did. And it has all served me well far away from my mother and the site of all my trauma."

"Trauma?"

He asked the question with a faint hint of mocking to his tone, but she was past caring what he thought about anything. It didn't matter.

"Yes, I found life at the palace quite traumatic. Did you not?"

"I do not think in terms of my own trauma," he said, lifting his glass of whiskey to his lips.

"Can you say that you were happy there? Because it seems that you were away more than you were ever there. Unusual for the heir to the throne, don't you agree?"

"I will never take the throne. And I will never have an heir. It dies with me. It will be turned over to the people."

"Your father will be devastated by that."

His grin took on a wicked curve. "I hope so."

"Revenge," she said. "You did mention that."

"Do you not take any joy in this?"

She frowned, looking down at her hands. "I don't know. If I'm being honest with you, I don't know. I came with you, so maybe I… Maybe a part of me wants to hurt both of them. Maybe. I would hope not. I would hope that…"

"You would hope that you were somehow more enlightened than me while offering to come back as my friend and help me in my endeavors?"

"Yes," she said. "I'm sorry if you don't understand that. I'm not sure that I understand much of anything in regard to my own feelings right now."

"Something I never suffer from. But then, I believe that is because I am honest. I am honest about what I want. I am honest about who I am."

"And you don't believe that I am?"

He stared at her for a long moment. "You are many things, *cara*. I do not believe that honest is one of them. But you are beautiful. And you will make an excellent weapon to be wielded against my father, and that is all I require of you."

With those words settled like a brand in her breast, the plane touched down.

They were ushered into a car, and they began to drive on the narrow, cobbled roads that felt like a distant dream to her now.

A part of a person that she no longer acknowledged. Eloise St. George.

Who wanted to be beautiful, like her mother. Who wanted to be special. Who just wanted, and felt so hungry for whatever might make her feel whole. Feel real.

The approval of her mother.

The attention of Prince Vincenzo.

That poor girl. She did not know what love was.

And you do now?

She knew what it was not. She would accept that as progress.

"I never spent much time in the city," she said, looking out the window as they moved away from the small brick buildings into modern skyscrapers. The business district in Arista was as bright and modern as any other major city. It was only around the edges that the ancient charm of the place was still preserved.

"Of course, you wouldn't have."

"We would travel with your father's staff. We spent most of our time in Paris. I haven't been back to Paris since I was fifteen."

"Why not?"

"I told you. I have been living and working in Virginia. Do you think that I have the funds to be a jet-setter? I took the check you gave me and I made something from it. But it was hardly enough to make me independently wealthy for life. I am on a budget."

"And your many benefactors since have not flown you off to Europe?"

"My many benefactors? Do you mean my employers? Because no."

"No, I mean your *lovers*."

"What makes you assume I have lovers paying for my life?"

He stared at her for a long moment. "Are you telling me that you don't?"

The way he looked at her made her stomach feel tight.

"I'm not telling you anything," she said. "I am asking you a question. What about anything that I am, or any of my life you have seen, suggests to you that I have an endless array of sugar daddies trotting me about the globe?"

"It is only that your mother…"

"Yes. My mother. We are not the same. We don't look the same. We don't act the same. My mother has spent the last twenty years with your father. Living a strange half-life. They cheat on each other, of course. My mother takes other lovers. But still, she is a creature of the night, wandering around European cities after dark because she can never be connected to him. Because she cannot have the notoriety she would prefer. Because she must trade that in for money. The most glittering, celebrated, reviled socialite America had to offer way back at the turn of the millennium, and now she is obscure. That's who you think I am? An undercover piece on the side? Managing to stay out of the tabloids because I have taken up with someone so lofty that I am a secret? Or perhaps you imagine I am more of a common tart, and none of the men that I associate with need to be quite so careful of the press?"

It wasn't the first time people had assumed things about her because of her mother. There was no excuse for it, ever. She hated it. It made her feel small and grim and sad.

"You forget," he said, his tone dark. "You forget what we all know to be true."

"You think I'm a whore. Go ahead and say it."

It wouldn't be the first time one of the Moretti men had accused her of such.

"I assumed you had continued on in the lifestyle you'd begun at the palace."

"Because you think you know the truth? Because of something your mother told you? As if she had any reason to…as if she would have ever wanted you to like me, Vincenzo."

"Be careful what you accuse my mother of," he said, his teeth gritted.

"Why? She was not careful of what she accused me of. And even if it were true? Are you better than me?"

"Eloise…"

"No. Admit it. You are just like your father. Just like all those sorts of men. You think you can judge a woman by the way she dresses, and you think that you know her moral character based on the amount of men you think she might've slept with. That doesn't teach you anything about a woman. How many women have you slept with? And were they wealthy? You have paraded all around the globe with great glittering creatures on your arm. What am I to learn about your morals from that?"

He laughed. Bitter and hard-edged. "You mistake me. I never said that I was better. I never said that I was better than my father. Or than you. I am simply different. I hardly lead a life worth canonizing. Nor do I pretend to. I am steeped in all manner of immorality, and I have never acted differently. And that is the only real difference between myself and my father. That and the fact that my liaisons affect only me. And I will not seek to flex my power over my people. That, perhaps, is my only real redeeming feature. I am not power hungry. I have power. I find that with it, I am able to ignore any appetite for more. I have money. I am not afraid of losing my status. I know who I am. My father is small. He fears being deposed. He fears being unmasked. He fears that in the end all that he is, all that he cares for and all that he pretends to be will be unveiled. Will be destroyed. I will see that it is. As for me? There are no surprises. There is nothing to destroy. I have been working to restore Arista to its former glory behind the scenes for many years. I will give all that must be given to the country and its people. And yes, I will continue on as a whoremonger. But I will not enforce morality that I do not myself believe in upon my people. I will not put on a mask. You mistake me. I do not care what you do. I do not care who you have slept with. And I do not care who is bankrolling your life. Only that I do not wish to be lied to."

"You have not earned the right to my honesty," she said, her chest feeling tight. "I don't like to give people access to my secrets."

"And why is that?"

"Other than the fact the press already tried to make me a public commodity? Somewhere in the middle of your secrets, all your insecurities are buried. And what do people love more than anything else? To use those against you. I will not expose myself to such a thing. I will not make myself an easy target. I refuse. So I will not prostrate myself for the enjoyment of any man. Least of all you."

"So long as you're a good actress, I suppose in the end it doesn't matter."

He shifted, and she smelled the spicy scent of him. Her entire being fluttered.

The real concern was that she would not have to pretend at all to act as if she was attracted to him. The real concern was that she wore it with obvious ease.

The real concern was that anyone might know.

But most especially, him.

The car pulled up to the front of a grand building made entirely of glass and steel. The windows reflected the mountains in the distance, and the intensity and magnitude of it sucked the breath straight from her lungs. This was his palace. A palace so unlike the traditional palace where they would go later tonight. The deliberate flex of his distinct power was obvious here. He was younger. A man who had earned his money, not a man who had taken it out of the pockets of the citizens of Arista. They got out of the car, and the doors to the building opened automatically. The lobby was stunning. All modern architecture that gleamed with gold rather than the expected chrome. It was not ornate or tacky, rather there was something like fire about it that made the entire place burn hotter.

The doors to the elevator had that same gold, brushed bright. He put his fingerprint on a panel, and the doors opened.

"This is my private elevator. It is the only way to get to my suite of rooms."

"And so you have made yourself the King of Arista after all."

The back wall to the elevator faced the city, and as they rose high above the buildings, looking out over the expansive view, she could see what she said being proven. He had no rejoinder, because there was nothing to be said.

"All of our things will be sent soon. You may have a rest."

"I should like some food."

"We are having dinner at the palace."

"Yes. But by then I will have a stomach full of anxiety, and I would like something to eat."

He gestured across the barren, modern space. The floors were black, the counter cement. But yet again the details in gold. "Be my guest."

She walked into the kitchen area and opened the refrigerator. She noted that the handles were also gold.

Inside were fruit platters. Meat and cheese trays. It was as if appetizers for an upcoming party had been prepared. And she took them all out, happily examining them.

"These will do nicely."

She put them on the countertop and uncovered them, scrounging until she found a plate and filling it with a generous portion from each tray. Then she hunted around until she found sparkling water and poured herself a glass.

And all the while he watched her, leaning back against the island, his palms pressed down into the surface, his forearms flexed.

"I have staff for that," he said.

"Well, I was able to dish myself an entire plate without you summoning anyone, so I think it all worked out in the end."

She looked around and saw that there was no dining table in the space. So she took it all to the low, leather couch that faced floor-to-ceiling windows that overlooked the city. She sat down and popped a grape into her mouth. "This is quite nice."

"Thank you," he said, dryly.

"I always try to be polite."

"What game are you playing?"

"I'm not playing a game. I feel that you are a game

player, and therefore cannot figure out what I'm doing. And what confuses you most is that I'm not doing anything. I'm not. I am not doing anything, and I do not wish to be doing anything, and I am no threat to you at all. I am simply me. I have changed. I was only ever the Eloise that you knew because of my mother. And I have worked very hard to become the Eloise that I am. Stop looking for the snake in the grass. It isn't me."

"How do I…"

"You came to me, Vincenzo. If you had not, I would never have come back here."

"You acquiesced easily."

"Yes. Because I meant what I said. If you need help, I wish to help you. You are trying to rescue your country, at least, as far as I can tell, reading between the lines of your grim threats. I respect that. Your father has done a terrible job with this country, and it sounds to me as if you are the only person willing to do something to save it. And the fact that you are willing to turn the power over to the people… For all your bluster I do believe that you are well-meaning. I do believe that you want to do the right thing by your country. The palace staff were always kind to me. Regardless of the drama happening between your parents and my mother. They were always so very kind. I feel… Even though it was isolated, Arista has been my home for as long as anywhere else. It matters to me what you're doing. So I'll help. But I don't want to enrich myself or anything like that." She ate a piece of cheese. "Though, I'm not averse to enjoying some nice food."

And for his part, he was actually stunned into silence, which was really quite something.

But it wasn't long after that her clothing arrived.

And she was whisked off to change yet again. Wrapped in that brilliant green gown that was now custom fitted to her curves.

And when they exited the hotel, the press was there. Flashbulbs went off, the melee surrounding them intense.

"Is that Eloise St. George? Your father's mistress? Where has she been hiding?" The press volleyed questions, a pounding insistent drum, and it took her back.

All the way to when she'd been eighteen and heartbroken, tender in her feelings for Vincenzo still and somehow being cast as a whore in a play with his father on the world stage.

Her heart was pounding so hard she thought she might vomit.

"Yes, it is Eloise St. George," he answered. "And you know the old stories about her. But you do not know the truth of how she came to be at the palace. Her mother has lived as my father's mistress since Eloise was six. Eloise and I have known each other since childhood. I, like many of you, blamed her for my father's behavior at the time. She was eighteen. My father was a king. I am not blameless, but the press hounded her, treated her as the villain in the piece. We are here to unmask the real villain."

"Your father's mistress?" one of the men asked. "It was reported that the indiscretion with Eloise St George was the only…"

"You will find that my father is economical with the truth as it suits. That the King has not held himself to the same standards that he holds his people. You may be quite shocked to learn just how deeply my father has let down Arista."

"Do you have proof?" another reporter asked.

"I have lots of proof," he said. "I will happily give it to you. But now I must take Eloise to dine at the palace. It has been a long time coming for her. I am here to tell my father that he is ruined."

He grinned then, the smile of a predator that made her shiver down to her bones. "And believe me when I tell you, you will have all the information you need to ensure the ruination is complete."

CHAPTER FIVE

HE ALMOST FELT sorry for Eloise. Almost. She was pale and drawn and quiet as the limousine inched ever closer to the palace.

She had been nearly silent ever since the reporters had ambushed them outside his penthouse. And it had only become more pronounced with each passing moment since. He could feel her dread, feel it radiating off her.

"You are nervous?" he asked.

For the first time he felt… He had miscalculated. She was hurt by all of this. More distressed than he'd assumed. He had thought her hard. He had made assumptions about who and what she was based on his belief in her guilt when it came to her relationship with his father.

And he'd let that form his image of her all these years. Anything to replace the one he'd had back when they'd been young.

They arrived at the palace, and he felt his own stomach tense. He felt her entire body go rigid.

He had not been back here since his mother had died. And it had been her death a year ago that had triggered this plan.

He'd come only to say goodbye to her, and he could still remember the stale feeling in the room. All the bitterness from so many years steeped in it.

It lingered. In the air. In him.

They got out of the car at the front entrance, the grand double doors opening slowly. The palace was a gleaming white, a testament to the unending purity of its ruler. The spires were gold. It was not an accident that in his own building he employed the use of concrete and gold. An echo of what his father was, and the lack of pretense with which Vincenzo presented himself.

Symbolism that no one would ever appreciate except for him, he had a feeling. And yet, appreciate it he did.

He took her arm, and the two of them stood at the threshold to the palace, and suddenly she began to… Laugh.

"What?"

"Oh, I just… This would've been my dream. When I was sixteen years old. Arriving at the palace with you. I would've felt… I would have felt like the luckiest girl in the world."

"Well, you are quite undermining my presence, at the moment. As it is intended to be a bit more ominous. Giggling is hardly the tone we want to set."

"What you're sharing with the world is ominous enough. We have to belabor it by acting like a funeral procession?"

"Did you want it to be a family reunion?"

"Hardly." She made a strange, strangled sound. "We are practically stepsiblings."

He nearly recoiled. "We are nothing of the kind. Our parents are not married."

They stopped and looked at each other for a beat. And he felt a burn start in his blood. But it wasn't just that. It was an unexpected solidarity.

He had thought to force her here, but she had offered to come.

As a friend.

Even after everything, she had offered that.

They were announced and led through the grand corridors of the palace, on through to the great dining hall, where his father was seated at the head of the table and there, at his right-hand side was Eloise's mother.

She looked up, her eyes like glittering bright jewels. Her fingernails were long, red claws.

She had not been permitted to sit in that position when his mother had still been living. And he could see that she took a great joy in flaunting this change in his face.

"How wonderful that you could join us this evening," she said, acting the part of hostess.

It made his stomach curdle.

"Of course."

"The other guests will arrive shortly," his father said.

And it took a moment. Just a moment. For Eloise's mother to recognize her. And a moment longer for his father to do the same.

"What is this?" his father asked.

"Oh," he said. "Eloise is here. As my mistress. I find that I have taken a great liking to her of late."

Her mother looked at her daughter with a dismissive sneer.

"That is impossible," she said. "She has gained at least two stone since she was here last. I should think that a man of your pedigree would have better taste."

What surprised him, as much as the moment of camaraderie he'd felt with her outside, was the rage he felt toward her mother just then. Had he not himself been hard on her when he'd first encountered her again? He knew he had been. But it was not this.

The way she looked at Eloise...

She hated her, he realized. Because she was young and beautiful, whatever the woman said. Her own daughter outshone her and she couldn't stand it.

"Oh, my taste is impeccable," he said. "And I find each and every curve of her body to my liking. More than that, I have decided to go public with it. And with our relationship."

"All the guests here tonight are well aware of the nature of my relationship with Cressida St. George. It is my inner circle."

"I'm sure, Father," he said. "But your cronies are one thing—the public is quite another. I have already spoken with the press. Of course, they all remember the one sin you were ever caught in. But you made sure to assassinate her character. To make it seem as if you were only a victim. But I have evidence to the contrary, and I will make sure the world knows. Not only of your sexual indiscretion but of all you have stolen from Arista. You have defrauded this land, and its people, and I intend to see your wrongs exposed, and made right."

His father began to turn a particular shade of purple, but it was then that the other dignitaries and diplomats began to line the table.

Eloise, for her part, looked subdued. Then as he made conversation with the men around him, making provocative statements about the economy of Arista, he felt her shrinking beside him.

And again the urge to protect her was strong. He could not explain it; he was here on a mission that concerned his country, his revenge. And yet he felt consumed by her. And that had not been part of the plan.

Tonight, he decided he would say no more to his father. Tonight, he made it his mission to speak only to the other men present. And he also left the table at the precise moment all of the other guests did. His father tried to catch him.

"Eloise and I are returning to my flat," he said. "I rather would like an early night with her. Surely that's something you can understand."

"You were raised with her," he said.

"And you took advantage of her," Vincenzo said. "Which I will not do. But you did that often, didn't you?"

"You will not make these things public," his father said.

"I already have."

But then his father reached out and grabbed Eloise by the arm. "If you wish to play the whore..."

"I never did," she said. "And you know it. But you let the story go out as it did because you thought it such a great distraction to the reality of what you were doing. I understand that now. That my image, my body, was something you could trade on. A way to try and play the victim. Someone got too close to the truth, but they were just wrong enough that being handed me as a scandal kept them from my mother."

Vincenzo only stood, frozen. There were few times in his life when he had felt that he might be outside his understanding. Once had been when Eloise had kissed him, and he'd sent her away in spite of a roaring need to drive himself inside her.

And now.

He'd had no idea. He never had.

"I didn't know why I came back," she said, her voice sounding strangely detached now. "But I realize now. It was to have a front seat at your deposition. You destroyed me for all the world to see, but I refused to let that be the last word. It will be mine. The last word will be mine. You could not force me to be your mistress, you could not shame me into vanishing and you will not cow me into silence. You are a twisted, perverse old man, and you may have made my mother your puppet, but you never succeeded in making me anything. Neither did you, Mother," she said, looking her mother in the eye. "All that I am, I am because of myself."

She turned then, walking out of the ballroom. He stood for a moment and realized that his place was with her for now. For had he not brought her here? Was her distress, her pain not his fault?

He had believed a lie for years. He had been his father's pawn much the same as anyone else, and it galled as much as the guilt that now assaulted him.

"Eloise," he said, following her. "Tell me."

"Now you want to know? You should have always known, Vincenzo. You of all people should have always known."

"How?" he asked, and yet he felt his failure like a howling beast inside his lungs.

"You knew me."

"I thought I did. But then you kissed me."

"And that made me a whore?"

"No," he said. "You said you loved me. I thought

anyone who loved me… I could not believe it. I could much more easily believe you were using me all along."

In those words was a sadness he never wanted to examine.

"I was never using you," she said, unshed tears in her eyes.

"Eloise…"

"After all of that I just wanted to start over. I never wanted to be here again. I never wanted any of this. I thought… I thought I could just put it behind me."

"But you came with me. When I asked. You came with me."

Her eyes glittered. "Yes. I did. I thought I was fine. I thought therapy fixed all of this but… I'm angry. I am angry. My mother made me hate my body—your father made me afraid of it."

And for the first time, true sympathy curled inside him. Not just the first time he had ever felt sympathy for her. Possibly the first time he had ever felt sympathy for anyone.

And he felt a black sort of blinding rage at his father that was different than the rage he had carried around inside him all this time. It was different.

They went back to the penthouse, and when they walked inside, he looked at her silhouette against the city lights below.

"Are you all right to continue?"

"I knew the history between myself and your father. Even if you did not."

"He did not ever…"

"No. But I fear that he would have."

"You're very brave, Eloise," he said, the compliment foreign on his lips.

She turned and looked over her shoulder, smiling. Her blond hair cascaded down her back in golden waves, and he had the urge to touch it, but also… In the wake of what she had told him, he felt he ought not to.

"Thank you," she said. "I do not feel brave sometimes. Rather I have chosen to hide myself away, and there are times when I question that. But I am happy. I am content. Is there more to life than that?"

"I am not happy or content," he said. "So I suppose we can debate whether or not there is more than that."

"Indeed." She looked at him for a long moment. "I wanted you," she said. "Please know that. It was not simply manipulation or loneliness. I know that I was too young. But what I felt for you was genuine. That means something to me."

Then she turned and walked into her bedroom, leaving him standing there feeling speechless. And there was nothing half so remarkable as that.

CHAPTER SIX

WELL, SHE HAD done it. She had confronted the King. She had spoken the truth.

She knew the King's behavior wasn't her fault. She knew that it was the kind of man the King was. It had nothing to do with the kind of woman she was. Nothing to do with anything she put off, nothing to do with the shape of her body. There was nothing wrong with her.

But she still felt shame, especially when the King had looked at her last night, and she hated that.

What a strange thing to be back. To be confronted with all these things that she had been convinced she had dealt with on some level. She supposed that she had. She wasn't reduced to a crying mess or anything like that. It was just that she felt… It was just that she felt. And tonight they were to return to the palace for a ball celebrating the five hundredth year of the Moretti Rule.

It was tonight, she knew, that Vincenzo would ensure it all burned.

She knew that because it would be poetic to him. Of that she was certain. This claim that he was going to disrupt the line, he would do it on the anniversary of his family's rule, because he liked the symmetry of it. Because he would like the poetic bent to the justice.

She wasn't sure justice sounded anything like poetry to her.

But it appeased some dark piece of her heart she'd thought long dealt with.

Who didn't want to stand before their abusers and tell them what they thought?

When the news had broken of her supposed relationship with the King she'd been devastated. And she'd lost the one ally she'd thought she had.

Vincenzo.

She had to wonder if, in the end, it was Vincenzo who had hurt her worst of all.

Because she'd never believed in her mother, or his father for that matter.

But she'd believed in him.

She shook off those thoughts and decided on a walk. She went down through the marketplace, away from the center of the city, and found a farmers market. She bought flowers. So many flowers. Enough that her arms were completely full by the time she left. Then she went up to the penthouse—her thumbprint granting her access for the time she was staying there—and began to place flowers in vases on every available surface.

When Vincenzo appeared, he was shirtless. There was sweat rolling down his chest, and his cheekbones were highlighted by slashes of red. "What the hell is this?"

"Oh," she said. "I thought you were… In bed."

"I've been out for a run," he said. "What is this?"

"I thought that some flowers would brighten the place. I love flowers."

He blinked. "I have never had flowers in here."

"You also don't really have any color. This is much nicer, don't you think?"

He shook his head. "I do not think."

"Do not be a beast, Vincenzo," she said, continuing to arrange the flowers.

He took a deep breath and crossed his arms. "I've been thinking about my father," Vincenzo said.

"Yes?"

"He is a bastard."

"No argument from me."

"If you do not wish to participate in this…"

Her fingers stilled, her eyes lifting to his. "Are you asking what I want?"

His expression was grim. "Yes."

Her heart felt tender. She could leave. She could go right now. Forget this was happening in Arista. He could complete his vengeance without her.

"Vincenzo, do you believe me now?"

"Yes," he said, his voice tight. "I am…sorry."

"Have you ever told anyone you're sorry before?"

He looked away. "I have never been sorry before. I am now."

She thought her chest might crack. "I accept your apology."

"Would you like to leave?"

"No," she said. "I might be having difficulty sorting through my feelings on the matter. And I am not entirely certain that I'm… Happy. Or enjoying this, but I do think it needs to be done. And in some ways I think it is good that I'm bearing witness to it. But in the meantime, I would like to collect flowers, and do things to make myself feel more comfortable."

"Of course."

"There is the matter of the gold dress…"

It was so revealing. And she had felt sick over that when he had first put her in it. For a variety of reasons. But now…

She did not want to act out of a sense of fear. Or a sense of shame. She wanted to be… Well, if he thought she was beautiful, then she wanted to be that kind of beautiful. For her. For him.

Maybe she shouldn't want to be beautiful for him. But she did.

Because it was a tender bloom in the center of her, of a girlish fantasy that had been as breathless as it was innocent. Something that she had lost later.

Something that had been tainted thereafter."You are worried about it?"

She was, but she…decided to let it go. "Really, the thing that I'm most worried about is having to dance."

"We do have to dance," he said.

"I figured as much. But we are making a statement, are we not?" She imitated his tone and arched a brow in what she hoped was a decent impression of his arrogant expressions. "We must make a show."

"Are you mocking me?"

"If you have to ask, I'm not doing a very good job."

"No one dares to mock me."

"I dare. And quite handily too. I am sorry if it disagrees with your royal constitution."

"I'm glad to see you are not quite so timid as you were last night."

"I was not timid in the end."

"No," he said, smiling. "You were not."

It was his smile that undid her.

"Shall we practice dancing?"

"No," he said.

"Please?"

"You wish to practice now?"

He gestured to his bare chest, and she could not help but take a visual tour of his body. Glistening and tan, with just the right amount of dark hair sprinkled over his muscles. His pectorals, his abs. She wanted to touch him. And the inclination she felt toward him was quite a bit different than the one she had felt when she was eighteen. For she had imagined gauzy things. Sweet kisses and touches, and him laying her down on the soft mattress. Here she could easily imagine his hot skin. Sweat slicked. She knew his mouth would be firm, and that his whiskers would scratch her face. She could picture him putting his hand between her legs and...

She bit her lip.

Her fantasies had certainly progressed, even if her experience had not.

But she could imagine—vividly—what she wanted from him. She wanted to inhale all that testosterone. She could remember vaguely being concerned about his chest hair back when she had been eighteen. In fact, she had been afraid that she would not like to touch it, which was a problem, as she did want him, she had told herself.

Now she wished to run her hands over his body, chest hair and all. She wanted to lick him. Even sweaty. Maybe most especially sweaty.

The desire was deep, and it was visceral. And she was not ashamed. She wasn't ashamed.

She was a woman. And he was a man. An attractive man, and she wanted him.

Her body was her own. But he could borrow it. And he could use it. She would greatly enjoy that.

"If you wish," she said.

And he took two steps toward her, his dark eyes blazing, and she realized then that he was certain he was calling her bluff. Instead, she took a step toward him and held out her hand. "Let us dance."

He pulled her up against him, and she could feel that his chest was damp through the fabric of her top. He was hard. And just as hot as she had imagined. She put her hand on his bare shoulder, could feel the play of his muscles beneath her fingertips. And he grasped her hand in his. "I have made it no secret that I think you're beautiful."

"It is only our connection that prevents you from finding me... How did you put it? Beddable?"

She was being more bold, more forward than she had ever intended to be.

And she felt... Giddy with it. Not ashamed. Not worried.

"Yes. I believe I did."

A great many words bottled up in her throat. He thought her a victim now, or something close to it. Did that mean he no longer found her beddable? Or did it mean he found her more so because he found her innocent in that way?

She didn't know. And she supposed the only way to find out would be to make an actual move on him. But she stopped herself just short of that.

And instead, tried to focus on what it felt like to be held in his arms. To follow the steady rhythm of the dance. Even though there was no music.

And the absurdity of it all would've made her laugh if she could breathe. But she couldn't.

"You're a very good dancer," she said, her eyes focused on his chest. The golden skin there. The muscle definition. The hair...

"Hazard of my upbringing."

"I didn't learn to dance."

"You seem perfectly competent at it."

"Oh, I am. I used to watch. I used to watch from upstairs. When your family would have balls."

"Your mother went."

"Yes," she said. "But there was... My mother enjoyed the attention. The drama. In a way that I never could. Anyway, it was thought that I would draw attention. The kind they didn't want. The kind they didn't like."

"I've never been able to figure out exactly what manner of sadist my father is. The way that he hurt my mother. And the way that he... The way that he treated yours."

"I think you'll find my mother quite likes being involved in the pain, whether she's dishing it out or taking it."

"That may be. But there is an element to it that I... I can't absolve him of. Not anymore. After knowing what he did to you."

"My mother knew. She is still with him. Do not absolve her simply because you are refocusing your anger. No, your father isn't a good man. There is no disputing that, but my mother is not a victim."

"Perhaps it is possible to be both. The predator and the prey."

She frowned. She wanted only to focus on him. On his body, on his beauty. She wanted to focus on the warmth of his body, the strength of his hold. The fantasy inherent in this moment, and not the reality of their lives. Never that.

One thing was certain—they had both suffered for the games their parents played. Whoever's door had most of the blame heaped at it.

"It will be fascinating," she said. "To be down in the ballroom tonight."

"Yes. No longer the secret."

Recognition bloomed in her chest. "I think I must want that."

"What?"

"I am marveling at my own motives," she said. "I cannot say that I have figured them out entirely. I have lived a quiet life these last few years, and I said that I would never return here. That I would never… That I would never see you again. And that I was happy for it."

"I see."

"Yet here I am. Dancing with you. Here I am, leaping headfirst into this retribution."

"Perhaps you are just as filled with hate as I am."

She smiled up at him, but she felt the expression falter as her eyes collided with his. "But that can't be. Because I have worked very hard and I…"

"All that therapy," he said. "You think you should be more enlightened than I am?"

"I know I should be," she said.

"Reality is often a difficult thing. What we might

like is not always what is. Aren't our entire lives a testament to that? Isn't all that we've been through a testament to that?"

"Maybe that's why I prefer the fantasy. Of gardens and a quiet life. A little stone house."

"I can see how it might appeal," he said.

She looked up at him again, and she felt something electric when their eyes clashed.

"You can?"

"For a moment. Like smelling the scent of roses on the breeze. And it catches you, for a breath. And then it's gone and you're left to wonder if it was there at all. I can sense it that way. I can feel it that way. The impression of a life lived quietly. Of a life lived only for yourself."

"I hadn't thought of it that way." But he was not wrong. She had removed every responsibility she might feel toward another person. Every hint of caring about outside expectations. She had sunk deeply into her own reality. Only her. Only her flowers. Only the things that made her happy and none of the things that didn't. And so she had been unprepared. Her emotions still in that same deep freeze when he had come to see her. She had been unprepared for what it would do to her. Unprepared for what being back in Arista would mean. Or maybe *unprepared* was the wrong word. Blissfully, intentionally disconnected from it.

But now she was here. And she felt anger. For the girl she had been. And a heady rush of need for the man that he was.

He felt like the reward she had been hoping for all this time. The reward that she deserved after living a life so disconnected. After being denied so many things when she was a girl.

And without thought, she moved her hand from his shoulder and slid it down the front of his chest. Pressed over where his heartbeat was, and she felt it raging. She looked up at him, her heart pounding an intense tattoo in time.

"Vincenzo…"

"That is enough," he said, moving away from her. "Tonight is the night that I tell my father no matter what. No matter how he tries to clean up after this, it is no use. I am his heir, and I refuse to carry the line forward. And he will have to face that."

"I admire your rage," she said.

"Why is that?"

She felt separation between them like she had been stabbed. "Because it's clean. And bright. Because it is…real. It is that which I admire most. The honesty in it."

"You seem quite honest, Eloise."

"I try to be. But then I wonder. If I have been the least bit honest with myself. I didn't think I was angry anymore. I thought I'd put it all away. What does it mean that I haven't?"

He stopped, his hand lifting, hovering over her cheek, as if he wished to touch her. To maybe offer comfort?

"You are human," he said, lowering his hand.

She ignored her disappointment. "Is that what you are? Human?"

"I cannot afford to be human. I must be the cleanup

crew. I must fix all that he has broken. And I cannot allow myself to be distracted."

He strode from the room, leaving her standing there. Her hand burned where she had touched him, and her heart... Her heart burned too. Her heart burned with an intensity that she could not identify.

She felt like she was on the edges of her own life. The pull to Virginia was strong, but she wasn't there. She was here. And she felt like... Something was going to break.

She was afraid that it was going to be her.

CHAPTER SEVEN

WHEN ELOISE EMERGED, ready for the ball, his gut tightened with the need that defied everything else. He'd had to walk away from her earlier. The touch of her delicate fingertips against his skin almost more than he could bear. He did not wish to be so attracted to her.

What he'd said to her when she was eighteen was just as true now. She was bound to him in ways she had not chosen. They were bound to one another in this sadistic farce.

He was a man who owned his appetites. But he was also a man who protected those weaker than himself. A man who did not believe in using his power against others. Eloise had chosen to be here, but he had to wonder how much of the past's sins had dictated that.

His father had hurt her unforgivably—he could see that now.

And it shamed him, tenfold.

Because even if she had slept with him, that would have been true.

He had somehow realized she was young and a victim of circumstance when she had kissed him. When she had come to his room.

And he had forgotten it all when he'd been hurt

by her. Had recast her as the villain the moment he'd found it convenient.

It shamed him.

But now Eloise was standing before him wearing that revealing gold dress and looking like a goddess reborn. Like she had just emerged from fire, a glorious avenging sexuality that he wanted to hold against his body. She was glorious. When he could think of nothing more poetic than his father having to witness her being part of his downfall. She was a fresh-faced glory, her cheeks pink and tinged with something gold like the dress, her lips a glossy rose with an underlying flame.

And he could not help himself. He wanted her.

But it was not Eloise who was unworthy.

It was him.

One thing was for sure, she might've had therapy. She might arrive in a place that she considered healthy, but healthy was the furthest thing from his mind. Because his life was not divorced of responsibility. Because he could not go off and live that quiet life that called to him like a rose petal on the wind. He could not. Because he had to save Arista. Because he had to make sure his father's legacy wasn't immortalized in glowing terms and song, but that he was remembered as he'd truly been.

He must.

And so if all the things inside him remained twisted, it was because they were twisted around these inevitabilities.

He could not be another man, and he would not seek to try. He would not turn away from all that he must do.

But he did not wish to turn away from the beauty that was before him either.

Whatever he might deserve.

He held his hand out, and she took it. A tentative light in her eyes.

And he wanted to banish that tentativeness. He wanted to tell her definitively that he would defend her. That he would slay every dragon.

Because he was piecing together these things, these events that had occurred. From the first time he had seen her when she was six years old to that time she had gone to his room and confessed her love to him in what he thought to be a brazen sort of manipulation. But if he saw it differently. If he looked at her differently, if he banished that cynicism that was so forceful inside of him...

Maybe she had loved him.

Maybe when she'd come to his room, when she'd kissed him, it had been with more sincerity and heart than he'd ever had inside his body.

A gift he had not known how to receive.

It made his chest feel like fire.

She had gone away and hidden, protected herself in the wake of his betrayal, because he could see that clearly now.

He had been the one who had wronged her.

Enormously.

He was not a man who understood love, but loyalty at least, he had made it a point to know. Honor. He had not acted with honor. She had been his friend, all because she had reached out to him. All because of her spirit, which was lovelier than his would ever be.

He had accused her of whoring herself out. He had paid her to leave.

She had gone away and made a quiet life for herself. And she was correct. He was the one who had sought her out. So if he removed all of his presuppositions and the deep, entrenched and unfair thoughts that he had been directing at her for all these years... He was left with the woman standing before him. Strong when those around her who should've protected her had not been. Filled with honor and integrity. With strength. A girl who had thrived in spite of the lack of care.

A wildflower left to grow on her own in the garden, who had fought her way through, without being consumed by weeds.

She was that wild garden at the house in Virginia that he had thought was unkempt. It was not.

For it tended itself, and it thrived in the wild.

Just as Eloise did.

They should all be so lucky as to have that kind of strength inside of them.

He himself? He was oriented to vengeance. But she had seen to her healing.

There was a power in her choice that he had never known before. That he had never seen.

They got in the limousine and were silent on the drive to the palace this time. His own thoughts were turning. He was ready for this. More than ready.

But he had not anticipated that so much of his thought would be with her. How could he have? For his entire opinion on her had changed in just a couple of days.

The palace was open, brightly lit and glittering.

Lights were strong over the courtyards, with guests spilling outside.

One of his father's perfectly immaculate glittering affairs.

These were not the sorts of debauched parties he had in secret. No. These were demonstrations of wealth and goodness, and only if you knew, only if you really knew, could you sense that hint of disreputability beneath it all.

But it was there.

And he knew it well.

The truth of the fact was that his father was often sleeping with his friends' wives. That there were no fences built by marriage vows, none that could not be handily crushed by the cavalier nature of the way all of these people treated relationships. But that was only what you would see if you wished to dig beneath the surface.

And none of the casual guests would. They would all simply enjoy the opulence around them and not dig at all into the glittering, terrible underbelly.

But, as he and Eloise walked into the ballroom, a hush came over the room, and he knew that his statements from yesterday had done their job. They had been in the media. And everyone here had heard the rumors, and here he was, and here she was. A bright beacon of truth. Substantiating those claims.

Here they were together. A reckoning.

"They know," he said. "And tonight, they have all turned up to see what will happen."

"It is amazing your father hasn't disbarred you from the event," she said.

"He won't. He won't because he knows that doing

so will only create more rumor. And at this point, the scandal is already out of his control. He will not wish to be pressed."

"And you will press him," she said.

"Without hesitation," he responded. "But first, a dance."

He led her out to the middle of the dance floor and pressed her luscious body against his. For a moment, he forgot where they were. For a moment, he forgot why they were here. Every eye in the room was on them. Every eye filled with curiosity, but he did not care. For what he wanted, what he really wanted was to have Eloise in his arms. Her soft skin beneath his hands.

She had become a symbol of his retribution. She had become a symbol of all of this. While she most of all was suddenly what he now wanted to avenge. More even than his mother.

As he looked at her angelic face, he could not explain why it had become suddenly the driving force, the driving need.

But it had.

She was the most important thing. She was everything.

Eloise.

The desire for her was like a fire in his blood, and for a moment, that thought gave him pause. Because he wondered if this heat in his blood was anything like his father's.

Vincenzo had never wanted a woman. Not a specific woman.

He desired women. He liked them in all their shapes and forms. But... He had never been sick with his desire for a specific one.

And here he was.

He wanted her above all else. He wanted her more than revenge. He wanted her more than his next breath.

He traced his finger along the line of her jaw, and he felt her shiver beneath his touch.

He lowered his head, a breath away. "You are beautiful," he said.

"I feel beautiful."

Not foolish. For she had said so many times that she feared feeling foolish. But she did not feel as if her body was the sort that would create the reaction that he anticipated, but he could not see what she saw. He could only see desirability. He could only see beauty. But he could also see that it mattered what she thought of her own self. What she thought of her body. And he cared about that.

Another foreign feeling. Caring about another person in this way.

He had cared only about justice for a very long time.

Now he found he cared about her feelings.

And that was a novelty.

But he could not call it anything half so light as a novelty, not with any honesty. It was a pain that started at the center of his chest and burned outward like a wildfire. He looked over her shoulder and saw his father. Watching.

Even the King was watching.

Good.

He hoped that he was anticipating what came next.

The gaze of his father made him refocus. On his revenge. And that was when he decided to lean in and taste her lips. He felt her breath draw in just as his mouth touched hers. And he tasted that sweetness.

That rose petal on the wind. That glorious hint that filled his lungs if only for a moment before vanishing. Like a bright white moment of clarity. Of possibility. And suddenly, with that soft mouth beneath his own, everything seemed possible. They seemed possible.

And when they parted, it was gone. A hint of a memory that might've been a dream, because all that remained was Vincenzo. And all that he had yet to do.

"It is time," he said.

He moved away from her and made his way over to his father. "Congratulations," he said. "On the long-standing lineage of the Moretti family. Is that not why we are all here to celebrate?"

"It is why I could not bar you from the festivities. Yes."

"A tragedy for you," he said, feeling his mouth curve into a cruel smile even as he spoke. "But I think what I have to say about the Moretti family is something that all the guests in attendance may wish to hear."

He turned and, with an effortless ease, projected his voice over the din of the crowd. And he did not sound like an unhinged voice in the street, rather he spoke with the confidence and authority that flowed through his veins. "The Moretti family bloodline is filled with poison," he said. "There is no one who knows this better than Eloise St. George and myself. We have joined together, united as one in this common belief. The Moretti line must end. And it must be exposed for what it is. You, who have sat here in riches while your people starved. Who have rained the judgment down upon them while you engaged in every kind of debauchery. While you kept a mistress for more than twenty years in the same home as your wife, flaunting her as an assistant, using state funds to support the lifestyle. And then attempting to manipulate her daughter into an affair with you, and allowing the media to crucify her when she refused you. Using your power and position and lording it over the women around you. You are a man with no honor. You are a man with no dignity. You are no kind of man. And I will take over the throne, and when I do I will begin to dismantle the line. Your precious bloodline. As destroyed as your reputation will be, once the truth I have about you is disseminated in the media."

"Whatever it is you're doing," his father said. "It will not work. The country needs me. The country needs the monarchy."

"The country needs nothing of the kind. I have been building the infrastructure right beneath your nose. Establishing the scaffolding required for everything to go on when you are no longer at the helm." His blood burned with anger, but this was different. This was a righteous, unending anger that flowed through him. And it did not feel toxic or calcified.

It was alive and so was he.

"Oh, yes. I have been pouring money into this nation for years. Under the guise of being an anonymous benefactor, foreign aid. Foreign aid you should be ashamed to accept given the amount of money that flows through your coffers. But you are not. Because you are greedy. Because you are corrupt. And when I ascend the throne, it will be to dismantle everything that you have built. The machine that you have created. And having me killed will solve nothing. Nothing at all. For even then you will lose your bloodline. I am not your ally, old man. And I have never been. And the line will die with me. For I will never have an heir. And the government will be turned over to the people. The Moretti line will not prevail for another five hundred years. It will not even prevail past the end of my life. I will deny you that. You will not live to see it, but you will live knowing it. You will watch the foundation of all that you are crumble. The rewriting of what will be in the history books after you are gone."

The room around them might have been a hundred yards in the distance, for in this moment, there was only him. Only his father.

"No one cares about a few women," his father sneered.

"Perhaps. Many do not. A small sin in this world. But it is not your only sin. And the rest? Do you think it was only my mother's life that spared you my wrath? I cared about her, but if I'd had all the evidence I needed to make sure your reign ended, unequivocally, when I revealed you, I would have done so on any given Tuesday. I don't require theatrics."

His father looked truly afraid now, and Vincenzo relished it. "I don't mind them, though." He grinned, and he knew it was filled with all the hatred that insulated his heart. "I have everything now. It is all in order. I was finally able to pay off one of your most trusted accountants to get me absolute proof of how you siphon money away from the people, and there may be those who will turn a blind eye to your sexual exploits, but what you have done to Arista? The name of Moretti will cease to exist. And what was it all for?"

He took a step closer to his father, and he felt as if someone had grabbed hold of his heart and taken it in their hand. Was holding it in place. Keeping it from beating. For he saw… Not the raging monster of his mind. But a man coming to the end of his years.

A man who was only a man.

"You are nothing but an old man who has left a legacy of pain. That is what you will leave in this world. It will be fixed when you are gone, and no one will think of you. You will die, and that will be the end of you."

"You would not dare. You would not dare do this. It does not benefit you."

"I don't care about power," Vincenzo said. "It is of no consequence to me."

"You… You think you're better than me. And here you are parading in with the same sort of whore that I have favored these many years. She would've warmed my bed if she had stayed longer. They all do in the end."

"That's a lie," Eloise said, her voice cutting over the sound of the gasps in the room. "I would never have warmed your bed. I denied you. When you came for me when I was only eighteen years old. I denied you."

His father's face contorted then, into an ugly, hateful sneer, and Vincenzo felt as if they were all watching him unmask himself. "You can say whatever you like, but the newspapers already spoke their piece. And people will always wonder."

"But I won't," she said. "And I am not hungry for a certain kind of reputation. I am only hungry for freedom. And I can have that. I will have it. You are nothing but a bitter, sad old man. Twisted. If you did not have power and money, no woman would touch you. And that is the difference between you and Vincenzo."

Vincenzo felt as if he'd been shot. Her defense of him, after all he had done.

"He does not crave it because he does not need it," she continued, all her righteous fire spilling from her, filling the room. "You do. You need to have power over the people that you manipulate into your sphere. Over the women that you manipulate into your bed. They must be afraid of you. You would've forced me, and we both know it. Even though the rumors leaked to the press were wrong, they were what rescued me. Because it was the rumors that made Vincenzo give me the money to leave. And I am grateful for that every day. Had I not been rescued by default of being sent away, I know that you would've forced me into your bed. You would've made me into another of your secrets. And I know what it's like to live my life as a secret. But I will not. Not anymore. Hiding was easier, because it allowed me to make my life mine. But I will not be cowed. Not for any reason. Not for anything. I am not afraid of you. I am not a powerless girl. And no one should be afraid of you. Everyone should know what you are, openly. So that no one is keeping your secrets, and no one is trying to pretend."

"You bitch of a girl," he said.

"That is enough," Vincenzo said, stepping forward. "Eloise is a woman. Filled with bravery and integrity, and she makes the world better for being in it. Something you will never ever understand. You are nothing but a coward. Your entire kingdom is built upon perfidy. It is built upon lies. And tonight it is finished. In the future it will be finished for good."

"You are dead to me," his father said.

Vincenzo turned. "I would love to say that you were dead to me. But you are not. You are very much alive. And until you are dead, you will not be able to be dead to me. Because I must fight against you. You have made it so. I refuse to allow you to exist as you do. To be as you are. What I want you to know is that you are a fool. Believing that I was simply distant. Believing that I was not secretly acting against you all this time. You are a man of great manipulation. But it did not occur to you that your own son might have secrets of his own. Did not occur to you that your own son might be hiding the truth of the matter from you. And of course it never occurred to you that you might miss something."

"You cannot do this."

"I have. The ball is in motion. All the information that I've compiled about you is being sent out to various news sources automatically tonight. And I daresay there will be a reckoning about what took place in this very ballroom. I cannot imagine that all your guests will remain tight-lipped. Many of them will be rushing to speak against you. To make it clear that they do not wish to associate with you in any way. They will all flee from you like rats from a sinking ship. Even your mistress would be wise to do the same."

"You cannot…"

"I have done my part," Vincenzo said. "The rest will unfold on its own. It is over now. You do not deserve silence. And no one here deserves protection. I would remember that when you all go out into the world. You must choose a side. I would advise you choose the side that stands against him."

He looked over at Eloise, who was burning bright, her breath coming in harsh, sharp bursts. Eloise. She would not be broken by this. Because she was not the fragile wisp of a creature he had deemed her when she'd come to his bed and kissed him. She was not the great manipulator he had allowed himself to believe she was thereafter.

She was strong. And she was brilliant.

And he was trying to think now of all that he could give her.

Make her your mistress.

No. It was impossible. That was the only thing that burned now. She could not be his mistress, because he would not dishonor her in that way. And he would not take a wife.

But she could be his. For the night.

He would give her everything they could have had then.

Because now triumph burned in his veins, and need burned in his gut, and he needed her. He needed her more than he needed to breathe.

He needed her more than he needed anything.

Like atonement.

Like redemption.

He took her hand and escorted her from the room.

When they were outside the palace, Eloise did something entirely unexpected. She threw her arms around his neck, and kissed him.

CHAPTER EIGHT

ELOISE COULD NOT explain what was happening to her. She couldn't explain the feeling that was fizzing through her veins.

But she felt like she was ready to crawl out of her own skin. She felt like she was ready for something. For something big. For something changing. Altering.

She needed him. As she had felt when she was eighteen, but this time that burned brighter and hotter.

This time she burned brighter and hotter.

Incandescent.

Rage.

She was so angry. For the shame the King had made her feel all these years. For the way she had been written about. She had tried to push all that aside, to reconcile it. But it was wrong, and it had hurt. She had been called a whore countless times, wrapped in the language of smug men wielding pens and trying to sell clicks.

And she had never let herself be angry. She had tried to move on. She had tried to let it go, but here she was, back in the thick of everything, and she could not let it go. She did not feel placid and healed and normal. She did not feel like a lazy day gardening. She felt like a thwarted warrior who needed only a sword so that she could take it out and cut off the head of her accuser.

She was furious. And right then she did want revenge. Right now she wanted satisfaction for all the things that she had been through. For the life spent ignored, for the girl that she had been walking these palace halls, for the young woman she had become who had fallen in love with Vincenzo only to be cruelly rejected. Who had been paid off by the one person she'd cared about, and he hadn't believed in her any more than anyone else. Who'd had to forge a life by herself. Who had only ever been able to find contentment by herself, and never with another person. And certainly never in the arms of another person.

It was hell.

And she felt like she was burning.

She had tried. She had tried so hard to be… Above it. But right now she was in it. And she was being roasted in these flames, and she wanted to burn more. Burn brighter. Burn until it was not only anger. Burn until she was not just a victim. She wanted to burn it all away. All of it. And so, without thinking, she kissed him. And it was everything she had ever imagined. More than that kiss out on the dance floor, which had sparked something in her. More than touching his chest during their dance lesson this morning—had it really been this morning? She could hardly believe it. More than anything. Ever.

It was all him. It always had been. And maybe tonight was about reclaiming something. Reclaiming something for her own. Reclaiming a piece of her that had never experienced satisfaction.

Maybe that's what it was.

And so she kissed him. He put his hand on the back of her head and held her close. Angled his head so that he could take the kiss deeper. And when his tongue touched hers, it was gasoline to the lit match that was Eloise.

They were standing there in front of the palace, and it might as well be a burning building behind them. Ready to explode with the powder keg they had set off there. And still they were kissing. Absurdly, and perhaps appropriately.

"Let's go," he growled against her mouth.

He growled.

He did want her.

And everything else could wait. All of the complicated feelings she had about tonight, all of her concerns for the future. All of it could wait until tonight was over. Because tonight she felt beautiful, and it didn't feel like it had teeth. Didn't feel like the cost of her beauty was her dignity or her agency. Didn't feel like her beauty could only exist if it took the shape her mother tried to force her into.

She felt both in and out of control in the most glorious, delicious way. And she wanted to claim it. As she staked a claim on herself and on him. He had been a wound. An old wound that had lived deep inside her, not because she didn't understand that their age difference at the time had made it perfectly reasonable that he had rejected her. It was that she had felt like she had revealed a part of herself, for the first time, to another person, and she had been rejected. She had felt fragile all these years. And now she felt… Reborn. Like she was reclaiming something that had been twisted and perverted, taken from her.

Tonight she felt giddy with her excitement over him. With the hope of what it might mean.

No, not a future together. He had made it abundantly clear that was never going to happen for him. And as for her...

She could not tie herself to this family. To this place. This was the end of it. Her eyes filled with tears, because she did not want to think of that. So she leaned in and kissed him again, and she pushed all thoughts of the future away.

They got into the limo, and he pulled her onto his lap. She put her thighs on either side of his and kissed him, uncertain where her confidence came from. Where her reckless abandon had come from.

She rocked her hips against the hard ridge of his arousal and she ignited.

She was slick and hot and ready for him, and a childhood crush had not prepared her for the desire she would feel as a woman.

No. It had not. "We still have to get into my penthouse," he growled. "Or I would strip you naked now."

The dark promise sent a thrill through her entire body. She would not be opposed to that. Not really. They could have the driver go around the block and he could take her here, right in the back of the car. They wouldn't have to pause to think; they wouldn't have to pause for breath. They wouldn't have to pause for anything, and that was what she wanted. Because thought felt like the enemy right now. She didn't want thoughts. She wanted feelings. Nothing more than the deep, intense feelings that existed between them. The unending desire that he had built inside her. It felt magical. And few things in her life ever felt magical.

She nearly laughed.

Because she could remember when she had been a girl, and she had thought that moving to the palace meant she was a princess.

There was nothing half so terrible as a nightmare adjacent to a fantasy. She knew, because she had lived it. She had never been a princess. She had been a ghost.

A ghost in her own life. A ghost in the life of those around her, and she would not do it. Not now. Not anymore.

And so she rolled her hips forward and reached between them, undoing the button on his pants and undoing the zipper as well, reaching her hand inside and gripping the hot, hard evidence of his desire for her.

His breath hissed through his teeth, and she marveled her own boldness.

But she was not a girl. She might not have practical experience of men and sex, but she knew all about it. She had read plenty of books that described the act in glorious metaphor and had seen quite a few TV series that had presented it in less than metaphorical visuals.

She knew that it was all right for a woman to be bold. In fact, it was appreciated.

And she knew what to do to follow her own desire. That felt somehow miraculously like a gift. Like an inbuilt sort of magic she hadn't known was there.

His head fell back onto the seat, his breath hissing through his lips. And she pushed herself off his lap, down onto the floor of the limo. She looked up at him, at the strong, hard column of his arousal.

She leaned in, flicking her tongue over the head of him. And he reached back, grabbing her hair and guiding her movements as she took him deep between her lips, sliding her tongue over his hardened length.

She was lost in it. In the glory. In her power.

For here she was on her knees with the most vulnerable part of him in her mouth. And he was at her mercy.

It didn't matter that she was less experienced. It didn't matter that she was younger. Here, they were equals. Here, on her knees before the Prince, perhaps she was even the one in charge of things.

It was a heady discovery. A deep, intense experience that she hadn't known she had wanted. But hadn't she spent all of her life feeling helpless? Surrounded by people with more money, more power and more powers of manipulation than she would ever have.

She was in charge now. She was.

He growled, bucking his hips upward, the hard length of him touching the back of her throat, and she steeled herself against that surge of power. And found that she loved it. Because it spoke of his lack of control. Because it spoke of his need for her.

She continued to pleasure him like that, until the limo pulled up to the front of the building. He looked down at her, his black eyes glittering.

"Maybe you should tell him to go around the block," she said, sliding her tongue from his base to his tip.

The tension in his neck was evident, the tendons there standing out, the tension in his jaw live with electricity.

"No," he said.

He righted his trousers, putting himself away and pulling her back up to the seat.

"We will finish this properly."

And she hated the underlying truth in those words,

because what he was not saying was that they would finish it in a bed because tonight would be the only night they ever had.

Because this was their only moment.

It made her feel a sense of profound grief, and she couldn't understand it.

She didn't want to understand it.

He got out of the car, then reached in, taking her hand and drawing her out onto the street as though she had not just been tasting him intimately. They looked for all the world like a proper couple who had not been engaged in sex acts in the back of a car.

It gave her a secret, giddy thrill.

It made her feel like she never had before.

Because she had given herself that quiet life, had disappeared into her garden and her flowers.

Those flowers that were simply beautiful as they grew and didn't have to strive for it. Those flowers that were not victimized for their beauty.

She had done it because it was healing, but her version of healing had had a cost. It was far too quiet. At the end of all things, it felt too sedate.

At the end of everything, what she had done was sand all the hard edges off her life, but with that she had taken the excitement. The thrill.

In truth, she had never really had a thrill. In truth, all of her life had been decided by others. There had been pain, there had been grief and sadness and neglect. There had been danger.

But no one had ever thrown her a birthday party. She had been surrounded by evidence that the capacity for lavish celebrations existed, but none had ever been wasted on her.

Not a kind word had ever been thrown her way.

Living amongst all that wealth… And no one had ever distributed even the smallest bit to her. She was fed, and she was clothed.

But she did not have beautiful Christmas trees and Christmas presents.

Because she was not a princess. And she never had been.

And so for this night, to seize the thrill of it all… It seemed worth it. But she mourned already that it could not go on.

At least she had a quiet life to return to. A safe life.

At least she had that.

The elevator ride was a study in torture, and they stood with just a scant amount of space between their bodies. And she did her best to breathe. To breathe in and out and to stop her thoughts. Her body was rioting with desire. She could still taste him on her tongue, and she was slick between her thighs with the anticipation of what was to come.

The elevator doors opened, and he walked out ahead of her and extended his hand, as he had done out on the street, but this time they were not going out into public. This time he was beckoning her into his lair.

This time he was inviting her to a private night of sin, and she was going to accept. She reached out, and her fingertips brushed his. A shudder went down her spine. The desire that was growing inside her was almost pain.

He drew her out, his dark eyes never leaving hers. Her mouth went dry.

No, it wasn't almost pain. Now it was pain. A deep, aching emptiness, and the desire to be filled by him.

She wanted him. She might be a virgin, but she knew full well what was going to happen here, and that she would receive it with great relish. She wasn't concerned about the pain.

Pain was familiar to her. And pain passed. That was one thing she had learned. You could live through unimaginable emotional pain. Betrayal, fear. You just had to find a way to get through the moment. A bit of physical pain didn't concern her at all.

It was amazing, really. That she had no nerves. That she didn't feel a sense of worry over what she did not know. Because she was with Vincenzo. And everything would be fine. That knowledge echoed deep within her soul, and she could not have explained it to anyone, let alone herself.

But it was Vincenzo.

The man she had fallen in love with when she was a teenager. The man she had never forgotten.

The man she had always wanted. This... This was inevitable in a way that she could never explain.

It felt right.

Sad in a way, but in a way that she was determined not to think about. Because this was their night.

The culmination of all that she had felt for him from the time she was a girl.

Vincenzo.

And then he swept her into his arms, and he kissed her, with a deep, unyielding need that stoked a fire down in her belly and made her feel like she was the flame itself.

She stood back away from him; she needed to do this. She reached around behind herself and grabbed the zipper tab on the revealing dress that she had worn all evening and unzipped it. Let it fall down to her waist, let it reveal her bare breasts. She needed to do this. To choose to reveal her body to him.

To stand proud in it.

Because it was the evidence of the shape that her life had taken. Of the things that she loved. Of the fact that she enjoyed baking bread and eating it too. That she liked cakes, and always had. That she also worked outside in the sun, and had freckles on her arms and shoulders from being out in it. That her nails were short because you could not garden with long fingernails, at least not nicely and easily.

This was the Eloise that she had chosen to be. And now she was choosing to give herself to him.

She pushed the dress down over her hips, leaving herself standing there in only her glorious, gold shoes and a pair of gold panties. She knew, because she had looked at herself in the mirror, that they made a slight dent in her hips, and she had known a moment of insecurity about that. Because it revealed her body was not perfectly taut or toned.

But then she looked at his face and saw the hunger there. She did not feel regretful about anything. About herself.

She took a step toward him, and she saw a muscle in his jaw jump.

"You are beautiful," he rasped, the words scraping over his throat.

Her cheeks heated.

"I'm glad you think so."

"I would never say that your body is made for sex. Not when it clearly accomplishes so many other won-

derful things. But I do believe that sex…with me…
may be one of its highest purposes."

She should not appreciate that. But she did.

She stopped, and she put her hand on his chest.
"Only if you concede that your body was definitely
made for sex. And most especially with me." His lips
curved into a smile, and it made her stomach dip. Because how often did this man smile? So rarely. If ever.

She began to undo the buttons on his shirt, slowly,
and there was an increased thrill to seeing his chest
when she was the one uncovering it. It had been glorious when he had come in shirtless, and she had danced
with him only this morning, but this…

This was unmistakably sexual. An unmistakable
expression of their need for one another. She moved
her hands over the hard planes of his chest, his stomach, then slid them back up to his shoulders, pushing
his shirt and jacket down onto the floor.

He was glorious. Just standing there in a low-slung
pair of black pants, all his hard-cut muscles on display.

He was physical perfection. In the classic sense.
A man who seemed carved from rock rather than
flesh, and yet he was hot to the touch, and she could
not deny that he was every inch a man. He made her
mouth water.

And she had thought that she wanted to lick him.
So now she would.

She leaned in, kissing his chest, then pressing the
flat of her tongue there, drawing it over his nipple and
up his neck, before biting the edge of his jaw.

And he moved, grabbing hold of her, taking her
wrists and pinning them behind her back, down at the
base of her spine.

"Little minx."

"Maybe."

She didn't feel like herself. Or rather, she did. She felt like herself unfettered, even as he held her there captive.

She had wondered what it might be like to live in a moment where she didn't carry pain or baggage from the past. Where she didn't carry inhibition, and she seemed to be living in that fantasy.

For everything just felt right. Everything felt free. And so did she.

He kissed her, holding her captive as he did so. And then he lifted her up off the ground and carried her back to his bedroom.

He deposited her at the center of the bed and reached out, hooking his finger through the waistband of her panties and dragging them down her legs. Then he took hold of her ankles, undid the delicate buckles on her shoes, one by one, slid them off and discarded them on the floor.

"Sit back against the pillows," he commanded. "And spread your legs."

For a moment, she knew embarrassment, because it was a frank command. And she did not know that she could withstand it.

"Spread them," he repeated, and so she found herself obeying, sliding back and leaning against the pillows on the headboard, parting her thighs, even though she felt as if there was a magnet between them trying to get her to put them back shut. To conceal herself.

It was one thing to stand before him bare, and imagine herself a classical painting, but quite another to do something so openly sexual.

This was not the kind of thing you could walk into a museum and see.

This was something else altogether.

But she did it. And when she saw the effect that it had on him, when she could see the outline of his arousal through the fabric of his pants, her embarrassment faded away. And she found herself unconsciously moving her hand toward the heart of herself, drawing her finger slowly through her own slick folds.

"Dammit, Eloise," he ground out. "This is not going to last as long as I wanted it to."

"But we have all night," she said, her breath coming in short bursts as her arousal began to reach a fever pitch.

The need for him combined with the teasing touch of her own fingers.

And the view of his desire for her.

"Yes," he agreed.

He kicked his shoes and socks off, and then moved his hands to his belt buckle, undoing it slowly before pushing his pants down his lean hips and revealing his flesh to her.

She arched her hips up off the bed, beseeching.

Because she was so hungry for him.

His lips curved slightly.

He wrapped his masculine hand around his own desire, squeezing himself, and then he made his way to the bed, still holding his arousal in hand. He slid his hand around the back of her head and forced her head upward, kissing her. Then he moved between her thighs and replaced the touch of her hand with the head of him. He slid it back and forth through her slick

folds, and she shuddered, that hollow sensation there
growing more pronounced. Growing wider.

"Please," she whispered.

"Not yet," he growled. He moved down her body,
kissing her breasts, sucking one nipple into his mouth
before turning his attention to the other one. Then he
kissed his way down her stomach, until his face was
scant inches from the most intimate part of her, his
hands on her hips. Then he started to lick her. He was
not delicate in the strokes he made against her body.
He was decisive. Firm. The flat of his tongue moving over the most sensitized part of her. And then he
moved his lips to that centralized bundle of nerves and
sucked it in deep.

She screamed. Her climax broke over her in a wave,
pounding against her, never-ending.

And when he came back to her, kissed her, let her
taste her own desire, there was no fear in her.

Only need.

The need for him that she'd had for so many years.

This man who had felt like the other half of her
soul at one time.

Leaving him had felt like losing herself.

But he was here now.

And he was there, between her thighs again, the
blunt head of him now probing the entrance to her
body. And she could feel herself stretching, could feel
a slight bit of pain.

Then he growled and thrust into her in one smooth
stroke, pain and pleasure bursting behind her eyes, for
this was what she had wanted. More than anything.
This was the answer to the need in her, and while
there was pain there, it was offset by the deep sense

of satisfaction that she felt. And she understood it. She understood why women did this even though it hurt.

Because it hurt not to. Because it was the only way to find true satisfaction.

Because there was no other answer.

He looked at her, his expression strange, but it faded. And then he began to move. Building the desire in her stroke by glorious stroke.

Impossibly, she felt need begin to build inside of her again. And when it broke over her, he went right along with her, growling out his pleasure as he found his own release. As he spilled himself inside of her.

And when it was over, he lay beside her, stroking her face.

"You should've told me," he said.

"I should've told you what?"

"You either have not been with a man for a very long time, or you have never been with a man at all."

She closed her eyes. She could lie. She could lie to protect herself. But why? This was tonight.

And they got to have tonight. And why should there be any lies between them?

"I have not been with a man," she said. "Not with anyone."

"No, Eloise," he said. "I was appalling to you."

"Yes," she said. "You were. But I'm used to that."

"I hate that even more. That it did not affect you because I'm just one of the many people who have treated you cruelly."

"The world is cruel, Vincenzo. And we either hide from it as I have done, or we learn to become cruel in it, as you have done. At least you fight for the right things. You try. You have honor."

And she realized as she said the words, just how true they were. That this was why it could only be one night. For Vincenzo had chosen his path, and she had chosen hers. And tonight they were able to meet in this bright place of glory. Tonight, they were able to meet at this place of pleasure. Where neither the world nor either of them needed to be cruel.

But she would have to go back. Because she had chosen her way, and he had chosen his.

And she had to admit to herself that his way... It was hard and sharp. Like living in a battlefield, but it at least helped people. What did her method do? It did nothing. It did not protect anyone else.

It made her feel ashamed.

But they had tonight. And she would not let anything else matter.

"Why have you not been with another man?"

"You know why not," she said. "You know why."

"My father."

"It's part of it. But I never felt like my body was right. And I never felt like it was mine. And I was afraid... I was afraid of becoming my mother. She has made terrible choices in the pursuit of men. In the pursuit of her desire for them. Or for what they can give her, and I never wanted that. You must understand, what happened between the two of us made me question myself in a very deep way. And I did not wish to question that. I did not wish to find myself lacking in that way."

"The very fact that you have a concern about that proves that you are not your mother."

"Perhaps."

"It doesn't matter. Tonight you are mine."

She smiled. "Yes. Tonight I'm yours.

They made love all night and slept in between. At one point he got up and made them a platter of fruit, cheese and honey. All the things that he already knew that she loved, and it made her ache. Because this could not last. Because she could not stay with him. With her Vincenzo. She had to get away from here. She had to go back to the safe space that she had created for herself. But they had tonight. And it had been glorious. That would be enough.

It would have to be.

When the sun rose up over the mountains, she dressed in the clothing that was hers and sneaked out of the penthouse. It did not take long for her to find a flight that would take her back to Virginia by way of England.

She turned her phone off so that when Vincenzo discovered that she was gone he would not be able to contact her. Because if he did… She would not be able to be strong.

CHAPTER NINE

WHEN HE HAD awakened to find that Eloise was gone, it had come as a shock to him. A shock that had faded with the passage of these many months, especially as the media storm that he had brought down upon his father, and on Arista, had had some unexpected results.

His father had abdicated. And fled before legal proceedings could be taken up against him. Whether or not he had taken Cressida St George along with him was a mystery, but she had vanished as well.

Leaving Vincenzo on the cusp of being crowned King. His coronation would coincide with the new year. Though it was merely a formality, as he was even now acting the part of ruler.

It gave him little time to ponder Eloise. But he did. In those quiet moments when there was nothing but the breeze and he thought of roses.

It was an impossibility, anyway. The two of them. An impossibility that they should ever have anything more than that single night.

It was perfect, poetic in many ways. As if they had somehow consummated the vengeance itself.

And yet he dreamed of her.

And he wanted no other woman. Though he told himself there was no time for women anyway.

He was rearranging a country.

He was not going to plunge them straight into democracy, but rather he was establishing oversight. Parliament. He would not abolish the monarchy overnight, for there was no practicality there.

The people were used to being ruled with an iron fist, and when it came to restrictions, Vincenzo was opening the floodgates.

There were many older citizens, however, who wondered at the security if they did not have a king.

And Vincenzo was happy to see that everything ran the way that he thought it should, and that everyone felt secure.

He was thankful, also, for his friends from Oxford, who had been his lifeline through all of this.

Rafael, bastard though he was, in every sense of the word, had been the acting Regent of his nation for years, waiting for his younger brother, the true heir, to come into majority.

Jag was well established in his own country, and Zeus was god of all he surveyed. Though he was not the ruler of his country as yet, he certainly behaved as though he ran the world.

It was not unusual for them to clear their schedules and fly to the nearest major city to meet up for a drink or two. Even less unusual for them to make video calls to one another. He felt privileged to be surrounded by them as advisors. Though he often thought it funny, given the hell they had raised in their youths. Age, he thought, came for everyone.

So it was not entirely unexpected when his computer chimed, and he answered, that the first face that popped up was Rafael. Followed by Zeus and then Jag.

"It's late here," Jag said.

"Apologies," Rafael said, but he did not sound at all sorry.

He could see that Rafael was in his study, a fire roaring behind him. It was cold in his mountainous country near Spain, as it was in Arista.

"You've never been apologetic a day in your life," Zeus said. "It's one of the things I like about you."

Rafael waved a hand, dismissing them. Then his black eyes met Vincenzo's through the screen. "You have not seen," he said.

"Seen what?"

"I knew it. For if you had seen it, you would've phoned us. Or, at least would've looked like thunder when you answered."

"I always look like thunder. The cost of figuring out how to repair a country so badly managed."

"No," Rafael said. "This is worse than the state of your country."

"What?"

Rafael picked up a newspaper and held it up. It took a moment for it to come into focus on the screen, but when it did...

"What is the meaning of this?"

"Why, it looks as though your lover is round with child," Zeus said, looking darkly amused. "So much for all of your proclamations regarding the ending of your line. It seems that your seed is prodigious."

"I will thank you to not speak of my seed," Vincenzo said, continuing to stare at the image before him.

For it was indeed Eloise. At a grocery store, with a very clear and obvious baby bump beneath her sweater.

"Why is this…"

But the headline made it all clear. The former lover of King Vincenzo, who had disappeared seven months prior without a word after dropping bombshells regarding the previous King of Arista, was now looking about as pregnant as one might be had they conceived during that time. So of course the speculation was that she carried the heir to the throne of Arista.

She carried the heir to the throne of Arista.

The truth of it hit him hard.

He had failed.

He had made one vow. He had said that he would not carry on his father's line, and that bastard yet lived, and he was likely bringing a child into the world. It filled him with rage.

"No," he said. "This must be… It must be doctored."

"You did not sleep with the delectable woman that you brought to help destroy your father?" Jag asked.

"That is beside the matter. I have slept with many women, and none of them have ended up carrying my child."

"Yes, but did you use a condom?" Rafael asked.

"Excuse me?"

"A condom," Zeus said. "They've been around for quite some time. Known by many names. French letters. Surely even in your little backward country you are familiar with the concept of keeping it under wraps."

"I…"

He had not used a condom. And he was only just realizing this. He had been… It had been an intense night. Filled with the revelations of the day and the rather unpleasant business of the ball. And he had been swept away. Just as she had been. But she was a virgin. He should've...

"Yeah," Zeus said. "No condom. Excellent."

"You must marry her," Rafael said.

"I'm sorry, am I taking orders from you now?"

"No," Rafael said. "But as the bastard in this group of legitimized men, I feel I must speak to my own experience. The Crown was denied to me. Because my father would not marry my mother. And here I am, doing all the work, planning my brother's wedding, in fact, so that he might take the throne. Managing all the things that come with it, as if I am a glorified nanny, all for want of legal documentation between my parents. I could've been king. Instead of a nanny."

"It is my will that none should be king," Vincenzo said.

"So abolish the monarchy. Carry on as you intended," Jag said. "There is no reason for you to change your plans. But Rafael is right. A real man does not impregnate a woman and allow her to go unwed."

"We do not all live in the Dark Ages," Zeus said. "I don't know. You could set her up in a very nice home. Adjacent to yours, if you ever plan on visiting the child. Though, children are quite boring."

"Thank you," Vincenzo said. "For your concerns regarding the entertainment factor of the child that I may have created. However, whether or not I find it amusing to become a father is irrelevant. If I am to become one... Then I will do as I must."

"You will marry her," Rafael said.

"Not because you told me to," Vincenzo said.

"Petulant," Zeus said.

"Hardly. As if you would obey the dictates of that asshole."

"Absolutely not," Zeus said. "I cannot be tamed. By anyone. But, I use condoms. So."

"God help you when you meet a vixen who matches the appeal of Eloise St. George."

It was foolish to even attempt to defend himself, and yet he did.

"I have met any number of vixens," Zeus said. "Minxes, scarlet women and temptresses. And still. No bastards."

"Marry her quickly," Rafael said. "We will all be at your wedding."

"We'd better be *in* the wedding," Zeus said.

"I should think so," Jag said. "It is the only wedding we are likely to take part in."

And all Vincenzo could think was that he would be incredibly, darkly amused if any one of them ended up in the position where they were forced to marry. "Just don't make it around the new year," Rafael said. "It is my brother's wedding."

"Yes," Zeus said. "He is marrying that fresh-faced little princess from Santa Castelia. She is quite delectable."

Rafael's face turned to stone. "She is barely twenty-two years of age. I would prefer you keep your opinions on my future sister-in-law and her beauty to yourself."

There was a thread of steel in his voice that was always present, but it was much more intense than usual.

He had not given full credit to the rather unfair nature of the situation Rafael found himself in. Because of course, he was a placeholder. For his younger brother, who he must herd through life as if he was his son.

All after their father gave no thought at all to Rafael himself.

But Rafael's problems were of no real concern to him right now. The biggest issue was the fact that he was going to be a father.

He was going to be a father.

He had never wanted this. He had sworn that he would not…

He was here in Arista, on the cusp of keeping his promise to his father. Working to dismantle everything.

But Eloise was carrying his baby. And that changed everything. Eloise, who he had not been able to stop thinking of since their time together. Eloise.

"I must charter a private jet to Virginia."

"When?" Zeus asked.

"Tonight."

Eloise was sitting at the kitchen table, solemnly looking around at all her decorations. She had imagined that when she was an adult she might have a different sort of holiday season. That she would decorate festively and cheerfully and capture the magic of Christmas that she had always missed as a girl.

She had always done her house up beautifully, and yet it still never felt… Magic. But even now, nursing a broken heart, she felt a tingling of magic. Because by next Christmas she would have a child to share the holiday with.

The thought made her heart nearly overflow.

She had been terrified, ever since she had taken that pregnancy test and it had come back positive. But she had known… She had known that she wanted the child. She had also known with perfect clarity that Vincenzo did not. He had vowed never to have an heir. It meant something to him. That promise.

Vincenzo was on a path. And nothing would change his mind about that path. Nothing. She didn't want their child to be a source of contention. She had returned to her quiet life, and that was a gift. She had her cottage; it was paid for. And she wanted the baby. She wanted to be a mother. And she had not fully realized what that would mean until this moment. Sitting there in her house surrounded by the Christmas decorations that had never really created the feeling in her that she wanted to have.

Holidays in the palace had been—as had everything—for the enjoyment of the adults. There had been parties she was not allowed to attend and gifts that had not been for her.

She had never had anyone to share it with.

She had never had family to sit by the Christmas tree with. And now she would. And her child… She would throw them birthday parties and Christmas celebrations. She would delight in their achievements and comfort them when they failed. She would do for her child what no one had ever done for her.

And there was something hopeful in that. In knowing that she could change something about the world. And knowing that she could take a little piece of the hurt inside of herself and transform it into something different. Into something new.

No, she could never have the relationship with her mother that she might have wished for as a child, but she could be the kind of mother that she had wished for. She would have another person in her life that she could love and…

Well, very much of her had wished that she could love Vincenzo but… This was better. It was.

She would raise the child far away from Arista. Far away from the palace, and all that pain. It would be better. She would be better.

No. She couldn't have Vincenzo.

But that was all right.

She had accepted that. Before she had gotten into his bed. She wished, just slightly, that she might have thought a little more clearly about the consequences of their joining. But…

Now? Now she felt happy. Even now, sitting there by herself with the snow falling outside the window…

There was a knock at the door. Skerret leaped onto the table and knocked her ball of yarn off onto the floor.

"Skerret," she scolded.

The cat jumped down, startling again when there was another knock on the door.

She got up, and she walked over to the door, looking out the side window. Her heart fell down to her feet.

Because standing there on the doorstep, snowflakes collecting on the shoulder of his dark wool coat, was Vincenzo.

Oh, she didn't know what to do. She hadn't wanted him to know about this… She glanced down at her rounded stomach. But she couldn't avoid him. He was here.

It didn't matter. She would simply face it. It was her decision after all. She was pregnant, and she wanted the baby.

She took a deep breath and opened the door. But what she was about to say died on her lips. Because she had forgotten how beautiful he was. Or maybe it was simply that a mere memory could not hold within it the intensity and brilliance that was Vincenzo Moretti.

"Hi," she said.

Well, that was just perfect. That was not at all what she had meant to say.

He looked down at her stomach, then back up at her. "It is true," he said.

"What's true?"

From the interior pocket of his jacket he took a folded-up newspaper and held it out toward her.

And then she recognized herself. Standing in front of a rack of candy bars, with her baby bump clear and visible. And the headline read: King's Lover Pregnant with Heir?

"Oh, no," she said. "I don't… Vincenzo, I don't know how they got this…"

"Do not tell me the baby is not mine, *cara mia*. For we both know that it is. You were a virgin when you came to my bed, and I hardly think that you leaped straight from my bed into a different one."

"How do you know?" She scowled, indignant at his assumption. "For all you know, I decided sex is actually quite fun and I should like to have more of it. Maybe I went straight from your bed to someone else's. I did leave very quickly." She was practically breathing fire. He'd thought all of this about her easily before, why not now?

Standing there in a rage as if she'd betrayed him, when she knew damned well, as did he, that he'd emphatically stated he did not want a child. As if she'd taken something from him when he had said from the beginning he wanted nothing to do with it.

"Do not play games, Eloise," he said. "I'm not amenable to them."

"Well, what you are or aren't amenable to is my highest concern, Vincenzo."

"Come with me."

She should have known that if he found out he would be inflexible, obnoxious and demanding. On account of the fact he was inflexible, obnoxious and demanding.

"I cannot come with you," she said. "I have a Christmas tree. And a cat."

"Is the cat not outdoors?"

"No. When it began to snow I brought Skerret in."

His lips flattened into a stark line. "That is a ridiculous name for a cat."

"Well, it just kind of… It fits her. Because she gets scared very easily. And also she is sort of slinky like a ferret. And so she's a Skerret."

"It is still ridiculous."

She was pregnant, he had come to take her away and they were debating the merits of her cat's name. "I can't go with you," she said forcefully.

"You can't or you won't?"

"It amounts to the same thing. And anyway, you said you didn't want a child. You in fact vowed never to have one."

"I did. But you are having one. So… It does not matter what I said."

"Yes, it does," she said. "Vincenzo, you can pretend it doesn't matter but it does. Look, you don't have to do anything with this child. I am prepared to care for him or her myself."

"You don't know what you're having?"

"No. I declined to find out. I wanted to be surprised. I know it sounds strange, but I'm very happy. The idea of being a mother... I didn't know that I wanted it. I had told myself that I would be better off living a quiet life by myself. But now... I quite like the idea of sharing it with someone. It pleases me. I'm very... I'm very content with the way things are turning out. You have to trust me. I... I'm not unhappy."

"You mistake me," he said, stepping into the cottage and filling the space. She had forgotten, too, how commanding his presence was. "I did not come here to see to your well-being, Eloise. I came here to claim my child. This is not a welfare check. This is a proposal. Or kidnap, if need be."

"A *proposal*?"

"You will marry me."

"That is a demand, not a proposal. And I will not," she said.

"You will," he said. "I am about to be King, and we must marry before my coronation or the child will be a bastard. Do you understand the implications of that?"

"I... I guess I don't. I... This isn't the Dark Ages. Surely that doesn't mean a thing."

"It does. It means he or she will not be able to inherit the throne."

"You did not want the throne to carry on," she said.

"I don't know what I want now," he said, shaking his head. "There was a way of things. That I had planned, and none of this fits into it. None of this is what I wanted. None of it is right. And yet it is what is. So I must adjust my plans accordingly, must I not?"

"I'm set to have Christmas here."

"It does not matter. You will come with me."

"Don't you want to know why I left?"

He looked as if she had slapped him.

"Why you left?"

"Yes. The morning after we… After we were together. Don't you want to know why I left?"

"Why then? As you are surely intent on telling me."

"I left because I could not stand the idea of…being in Arista any longer. I do not want to be in the palace. All of it, the royal protocol, the location, the walls themselves are nothing more than a terrible memory for me. And it is not something that I can…fathom living with for the rest of my life. Vincenzo, this is my home. And in it I made a place for myself, and I do not wish to go back to being that sad girl lost in a royal life that she was never meant to live."

"I am not my father," he whispered.

"I didn't say that you were. But that does not change the fact that I do not feel at home there. Nor do I want to."

She had just been sitting there, feeling excited about her future. About what she might have with her child. She had been imagining the simple, quiet life where they did not have to consider anyone. Where they did not have to conform, or hide in the shadows.

The very idea of returning and marrying Vincenzo… And he was to be King! It was everything she didn't want. It was so many connections, so much responsibility. It was a nightmare.

"No. I cannot."

"Come back with me," he said.

"No, Vincenzo."

"You must come back with me," he said. "Or I will have no choice but to take the child."

"You wouldn't." She searched his face, tried to put aside her own fear, her own anger and see what on earth he was thinking. Feeling. He'd said he didn't want this, and yet here he was. One thing she knew was Vincenzo was a man driven by his own code of honor, consumed by it, and it didn't matter if she could make sense of it or not. When he decided something, it was the way of things. "You don't want the child," she reminded him. "You said as much yourself."

"I said I didn't want a child. Now there will be one. And that is simply the way of it. I am not turning away from my responsibility. I will not do it. I am a man who knows what is right. And I will do it. I will do my duty. In this as in all things." His voice sounded shattered, and it was the only thing on earth keeping her from lashing out at him entirely.

The only thing that was pressing her to go with him.

"So you really will blackmail me, then?"

"If I have to. I was always willing to, Eloise. That must've been clear."

"I'm bringing my cat," she said.

He looked down at the small creature, the disdain he felt for the little scrappy tabby apparent. "It shall not be loose on the plane."

"Of course not," she said. "What a silly suggestion. She cannot be loose on the plane. It would terrify her. She will be in a crate."

"And what else?"

"What do you care what else I want? It does not matter to you."

"It may shock you, Eloise, but your misery is not actually my goal. What I want is my child."

"Why?"

"Is it not the most natural thing in the world to want your child?"

She stared at him. "You and I both know that it is not. You cannot simply expect that someone will. Did my mother really want me?"

"Eloise…"

She shook her head. "You might be able to take the baby from me, but you cannot force me to marry you. And then the child will not be legitimate."

"Eloise…"

"No. I know that I don't have a lot of power here, but I have had so little choice in my life, Vincenzo. Surely you must want to do better for me than my own mother did. Surely you must want more than to hide me away in this place. Surely I deserve more than that."

"What is it you want?" he said.

It came to her in a moment, because the truth was, it would be… A wonderful thing for her child to know its father.

It was only her fears of that palace, of that life, that truly held her back.

"Make me a beautiful Christmas there at the palace. Show me that there's something there other than what I remember. Other than that dreadful…awful empty feeling that I always get in the palace. You show me. Show me that there is something else. Show me that there can be more. That there can be happiness."

"As you wish," he said. But he looked angry. And he did not look happy at all.

"Gather your cat," he said.

"And my Christmas tree," she said. Because on this she would not budge. And maybe she was just throwing out a ridiculous thing she did not think that Vincenzo could or would accomplish. But if she was going to subject herself to being married to him, if she was going to go back there, she needed him to try. But as she packed her things to go, her heart nearly cracked with an unimaginable grief at the thought of leaving this place.

This safety.

And then Vincenzo went into her living room, picked the tree up and put it over his shoulder. Three ornaments dropped on the floor. "Be careful with that," she said.

"You told me you wanted to bring your tree. I cannot guarantee the manner in which it will arrive."

"I don't…"

"The plane is waiting. I will drive us there. And I will strap your tree to the roof."

"You really will?"

"Yes. Make your commands of me, and I will show you that I am equal to whatever task you assign. You asked me once if I wanted a quiet life. The truth of the matter is, I do not get to choose that. Because of my birth. Because of who my father is.

"The same is true for our child. And I do not want to limit their choices. And you…"

She nodded slowly. Because she knew. She knew she had a responsibility to her child. To their child. To doing what was best for them. No matter what. It was the one thing that his father and her mother had not been able to do. They had not been able to think of anyone else. They had thought only of themselves. And she could cling to her quiet life, her desire to stay away from Arista, but if she denied her child that which they were due by rights, if she denied her child the chance to know their father, when Vincenzo clearly wanted them? Then she would not be any better than her own mother. She simply could not do it. "Let's go."

And she knew she had no choice, not because he would pick her up like the tree and carry her out if she refused, but because there simply wasn't another choice. There simply wasn't.

CHAPTER TEN

"You've done what?"

"I brought her back to the palace," he growled at his computer screen, and more specifically at Rafael.

"Did you kidnap her?" Zeus asked.

He shrugged. "Borderline."

"No one likes an indecisive kidnapping, Vincenzo," Zeus said.

"It was decisive enough. She is here, is she not?"

"Is she *marrying* you?" Rafael asked.

"Most likely."

"Most likely," Jag said. "That is…"

"Weak," Zeus said.

"Mmm," Rafael agreed.

"I cannot force her to marry me."

"Untrue," Jag said. "You can absolutely force her to marry you."

"Perhaps I do not *wish* to force her to marry me," he said.

"And why not?" Rafael said.

In truth, Vincenzo did quite want to force her to marry him. When he had opened the door and seen her standing there, round and pregnant with his child he had… Well, he had picked up her Christmas tree, tossed it over his shoulder and brought it back with them to Arista! That was how strange and primal the response had been to seeing her like that. All he had known was that he would do anything to have her.

And yes, he actually would force her to marry him. If he had to.

"I am hoping to make her think it was her idea," he said.

"Oh," Zeus said. "That is smart."

"All she has asked is that I give her a Merry Christmas. She said if I can make her forget how difficult life was here at the palace when she was a child then she might be more… Amenable to staying with me."

"Buy her a pony, then," Zeus said.

"She did not ask for a pony."

Zeus looked at him as if he were insane. "All women want a pony."

"Then I will buy one. I will fill a stable with them for her. I will do it now."

"No one likes a reluctant gift giver," Zeus said.

"I do not care about any of this. Not ponies or Christmas."

His words landed in this group of men, for none of them had ever experienced the kind of happiness many associated with the holidays. They had never spoken of it, he simply knew.

Because they had never spoken of it.

That silence spoke volumes, like many other silences they had shared over the years.

"Let us send gifts," Rafael said. "To welcome her. Your new Queen."

He narrowed his gaze. "You don't need to do that."

"Yes, we do," Jag said. "I will have…" He snapped

his fingers. "Yes. I have an idea. All will be sent tomorrow."

"I…"

"It is settled," Rafael said.

"Settled," Jag confirmed.

And then they vanished from the screen, and Vincenzo had a feeling he would not enjoy what came next.

He pushed the button on his desk and summoned the house manager. Who came quickly. "I wish to decorate the palace for Christmas. Every single room. From floor to ceiling. No expenses to be spared. The money is to be taken from my personal account. None of the money shall come from Arista."

"Your Majesty…"

"It is for Eloise. We must make this place beautiful for her. For she is to be my Queen," he said.

The manager looked delighted at that. "Your mother would be very pleased," the woman said.

"Perhaps," he said. "Perhaps not." He could not imagine his mother being happy with him taking Eloise as his bride. Considering the history of it all.

"Well I am pleased," the house manager said. "She was always a nice girl. Very quiet. She never got the childhood she deserved."

A strange pang of regret echoed in Vincenzo's chest. "No," he said. "She didn't."

One thing he was utterly determined in—he had been given a challenge to woo his princess in a specific way, and he would do it. He might not understand finer feelings. Might not be a man who knew much about emotion. But he had a capable staff more than able to ensure that any decorating needs might be met.

And when it came to him personally… Well. He

knew about seduction. And that, he was confident, would do the real work.

One thing he was certain of. Eloise would not be able to resist him.

Let his friends send gifts. He would take a different approach.

Eloise didn't emerge from her room until late. She was jet-lagged and had a terrible time sleeping the previous night. She felt out of sorts and unhappy to be back at the palace. Except... It was not that simple. It was not so simple as unhappy. Because in spite of herself that was something that she wanted—to be close to Vincenzo.

And she couldn't even be angry about the fact that he wanted their child.

No. What frightened her was the warmth that filled her at the thought. What frightened her was how much she wanted him to want their child.

When she emerged, she was met with a sight she had not expected.

It was magic. There were twinkling icicles hanging from the ceiling. Glittering rich green and red garlands swirled around every column, every balustrade. Every bannister. Wreaths were hung on every wall. There were gold candelabras with lit white taper candles casting a glow over the room.

The white palace was bedazzled. And trees. There were trees in every room. When she went into the dining room, there were four trees. One that stretched all the way to the ceiling, impossibly tall, two beside it a bit shorter. And in the center, her humble little tree that had come all the way from Virginia. She could not believe it. She simply couldn't believe it.

"I..."

"Good morning."

Elizabeth, the housekeeper, came into the room. She had always liked Elizabeth. There was a distance between them that had been ordered by the King, but she had never felt any chill coming from the other woman. And now, with the King gone, there was no reservation at all.

"Breakfast is set to be brought out upon your arrival. If you are ready?"

"Oh," she said. "Yes, I am."

"Coffee?"

"Herbal tea. Thank you." She had been quite happy that coffee didn't sound appealing, since strictly speaking you needed to limit it with pregnancy. She had thought it sounded unimaginable, but then she had attempted to drink the permitted one cup, and her stomach had turned.

All for the best.

"Right away."

She was only left alone for a moment when the double doors swung open, and one of the other members of staff, Pietro, came in and bowed with a flourish. "Ms. Eloise," he said. "Some gifts have been sent for you."

"Gifts?"

But she did not have to wait to see what that meant. For in through the doors came a veritable procession of staff. The first wave of them carrying bowls made of precious metals. Inside of them was dried fruit that sparkled like jewels. There were flowers, crystal bottles of perfume and woven rugs.

"From Sheikh Jahangir Hassan Umar Al Hayat," one of the men said, placing all of the bounty on the table in front of her. She sat down, overwhelmed. "Sent upon a hand-carved troika, for the lady to keep as her own."

"I... That's incredible."

"There is more."

Following that came another wave of staff, carrying baskets filled with olives, platters of cured meat, fruits and nuts.

"From Regent Rafael Navarro. The finest goods from his country." He handed her a stack of papers. "Also stocks," he said, "in the Regent's personal company. Should you need to make a bid for your freedom."

Eloise blinked. "Oh, well, that is very nice of him."

And then, at the very end, came a young woman, with a very small horse on a lead.

A horse.

"This is from Prince Zeus. With the message that, if at all possible. women should be given the world. But failing that, they ought to have a pony."

And she couldn't help it. It was ridiculous. She laughed. "How wonderful."

She looked up then and saw Vincenzo standing in the doorway looking like a thunderstorm.

"That bastard did not send a horse into my palace."

"Who?"

"Zeus," he said curling his lip. "I should've known he would do it."

"Who are these men who sent these gifts?"

"They are my..." He looked like the word he was about to say was causing him pain. "My friends."

Her eyes widened. "You have *friends*, Vincenzo?"

He arched a dark brow. "Endeavor to not sound so surprised about it, Eloise."

"Well, I am."

"They did not decorate the palace," he said. "I did. Well, I had it done."

"It's glorious," she beamed.

Her breakfast came out, which took the form of baskets full of pastries, butter, jam. It was all a bit much.

"I don't think I will be able to eat all of this," she said, considering the fruit baskets as well.

"I will help."

He sat down next to her. Next to her. This man who was King. It was such a small gesture, and yet it felt…

Don't go romanticizing things like this.

He wanted something from her, and he was willing to do anything to get it.

Yes. And she had wanted him to. So was it so bad that he was acting consistently in that manner? She swallowed. This was all she had wanted. All those years ago.

Well, she had wanted to kiss him. But there was something to this simple connection, here in the palace that… It felt intimate in a way. It felt right.

And no, it wasn't simple. It was complicated. All of this was complicated. There was a horse in the dining room for crying out loud.

"The horse should probably be taken outside," she said.

He nodded. "Have the pony taken to the stables," he ordered.

"I will go see her," she said. "After I'm finished."

"I do not think you have hurt the pony's feelings."

"I shouldn't like to hurt the pony's feelings."

"And how is… Skerret finding his new residence?"

"I believe he quite likes the back right side of my bed. Beneath it. He has not come out. But he has eaten. And has used his box."

"Good to know," he said.

"It will take some time to adjust. The palace is very large."

She didn't just mean the cat.

She stared at him, and she knew that he didn't really care how her cat was finding the adjustment. He was trying. She just wished she could understand more deeply why. Because he had said so firmly that he didn't want a child. And she could understand him making gestures toward it now out of a sense of duty, but the degree to which he seemed to be taking up the cause was… That was what she could not understand.

"Why do you want this child?"

"Because it is the right thing to do."

"Is it only important to do the right thing? In this way?"

"My father never did. Not on behalf of anyone but himself. All I know is, in this life, I will make the decision to do what I know to be right. Whether I understand it, whether I want to… It is the path I have chosen."

"Right. That path of revenge."

"I removed my father from the throne, essentially. And now here I am, striving to set the nation on a better path, but grappling with the reality that the people are not completely happy with the idea of losing the monarchy. Even though they had no real love for my father. They like a symbol. And I am trying to affect change…"

"But it isn't as easy as coming in and ordering things to be done your way?"

"Do not sound so pleased about that, Eloise."

"I'm not. Actually… Vincenzo, you must know one wonderful thing about going off and having my simple life is that I have not been responsible for anyone else. Skerret. She is the only thing I've been responsible for all this time, other than my own happiness. And that is very easy. It is very easy. What you must do… It isn't. You are beholden to an entire nation, and I do not envy you that position. I never have. I was so happy to leave Arista. So happy to escape all of this. But you are right. There are other things to consider. I cannot face the idea of our child growing up in this palace as it was for us."

"It will not be."

"Down to ponies in the dining room. Apparently."

"That was not me," he said. "Let me make that very clear."

"Not wanting to take credit for your friend's idea?" A smile tugged at her lips, in spite of everything.

"Not wanting to take blame."

"She's very charming. And perhaps our… Perhaps our child will enjoy riding." Her eyes stung. "We get this chance. Not just to do this because it's right. But to give our child what we did not have."

"And that is?"

"Love."

"What is love to you?"

It was not a question she had expected him to ask. "You know," she said. "Love."

"I confess that I do not. I was never exposed to love as a child. Nor have I been exposed to it as an adult.

At least, not in any way that I recognize." There was a cool detachment to his voice that was somehow more painful than a wrenching sob, and Eloise could only stare, stunned at the pain his admission created in her. Stunned at this easy admission of his own deficits. And even more, that he did not seem hurt by it. Only accepting. "On top of that, we have very different ideas of what love is presented throughout time in history. There is, of course, the modern concept of loving yourself before all others. There is romantic love. The love of a friend. There is the classic biblical interpretation. Love is patient. Love is kind. It speaks more of a concept than anything specific. So what is it you mean when you say *love*?"

She was taken aback by that absolutely, because she found she did not have an answer. Because it was only a feeling, and he wanted to know what it looked like practically.

"I…"

"You say that you want our child to have love, because as a society we're encouraged to talk about love as though it is free and easy. As though every parent loves their child, and every child their parent in return, but we know that is not the case, do we not?"

"Yes."

"And then there is romantic love. Look at my parents' marriage. Is that love, do you think?"

"I do not think your father or my mother have ever truly loved anyone."

"And yet, I imagine they would say they do. Maybe they didn't think that they do. Because we are conditioned to believe these feelings simply are. That they are easy. That they are created inside of us perhaps the same time as our physical hearts. But what is love in a meaningful sense? In a way that you can touch, and a way that you can taste and feel. What is it? Because if it is not an action, then it does not matter, does it? So when you speak of loving our child, if you mean I will care for them, if you mean I will offer support. Yes, I will. All of those things. Everything we did not get from our parents. In the same manner that I'm delivering your Christmas."

"But to you that isn't love?"

"I think perhaps love is a mass societal hallucination," he said, his voice grim. "If less people professed it as easily as they sneezed, then perhaps it might return to some original weight. Perhaps there would be something to understand. But I find myself cynical about the concept."

"Your mother loved you, surely."

He lifted a shoulder, and his gaze grew distant. "If she did, she never said. But my mother was the most stable influence in my life, that is certain. She saw to her duties, she inquired about my well-being. She was a good queen, and for all that my father offered her no recognition. Nothing but scorn."

She could hardly breathe after that scathing takedown of the entire institution of an emotion that she had believed to be the greatest thing in the entire world. Except... He had made it feel cracked. Crumbling. Was love and care the same thing? Duty and responsibility? Because when she thought of what she had been denied by her parents, those were the things that she would list. And yet it felt like there was more. Something self-sacrificial. Something self-sacrificial by choice.

"Would you have rather your mother said it?"

"Maybe at one time. But in the end of all things, it doesn't matter."

"You have a very grim view of the world."

"Is it? I don't think so. I think what is grim is how cheap words have become. We say them, we ask for them, we do not think about what they might mean. What they should mean. Perhaps if we did, people like our parents could not exist in such denial about their own behavior."

"Do you think they are in denial?"

"I hope so," he said. "Because if either of them has any real idea of the depth of their own depravity, if they realize how morally bankrupt they truly are and choose to walk that path anyway, I find that infinitely more upsetting."

"I suppose," she said. She felt chilled, all the way down to her soul.

She looked at him. And she felt like she understood something deeper about him than she had before.

She had wondered why. Why he wanted this child when he had been so dead set against the idea of children at all. Why he had come to get her. Why he wanted to marry her.

But she could see that he was actually a man of great depth and feeling, though ironically, after his previous statement about the awareness a person had of themselves, she knew that he did not see himself that way.

But he was a man who wished to intensely understand love before he ever professed it. And she realized, that was the cost of him.

She had escaped to that simple life, and nothing would ever be simple with Vincenzo. She let that sink in deep. Down through her skin, down into her blood. Her bones. Yes. Being with him would be a choice. A choice that would take her far away from where she had been before. From what she had known.

But perhaps she was ready now. Strong enough now. Perhaps she could be with him. She leaned in, across the small space of the dining table, and she pressed a kiss to his mouth.

He went still. And so did she. And it was like fire in her blood. Fire that joined in with that deep acceptance of the fact that there was no simplicity with a man like him.

And there never would be.

"I wish to go for a ride in the troika," she said.

"The pony cannot pull the troika," he said.

"Perhaps not. But we are in a winter wonderland. And you have promised me Christmas."

"I did. But I must call my friends first and tell them what manner of monster they have created."

"And what manner of monster is that?" she asked.

"Well, a kind very similar to them, I suppose."

"Tell me about your friends," she said.

"There isn't much to tell," he said, straightening. "We met at Oxford."

"I find that very interesting."

"What exactly?"

"Well, that you have friends. I wasn't trying to be mean when I said something about that. I don't really have friends. I have made casual acquaintances in the world of horticulture. Don't laugh. But I have never really known how to…" What she was about to say was dishonest in some ways. "I have struggled in my life to know how to connect to another person. Weirdly, my upbringing isn't very relatable."

It was one reason, she supposed, that it had been him from very early on.

"We are connected very much by similar pain," he said. "Each of them has their own… Difficulties. We are wealthy, powerful men, by any standards. And that made others in our sphere either seek to use us— which is foolish, because none of us would allow it— or it made them hate us. We found each other, and over the course of years confessed the great bleeding wounds our parents had left in us. You can have the entire world at your feet and still be missing a great many things."

She knew that to be true.

"If you want your troika ride, I suggest you get ready. I will have the staff prepare the horses in the stable. And I will have an outfit appropriate for the weather sent to you."

"Oh…"

"I think the word you're looking for is *thank you*."

"Yes," she said. "Thank you." And she suddenly felt foolish that she had kissed him. Because he had kissed her back, but it had been solicitous, not filled with heat.

But then, perhaps he was not attracted to her when she was like this. She was incredibly round. She could not blame him. She was surprised, honestly, that she was attracted to him still. She would've thought that her present condition excluded her from such feelings. How interesting that it did not. For she felt as if she would happily strip off all her clothes and climb into his lap, baby bump notwithstanding.

"I will meet you in an hour."

"All right."

CHAPTER ELEVEN

IN THE END, Vincenzo decided to prepare the horses himself and did the rigorous task of getting them in the bridles on the troika. He would be sending Jag a picture of his middle finger later.

But it was a lovely sleigh, with intricate hand carvings on it and he knew that the gold leaf paint contained real gold, because Jag would never settle for anything less.

When Eloise appeared, it was like the sun coming out from behind the clouds. She was wearing a furry white hat, and a long white coat with fur around the edges. It went all the way down to the ground, sloping gently over her bump. There was a border of blue thread that ran from the collar all the way down to the floor.

She looked like a snow queen. Standing out there in the cold, her cheeks red, wisps of blond hair escaping the hat. When she had kissed him earlier, it had taken all of his strength not to clear the table and ravish her upon it. But he knew that he could not. He was trying to convince her to marry him, and ravishing her in her present state was not going to help with that. He had to show her that they had something that went beyond attraction. Attraction they knew they had. That was not up for debate. Attraction was what had gotten them into this situation in the first place. But she was asking for something else from him, and he was determined to give it. Determined to secure her acceptance of marriage.

His staff had packed a grand lunch in the sleigh, and they had placed thermoses of hot chocolate in the front. He wished that he'd asked them to add liquor to his own, but he had thought that it might be distasteful, considering Eloise's condition.

Still, he regretted it now.

"Oh," she said. "It's beautiful."

One of the horses shook their head, tossing their caramel-colored mane. And the harness jingled. There were, of course, bells upon the red leather straps.

"This is a Christmas fantasy," she said, her eyes jewel bright.

He had noticed that when they had flown on the private plane, she did not seem inured to excess. She had been raised in the palace, and yet, she did not seem to take luxury for granted. But perhaps that was because she had been kept adjacent to it, rather like an urchin with her nose pressed against the glass. For she might as well have been, as the use of it was denied to her.

It made him want to give her everything. Everything she had been denied.

"Leave it to Jag to go over-the-top."

"It's wonderful. I do rather wish Zeus's pony could lead the team."

"He will have to be content with being a stand-in in a live-action manger scene. That is perhaps more to his scale."

"Poor little thing. I'm afraid to ask why the pony. It seems as if it's some sort of inside joke."

"Zeus is under the impression that all women want a pony."

She laughed, the sound crystal like the snow all around them. "You know, I don't think he's wrong."

"He would tell you that he never is."

"And what do you think?"

"I think he is only wrong when he disagrees with me."

"I see."

Then they got into the troika, and there was a soft blanket inside, mottled gray and thick and plush. He draped it over her lap. And when she looked at him, her cheeks were crimson.

"Yes?"

"Nothing. No one has ever taken care of me before."

"Did you not ask for care? Is that not what a request for Christmas is?"

"I like it. But it occurs to me I have never really taken care of anyone either. And I suppose I will be. Soon." She looked down at her stomach and placed her hand on the rounded bump there."

"I have never cared for anyone either."

"I don't think that's true," she said. "You have your friends. And it sounds to me like you've been there for each other when you've needed one another. I think that is quite commendable."

"I will accept any and all commendations as they come," he said.

"Naturally," she said.

He took his seat in the driver's spot and picked up the reins.

"It did not even occur to me to ask you if you knew how to drive it. Why would you know how to drive a Russian sleigh?"

"It is easy," he said, slapping the reins gently and urging the team forward.

These horses were soft mouthed and easily steered, the best. And the sleigh moved smoothly through the snow. They went away from the grounds of the palace, toward snow-dusted pines, going along the path that went through a thick canopy of trees.

She looked around, an expression of wonder on her face. "I half expect to see a lamppost."

He chuckled. "How about if I offered you some Turkish delight in exchange for betraying your entire family."

"You have essentially done that. But my family was easy to betray." She sighed. "Turkish delight really isn't good enough to justify that sort of betrayal. Not if your family is good."

"Is that your firm stance?"

"Yes. I would need chocolate cake."

He chuckled. "Good to know."

"I am happy," she said quietly. "That your father has lost the throne. I am happy that my mother has lost her position here at the palace finally. I am... I am glad they were exposed. And I have to wonder what all that therapy was for if I can still take such pleasure in their downfall."

"I believe that is just called being human."

"It is an inconvenient thing. To be human. I think I tried really hard not to be."

"What do you mean?"

"Moving away the way that I did. Going off on my

own, ensconcing myself in gardening and all of that. It was my very best attempt at not being vulnerable."

"You can hardly be blamed for wanting to avoid vulnerability."

"Maybe. But I wonder about all I have missed. And how… Well, how deeply in denial I am about my own human nature. I do not think I am half so benevolent as I let myself believe. When you and I met in the garden all those months ago, I told myself that I was going with you as a friend. But by the time I left your bed that morning, I knew. I knew that I was glorying in their destruction. And I was so judgmental of you. I felt above you. I felt better than you, but it was not fair."

"Do not be concerned about that. I feel better than most people."

She laughed. She couldn't help herself. She utterly howled. "I imagine you do." They lapsed into silence again, as the troika went deeper into the trees, the bells jingling.

"We shall take the baby out like this," she said, "for Christmas."

"Shall we?" he asked, his chest getting tight.

"Don't you think we ought to make some Christmas traditions?"

This was the first time she had really talked like she would stay.

"I don't know. Do you think they are important?"

"I do," she said.

"And how will we know?" he asked. "How will we know what matters?"

"Well," she said slowly. "I would think, we should try and remember everything that it felt like we were missing back when we were children. And make sure our child does not miss that?"

"A long list," he said.

And he suddenly wondered if he had never wanted a child because he wanted to end his line, or if he had known that…

That it would be difficult for a man who had never experienced having a real father.

A father who cared.

He wanted to be the right kind of father.

And he had no real idea what that meant.

Right then, he made a decision to show her something he had never shown another person. As the road forked, he went to the left, and it narrowed and went windy, and the ground became thicker with snow as they exited the trees.

"Where are we going?"

"You'll see."

They rounded a curve, and the mountains in front of them disappeared. And about twenty feet ahead, so did the snow.

"Vincenzo," she said, putting her hand on his thigh.

"No worries."

He stopped the team of horses, just at the edge of a ravine that overlooked a crystal lake, frozen over with ice, the sun sparkling over the surface.

"Vincenzo…"

"It's beautiful," he said. "Is it not?"

"Yes. What is this place?"

"I used to come here as a boy. It is part of the un-spoiled wilderness in Arista. As far as I know, there is no path to get down to the lake, though I thought as a boy of many different methods to try and get there.

I wanted to be part of the wilderness. Most of all, I wanted to escape the oppression of the palace. And so I used to come here. And I used to sit. And I used to think of escape. But there was no way to escape. Not from where I was. It was then that I had to accept that…in the end of all things, I had to turn back and confront the evil in my world. I could not simply run away into the wilderness. There was no path."

"That must've been terrifying to realize as a child."

"Did I ever tell you when I realized that my father was bad?"

"No," she said.

He had never told anyone this story. Not even Rafael, Jag and Zeus.

"When the antiliquor laws in Arista went into effect, I remember seeing my father drink a glass of wine with dinner every night. And when I tried to question him about it, he said that some men made the rules, and others had to live by them. And I knew it was wrong. Down in my soul, I knew it was wrong. That one life should be lived here in the palace, while another would be lived among the people. I knew that his control was simply for the sake of control, and not out of conviction. And at first, like I said, I wanted to run. But I realized someone had to fix it. Someone had to. And the longer things went on, I only saw more contradictions between the rules my father made in the edicts he issued and the way that he lived. And no one did anything to stop him. No one spoke against him. I realized that person would have to be me."

She nodded slowly. "What a terrible realization."

"It was a powerful realization, and I am glad for it. You cannot wait for others to do the right thing. It is up to us. Each of us. We cannot claim something is not our problem. If it exists in the world, it is a problem for all of us."

"You are a very good man. You cover it quite skillfully with hardness. But you are a warrior."

He did not know what to say to that, so he simply looked out at the view. He felt like a warrior at times. But rather than wearing armor, his whole body was covered over in a protective layer. Calcified. He looked at her, and he felt drawn to her. Pulled toward her like there was a magnet between them. Something he could not deny.

But she had wanted a nice outing; she did not ask to be ravished. Again, he would have to practice self-control. Damned inconvenient when he wanted to do anything but. "We should go back."

"We haven't even had a hot chocolate."

"I do not wish you to catch too much of a cold."

"I'm fine. I'm pregnant. I'm not broken."

Pregnant. With his child. They really were standing on the brink of everything changing.

But it was not that escape he dreamed of as a boy. And it wasn't that simple life she had talked about either. It was something else. Something he couldn't say that he understood.

"The doctor said you were healthy?"

She nodded. "Yes. I had my standard checkups and…"

"Are you due another one?"

"Soon. But I'm not concerned."

"Good to hear."

"Women have been doing this for a very long time."

"Yes," he said. "But it is not always safe."

"But there's no reason to believe that mine will not be."

Suddenly, his chest went tight, clutched with something unfamiliar. He could not figure out what it was. He had never experienced anything like it before in his life. He had the sudden urge to grab her and gather her up close to his chest. And all around him the world seemed precarious. The trees laden with snow that might tip from the weight of it. The precipice in front of them, and the lake down below. All of these sights that he had wanted to show her suddenly seemed like they might rebel against them both. He was aware of how fragile she looked. In all that white.

He had been prepared to seduce her, to entice her into his plan of vengeance. He had made love to her that night months ago with both of them burning white-hot from battle, the thrill of victory.

And now it was his own need. A great, ravenous beast that burned in him like a monster he feared could consume them both.

But she was pregnant with his child. He could not touch her like this.

"Let's go," he said.

The farther away they got from the precipice, the more the feeling faded. But he only wished that he could understand what had started it in the first place.

Or perhaps, he did not.

CHAPTER TWELVE

ELOISE COULDN'T UNDERSTAND. Vincenzo had been so sweet to her today. And it was weird. Because he was many things, but he was hardly sweet, and he was being solicitous in a way that... It seemed odd. She had kissed him this morning, and he had not done anything to follow up on it.

She paced back and forth in her room, wearing a soft, gauzy white nightgown that made her feel elegant, or rather like a cloud. A round, fluffy cloud. Perhaps she simply didn't appeal to him. He had been sweet to her on the trip in the troika. And he had shown her the view of the water and she felt... In many ways she felt closer to him than she ever had. But she missed the heat. She missed the fire. And she hoped that this was not the compromise that had to occur. That in order for them to have conversations. In order for them to connect, in order for them not to be bogged down in misunderstandings and recriminations, they had to be... Friends.

Not that there was anything bad about being friends. But she wanted the fire. He had always felt like more to her than that. A connection that had come from nowhere. A connection that had taken root deep inside of her chest. He had never been anything quite so bland as a friend, and she did not wish him to be now.

She remembered the wildness between them, that moment when they had been rejoicing in their accomplishments. In taking down his father.

She was remorseful about that emotion, but there was something about the dark edge of that experience that had affected her. That had made her feel... Wild.

Did she have to be glorying in something so dark in order to experience that kind of explosion of passion? In order to create it in someone else?

Without thinking, she exited the bedroom. She began to walk down the hallway, her throat dry. Her heart was thundering in her chest.

She already knew what she was doing without it even forming in her mind as a coherent thought. She wanted him. And she wanted to be brave.

She was trying to find a way to join up these pieces of herself. This girl who loved planting, who wanted a Christmas and who wanted birthday parties. Who wanted these soft, simple things. And who felt the dark turn to light when her enemies were slain, and who wanted to tear Vincenzo's clothes off and wanted him to do the same to her.

Who had gloried in the animalistic need between them, and who had sat in the troika watching the falling snow all around them. Who had enjoyed the silence and that lake view.

Because it was all inside of her. All the same, but right now it felt distinct. Separate. She had been certain that he had chosen a path and she had chosen another and those paths could not meet.

But they could. They did. She had the feeling they

met at that cliff side. Tranquil beauty and a sense of danger.

But she could not quite figure out how to make sense of it. That's what she was searching for now.

She had the sense that he would not be in his room. She knew where his study was in the palace. Where his father's had been before him. It was funny to wander around the palace now, this place that had always been filled with dark foreboding, but now was covered in icicles and lights. All for her. And he didn't understand it, but he had done it anyway, and surely there must be something of emotion in that.

Or he's just trying to manipulate you.

What was manipulation? And what was caring?

Did either of them even know the difference?

Her heart was pounding in her head now. Making it difficult to breathe. She pushed open the door to his study and found him there, sitting at the desk. There was a fire in the grand fireplace, and she could see snow falling outside the window in the darkness.

"What are you doing here?" he asked.

"I came looking for you." She walked toward him.

"Is everything all right?"

"Everything is fine. It's just… It's just that… Am I repulsive to you now?"

"What?"

"Me. In this…" She swished her nightgown around. "In this shape. Do you not want me?"

He stared at her from the desk, the firelight illuminating the hollows of his face. His eyes looked black. Like coal.

"Is that what you think?"

"Yes. I kissed you."

"You did. And asked me to take you on a sleigh ride."

"And you did not try to kiss me."

"No. But you did not ask me to. You asked me for a ride in the troika."

"And you gave it to me. And I appreciate it. But I did expect you to try and…"

"I thought that you wanted me to give you Christmas."

"I want both. I want Christmas, and I want you to look at me as if you want to devour me. I want conversation, but I also want you to kiss me."

"A kiss… Eloise, I could not stop at just a kiss."

"You couldn't?"

He stood and rounded the desk slowly, his mannerisms that of a prowling cat. "Eloise," he said, his voice frayed. "It is a torture to be so near you and not touch you. To see your body so luscious and round with the evidence that you carry my child, and to keep my hands off you. I have wanted nothing more than to grab hold of you and crush you to my body from the moment I first saw you standing in your house. But I have been restrained, because I did not want to put you under undue stress. And I have commanded that you marry me. And I am… I am at your mercy," he said, the words splintering like thin ice. "I would not wish to do something to distress you, for fear that you would refuse me."

"You're afraid that I will refuse you?"

"Of course I am. You have not agreed to be my wife. You have not agreed to be mine, and it all hangs by a thread. This balance is… It is precarious." He dropped to his knees before her, and she startled. Then his thumb was at her ankle, massaging her there. And he continued up, sweeping the nightgown up her thighs, past her hips, and pulling it over her head, leaving her completely nude in the firelight. And she felt… She felt beautiful. The way he looked at her, the way the fire glowed across her curves. He made her feel like a goddess.

"*Diana*," he said.

And it made her feel warm all over, because she knew that he was thinking the same that she had been. A goddess.

"Goddess of the hunt. But it is I who would have been in pursuit of you."

"I'm the one that came to your study," she said, her breath a whisper.

"Perhaps… Perhaps we hunt for each other."

"Perhaps," she said, the words coming out soft as a feather.

He stood away from her, unbuttoned his shirt slowly, his body bathed in an orange glow. The dips and hollows of his body highlighted by the harsh flame. He removed all his clothes, and he looked like a god himself. Or perhaps simply… A predator. Like he had said. Perhaps they both hunted one another. Then he moved to her and kissed her. But this was not tentative. Not the polite kiss between two people seated at the dining table, where others could walk in at any moment. It was deep and hard, carnal. It held in it the promise of everything he had just said. It made his words into truth, as he devoured her mouth, licking deep and stealing her breath away. He kissed her neck and then moved down to her breasts. He cupped her, squeezing them, drawing his thumbs over her nipples. "Beautiful," he rasped. "I love your curves. You were concerned, about your roundness, even before you carried the baby. I find you lush. Feminine. Exquisite. And this new shape... It is unbearable. I cannot breathe for how exquisite you are."

She moaned as he lowered his head, drawing one tightened bud between his lips and sucking hard. She was so sensitive there now, she felt it all echo between her legs. Felt her desire for him erupt like sparks. She was very nearly there, just from the attention to her breast. He sank lower, trailing a line of kisses over her rounded bump. And she felt the baby shift inside her. He stopped and looked up at her, his expression fierce. "Was that?"

"Yes," she said, softly. "The baby moves."

He got to his feet and pressed his palm against her stomach. "It moves?"

"Yes," she said.

He caught her gaze and held it there for a long moment. And something swelled inside her chest, and she was sure looking into his eyes the same thing was in him. And she wanted to tell him. Wanted to say it.

Because this was love. It was pure, and it was real. And it was more than a responsibility. It was more than an attachment. It was a miracle. A miracle that defied explanation. "It is incredible," he said.

"I know," she said.

He kissed her hungrily then, breaking the softness of the moment, driving her back and then guiding her gently down into a chair. Then he knelt down before her and spread her legs, lifting her thighs up over his shoulder and tasting her as he had done the first time they were together. She gasped, arching into him, enjoying his loss of control. But it was the combination of this moment and the moment just prior that sent her over the edge. That fierceness in his face. The realization that this was real. Everything.

She sobbed out her pleasure, and he rose up from the floor, picking her up off the chair and wrapping her thighs around his body, before seating them both again. Then he thrust up inside her, and she let her head fall back. He gripped her hips, driving up into her, his eyes wild. And she lost herself.

Because here it was. The sweetness combined with the passion. Need combined with want too.

The simplicity of creation, of life and the dark broken pieces of their desire for one another. It filled her. Consumed her. Changed her. This man, who was the father of her child, her future husband, her lover.

He was everything, just as she was.

He was a warrior, a protector. He could touch her gently and with passion.

And when her desire broke over her, it burst behind her eyelids with every color under the sun, bright and brilliant, sweet and pastel, dark and rich, and for the first time she understood what it was to be Eloise. Not Eloise ignored. Not Eloise hidden. But Eloise, fully in charge of herself. In command of her desires. Then he cried out his own release, and their eyes met. And right then, she felt whole.

He rested his head against her neck and whispered, "I smell roses."

She didn't know what it meant. But it felt like a declaration. "Vincenzo," she whispered. "I'll marry you."

He looked up at her, the intensity in his gaze burning hotter than the fire. "You'll marry me?"

"Yes."

"We will marry on Christmas Eve."

"Yes."

He gripped her chin, holding it tight. "Say it again."

"Yes," she said again.

CHAPTER THIRTEEN

"WE ARE GETTING married on Christmas Eve," he said, speaking to his friends through the computer screen.

"What a shock—Vincenzo Moretti's had his way," Jag said.

"It was the stock options," Rafael said.

"I think we all know it was the pony."

"It was the troika," Vincenzo said.

"Is that what the kids are calling it these days?" Zeus quipped.

"I expect you all to be there."

"Absolutely. I would not stay away from court if you were being sentenced to life in prison," Jag said. "I will certainly not miss your marriage."

"Nice," Zeus said.

"You're doing the right thing," Rafael said. "It is right that you marry the mother of your child."

"Do you always do what is right, Rafael?" Zeus asked, his tone dry.

"Yes. Do you not?"

"I think you know I avoid it at all costs whenever possible."

"Not me. Honor is everything. It is all a man has," Rafael responded.

"Well," Zeus said. "We all have thrones. You do not. At least not permanently."

"It may shock you to learn I don't care," Rafael returned.

"Enough of this," Vincenzo said. "You must all come, and you must all be kind to her."

"Of course we'll be kind to her," Jag said.

"*You* are another matter," Zeus finished.

"Friendship is overrated," Vincenzo said. But he did not think that was true. Friendship had been the only good thing in his life. The friendship with these men. But then there was Eloise. The memory of last night made him burn. Eloise was perfect. Brilliant. She had been exquisite in the firelight. All glowing curves and pleasure.

"We will see you Christmas Eve," Zeus said.

"See you Christmas Eve." He rang off the call and paced the length of the room. There were only three days until the wedding. And he intended it to be a massive celebration. He would make a wedding so bright and brilliant that Eloise would be radiant with it. And he found that drove him most of all. Something had changed inside him that night all those months ago. He had begun to want things, not for himself, not for the greater good, but for her. When he was in her arms, what seemed faint became all the more clear. As if the intangible suddenly made sense in a way it never had before.

It was a feeling that rested somewhere next to the fear he had felt when he was out in the troika with her. But it was something different. Something more. And when he had put his hand on her stomach and felt the baby moving...

It had made everything all the more real. That was certain.

He left his study and went down to the dining room, where she was already sitting, chatting with the housekeeper. The smile on her face made him stop where he stood. She was radiant. But there was something more. There was something to the light in her expression. Something bright in her eyes. And he could not fully fathom what it was. Only that it immobilized him. Utterly. Completely. He didn't think he had ever seen anyone look quite so happy in this palace.

Perhaps it would be all right.

"All plans are going forward for the wedding," he said, moving deeper into the room.

"Oh, good," she said. "A Christmas Eve wedding really is so exciting."

She beamed. The smile quite unlike anything he had ever seen before. She was beautiful.

One of his staff came in then, holding an envelope. "A message for you," he said, addressing Eloise.

"Oh," she said. "Thank you."

She took the envelope from his hand and opened it. As she began to read, her expression fell. It was like a light had been extinguished, and it made his chest seize up.

"What is it?"

"It's nothing," she said, holding the letter close to her chest.

"It is something," he said. He held his hand out, the demand obvious. She gave in, placing the paper in his palm.

He looked down at the letter. And his blood turned to ice.

Congratulations on whoring yourself out to royalty. Do you honestly think you're any different from me? You're smart, though. You're carrying the heir. But all your principles, and his, look foolish. You are no different. Just remember that.

It was from her mother.

"That snake," he said.

"She's not wrong. Except… She's all wrong." She looked up at him, but her expression was sad now, and he hated her mother for that.

"Explain."

"It's not the same between us as it was between her and my father. And I am not carrying this child to get your money. You know that."

He did. Because she had been happy to hide the baby away from him. He did not suspect Eloise of being at all like her mother. But still it was a terrible thing, to watch that haunted look in her eyes. Because no matter what she said, she felt the pain from this letter very deeply. It didn't matter that she shouldn't. It didn't matter that she knew she wasn't her mother. She felt it.

And he felt a burden of responsibility for causing this pain.

"Is it bad?" he asked. "Being here?"

"I'm not going to pretend it's my favorite."

"Of course not," he said.

"But… Where else would I be?"

He gritted his teeth together. "Yes. Where else…"

But in his mind's eye, he saw her back in her garden. Surrounded by her flowers.

That was where she would be.

If not for him. If not for this.

She had been brave, a warrior in all of this, but she had not chosen this path in the beginning. He had. Or rather he had been put on it in a way that felt fated. Unavoidable.

But she wanted love.

And he did not know what it was.

The evils of the past would always be there. This letter proved it.

He had dragged her back into hell along with him, and he did not know what to make of that revelation.

"I am taking dinner in my study tonight. I hope you enjoy your meal."

Then he turned and left her there, feeling like a coward. Feeling ineffective. Feeling like...

He felt like an ass. And he was.

But there was nothing to be done about it.

CHAPTER FOURTEEN

HE HAD BEEN distant for two days. And now it was the eve of their wedding, and she didn't understand. She didn't understand why this man, who had taken her out and showed her his favorite view, something he had never shown anyone before, was suddenly like a stone again.

Because she and Vincenzo had nearly become friends, and then after the way they had made love by the fire, it had all become more. And she just couldn't credit what had happened because of this distance between them. It was disturbing and upsetting. And she wished... She wished that she knew exactly how to reach him.

What is love?

She had been thinking so much about that statement. And she knew the answer, but she didn't know how to tell him. That was the problem. Because she knew that she loved him. And she knew that she loved their child. And that he did too. She had seen it in his eyes when he had felt that miracle. But how...

You have to tell him.

But it scared her. The idea of telling him. Because she had tried... It reminded her of being eighteen. Of trying to forge that connection between them that he had not felt at the time. It reminded her of that humiliation. Of that sadness. And she didn't want to experience it again.

But what other choice was there?

She had had a moment of wholeness. Of being Eloise as she was intended to be. Rather than Eloise, fragmented by the life she had been given. But she would live her entire life in fragments, only experiencing that blinding, wonderful feeling of being complete when he was inside her. When she had a feeling that she might be able to experience it all the time. Yes. She might.

And wasn't that worth it? Wasn't that worth the risk?

It was only her feelings, after all. And whatever happened with those, she could survive them. It was only feelings.

She had a doctor's appointment today, and he was going to accompany her. She had been wanting to leave the gender of the child a surprise, but having a scan done this late in the game might reveal everything.

But it would be okay if he... She wondered if he would connect even more, having seen the child. Knowing if it was a son or a daughter.

Those thoughts were all swirling around in her head when the doctor arrived at her bedroom.

How different it was to be treated when one was going to be a queen. The doctor was followed closely by Vincenzo, who appeared in a cloud of ferocity and intensity. As he was wont to do.

But this seemed even more pronounced than usual.

"Good afternoon," the doctor said. "It is an honor to treat you today."

"Oh," she said, feeling her cheeks heat. "Thank you."

"Let us get this started," Vincenzo said.

She readied herself, lay on the bed and waited.

The doctor shifted her nightgown, pushing it up over her bump. Then put a warmed gel on her skin, gliding the Doppler over the top of it.

And then the sound of the baby's heartbeat filled the screen, and she saw the silhouette of their head. An arm pressed right up by their face.

"Vincenzo," she whispered.

She hadn't seen the baby in a few months, and it was incredible how much more like a baby it looked.

"Oh, Vincenzo."

She heard Vincenzo draw close to the bed, and then felt him as he dropped to his knees beside it. She looked at him, at the way his dark eyes were rapt on the screen. The doctor was moving over various parts now, the baby's belly, legs, feet. Then back up to the head, where they could see the profile.

Vincenzo said nothing. His face was simply set in stone, caught somewhere between terror and awe. She understood. She felt that way too. "This is it," she whispered. "Vincenzo. This is it."

And she knew that he understood what she meant. This was love. It was as certain as she could ever be that he would understand. Because she could see it. She could see it in his eyes. And she felt it reflected inside her. This terrifying, momentous, wondrous thing.

"And do you want to know the gender?" The doctor asked.

"No," Vincenzo said. "No."

But there was something strange in his voice that she could not quite understand.

The doctor finished the exam, and then Vincenzo

turned to leave at the same time as the doctor. "Stay with me," she said.

He stopped.

Skerret chose that moment to come out from under the bed and jump up onto the mattress. Investigating the extra person in the room, not brave enough exactly to take on two. The little gray creature was no less mangy now in looks than she had been when Eloise had first adopted her. She would always look like a ditch cat. There was no getting around it.

"I think Skerret is requesting your affection," she said, feeling mildly amused when she jumped down from the bed and wove between Vincenzo's legs.

"Skerret will have to be disappointed on that score."

"She's not afraid of disappointment. In fact, I think she's quite inured to it. She'll wear you down eventually."

She felt for a moment like she was actually talking about herself.

"And how have you been? Since your mother's letter?"

She frowned. "Oh. It's not unexpected. She's spiteful. It has nothing to do with us. Nothing to do with where we are going."

"I do not think we should get married."

"What?" she asked, feeling as if she'd been struck, the pain of those words a physical blow.

"I do not think we should get married. I think you should go back to Virginia." His words were hard, and so was his face.

She felt as if the bottom had dropped out of the world.

"Are you... Angry at me?" It was all she could think. That she had done something wrong. Again.

He had sent her away once before with offers of money because he believed the worst of her. Had something happened again?

"Vincenzo," she said, a pleading note in her voice. "What is it? You know I am… You know I care for you…"

"It is not you," he said. "But this place… There is poison in these walls. And no amount of Christmas lights is ever going to make it different. You deserve better than this. Our child deserves better than this."

"Better than being the heir to a throne? Better than this country?" Tears filled her eyes. "Better than having his father?"

"I will still be his father. But if we do not marry, then he is not the heir. If we do not marry, then… All will go according to plan on my end, and you will not have to spend your life trapped here."

"Did I say that I was trapped?"

"No. You didn't. But I see it. I see it even if you do not."

"You… You utter bastard. I did not ask you for this." Anger boiled over inside her. He was talking about walls, but the only wall here was him. He was so hard. And he would not tell her the truth. He was shut down and merciless in his coldness, and what was she supposed to do with that? "How… How can you do this? After you've just seen our child?"

"This why I have to do this. It is why I have to."

"I love you," she said. "I love you, Vincenzo, and I didn't tell you this before because you want to know things about this feeling that I don't think I can answer. Because it is something in my blood. Something that feels as much a part of me as anything else that I am. And I cannot come up with a way to explain. I cannot think of how I might define it. I know that you want that. But I can only tell you what I feel. In my heart. And it is love for you. A love that has been there for… Well more than ten years. I love you. The more that I get to know you, the more that I feel it. And it is more than simply wanting to take care of you. Wanting to protect you. Wanting to sleep with you. I am carrying a piece of you inside of me. This evidence of the passion between us…"

"Yes," he said, "and I am the result of my mother and father's union. But there was no love between them. What of your father? You've never even met him. That is not evidence of love, Eloise. It is simply an aftereffect of sex."

"But the child…"

"I don't feel it," he said. "I don't feel it. You said this was it. And if I cannot… I refuse to have our child grow up as we did. I refuse it."

He didn't feel it. He didn't feel it even for their child.

"Maybe it is because I never saw it," he said. "Never heard it."

"Neither did I. But I still know enough to understand it when I am fortunate enough to have it. Why can't you?"

"Perhaps I'm just broken, more so than you."

"Your friends," she said. "Do you not love them?"

"It's different."

"It's not. It all comes from here." She pressed her hand to his chest. "It all comes from here. From who you are. And I cannot… How can you think that there isn't love there?"

"I will send you back to Virginia."

"No," she said.

"I am sending you back."

"You can't."

"Then you will live here as you did as a child. Ignored. Unwanted. Is that what you would like?"

She drew back, feeling as if he had struck her. He might as well have.

"Vincenzo…"

"I will ready the plane immediately."

"Vincenzo!" She screamed his name, because he would not yell. She unleashed her fury because he had closed everything inside of him.

And he stood there, his breath coming hard, his chest heaving with it. "It is not this place that is poison, Eloise. It is me. It is my blood. And I will not poison us all."

And that was how she found herself bundled onto a private plane, numb. Crying. She had no recollection of the flight. None at all. She was just suddenly standing in front of her door in Virginia with the snow falling softly behind her, and her cat carrier in hand.

She walked inside and looked into the corner where her Christmas tree had been. She realized it was still at the palace. And for some reason it was that, that stupid thing, that made her burst into tears. That made it all feel like too much. For some reason, it was the tree that pushed it beyond the pale. She began to weep. Like her heart was broken. Because it was. Because she no longer had Vincenzo, and nothing would ever be right again.

You have your child.

Yes, she did. And her simple life. Except Eloise was

not simple. Not anymore, and perhaps she never had
been. Eloise had learned to want it all.

And taking half felt unacceptable.

He did not expect his friends to show up early. But
they did.

And he was drunk.

"What the hell is this?" Zeus asked.

"Nothing," he said, straightening at his desk, feeling worse for wear.

"Liar," Rafael said. "You look like hell. And you
smell worse."

"I find you offensive in every way," Jag said.
"Where is your woman?"

"She is not my woman," he said.

"Then something's changed," Rafael said.

"Nothing has changed. I simply realized that I was
allowing her to live through what we had already endured as children. It was not right. I sent her home."

"You did what?" Jag asked. "You sent your pregnant
fiancée home the day before your wedding?"

"It had to be done."

"Did it?" he asked. "I do not believe you."

"I didn't ask for your belief, friend. I, in fact asked
for nothing. Least of all for the three of you to be standing in my study."

"Too bad for you," Zeus said. "This is what friends
are for. Get yourself together."

"I'm together. I am doing the right thing."

"You're not doing the right thing. You're doing the
easy thing," Rafael said. "You saw her struggling,
and rather than doing something to fix it, you sent
her where you didn't have to look at it. Rather than

doing the work to figure out exactly how you needed to change this place so that it was not the same place that you grew up in, you removed her. And you're going to what? Sink away in your misery?"

"How dare any of you lecture me on feelings."

"You do not have any, you are a coward. Not a King."

"And you are in my palace."

"How quickly he has come to view it as his palace," Jag said. "For all his talk of not even wanting the throne."

"What would you have me do? You'd have me keep a woman with me who professes to love me when I cannot offer her the same in return?"

Zeus lifted a brow. "I am hardly one to advocate for the institution of marriage, or love. But I can hardly see why you're standing there acting as if the woman carrying your child being in love with you is some conundrum you cannot get past."

"Because of her happiness. It is for her."

"Or is it for your own protection?"

Vincenzo didn't want to speak to them anymore. Instead, he strode out of the study and down the stairs, and before he knew what he was doing, he was walking. In the snow. Walking until he reached that spot on the hill that overlooked the lake. The wind whipped up furiously around him, his coat blowing around his knees. He stared into the snowflakes, which burned holes through his skin with the freezing cold.

But he didn't care. "Eloise," he said.

This is it.

He could not understand what she meant. He couldn't. Because all he felt was pain. The same pain that had been in his chest from the time he was a boy. When he looked at his mother and saw her sad. When he looked at his father and found him lacking. When he felt lonely. When he had been isolated as a boy. This feeling was...

He thought of his mother again, and a great pain burst in his chest.

This is it.

He recognized this feeling as grief. Not as love. And then he saw his mother's face.

I love you.

The words exited his mouth before he could even think them through.

He looked at his mother, and that was what he thought.

But it was painful. It was not a glory.

No one has ever said it to me.

No one except for Eloise.

And then, even in the midst of the snow, it was like he could smell roses.

And he knew.

It wasn't the simple life that called to him. And it wasn't a rose petal on the wind.

It was Eloise. And loving her.

Love had been grief for all his life because there had been no one there to return it. And when he had looked upon his own child, he had felt that same pain because he felt ill-equipped to deal with it.

But Eloise was right. It was love. And it was something more than he had ever imagined it could be. Because pain was part of it. And perhaps this was why people did not love in this way. Unless they couldn't help it.

Unless they had to.

He loved her.

He loved her. He loved their baby.

He had loved all along. He had loved his mother, who had never said it to him as she wallowed in her own grief. He had loved his father, even while knowing the man was flawed.

Love had always been inside him.

And now, it finally had a chance to take a shape other than this pain.

If only Eloise did not hate him.

He hoped that she didn't. To have come this far, only to lose love again would be unbearable.

He walked back to the palace, completely unaware of the cold now. "We must go," he said to his friends. "To Virginia."

"Really?" Zeus asked. "That's so surprising. You had a change of heart after your isolated self-flagellation walk."

"Shut your mouth for once and gather up as many Christmas decorations as you can. And we must make sure to get her wedding dress."

CHAPTER FIFTEEN

SHE HAD NOT put up a new Christmas tree, and she was slightly regretful. There was no reason to compound her misery, after all. And yet part of her wished to. Wished to wallow in it. In the pain of not having him with her.

Vincenzo.

She loved him. The fact that he had done this to her didn't change that.

It was Christmas Eve, and she was miserable.

Skerret was sitting by the fire in the sweater that she had knitted for her, looking as fine as a ditch cat could.

"At least one of us is content."

The cat said nothing. She only stared back with contemptuous yellow eyes.

Then suddenly there was a knock on the door, and she had a terrible flash of the two other times this had occurred. But twice was perhaps possible, three times, after he had so soundly rejected her, was not. But who else would be at the door on Christmas Eve?

She scrambled out of her chair and waddled to the door.

And when she opened it, it was not just Vincenzo standing there, wearing a dark suit, but three other men, just as tall and imposing, and all so handsome it was stunning.

These men had to be his friends. They had all gone to school together. How had the women on campus gotten anything done?

"Oh," she said.

"She's beautiful," one of the men said.

"Luminous," another said, walking in past her.

"A goddess," said the third. And then suddenly all but Vincenzo were in her house.

"Agreed," Vincenzo said. "I have brought your wedding dress. Because I would still very much like to marry you."

She blinked, then took a step out of the house, closing the front door behind her and isolating them. "What?"

"I realized something. I realized that I love you. Because I found an answer to my question. I was wrong. Love is something born into all of us. What I think we learn is how to suppress it in favor of selfishness. What I think we learn is to ignore it when it hurts too much. And so, for me, all love was pain. When I looked at our baby, all I saw was grief, and when you told me you loved me, all I felt was loneliness. Because that is all I have ever known when it comes to love."

"Oh, Vincenzo."

"You do not need to pity me. For I was a fool. And I hurt you. I regret that. Bitterly."

"But…"

"But I'm here. I'm here because I love you. I'm here because I want you. I've never said those words to anyone. I have never realized that feeling before now.

And I hope that is enough. I hope that it is clear that what I say is true."

"Even if I didn't believe you, I wouldn't be strong enough to tell you no." She flung her arms around his neck and kissed him. "Because I love you. I was willing to love you through you figuring out what love was. I didn't need to hear it back right away."

"I know," he said. "But I was just so... I cannot explain." He shook his head. "Except that I was terrified. And I hated admitting that. More than anything."

"I'm sure."

"Zeus is ordained. And he is ready to perform the wedding now. I'm ready to marry you now."

She blinked back tears. "That's good. Because I'm ready too."

From behind the garment bag he pulled a bouquet of roses and extended it to her. "When you told me about your simple life, I could feel the longing for it in a fleeting way. The scent of roses on the wind. But I realized today it was deeper than that. It was my longing for you. Not simplicity. But simply to be where you are. And I got these roses because, for me, it is that intangible thing made real."

She put on her dress, floaty and ethereal, skimming over her bump, and clutched her roses to her chest, looking at herself in the mirror and feeling... Whole.

They were all out in the garden. In the snow. And as she and Vincenzo exchanged vows, just them and Vincenzo's closest friends, she felt she understood love in the truest, most complete way possible.

"I now pronounce you husband and wife. King and Queen."

"You cannot pronounce me King," Vincenzo said. "There is to be a coronation."

"I can pronounce you whatever I like," Zeus said. "I'm officiating."

And with that, they kissed. And it didn't matter what they were called. It didn't matter if the monarchy was abolished or not. It didn't matter if they lived in this cottage in Virginia, or in the palace. They were each other's home. And that was all that mattered.

The coronation was met with great enthusiasm by the people of Arista. Jag and Zeus were in attendance, but not Rafael, who had the wedding of his brother to see to. And it was shocking when they heard the news later. That the wedding had not in fact gone on as intended. But the bride had been taken—by Rafael himself!

"Now that was unexpected," Zeus said.

"Entirely," Jag said. "He never breaks the rules. Or does anything half so interesting as kidnapping women."

"There is a story there," Zeus said. "And I am going to get it."

Eloise thought that she had been filled up with love, more than she could ever hold inside of herself, with her husband, his friends, the people of Arista. But when their son, Mauro Moretti was born, they knew different. Both of them. And they found that the miraculous thing about love was the way that it expanded. To fit everything. The way that it colored every breath, the way that it informed absolutely everything.

After much restructuring, and a vote, it was decided that Arista would retain the monarchy, at least as stabilizing figureheads. And the people were happy to welcome Vincenzo as their King, and Mauro as the next. Especially with more freedom to choose the laws of the land and the knowledge that their leader was just. And that his son would be raised in the same way.

That summer, they went back to Virginia. And spent time in the garden where Vincenzo had first found her.

She had planted roses. Everywhere. For they would always be that concrete symbol of their love. And much to her surprise, with the baby strapped to his chest, Vincenzo rolled up his sleeves and knelt in the dirt beside her, digging a hole with his hands for the new rosebush she had bought.

"I never thought I would see King Vincenzo Moretti on his knees in the dirt, much less beside me."

"And I never thought I would be loved. Yet now I find myself overfilled with it. And I've never been so happy."

"Neither have I, Vincenzo. Neither have I."

There were no sad places left in the world for them. No dark, deep hollows of loneliness. For their love filled them up.

Eloise had wanted a simple life. And in some way she supposed she had one.

Simply perfect.

She started humming.

* * * * *

COMING SOON!

We really hope you enjoyed reading this book.
If you're looking for more romance, be sure to
head to the shops when new books are
available on

Thursday 23rd December

To see which titles are coming soon, please visit
millsandboon.co.uk/nextmonth

MILLS & BOON

THE HEART OF ROMANCE

A ROMANCE FOR EVERY READER

MODERN

Prepare to be swept off your feet by sophisticated, sexy and seductive heroes, in some of the world's most glamourous and romanti locations, where power and passion collide.

HISTORICAL

Escape with historical heroes from time gone by. Whether your passion for wicked Regency Rakes, muscled Vikings or rugged Highlanders, aw the romance of the past.

MEDICAL

Set your pulse racing with dedicated, delectable doctors in the high-pre sure world of medicine, where emotions run high and passion, comfort love are the best medicine.

True Love

Celebrate true love with tender stories of heartfelt romance, from the rush of falling in love to the joy a new baby can bring, and a focus on emotional heart of a relationship.

Desire

Indulge in secrets and scandal, intense drama and plenty of sizzling ho action with powerful and passionate heroes who have it all: wealth, sta good looks…everything but the right woman.

HEROES

Experience all the excitement of a gripping thriller, with an intense ro mance at its heart. Resourceful, true-to-life women and strong, fearless face danger and desire - a killer combination!

To see which titles are coming soon, please visit

millsandboon.co.uk/nextmonth

MILLS & BOON

Coming next month

ONE SNOWBOUND NEW YEAR'S NIGHT
Dani Collins

Van slid the door open and stepped inside only to have Becca squeak and dance her feet, nearly dropping the groceries.

"You knew I was here," he insisted. "That's why I woke you, so you would know I was here and you wouldn't do that. I *live* here," he said for the millionth time, because she'd always been leaping and screaming when he came around a corner.

"Did you? I never noticed," she grumbled, setting the bag on the island and taking out the milk to put it in the fridge. "I was alone here so often, I forgot I was married."

"*I* noticed that," he shot back with equal sarcasm.

They glared at each other. The civility they'd conjured in those first minutes upstairs was completely abandoned—probably because the sexual awareness they'd reawakened was still hissing and weaving like a basket of cobras between them, threatening to strike again.

Becca looked away first, thrusting the eggs into the fridge along with the pair of rib eye steaks and the package of bacon.

She hated to be called cute and hated to be ogled, so Van tried not to do either, but *come on*. She was curvy and sleepy and wearing that cashmere like a second skin. She was shorter than average and had always exercised in a very haphazard fashion, but nature had gifted her with a delightfully feminine figure-eight symmetry. Her ample breasts were high and firm over a narrow waist, then her hips flared into a gorgeous, equally firm and round ass. Her fine hair was a warm brown with sun-kissed tints, her mouth wide, and her dark brown eyes positively soulful.

When she smiled, she had a pair of dimples that he suddenly realized he hadn't seen in far too long.

"I don't have to be here right now," she said, slipping the coffee into the cupboard. "If you're going skiing tomorrow, I can come back while you're out."

"We're ringing in the new year right here." He chucked his chin at the windows that climbed all the way to the peak of the vaulted ceiling. Beyond the glass, the frozen lake was impossible to see through the thick and steady flakes. A gray-blue dusk was closing in.

"You have four-wheel drive, don't you?" Her hair bobbled in its knot, starting to fall as she snapped her head around. She fixed her hair as she looked back at him, arms moving with the mysterious grace of a spider spinning her web. "How did you get here?"

"Weather reports don't apply to me," he replied with self-deprecation. "Gravity got me down the driveway and I won't get back up until I can start the quad and attach the plow blade." He scratched beneath his chin, noted her betrayed glare at the windows.

Believe me, sweetheart. I'm not any happier than you are.

He thought it, but immediately wondered if he was being completely honest with himself.

"How was the road?" She fetched her phone from her purse, distracting him as she sashayed back from where it hung under her coat. "I caught a rideshare to the top of the driveway and walked down. I can meet one at the top to get back to my hotel."

"Plows will be busy doing the main roads. And it's New Year's Eve," he reminded her.

"So what am I supposed to do? Stay here? All night? With *you*?"

"Happy New Year," he said with a mocking smile.

Continue reading
ONE SNOWBOUND NEW YEAR'S NIGHT
Dani Collins

Available next month
www.millsandboon.co.uk

LET'S TALK
Romance

For exclusive extracts, competitions
and special offers, find us online:

f facebook.com/millsandboon

🐦 @MillsandBoon

📷 @MillsandBoonUK

Get in touch on 01413 063232

For all the latest titles coming soon, visit
millsandboon.co.uk/nextmonth

JOIN US ON SOCIAL MEDIA!

Stay up to date with our latest releases, author news and gossip, special offers and discounts, and all the behind-the-scenes action from Mills & Boon...

 millsandboon

 millsandboonuk

 millsandboon

It might just be true love...

MILLS & BOON
Desire

Indulge in secrets and scandal, intense drama and plenty of sizzling hot action with powerful and passionate heroes who have it all: wealth, status, good looks…everything but the right woman.